TIM AKERS

KNIGHT WATCH

A Baen Books Original

Baen Publishing Enterprises
P.O. Box 1403
Riverdale, NY 10471
www.baen.com

ISBN: 978-1-9821-2485-4

Cover art by Todd Lockwood

First printing, September 2020

Distributed by Simon & Schuster
1230 Avenue of the Americas
New York, NY 10020

Library of Congress Cataloging-in-Publication Data

Names: Akers, Tim, 1972- author.
Title: Knight watch / by Tim Akers.
Description: Riverdale, NY : Baen Books, [2020]
Identifiers: LCCN 2020022155 | ISBN 9781982124854 (trade paperback)
Subjects: GSAFD: Fantasy fiction.
Classification: LCC PS3601.K48 K56 2020 | DDC 813/.6—dc23
LC record available at https://lccn.loc.gov/2020022155

Printed in the United States of America

10 9 8 7 6 5 4 3 2 1

DEDICATION

For my mother,
who does in fact drive a Volvo. You're the best.

CHAPTER ONE
DRAGONSLAYER

I killed my first dragon with a blunt sword and the engine block of a 1977 Volvo station wagon. It was my mom's car. I don't think she'll ever forgive me, but in my defense, that dragon was a real asshole.

This all happened at the fighting competition at my local renaissance faire. In case you're not in the nerd know, a ren faire is a place that adults go to pretend they're living in the Middle Ages. Full metal armor, overpriced beer in equally expensive steins, some light bard-work with a side of bustiers, and a plethora of mud. It's a good time, completely harmless, and the sort of place you might expect to see a frustrated college student living out their dream of being a knight.

The thing you shouldn't expect to see is a dragon. Because, and I can't emphasize this clearly enough, dragons aren't real. No more real than wizards, or flying carpets, or werewolves. No more real than struggling English majors who become actual knights. Or at least, that's what I believed going in.

For now, though, I was running late.

I was staying with my parents over the summer. My penultimate year in college was going well, but just before the term ended the apartment I was supposed to live in next year fell through, followed shortly by the job that was supposed to pay for half that apartment and the roommate who was supposed to cover the other half of the rent. It was like the gods were knocking down my hopes and dreams, one at a time. Oh, and my girlfriend left me. Cool. Good end to a year.

Discouraged, I had returned home for the summer. It was kind of weird. I hadn't been home for more than a weekend since I left after high school. I had kept in touch with friends online, and in some ways it was like stepping back into high school all over again. My old pal Eric welcomed me back into his D&D campaign as if I hadn't missed a session, and the various dramas, traumas, and gossip that I thought I had escaped resumed without missing a beat.

The best thing that had come out of this was the local ren faire. I used to go every year, but in college I had gotten involved with the statewide faire, a much larger and more professionally run event, but it somehow wasn't as fun as the local deal. I had started fighting again and was quickly moving up the ranks of the tournament scene. That fateful weekend was the regional competition, which would maybe get me back to the state level, if I was lucky. Eric was coming along, and he told me he had a surprise waiting at his house.

"Please God, not another story. Please God, let it not be another story," I whispered to myself as I gathered my gear. Eric was kind of a writer, in the way that a thunderstorm was kind of a bath. He produced an endless deluge of elves and heroic farmers and whispering woods that dripped with primeval... evil. That sort of thing. And as his friend, and too polite to decline, I had been exposed to all of it. If you have to write a hundred bad pages to produce one good sentence, then Eric was well on his way to produce thousands of good sentences. I just hadn't seen any of them yet.

"Did your watch stop again?" my mother called from the bottom of the stairs. I whipped my phone out of my pocket and stared at the blinking zeroes. I tossed it into my bag. Stupid phone, always flipping out.

"No, Mom!" I lied. "My phone is just fine."

"Then you know how late you are?"

"Yes, I know how late I am!"

"Because Eric lives fifteen minutes away, and you'll need time to park, use the potty before—"

"Mother!"

"Use the potty before you go, and I don't know how long it takes to get back into your fancy pants after that, but I imagine—"

"Mom! It's fine! I'm just a little late. Eric won't mind."

Mother left her post at the base of the stairs, though I could still hear her grumbling all the way to the kitchen. I tossed the last few supplies into my bag, strapped my sword and shield together, and hurried downstairs.

"Did you eat your snack?" Mom yelled as I hit the front door. "Because your tummy—"

I didn't hear the rest of it. I hammered down the stairs to the porch, fumbling in my front pocket for the keys to my little hatchback. Gear went into the back seat, then I squeezed between my car and Mom's ancient station wagon, carefully opening the driver's side door and shoehorning my way into the car.

"Fourteenth Century, here I come!" I shouted and turned the key.

The Fourteenth Century was already waiting for me. There are no cars in the Fourteenth Century. And there was no working car under my butt. Nothing happened. Not even a whimper from the engine, or the clank of a dead starter, or anything. Just the click of the ignition, and then silence. I laid my head against the wheel.

"Okay," I said. "Now I'm late."

Eric's neighborhood was a little older than mine, a little nicer, and a whole lot out of the way. I turned down his street going too fast, the screeching tires of Mom's dilapidated Volvo drawing the stares of a group of mothers on the corner. I cued up my *Monster Manual* voice.

"Beware the feral packs of soccer moms. Disapproving glare, plus ten to hit, applies the existential horror debuff. *You don't look like you're from around here. What are you doing with your life?*" I rolled past them with a wave. "Ladies." They turned back to their strollers in disgust.

Eric's house was at the end of the street. Tall trees surrounded the yard, and the main house felt like a forest retreat, rather than the suburban mansion that it actually was. I rolled up the driveway and came to a halt in front of his porch. Eric was leaning against the front steps, his iconic beer stein in hand. He was a little heavy, his curly hair sticking out in bits and bobs around the crushed velvet of his bard hat. I had never known Eric to play an instrument, or sing, or show any musical inclination, yet he insisted on wearing a bard outfit to the faire every year. I think he just liked the tights.

"Oh, dude! The mom-mobile! What happened to the hot hatch?" he asked. I got out of the car, slammed the door like a cannon shot, and shrugged.

"Wouldn't start. Probably something to do with the ignition or, or the alt . . . altro . . ."

"Sure, it's definitely one of those things, and not the fact that you break every complicated thing that you touch," he said, bouncing down the stairs and throwing his cooler into the back. My mom's station wagon was the old kind, a Volvo with steel doors as thick as tank armor and an engine that ran on high-grade coal. When Eric slammed the back door shut, it made enough noise to scare a flock of birds out of a nearby tree.

"Well, it'll get us to the faire. You ready?" I asked.

"They might not like us bringing something this old into a renaissance faire," Eric joked. He hauled a cooler down the stairs and slid it into the back, along with an authentic lute case that probably contained various grains of vodka, and his boots. "It strains the realism of the experience. Might want to trade it in for a couple of horses and a wagon."

"You don't like the ride, you can drive," I said.

"No, it's cool, man," he said, getting into the front seat. "Besides, I tore up my license. Living old school!"

"Why the hell did you tear up your license?" I asked.

"Historical authenticity," he said, waving his fingers like he was casting a spell. "Don't want to mess with the ren faire mojo."

"Oh yeah? And all the gear in the back?" I asked, opening my door. "How authentic is that Yeti cooler?"

"There is power in anachronism," he answered. "And ale."

"Well, as long as you know what you're—"

The front door of Eric's house slammed shut, and someone strode out onto the porch. I looked up, and my heart sank.

Chesa Lazaro glared down at me from the shadow of Eric's porch. She competed in the archery competition every year, and of all the competitors, she probably leaned into the elf-fantasy the hardest. She wore her ears and costume to every match. She spent as much time and money on her outfit as most people did on their wedding gowns, and it showed. This year's version of Elven Warrior Princess was a knee-length armored dress with splint mail leggings and high laced leather boots trimmed in gold. Light breastplate and shoulders were done in leaf-shaped metal scales, tinted the color of spring grass and also trimmed in milky gold. Her glossy black hair was pulled back in a dozen braids, woven through with golden thread. The tan tips of her fake ears poked through the plaits, indistinguishable from her coppery skin. Glittering black paint covered her high cheekbones in a false tattoo that was a cross between a butterfly and a switchblade, hiding the spray of freckles that had first caught my attention years ago. Her eyes, dusty tan with a hint of green, glared at me. We were a thing for two weeks the summer before I left for college, and Eric never missed an opportunity to remind me how badly I'd screwed that relationship up.

"Leaving without me again?" Chesa asked.

"Hey, Ches!" I said half-heartedly. "Good to see you." I ducked into the car and lowered my voice. "What the hell, man?"

"Surprise!" Eric whispered back, his pudgy face framed by jazz hands.

Chesa threw her bow and quiver in the back, along with a leather pack that looked like it came out of the props department for *Elf Wars: Revenge of the Elf Lord*. I twisted around in my seat.

"You guys are bringing a lot more stuff to this faire than I am. Something I should know?" I asked.

Chesa sniffed. Eric shrugged. I put the Viking bitchwagon into gear and rattled down the road.

The drive to the faire was about as long and awkward as you could imagine. Eric talked about his latest story, which had something to do with mildly erotic tree people and a lot of adjectives. "I'm doing some great work with adjectives," he confided to me. "Really, really, really great work."

When we got to the faire, Chesa disappeared into the crowds. While I was gathering up my gear, I snagged Eric by the elbow.

"What was that all about?" I asked, nodding in Chesa's direction. "Are you guys a thing?"

"Holy cow, no. I mean, I would, don't get me wrong, but this," he motioned to his body like he was presenting a movie trailer. "This is not the ideal elf body. We've just been hanging out. She's a cool girl."

"I know she's a cool girl, Eric. That's why she hates me so much."

"Yeah, well. She needed a ride. Don't make a thing of it."

I gathered my gear out of the back of Mom's car under Eric's watchful eye. After I closed the door, he stood there looking at me. He seemed a little nervous.

"You waiting for something?" I asked. He shuffled his feet and pulled something out of his pocket.

"I just . . . I got you something. For luck." He handed it to me. It was a kerchief, black with white runes on it. "It's a favor. You could tie it to your sword or something."

"A favor? Are you my lady fair now?"

"No, no . . . it's just . . . it's good to have you home. And I know you're going back to college at the end of the summer, and I'm not sure how many days like this we'll have. So, I thought it'd be nice to have a souvenir or something. I don't know. It felt like something I should do."

I was touched. A little creeped out—but touched. I unfolded the kerchief and looked it over. It was . . . complicated.

"This something from one of your books?"

"It's the war banner of the Lost Empire of the Mage Witches. Dinndero-Dannion the Delft flew it as he rode to war against the Inerrant Emperor." Eric cleared his throat and continued in a false bardic falsetto. "The slick, ichorous, sodden legions plunged, dark and endearing, into the clamoring emptiness of the endless, breaking—"

"Right, got it. I'll do it proud," I said, knotting the kerchief around the hilt of my sword. He smiled. "You going to be at the match?"

"You betcha! Wouldn't miss it for this world, or the next!" He slung his lute o' vodka over his shoulder and tipped that ridiculous hat. "Good luck in the lists today, Sir John of Rast! Maybe I'll sing to your victory!"

"Please don't," I said, then buckled my sword in place and closed the gate on the Volvo. "I have enough trouble without your ballads of whoa."

CHAPTER TWO
ENTER THE HERO

I worked my way to the tournament ground, which was tucked into the far side of the faire, past a lot of vendors selling armor, leather corsets, and quite a bit of grilled meat. Usually I would stroll through, taking in the sights, sounds, and smells of the faux renaissance. The people were the best part, mostly because they were genuinely, thoroughly happy. A rare thing these days. It was a delightful place. But as I said, I was running late. I could already hear the marshal's call, and the reading of the lists. If I didn't hurry, I would miss my place in the tournament.

I was competing in single-hand and shield, or sword and board as it's known in my circle. I'm not a big guy, tall and skinny and probably too gangly to be graceful, but for whatever reason I'm good with a sword. Call it a gift, or a curse, since there's not a lot of demand for expert swordsmen this side of the sixteenth century. I always felt like I missed my time slot, like I should have been born in an age of knights and castles, rather than smartphones and fast food. These tournaments gave me a chance to connect with similarly displaced heroes and spend a weekend forgetting about the disappointing convenience of the modern world. I made some of my best friends at these things. Sometimes I wonder what happened to them all, if they think I'm dead or, worse, if I finally gave in to the mundanes and spend my weekends brewing mediocre beer or having opinions about politics. Thank the gods, nothing could be further from the truth.

Anyway, regionals. I fought my way through the first couple

brackets, handling my opponents with ease and honor, never striking when they were down, always letting them reclaim dropped weapons or recover from slippery footing. The chivalry part of this is important to me. You can win and be a dick about it, but that's just a more complicated way of losing. We're grown-ass men and women out in a field hitting each other with wooden swords on the weekend. Might as well have fun doing it.

I did well enough in the initial rounds to earn a place in the finals, then sat nervously on the sidelines while the finalists for two-handed sword, polearms, acrobatic dagger, and siege bow fought their bouts. The champion for acrobatic dagger caught my eye; she was short and fast, rolling from shoulder to heel and up again, her black braids swirling through the air as she circled her opponent. Acrobatic dagger was supposed to be a combination of throws and dodges, but she never touched her opponent until her padded dagger went into the target on his back. It was a thing of beauty. The audience gave her the round of huzzahs that she had earned, then the marshal marched into the ring and raised his baton.

Chesa showed up in the lists for siege bow but seemed to be off her game. Her initial flight went wide, and she stormed off the range in a huff. She had quite a following among the group of fairegoers who embraced the elven ideal and was escorted into a nearby grove by a group of pointy-eared cosplayers.

"Sword and shield!" the marshal called, and I scrambled to my feet. "For the Duchy of Elderwood, Sir John Rast, champion of the lists, bulwark of . . . of . . ." the marshal peered down at his sheet. Finalists usually had more accolades, but this was my first time in the big ring. The marshal gave up and flourished in my direction. "Sir John!"

There was a scattering of applause around the ring as I stepped over the barrier. "Get 'em, John!" someone in the crowd yelled, and I turned to see my friend Eric raising a stein in my direction. He had a girl on each arm, and three more circling. Typical. Eric was the kind of guy who only seemed truly alive at the faire. Real world Eric couldn't start a conversation with a girl without preceding it with "Well, actually . . ." and rarely got to finish his sentence before the lady walked off. Faire world Eric was witty, constantly surrounded by women, and perpetually drunk. It was something like magic.

I waved at him, then turned back to the ring. As my eyes swept the crowd, I caught sight of dagger-girl. She was leaning against a tree, smirking as she juggled a dagger in one hand. When she raised her brows at me, I realized I was staring and quickly turned away.

My opponent was waiting on the other side of the barrier. He wore the bare minimum armor required by rule, preferring to show off the kind of body that a paleo diet and slavish devotion to Crossfit will get a middle-aged man from the suburbs. His shield wasn't much bigger than his fist, while his sword was everything Freud could have wished for, long and black and as thick as my leg. His chest was heaving, as though he had spent the previous twenty minutes screaming into a shoebox. The marshal waved his baton in the man's direction.

"And for the Outlands, Kracek the Destroyer, Champion of the Feral Gods, Reaver of the Black Lagoon, Breaker of—"

The rest of marshal's introduction was drowned out by Kracek's war cry, a bloodcurdling scream that was quickly taken up by a dozen or so similarly dressed followers in the crowd. Kracek raised his compensation unit over his head, then kicked down the barrier and strode onto the field of battle.

Remember that thing I said about chivalry? Most folks feel the same way. But not all. Not Kracek the Destroyer, Champion of the Feral Gods, and extreme phallus rampant.

Kracek's real name is Douglas Hosier, and he's a property attorney from the suburbs. He drives a white Camaro, claims to date a Canadian model behind his wife's back, and is fighting a losing battle against a receding hairline. I get the feeling Douglas expected more out of his life than what he's gotten and is channeling that frustration into Kracek. He and his band of emotionally damaged men have been expelled from every duchy and protectorate this side of Cairo but, being a bunch of lawyers, somehow kept finding a way into the lists.

The marshal glared at the damaged barrier, then walked to the center of the ring and raised his baton. We squared off, Kracek's chest still heaving, my hands sweating through the thick padded mittens of my armor. Kracek grinned.

"I'm going to annihilate you, kid. I'm going to beat you so hard, your mother's going to be sterile. You'll be running back to—"

"Begin!" the marshal shouted. Kracek bellowed his disappointment at modern social norms and charged forward.

This was normal. Kracek and his type fought linearly, charging or charging faster. I gave some ground, presented my shield and winced as Kracek chopped at it. There were rules about force of blow, but Kracek always danced the line, a hair's breadth away from disqualification with each attack. He forced me back again, then slammed his shield into my sword, nearly knocking it from my grip. The tip of his shield caught my hand. The marshal called halt, separating us with his baton.

"No blows with shield, a demerit and reset."

"He swung, I blocked," Kracek growled. "What's the problem?"

The marshal didn't answer. Kracek shook his head and slouched back to the middle. "Judge is on your side, little man. Cowards like you, always hiding behind the rules…"

"You've got issues, man," I mumbled. He whirled on me, shaking that ridiculous sword in my face.

"I do! I do have issues! Screw your issues, that's what!"

"What?"

"You know what I mean!"

"No, I … I really don't."

"You're gonna know! You're gonna remember the might of Kracek!"

"Right, yeah … you mentioned that." I glanced at the marshal. "He mentioned that, right? There's not an echo or something."

"Taunting!" Kracek shouted. "Taunting, one demerit!"

"Demerits are for me to give out, and for you to earn, Mr. Hosier," the marshal said primly. "Now please reset before I am forced to disqualify you."

"Stupid rules!" Kracek the Hosier yelled. He stomped back to his position, flexed in the manner of a man about to eject his bowels, and shouted. "Kracek!"

I was just bringing up my shield to the guard position when a column of fire erupted from Kracek's mouth and slammed into me. The flames curled around my shield, licking at the cheap linen tabard my mother had sewn for me for my birthday. The heat crisped my eyebrows and filled my lungs. I backpedaled, dropping my sword and shaking my shield off my arm. The metal sizzled as it hit the grass, and pain prickled along the length of my forearm. My gloves were ash. I turned to stare at the marshal.

"There's no way that's legal!" I barked.

The marshal was staring at Kracek in disbelief. His baton was smoldering, and the shocked look on his face had as much to do with his horror as his lack of eyebrows. Then he turned and ran into the crowd.

"You're just gonna . . . just run? Come on, man! I didn't—" I glanced over at Kracek and shut right the hell up.

Kracek was hunched over, with molten fire dribbling out of his mouth. He was larger, and his pale, suburban skin was glowing like beaten copper. He tossed his rattan sword to the ground, then rolled his shoulders and looked around.

"Kracek's true form has become apparent. Kracek is displeased," he muttered, casting angry looks around at the crowd. "Kracek must fix this problem."

"Kracek must be on drugs," I said. "Seriously, man, get a therapist. You have some stuff that needs resolution. Honestly."

"Kracek will start with you," he answered. He took a step forward, and his boot burst open. Talons spilled out. Scales crawled up Kracek's leg, and his shoulders heaved, splitting open to reveal mucus-slick wings. When he smiled, Kracek's teeth looked like a band saw, as sharp and as bright as steel. Flames flickered in his eyes and across his black tongue. I took a step back.

"Or I'm on drugs. That could be," I muttered. "Eric, am I on drugs?"

A scream went up from the crowd, joined by a hundred others, and the grassy field of the St. Luke's Community Soccer Field and Recreational Facility became a stampede. Kracek grew and grew, arms elongating, belly bloating, wings stretching up until they topped the trees. He took a deep breath, and the stink of sulfur and ash filled the air. For some reason, I pulled out my padded dagger, then pissed myself.

A blur knocked me aside, sending me flying ten yards. I landed in a heap on top of the ale stand, breaking through the tent and smashing barrels of overpriced PBR. A flash of light filled the sky, and flames roared over my head. Even with my eyes squeezed shut, I could see blood-red flames. When I opened my eyes, dagger-girl was staring at me.

"Take a knee, mundane. The heroes have arrived," she whispered. Then she hopped over the smoldering remains of the stand and bounded toward Kracek.

Toward the dragon.

CHAPTER THREE
THAT VIKING BITCH

Dagger-girl hopped across the field, dodging a tail swipe as she ran directly at the beast's gaping maw. The grass under her feet turned to ash as the dragon tried to burn the flesh from her bones. She bounced into the air, executed a mid-leap pirouette, then landed on the dragon's back and started stabbing.

The dragon, I thought. *What the hell is going on? When the council hears about this, they're going to have a fit!*

"Eric!" I shouted. Crowds of people were streaming away, stampeding over the vendor tents and fleeing into the forest at the edge of the field. I caught a brief glimpse of Eric's ridiculous bard's hat as he ducked behind a tree.

At least he's safe, I thought. I started in that direction, but my foot caught on something hard and round.

It was a skull. It bounced away, chunks of scorched flesh flaking off as it rolled.

I put my hands on my knees and threw up, most of it splashing back into my face, since my helmet was still buckled down. I ripped the visor off and threw up again, kept at it until my stomach was more than empty.

The air sizzled as a stream of flame lashed overhead. It passed twenty feet above me, but the heat singed my nostrils and burned off the bile on my tongue. I spat and looked around. What I saw changed my life.

Dagger girl was dancing around the dragon, the same way she had danced around her opponent in the ring. Kracek (were his scales receding around the crown of his head?) followed her, craning his sinuous neck and spraying jets of flame, always missing by inches. He bellowed his frustration, and the trees shook. The girl landed on the dragon's back again, punched down a dozen times in the space of a second, then bounced away. A stream of viscous blood followed her through the air, trailing from the glowing twin daggers in her hands. Kracek's screams changed to pain, and he reared up on his hind legs and stretched his wings to the sky.

"Flimsy mortal! Kracek will sear your flesh from your bones and boil your blood in your skull! Flee before the might of Kracek! Flee before the champion of the Outland realms!"

"Gotta catch me first, snakeface!" the girl shouted. She landed in front of the dragon, crouching with both daggers spread wide like wings, that smirk still on her face. "You're getting slow in your old age. Slow and stupid."

"Respect your elders, child," Kracek said. His voice hissed through my mind, and flames licked his teeth as he spoke. "I have been in this world longer than any of your kind."

"And now you've overstayed your welcome," she answered. "Time to go!"

She leapt forward, but just as her feet left the ground, Kracek poured a stream of fire from his jaws. Twisting, she was somehow able to avoid it, but as she tumbled away the dragon whipped his massive tail forward, catching her in the back. She flopped like a rag doll, bouncing through the charred grass before coming to a halt. Kracek laughed, crashed back down on all fours, and strolled languidly toward her still form.

"Oh man, oh man, oh MAN," I whispered to myself. What should I do? I couldn't just sit here and watch her get killed. I looked around at the smoldering stalls. The vendor next to the ale house was a weapon maker. None of the blades were sharp, but they were good steel, and the dragonfire that had destroyed the craftsman's shed hadn't touched them at all. I snatched one of them up and ran at Kracek, waving the sword over my head and yelling.

"Hey, you scaly freak! Over here! We haven't finished our match yet, you cheating son of a bitch!" Not my most eloquent taunt, but it served the purpose. Kracek paused and craned his horned head in my direction, then let out a derisive snort that scorched the ground at my feet.

"We are not playing games anymore, Sir Burbia. Go back to your foam swords and your weak ale. You have a cubicle to fill on Monday."

I let out a furious roar and charged in. Kracek's wing brushed the air above me, buffeting me, nearly driving me to my knees, but I kept going. His nearest leg rose up. I looked up at those blackened talons, sticky with blood, each one as long as my forearm and wickedly sharp, and I realized I was in over my head.

"For Elderwood!" I shouted weakly, my voice cracking as I swung the dull blade against his muscular claw. The steel sang in my hands as it struck scale. The sword snapped in half like an icicle. I stood there, holding the broken hilt, staring at my death. For the second time that day, someone else saved me.

A trio of bright arrows blossomed from the dragon's claw. Kracek howled and reared back, thrashing his tail across the soccer field, tearing chunks of sod up with those talons. I staggered to my feet and backed away. Chesa's voice reached me over the din of Kracek's rage.

"Get out of there, you moron!" she shouted. I glanced back to see that she stood at the edge of the path that led to the parking lot. God, she was beautiful. What the hell was I thinking, leaving a girl like that behind just to test the waters of single life at college? Let me tell you, those waters are not the kind of place "I play with blunt swords on the weekend" makes a lot of progress. Maybe I should move home. Maybe I could—

"Impudent mortal!" Kracek bellowed, snapping me out of my reverie. I whirled back around and shrieked. There might have been additional pissing. I'd rather not discuss the details.

Kracek's claw fell on me, but just as his talons were about to reach my face, a blade of shining steel flashed between us. The tip of the dragon's claw fell to the ground. Kracek shrieked and reared up, beating the air with his wings. A heavy hand fell on my shoulder and pulled me back. A knight, there was no other word, stepped between me and the dragon. He was in full armor, the steel of his plate shining with runes. His double-handed sword blazed with the light of the sun. He looked at me over his shoulder.

"Get outta here, kid. This is tough enough without trying to keep the idiots alive."

I was about to answer when a pillar of flame fell on us from the dragon's mouth. The knight didn't have a shield, but as the fire roared close, a purple dome surrounded us. The shriek of burning air fell hush. I scrambled to my feet, nearly bumping into a black man in exquisite robes, carrying a silver staff. Tattoos of light swirled around his left eye, and glowing rings spun above his clenched fist. His pale eyes were fixed on the dragon.

"Clarence is correct," he said. His voice reminded me of a professor, almost too precise, his enunciation as sharp as lightning. "You are no good here. Take your bravery and go home."

I was about to protest when Kracek roared again, and another wave of flame singed the air. The knight howled in pain, and the mage flinched back. I turned just in time to see the knight, armor still smoldering, run up the dragon's arm and start hacking at Kracek's throat. I ran all the way to where Chesa was standing before I realized it.

"Are you an idiot? What the hell were you thinking?" she snapped as I ran up to her. "You could have gotten killed!"

"Good point," I said. I grabbed her elbow and pulled her toward the parking lot. "Let's go not get killed."

Most of the cars had already cleared out, though there were enough smashed bumpers and broken glass in the lot to indicate it had been a hectic retreat. There were dents all along the side of Mom's Volvo, which would have taken some doing, considering that the thing was built like a tank. I tore open the door and got in. Chesa dropped into the passenger seat, her complicated costume tangling awkwardly with the belt. She tossed the bow over her shoulder and into the backseat. She started banging on the dashboard.

"Go, go, go! This is not how princesses die!"

I dug the keys out of the glove compartment, then slammed them into the ignition and twisted. The engine grumbled at me, grating and clanging and sputtering with each turn.

"Come on! Come on!" I shouted. Stuff broke around me all the time, from cars to computers to expensive espresso machines. Mom wasn't going to be happy when I brought it home with dents in the door. "Not like she'll believe this story anyway," I muttered. "Come on, you Viking bitch, start!"

"What did you call me?" Chesa asked. "This is not Viking. This is late-Tolkien elf. I don't know how you could possibly confuse the two."

"I am talking to the car! The car is obviously a bitch, Chesa! I don't know why I have to explain this." I kept cranking the key back and forth, pumping the gas, even as we argued.

I was about to give up and just run when the engine roared to life. I shouted victory, slammed the door shut, and dropped it into gear. Glass popped under my tires as I backed out of my spot, then I cranked the wheel around and lurched toward the exit. I was halfway across the lot when a cacophonous wave of violence swept over the asphalt.

An explosion blossomed over the soccer field. I couldn't see what was going on over the berm, but I could hear screaming, and Kracek's hideous laughter. The tips of his wings fluttered through the air, and bright, blinding flame washed across the field. The screams got louder, and worse.

"Holy Ydrissil," Chesa breathed. "I had no idea it was going to be like this. I had no idea, I swear . . ."

"This is well outside the bounds of your usual ren faire experience, yes," I said. I slammed on the brakes and stared toward the field, fingering the transmission.

"What are you doing? John, what are you doing!"

"Ah, to hell with it," I muttered. "Chesa, get out."

"No. No, no, no. You're going to do something stupid, and then it's going to be my fault for not stopping you. You're just trying to impress me, and I've got to tell you, it's not going to work. You're not a hero, John."

"Maybe today I am. Now get out."

She stared at me for three long seconds, then fumbled the seat belt off and rolled out of the car. She slammed the door shut and leaned down to the open window. "Boys are idiots."

"Yup," I said, then threw the car in reverse, spinning the station wagon's balding tires as I spun around. "Can't take the car home in this condition anyway." I pointed the hood toward the walkway that led to the fields, pulled the seat belt across my shoulder with one hand while I steered with the other, and floored it.

There was a barrier to prevent this very thing from happening, but it was made to stop ambitious suburban parents from driving their precious German SUVs onto the sidelines, not to stop a chunk of Viking metal at top speed. I crashed through the barrier, slewed back and forth on the loose gravel of the path, then reached the field. The shocks bottomed out in the drainage ditch, and for a brief moment I was airborne, flying like a Valkyrie toward the dragon, and destiny. I planted the nose in the mud, sawed the wheel back and forth as the tires bit into the sod, then lay into the accelerator and started screaming.

The heroes were in a bad way. The knight was down, dagger girl was on fire as she danced away from the dragon's claws, bloody rents in her leather armor and desperation in her eyes. The mage, if that's what he was, knelt beside the fallen knight. There was blood coming from his eyes. He turned and looked at me, his eyes going wide and white as I barreled toward him. Then he grabbed the knight and rolled out of my path.

The dragon heard me at the last second. He was focused on the girl and her shining daggers and gave no thought to an engine roaring ever closer, not until it was too late. Kracek swung his sinuous neck toward me, wide head just off the ground. His golden eyes flashed wider for just a second, and flames curled around his jaws as he breathed in, ready to obliterate me, Mom's Volvo, and the everything in between.

I put the hood of the car into his jaw, going about forty miles an hour. The front of the car crumpled, and I was thrown against the seatbelt, hands smashing the wheel as my head snapped forward like a whip. I saw the hood erupt and the engine, old and heavy and still spinning, shoot out of its moorings and through the dragon's skull. The dragon's teeth shattered like delicate china. The black slug of the engine tore through Kracek's head and punched out the other side, taking whatever suburban frustration and mystical wisdom a dragon posing as a property lawyer might contain along with it. The dragon's neck whipped through the air like a firehose, spewing molten flame across the field. He deflated, scales shuffling to the ground, wings withering like spiderwebs in the wind. Then he dropped to the ground and was still.

With numb fingers I snapped the seatbelt off, shoved open the crumpled door, and got out of the car. The two people still standing stared at me with open shock. I tried to wave, lost control of my arm, my shoulder, and then my legs, following my hand to the ground. I lay there for what seemed like a long time, breathing in scorched grass and wondering if the ringing in my head would ever stop. A shadow fell across my face. I looked up and saw the mage and the girl, staring down at me. The girl looked furious.

"Who's this guy?" the mage asked.

"An idiot," she said. Then she turned away and ran to the fallen knight. The mage leaned over.

"Even idiots can be heroes," he said. He pressed his palm against my forehead. There was a bright scarlet light, and then nothing.

I woke up in a very different kind of place.

CHAPTER FOUR
MUNDANE ACTUAL

The first thing I smelled was mildew and antiseptic. When I opened my eyes, the dim light of a pair of candles flickered over stone walls and a white ceiling, spotty with water stains and mold. I coughed, and the sound echoed. I tried to sit up, but the sheets wrapped around my shoulders were as tight as a straitjacket, and just as comfortable. I took a deep breath and was alerted by my nervous system that I was actually in a lot of pain, maybe enough pain to kill me, certainly enough to keep me still and whimpering for the immediate future. So I continued to whimper. This drew the attention of my attendant.

"So, not dead then?" The speaker appeared to my right, nothing more than a dim shape in the candlelight. He tucked some bit of restrictive sheet even tighter around my shoulders, then leaned in close. I was surprised to see he was wearing a pair of vintage sunglasses, the kind with thick black plastic frames, and lenses as black as midnight. Long, curly brown hair spilled out on either side of his face. He was dressed in a dingy white blazer and blue jeans. He tapped my forehead. "That's a pity. We could use another dead guy around here."

"Where am I?" I croaked. My throat was as dry as uncooked rice. Mr. Cool Shades went to a nearby table and returned with a stein of water, then slowly poured it over my face. I gasped for breath, getting more of it into my lungs than my belly, while the rest soaked into my sheets. "What the hell?"

"You're in Mundane Actual," he said, and you could hear the

23

capitals. He returned the metal cup to the table. Both it and the candelabra on the table looked like props from the renaissance faire. "This is as far as we can take you for now."

"Not a hospital? I feel like I should be in a hospital." Cold fear crept into my gut. "Have you . . . am I being kidnapped?"

"Maybe. Or maybe you're dead. We'll get into that later." He leaned against the table and folded his arms. Now that my eyes were adjusting to the light, I thought I could see a dim glow behind his shades, as though his pupils were burning. "It's really an interesting question, about free will, and our right to choose what the universe may have already picked out for us. Did you stop having a choice when you drove your wagon into our friend's face, or was it sooner? Or later? Or are you making choices at all. See, in the sixteenth century—"

"Enough of that, Matthew," a familiar voice said. The man I thought of as the mage appeared at my feet. I mean that literally; he wasn't there, then he was. "I'm sure our guest has enough issues without your existential rambling. How are you feeling, son?"

"Like I was in a car crash with a dragon, then tied up and left to die of thirst. So, you know, pretty great."

"Oh, you're thirsty?" Matthew asked. He turned back to the table. "You should have said something."

"Why did you pour water on my head?"

"Why would I pour water on your head if you were thirsty?" he asked.

"Exactly!"

"I don't think I understand your question." He presented the cup again, holding it next to my shoulder. I looked from it to his face, then to the mage.

"Matthew," the mage said. "He can't very well take that cup from you if his hands are tied, can he?"

"Right, right. Mundane. I forget." He jerked the sheets free of my chest, setting off a whole new round of misery and pain. I had a moment to stare at the cuts and bruises across my chest before the pain hit me, and then I wasn't very thirsty for a while. When my senses returned, I carefully levered up onto my elbow and took the cup. The water was cold and stale, thick with silt. I almost spat it out, but my dry throat demanded otherwise. As I was gulping down the last of the water, a lot of stuff clicked in my head. Dead bodies on a field, and my friends disappearing into the woods.

"I have to go," I said, trying to stand. The mage made no effort to stop me. He didn't need to. Gravity and the pain in my chest were enough. I settled back on the bed. "I mean . . . I have to find out what happened to my friends. To the people at the park."

"A lot of them died," the mage said simply. "But not so many we can't fix it. With the news, that is. Dead is still dead, even here."

"Oh, God. Oh, hell . . ." I said. I was starting to feel sick again. "Do you know if my friends made it out?"

"Who were they?" he asked. "We're compiling a list for the media teams, so they can start on direct contact. If you have their names . . ."

"Eric Cavanaugh and Chesa Lazaro. They were dressed like . . . like . . ."

"Elves. The girl at least. We've had our eye on her for a while." The mage stood up and pulled a small notebook from his robes, then conjured a pen of pure light and wrote in it. I was still staring when he snapped the book shut. "She's fine. But we're not sure about Eric. Cavanaugh, you say? I'll have the cleanup crews look into it."

"Cleanup crews? Media teams? These are people we're talking about! People who have died."

"Yes, I understand the concept. I wouldn't worry just yet. Some of them we can retrieve. Their bodies might not yet believe they're dead, and then it's just a matter of talking the flesh back into the game. Like I said, we're still compiling the lists. I'm sure your friend will show up. And while we're at it." He lifted the notebook again. "What's your name?" the mage asked.

"John. John Rast," I said, "What's yours?"

"Sir John Rast? So you gave your actual name to the lists." He made his note and tucked the book away with a smirk. "Don't most folks make up something more . . . interesting?"

"I'm as interesting as I need to be," I said defensively. Truth was, I couldn't come up with anything better. "What's your name? Merlin? Gandalf? Tim?"

"Furaha na Nguvu ya Tembo," he said simply. "Or is that too interesting for you?"

"Few Harry na—"

"Tembo for your lazy American tongue."

"Fair enough, Tembo," I said, then swallowed more water and held the cup out to be refilled. Matthew just stared at it for a while. I looked at him. "Is there more?"

"Yes?" he answered, genuine confusion in his voice.

"May I have some, or is there some special way of asking for water in this place?"

Tembo took my hand and guided the cup back to my mouth. It was full again, and I realized the table didn't have a pitcher on it. Bile burned through my throat. I dropped the cup and rose to my feet, ignoring the pain in my chest. The sheet fell to my knees, and I was thrilled to discover that I was completely naked and not doing a lot for my reputation, considering the cold and injuries. I snatched the sheet up around my armpits—ignoring the stabs of pain in my chest—and stood there, shivering.

"Seriously, what the hell is going on!" I snapped. "There was a . . . a dragon, and those lights, and the girl with the daggers . . . and a DRAGON! Do you have any idea—"

"Yes, yes, we know. We were there." Tembo held up one hand, like he was arguing politics with a drunk relative, rather than discussing the particulars of a dragon on a suburban soccer field. He put a gentle hand on my shoulder and pushed me down onto the bed. "I think that's enough weird stuff for one day."

"No! You're not going to put me to sleep again, buddy! I want some answers, and . . ." I doubled over in pain as something tore loose in my chest. I leaned against the bed and tried to breathe. When the agony had passed, I continued. "Scratch that. No answers. I don't need to know what sort of nonsense you're up to. I just want to go to a nice, normal hospital, with nice, normal doctors and boring cups that don't fill themselves."

"That would be foolish," Matthew said patiently. "You're in the best hospital in the world. In all the worlds. Besides, we've got some questions for you and your friend."

"Questions for me? For me! What on earth could you possibly want to ask me?"

"I had forgotten how curious mundane conversation can be. What on earth, indeed. On earth." Matthew chuckled and rubbed his thigh, then seemed to lose track of the conversation as his palm chafed the blue leg of his pants. "Man, I miss jeans."

"Later," Tembo said. "For now, one more weird thing, and then you promise to stay calm until we can get our boss down here. Okay?"

"Hospital or I start screaming," I said. "I don't care where this is, someone's going to hear me."

"Sir John, you have no idea," Tembo said. He pinched the bridge of his nose in frustration, then motioned to Matthew. "St. Matthew, ease this man's pain, will you?"

"You're sure? I've only got so much, and Clarence—"

"Clarence will be fine once we get him back to his domain. Esther hates it when she has to spend the first part of an interview convincing a Mundane that the world really is an interesting place. Our friend needs a little persuasion."

"Sure thing, Tem," Matthew said. He whipped his sunglasses off. The light I had seen through the shades before wasn't fire at all. His eyes shimmered, like the sparkle that comes off diamonds in those jewelry store commercials, the purest, most unbelievable light. He held his hands forward, palms up, leaned his head back, and closed his eyes. The shimmer lingered, then flared into brilliance. Pure light washed over me, filling me with warmth and hope and comfort. I collapsed back onto the bed.

My pain was gone. The skin on my chest was smooth, the scabs gone, and whatever had been grinding in my ribs was replaced with a comfortable warmth. When I sat up, there was no discomfort. Not even my muscles ached, and the mottled purple bruises where the seatbelt choked me had disappeared. I stared down at my hands in wonder.

"What did you do?" I asked.

"You might call it a miracle, if you're that type," Matthew said. He folded the sunglasses and put them in his pocket. The light in his eyes was gone, replaced by dull brown irises and bloodshot whites. "That's all I've got, Tem. Clarence will have to wait until we get across the threshold. I need to get back to the Brilliance, spend some time with the light, before I can heal anyone else."

"You couldn't have done much for him with that little radiance, anyway," Tembo said, nodding grimly. He motioned toward the door. Matthew clapped my shoulder, then turned and left. The mage settled onto the edge of my bed.

"Is that proof enough?" he asked.

"Proof of what?"

"Impossible things. There are going to be a few of them, from here on out. I can't really say more than that. Not until the boss gets here."

I looked down at my hands, flexing the fingers, rolling my wrists. I was healed. I nodded my head.

"Sure," I said. "That's proof enough. So who's the boss?"

"I'll let her do the introductions. For now, simply know that you and your friend are lucky to be alive and not in chains. Took some convincing to keep Bethany from filling you full of holes. Clarence spoke well of you. Of your bravery, at least, if not your ability."

"Wait," I said, as his words finally settled on me. "My friend? Is Eric here?"

"I do not think that girl would answer to the name Eric," Tembo answered. "She seemed quite keen to know if you were hurt. Though I'm not sure that's to your benefit."

"Ah," I said, and the bottom dropped out of my stomach. "Chesa. Great."

CHAPTER FIVE
FERAL JANITORS

After Tembo and Matthew left, I took the time to explore the room I was in. I wouldn't usually use the word "explore" in this context, but this was definitely an exploration. There was a worryingly large pile of bloody towels at the foot of my bed. I pushed them around with my toe, trying to decide if it was enough blood loss to cause hallucinations. Maybe, maybe not. I snatched up the candelabra and started into the darkness, away from the door. Turns out I was in a long, dark hallway with beds every fifteen feet, and no windows. The light from the candelabra never gave me more than five feet of illumination, and the farther I got from my own bed, the dimmer the candle's flame grew. I went until the wick was a dim glimmer, then turned back. The hallway could have gone on forever, for all I could tell. It certainly went for a hundred feet.

With the uncertain void stretching out beside me, I found it difficult to sleep, despite Tembo's warnings about the rigors ahead. I finally settled into a restless doze, my mind running through the events of the day, the impossibility of dragons, and the strange man with the glowing eyes. There were a lot of weird things going on, and my mind was reeling. But mostly I was worried about Eric and Chesa. Eric, because he was my friend, and Chesa, because she wasn't, and I wasn't looking forward to having to explain what had happened. Especially since I didn't really know what had happened, or where we were, or anything. Maybe she would have some answers. Hopefully.

I was sleepily mulling the possibility of slipping out before my interview with this boss person when the door opened, and two nondescript men in gray coveralls came in. I heard their voices before the door opened, and they sounded perfectly normal, which made their arrival all the more shocking.

"There were three of them, big as dinner plates, just scuttling around behind the fridge. Dinner plates, Mike!" The speaker was short and thin, his head and hands too large for his body, dressed in gray coveralls. His companion was nearly his twin. The light from the outside hallway blinded me for a second as they came into the room. There was something wrong with their hands... "So, being the kind of man that I am, and not the kind of man you are, I got the zippo out of the garage—"

"Gods, Jerry, you're a wreck." The other man said. I sat squinting up at their dim forms as they busied themselves at the foot of my bed. "A zippo? For roaches?"

"Roaches the size of dinner plates, Mike. Keep your eye on the fine details of the story. Never step on anything larger than your foot, my mom always said. Zippo it is!"

"But still..." Mike bent down, briefly disappearing beneath the bed. "Your mom lived in a swamp. Not much danger in setting everything ablaze when mphlumphlgump."

"You are keen to recognize the danger of my position, Mike, keen indeed. But there was nothing for it. The roaches had drawn the wrath of Jerry Left! I dialed the zippo to what was surely an appropriate setting, primed the wick, and set about purging my kitchen of this nightmare. Have you ever burned a roach, Mike?"

Mike made a gagging sound, which drew a chuckle from Jerry. "Popcorn, my friend. Their shells erupt in the most satisfying way you can imagine. Of course, the refrigerator defrosted in an explosive manner, but at least the melted ice put out the lingering flames from the cabinets. All according to plan."

"Excuse me," I tried to interject. Jerry waved his hand at me dismissively.

"A moment, boy. Never interrupt a good story."

"This doesn't feel like a good YAURGH!" I screamed.

Screamed, you understand, because I finally saw what was wrong with their hands. Jerry gestured at me, not with fingers or palms or knuckles, but with something that could have been mistaken for a mop made of octopi, purple-black tentacles squirming over shining beaks, suckers puckering open and closed. So I screamed. Reasonable.

Jerry turned pale white in the blink of an eye, and the sudden contrast revealed the rest of his form. Which was boring in a comfortable way. He put a perfectly normal human hand to his chest, breathed in sharply, and blinked at me in shock. His other hand, the left hand, squirmed into a tight ball, like spaghetti around a fork.

"Son of a bitch!" Jerry finally squeaked out. "What's wrong with you?"

"What's wrong with *you*?" I echoed, pulling myself upright and drawing the sheets around my shoulders. "With your hand?"

"Glumphrgurgle," Mike said as he stood up. Several bloody towels were hanging from his mouth, and his throat was distended with the rest of the pile. He stared at me in confusion. "Phlrbub?"

There was more screaming, more confused hand and tentacle waving on the parts of Jerry and Mike (Mike's right hand was a match to Jerry's left, otherwise the two appeared to be twins), and finally an unfortunate retreat from the bed that ended with me getting tangled in the sheets. I fell onto the stone floor in a heap.

"Will you stop that!" Jerry shouted at me. He and Mike were both on top of the bed, clutching each other and mincing their feet. "They startle very easily!"

"They?" I asked. "They who?"

"Left and Right," Jerry answered. He held out his grotesque hand. It was nearly normal size, the tentacles wound tightly together, and two large eyes with figure-eight pupils, staring out at me. "I've been through one evacuation; I don't want to do that again!"

"Hansuh flitch," Mike mumbled around the towel in his mouth. He distended his jaw, worked his throat, and drew the rest of the towel into his belly. His skull reassembled itself, and he wiped his blood-flecked lips. "I mean, a real serious bitch."

"What is happening to my life?" I pressed the heels of my palms into my eyes, rubbing colors and shapes into the darkness, until I remembered I was naked and alone with two men who ate laundry and had tentacles for hands. When I opened my eyes, they were still staring at me tentatively.

"Are you done screaming?" Jerry asked.

"I don't think I'll ever be done with it, no. But I don't think there are screams enough in the world to cover this situation, so . . ." I stood up, wrapping the sheets around my waist. "What the hell is going on now? Are you the boss?"

"Oh, gods no," Mike said with a disturbing smile. "Gods, the boss. Ha! I mean, really big ha!" His laughter sounded like something he practiced in the mirror, right along with that smile. "No, we're just the janitors. The tame ones. Not the other ones."

"There are feral janitors?"

"Where do you think the smells come from?" Jerry asked, matter of fact.

"What? Never mind. Never-freaking-mind. What do you want?"

Jerry pointed to Mike's belly. "The towels, of course. And that sheet, frankly. You've made quite a mess out of it."

"Well, the sheet is all I have to wear right now, so—" Jerry interrupted me with a sinuous handwave, then produced a pair of coveralls much like their own, only black. He set them on the bed. "Now, the sheet, if you please."

"Some privacy?" I asked. "Turn around, or something?"

"We have a lot of eyes," Mike answered. "There wouldn't be much point in it. Though if it makes you feel better—"

"Nope, no, never mind. I don't want to know about your eyes. Just wait outside. I'll throw the sheet out when I'm done."

"We're supposed to take the sheet with us," Mike said. He rubbed his belly, looking nervously at Jerry. "He could run away with it."

"I'm not going to steal your . . . my life! What is— Never! Mind!" I picked up the coveralls and started unfolding them. There was a patch on the chest, an elongated hexagon that resembled a templar's helm, but with an ankh instead of a cross. As I pulled them on, I noticed Jerry and Mike wore a similar patch on their shoulders. With some clever balancing I was able to get the coveralls on without completely abandoning my decency. I threw the sheet at Mike. "Happy?"

"We were supposed to wash him—" Mike said nervously.

"Nope! No! Get out! Go and keep going until you're far away, both of you, go!"

I hustled the janitors out the door, then sat down on my bed and wondered about . . . well, a lot of things. When Tembo came through the door a few minutes later, I was perched on the edge of my bed, about to burst.

"I know I've asked this before, and I know I'm starting to repeat myself. But you have to understand my position. This is weird. All of this. And maybe it's not so strange to you, considering your whole light tattoo, interesting name, silver staff deal. But I'm starting to freak out. So can you please, seriously, please, tell me what the hell is going on?"

Unfortunately, I said all of this in one breath, too fast for the words to properly form. Tembo raised his eyes at me.

"Pardon?" he asked.

"That's really all I've got. It's a lot of little things, or big things, but it would take too long to list them all. You know all this isn't normal, right? So answer my question. What is going on?"

"A good question, but one without a single answer. Usually by this point in the initiation—"

"Initiation? Like a cult? You're a cult, then?"

"Listen, you're going to get yourself worked up. Just come with me."

"No, I have not gotten myself worked up. If anything, I have gotten myself worked down, which is kind of a big deal considering what I've been through. Two guys with squids for hands have gotten me worked up. They wanted to wash me, Tem. They didn't have buckets, Tem, or water. Or normal hands, Tem!"

"The janitors can be disconcerting. An unfortunate offshoot of some early twentieth-century writing that got out of hand. Most of them are friendly, but a few . . ." he shrugged. "Anyway. I thought you would still be asleep when they arrived."

"How is that better? Why do you think it would be better for me to wake up to that?"

"They exude certain chemicals that, upon contact with the skin, send the victim—"

"HOW IS THAT BETTER, TEM?"

"Enough shouting. The boss is waiting for you. Are you comfortable in your new clothes?"

"Sure, why not. What's the deal with this?" I asked, flicking the patch on my chest. "Feels like military. This a government agency?"

"The boss got into a weird space in the 80s. Started talking about brand awareness and market placement. Wanted logos. That's the only part that stuck."

"Logos. Like a sports team?" I asked.

"I prefer your military analogy, John. So will the boss."

"And who is the boss?"

"You'll see. Come on, she's waiting." He turned toward the door.

"Does our little sports team have a mascot? A theme song? Maybe a name?"

"Knight Watch," Tembo said impatiently. "And don't ask about the song," he muttered. "I hate the damned song."

I'm not sure what I expected from the secret headquarters of a magical organization that called itself the Knight Watch. Maybe something between the lair of a Bond villain and dinner at Medieval Times, with a dash of Hogwarts thrown in. What I got was mildew, crumbling drywall, and flickering fluorescent lighting. Tembo looked terribly out of place in his deep blue robes and impeccable manner. I could see how the janitors felt at home, though. I stepped through the door and immediately felt safer. How could things like dragons exist in a world with this much fluorescent light? Surely it had all been a trick of the mind. Surely, I was just in a theme park on the outskirts of town. Surely.

"I have to tell you, Tem, I was hoping for a little more magic. You could at least—"

"You!" The word froze me mid-sentence. I turned slowly toward the source and tried to smile. Chesa was standing in a doorway across the hall. Her elf costume was rumpled, the edges charred, her fey-ears hanging despondently from her lobes. "What. The hell. Have you done?"

"Oh, hey, Ches." I took a step back and bumped into Tembo, who was a lot more immovable than his gentle manner would suggest. "Glad to see you're okay!"

"Okay? John, I am anything but okay. Do you see this!" She grabbed the edge of her armored skirt and held it up. The plasticard scale mail was charred. "This is four hundred dollars down the drain. And these ears!" She plucked one of the prosthetics out of her hair and waggled it at me. "Custom made. I had to send a plaster of my skull to freaking China for these things. Someone in China has my head, John! And now they're ruined." She tossed it to her feet. Half a second later, Jerry the squid-handed janitor crept out of the doorway Chesa was standing in and reached for the discarded ear. Chesa stomped on his slithering fingers. She shot him an angry look. "And these guys! Don't get me started on these guys!"

"I think it's safe to say that everyone finds the janitors equally disturbing," I said. "Look, there's a lot going on. I'm sorry about your elf-stuff, but—"

"Are you in charge?" Chesa snapped. She was staring at Tembo. The big mage shrank back a little bit.

"Thank the gods, no. We were just going to see the boss, actually, if you want to join—"

"Damn straight we are," Chesa said. She started down the hallway, leaving us behind. Tembo shot me a look.

"Your friend is doing very well, considering the circumstances," he said.

"I take it you didn't have to convince her about the nature of miracles?"

"We did not get that far in our conversation," he said. "Who knows, she may survive this encounter with her mind fully intact."

"Fully intact? Am I not fully intact?" I asked.

"A question for later," he said briskly. "For now, Miss Chesa is getting away, and about to make a very wrong turn." Tembo hurried forward, calling after Chesa. "Excuse me, miss? You will want to go left at the intersection. Do not concern yourself with the sounds—" A roar of agony tore through the hallway from the door Chesa was about to open. She hesitated, looking unsure for the first time since I had seen her that morning. Tembo caught up with her and clapped his approval. "Very good. We will go this way. If you please?"

Chesa arched her eyebrow, first at Tembo, then at me, then the mysterious door. But she turned and marched in the direction indicated. By the time I reached them, the room with the roaring was well behind us.

"So what the hell's back there?" I asked Tembo. He lowered his voice and spoke without turning to me.

"We are trying to explain Clarence's injuries to his archenemy. It is not going well."

I glanced back just in time to see St. Matthew dance out of the room and slam the door behind him. A flare of light outlined the doorframe, and smoke poured into the hallway. When he saw me, Matthew waved and smiled, as though there was nothing unusual about a screaming, burning room.

"Weirder by the step," I said. Then I hurried after Tem and Chesa.

CHAPTER SIX
BOSS FIGHT

Tembo led us through winding hallways, illuminated by the buzzing, flickering fluorescents, sweeping past dozens of closed doorways. Most were just dented steel, but a few were barricaded shut, and at least one was actively on fire. No one seemed to mind. A squad of soldier-looking types, both men and women, squeezed past us, their olive-drab coveralls bolstered with ballistic armor and complicated tactical vests, though all their holsters were empty. Their eyes followed us curiously. I returned the favor, while Chesa stuck her chin out and ignored them completely. After they turned a corner, I caught up with Tembo and pulled at his robes.

"So you're not a government agency, you claim you're not a cult . . . but you've got squads of heavily armed SEAL team cosplayers wandering the hallways. Tell me, the leader of this little organization, does she have a heavily highlighted copy of the Bill of Rights hanging on her wall?" I asked.

Chesa snorted, but quickly wiped any trace of amusement from her face. Tembo shrugged.

"You are quick to pass judgment on people you have never met, Mr. Rast," he said. "I am sure that has served you well in your relations with your many friends."

"Point taken," I said. "And I'll also take that as a yes on the constitutional fetishism."

"He has a point, though," Chesa said. "What's with all the soldja boys?"

"That was the containment team at the soccer field. Most have never seen a dead dragon before. All they know is that you did that, apparently by mistake. You already have a reputation, Mr. Rast."

"You had a team of guys with guns, and you left it to me and my car?" I asked.

"The Mundane Actual teams have limited influence in these matters. They did what they could, but it isn't much. Believe me, they feel the same frustration as you. It takes time to adjust to the new unreality. People like that, they are not accustomed to feeling helpless."

"A common problem here, I imagine."

"Common, and terribly unnecessary. This is one of the few places we have true control. People like me, that is. And people like you."

"What's that supposed to mean?" I asked. Tembo only smiled.

"Keep talking like that and John's going to start thinking he's a hero. Doesn't take much to drive into a propane tank and blow a soccer field half to hell," Chesa grumbled.

"Yes, I forgot. Miss Chesa has not yet been converted to the unreal world," Tembo said. "So how would you explain these things? The dragon that we all know you saw, and the janitor?"

"Not to mention the burning door back there," I said. "That didn't seem to bother you."

"I'm not a rube," she answered. "I cosplay at the highest level. A couple tanks of propane, three men in a rubber suit, and a little laser-enhanced CGI may fool most people, but not—"

"You should have saved Matthew's little miracle for her," I said.

"Frankly, you were much closer to a total breakdown," Tembo said. "Chesa is handling this better than most. I will leave it to the boss to convince her. Now, be polite." He turned on his heel and gestured to a door. It looked newer than the rest, and the lock on the door was a combination keypad and swipe card. Tembo knocked, then stepped back. The door opened.

"You aren't coming with us?" I asked.

"I am not allowed in such places. For my own safety, I am told," he said. Tembo bowed slightly, then turned and walked away. He was humming to himself, and the tune bored a hole into my skull. He looked over his shoulder at me. "She is waiting, my friends. Hurry on."

This was the first time I had actually been alone with Chesa since the dragon attack. She was standing there, arms folded, staring daggers at Tembo's retreating back. I cleared my throat.

"I see you're still the best at awkward silences and even more awkward friends," Chesa said. She turned on me. "Really, John, you should try practicing on normal humans one of these days. There's just no substitute."

Before I could answer, she pushed open the door and stepped inside. Unsure if the door would lock behind her, I had to scramble before it swung shut in my face. Flustered, it took me a long second to get my bearings of my new surroundings.

Unlike the hallway, this room was clean and white, with sound tiles on the walls and a microphone hanging from the ceiling. A window in the opposite wall looked into an empty control room. The microphone was suspended above a vinyl-topped card table and two folding chairs. The door shut behind me, and immediately it got eerily quiet in the room.

"Cool, soundproofing," Chesa said quietly. "They could murder us in here and no one would have any idea."

A door next to the control room window unsealed with a pop and then opened, allowing a middle-aged woman in tactical gear to enter. Two guards, like the ones from the hallway except actually armed and more hostile than curious, flanked the doorway. The woman was carrying an open folder in one hand and a rotary style grenade launcher in the other. She had long, steel gray hair nearly contained in a bun on the back of her head and walked with the sort of authority I usually only saw in movies about the end of the world. She read from the folder as she walked, mouthing words and frowning. She pulled one of the folding chairs out with her toe, sat down, and motioned to the opposite chair without looking up. There was only one chair. Chesa and I looked at each other. Eventually, the women looked up.

"There are two of you," she said. "Is that new?"

"I'm sorry?" I asked. "New in what way?"

"Have you always been two people, or is this new? Am I looking at a Janus situation? Do I need to have the two of you bound into shackles of fell-born steel and welded back together, one piece of soul at a time?"

"Try it and I'll tear your eyeballs out," Chesa said simply.

"It's not new," I said, before the steel-haired woman decided to use the rather large grenade launcher in her hands. "For us, anyway. We've always been different people. I mean, these people. I've always been me. And Chesa's always been Chesa. Right?"

"So you'll probably want different chairs, I assume. One for each of you," the woman said. "Can someone get me another chair?"

One of the guards snapped to attention, then hurried out the door and returned mere seconds later with a folding chair, which he deployed right behind Chesa, then returned to his place at the door. The whole operation took no more than ten seconds. It was as if they had a stockpile of folding chairs just out of sight.

"So we're good? You can sit down now? I'm not missing anything?" the woman asked.

"Pretty sure we're missing something," Chesa said, but she sat daintily in the chair, crossing her long, armored legs. I realized I was staring and fumbled my way into my seat.

As I sat down, the woman leaned the grenade launcher against her chair. Chesa cleared her throat and shifted a little farther away.

"We're hot?" the woman shouted. When no one answered, she twisted around and looked at the empty control room. "Miriam, are we good to go? You can hear me? Okay. First thing, I'm going to need your name. Rast, we have on record." She pointed at Chesa, who gave her full name. *Chesa Glorious Lazaro.* I always thought she was making up the middle name, but she insisted it was real. After Esther had finished writing this down, she turned back and looked us both up and down. "Sounds familiar. Might be something in the archives on you. And Rast, you're looking rough. The janitors didn't wash you?"

"I was already awake," I said. She nodded, as if that explained everything. "You're the boss?"

"Cellular degradation and the inevitability of death are the true bosses, aren't they?" She asked, then lay the open folder on the table. I could see pictures from the day's events. The crumpled front of Mom's car, burning faire displays, the torn sod of the soccer field . . . all of it framed by the mound of scales and muscle that was Douglas "Kracek" Hosier. Chesa creased her brow and leaned forward to examine the photos, then opened her mouth as if to ask a question. She never got it out, and the woman continued talking. "But yes, I'm as close to a boss as the Knight Watch has. Not an elite, mind you. Just the organizer. Esther MacRae."

Chesa was still going through the photos. She picked up a picture of Kracek's broken skull lying next to the ruin of Mom's car. I glanced over at her. Deep confusion was running through her eyes.

"They didn't give us a secret decoder ring when we woke up. Or much of an explanation at all, so you're going to have to go slow," I said, then nodded to Chesa, hopefully in a way that Chesa didn't notice. "Maybe slower for some of us than others."

"Gods, I hate when I have to do this part . . ." Esther said, rubbing her eyes. "What did they tell you?"

"Let's start easy. What's an elite?"

"Tembo, Clarence, Bethany . . . maybe you. Folks with an affinity for the unreal. They have a connection to their mythic identities and are able to affect the myths. They really didn't explain this?"

"This is a dragon," Chesa said.

"Yes. And your friend here killed it with his car. Which is impossible." Esther fixed her steely gaze on me, and I found myself squirming. "And impossible things interest me."

"But . . . it's . . ." Chesa looked up at me. "That's a dragon. Where are the propane tanks?"

"Yeah. Not your typical renaissance faire," I said.

"We can add renaissance faires to the things I hate. Just tempting fate, those places. We try to keep the mythics away from them, but Kracek had a lot of influential friends, and let's be honest, if a dragon wants to go somewhere, you're not going to stop him by waving around a copy of the Treaty of 1876 and threatening to start an inquiry."

"No, I suppose not," I said. "So he wasn't supposed to be there?"

"None of us were. But the actuator picked up some weird activity, and then we found out the dragon was in attendance, so we mobilized the team and set up a perimeter. And then you happened, and all hell broke loose." She shuffled her papers and then pressed her palms into the table. "Which brings me to my next topic. I've got some questions for you, Mr. Rast."

"Please just call me John. My father—"

"God, please don't say your father is Mr. Rast," Chesa snapped. "This is serious business. Do you realize that this is a dragon?"

"We'll get to that later. After you've answered my questions," Esther said.

"Actually, let's start there," I said. "Why don't you explain how a dragon came to be in a soccer field during a renaissance faire? Because that seems kind of important."

"This is my interview, my safe room, and my team. So we're going to start with my questions," Esther said. "Unless you think you can make it to that door before my guards bring you down."

I looked up at the guards, both of whom looked eager for us to try. I didn't think they would shoot us, but I also didn't want to learn the sorts of nonlethal methods they had at their disposal. I glanced over at Chesa. She shrugged.

"Always good to start with a threat," I said. "Sure. What are your questions?"

"This is your car?" she asked, flipping a photo across the table to me. I looked down.

"My mother's car, actually. She's going to kill me."

"Do you know where she got it?"

"Not really. She's had it for ages. I think she got it used."

"Anything unusual about its origin? A used-car lot she had never been to, for example, and was never able to find again? Might it have been a gift from a one-eyed man with a little dog, who appeared in her dreams and offered great power, if only she would keep the car safe for a thousand years? Just as an example."

"Just as an example," I echoed. "That's an awfully specific example."

"It's happened before. Only that was for . . ." she shuffled the papers in her folder, finally reading from one of the many handwritten pages. "For the care and protection of a boiling cauldron of giant's blood." She glanced up at me again. "So no?"

"No. There might have been a down payment, but I sincerely doubt it was in blood, or for blood, or written in blood," I said. "It was just a car."

"No. No it wasn't. 'Just a car' doesn't kill a dragon. And what about you, Mr. Rast. You seem suspiciously comfortable discussing blood contracts. Have you ever spoken to a goat?" I stared at her for a long moment, hoping she would hear the words she had just said and choose to say something else. Something rational. When she simply returned my stare with that same no-nonsense look on her face, I gave up. I shook my head. She nodded, glanced down at her notes, and continued. "Danced with, or on top of, or through, moonlight?"

"I'm not really a dancer."

"He is *not* lying about that," Chesa said.

Esther nodded noncommittally and shuffled through her papers.

"Have you ever engaged in drinking competitions with any of the elder races? For the purposes of this question, I would accept dwarves, darrow, underkin, feral janitors, certain Presbyterians, and any of the usual types of devil." She had a checklist, and a pen at the ready. "Ring a bell?"

"I once drank beer out of a boot in Cincinnati," I said. Her eyebrows went up.

"Possible Germans," she said as she wrote herself a note. "But nothing else?"

"I'm not even sure how to answer that question," I said. "I've lived a nice, boring life. I'm a nice, boring person. There's nothing interesting about me."

"Also not a lie," Chesa offered helpfully. She was getting over the dragon thing pretty well, to my unending misery.

"Nice, boring people do not kill dragons," Esther said. "Though you're right. Outside of your sword-related hobbies, there's not much to commend you to the life of a hero." She fanned out her papers, tapping absentmindedly on the scroll to the side. "Must have been the car."

"I think I've had enough of this," I said. "And, though I'm getting a little tired of asking, I'll give it one more go. What the hell's going on here?"

She ignored me, scanning through the papers and muttering to herself. Finally, she called over her shoulder. "Turn it off, Miriam. Investigation's over."

"Investigation?" Chesa asked. "You think we had something to do with this . . . this . . ."

"It's a dragon. Just get used to it," I said.

"I do," Esther answered over me. "Or more accurately, I think it had something to do with you. I don't know what, yet, but I'm really looking forward to finding out." She moved the papers around on the table, then drew a whole new sheaf out from the back of the folder and set them in front of us.

"What are these?" I asked.

"Applications," she said. When neither of us said anything, Esther creased her brow. "You want the job, don't you?"

"And what job is this?" Chesa asked warily, in exactly the same way you'd ask a crazy person which voice in her head she was talking to at the moment.

"Heroes," Esther answered. "We're in the hero business."

CHAPTER SEVEN
THE HERO BUSINESS

"A job? You're offering us a job?" I asked. "You're crazy. No. Wait. This is crazy. All of it." Chesa was staring down at the application like it was a thinly smeared turd that she had just found at the bottom of her lunch salad. "All we want to do is go home and forget this even happened!"

"Not many people make it this far," Esther said, squaring the pages and closing the folder. She pushed a couple of pens in our direction. "Again, not a threat, but most people die before we get them in this room."

"The janitors?" I asked, cringing.

"John, you and Chesa experienced a complete collapse of the mundane world. You more than her, but it's clear you're both involved, or you wouldn't have ended up here. All those people picked up by the containment team are now telling the police stories about a gas accident. Even the first responders have formed a convenient fiction about propane storage and a fire-breathing carnival prop that went wrong. The evening news will cover it without mentioning dragons, or swordfights, or any of that. The mundane world will go on thinking this was a tragedy and nothing more. But not you. You saw, and killed, a dragon. With a car."

"Yes?" I said.

She slammed the folder down on the card table. "It shouldn't be possible!"

It was all I could do to not laugh in her face. She didn't seem the kind of woman who dealt well with laughter, even in laughter-appropriate environments, which this was not.

"That shouldn't be possible? That?" I finally snapped. "Lady, have you walked outside this room? There's a guy with an octopus for a hand, another whose eyes glow and can fill a cup with his mind, and I'm pretty sure Tembo is more than a clever sleight-of-hand guy! So if you think driving a car into a dragon is an unreasonable strain on your credulity, boy, have I got news for you!"

She waited patiently while I yelled, watching me as I paced back and forth in front of the card table. I didn't even remember getting up. Chesa was watching me curiously, clearly waiting for me to run out of steam. Eventually I got dizzy, either from lack of blood or general hysteria, and sat back down. But I kept yelling for a while.

"And the girl with the daggers! I knew there was something kooky about her, I knew it! No one fights dagger like that, but there she was, jumping around like a horsefly at a picnic, one place in one breath, completely gone the next. And *Clarence*? First off, what kind of name is Clarence? And what was he thinking, with that 'This is tough enough without keeping the idiots safe' line? Could he have been more of a jerk?"

"Clarence nearly died on that field. He may walk again, someday, but he may never again carry the sword into battle outside of his domain. So. A little respect."

"Look, this hasn't been my best day. You have to admit that freaking out is a perfectly acceptable response in this situation. So why don't you stop screwing around and tell me what this is all about?"

Esther tapped the folder against her palm for a while.

"Are you going to take the jobs?" she asked.

"We don't even know what you're offering," I said. "And furthermore—"

"I'm in," Chesa said. She scratched her name across the bottom line of the application and flipped it back to Esther. "You probably have some magical way of filling the rest of that out. I'm no sucker."

I turned to her slowly and blinked once.

"But, but . . . the dragon," I said.

"Sure, a dragon. And monstrous janitors, and knights, and mages . . . it's pretty clear what's going on here." She snapped her fingers and smiled. "This is the entrance exam for some kind of magical realm. Next level Hogwarts bullshit. I can't sign up fast enough."

"Ten seconds ago, you didn't believe in dragons at all. Now you're fully on board? Just like that?"

"Of course. I can't believe you aren't," Chesa said. "John, the only thing I ever liked about you was the fact that you wanted to be a knight nearly as badly as I wanted to be an elven princess. And," she deflected her attention briefly to Esther. "Correct me if I'm wrong here, sister, but I'm pretty sure we're being offered the opportunity to do precisely that."

There was a long moment of silence. I raised my brows at Esther.

"Right?" I asked.

"More or less. You'll have to figure out your roles on your own, but that stuff is often driven by internal priorities and your connection to your own mythic past. It works differently for different people. I can't make any promises."

"Elven princess!" Chesa sang. She sprang to her feet and pirouetted around the room, bopping each of the guards on the nose and even smiling at me once, briefly, before she returned to her chair. She sang the whole way. "Princess princess elven princess yay!"

When Chesa was settled, Esther looked at me and gestured to the paper.

"And you, Sir John of Rast?"

I didn't answer. I just signed the application and shoved it across the table. I was a little miffed at how quickly Chesa was accepting all of this. I was the one who had killed the dragon, after all.

Esther collected the applications, squared them up, slipped them into her folder, then nodded.

"You can turn it back on, Miriam."

"You know there's no one in that control room, right?"

"A lot of our staff is already dead, or at least stuck somewhere between living and dying," she said. "You'll get used to it. So. This is how things work. The world, unreal and mundane, fantastic and drab. This is the secret that will change your life.

"Myths are real. They're not true, not in the way you think about truth, but they're very real. Dragons, djinn, oni, the Ramayana and Tuatha De Danann . . . you name it, I've seen it, tracked it, and then either killed it or given it a stern lecture and made it sign a release form. There's even some stuff out there we don't know the origin myth for, the legends of dead traditions, forgotten by everyone but the legends themselves. But they're out there, and they're just as dangerous as the rest."

"Get to the part about elves and unicorns," Chesa said anxiously.

"Don't interrupt. I'll lose my place." Esther looked up at the ceiling and started mumbling to herself.

"Djinn, lecture, dead traditions, dangerous...right. Got it." She cleared her throat and continued. "These things aren't content to live on in storybooks, or in the dreams of children. They break loose into the world, using their powers to manipulate and control the simple minds of mundane humanity. And the mundane world has little defense against them. The world has passed so far from its mythologies that unbelievable events are just that...unbelievable. Reality warps itself in such a way that the mundane world is protected from these unreal creatures. Djinn appear as charismatic humans, dragons mask themselves as accountants, or CEOs, or rock stars, and trolls make history in professional sports. Even—"

"Wait, sports?" I asked. "You're saying mythological creatures come to earth, disguise themselves as humans, and...play baseball?"

"There was a devil, a goat, who lived in Chicago. One day—"

"No, never mind, I don't want to know. But why would they disguise themselves? Why not just, you know...be a dragon?"

"Given a choice, I would be a dragon, personally," Chesa said. "The most beautiful dragon. With shimmering scales, and—"

"Don't make me regret bringing you in on this, lady. We could just wipe you and drop you in a cornfield somewhere, and then it's between you and your therapist." Esther rubbed her face in frustration then started over. "It's not a disguise. It's reality, protecting itself. I imagine Kracek would have preferred to walk around in his scales and claws if he could. But reality wouldn't let him. Kracek truly was Douglas Hosier. He was able to tap into certain powers of his kind...mind control, weaponized greed, even physical strength... but when those powers manifested in the mundane world, reality would twist itself into a knot trying to hide them. Rather than mind control, Doug would just be a very convincing speaker, with a knack for the stock market and too much gym time. It's not an illusion. It's just a false reality."

I sat back in my chair, mind spinning. Somehow, I was beginning to accept dragons. But this reality twisting thing, this was a lot to get my head around. What was the difference between Kracek the dragon and Kracek the Hosier? When did he stop being a suburban accountant and start being a dragon? While we were fighting? After? When he started to change? It was all very confusing.

"You clearly have questions," Esther said. "But first, I want to make something clear. Almost no one knows this. There's not some big government coverup, no ancient order running the world from behind the scenes. Mythological creatures are rare and, for the most part, happy to go unnoticed. There's a djinn in Sacramento running an In-n-Out franchise, and you'd never know the difference. Folks like that, they're not the problem. It's the ones that slip the leash and start causing havoc—burning down farmyards or writing reality-destroying poetry—that we concern ourselves with."

"We," I said, gesturing to the room. "The Knight Watch."

"The Knight Watch," she said, nodding.

"It's a terrible name."

She creased her brow and leaned back, looking like I had confessed to murder.

"It's a great name. Like nighttime, only a knight, and we watch. Knight Watch. What's the matter with you, you don't like my name?"

"Your name? So this is a new operation? Myths have been roaming the world for centuries, doing whatever it is they want to do, but now you've decided to get involved? One of them eat your family or something?"

"I am not in the habit of discussing my age, or my history, certainly not with new recruits," she said. "Rest assured that Knight Watch is well established. We know what we're doing. The team that you're going to be joining goes back to the Middle Ages, long before these things were myths that no one believed in. We have history and training on our side. If you hadn't stepped in, we would have taken care of Kracek, probably without having to kill him. The dragons don't like it when one of their own gets killed. That's where the elites come in."

"Everyone keeps using that word. Elites. That's Tembo, right?"

"The whole team, yes. You've met Tembo and St. Matthew, and Bethany, as well as Clarence during the operation. There are others, spread around the world, across different time periods and specializing in different kinds of myths. There's even a crew whose whole job consists of chasing down ghosts on social media. But your team, the ancient team, these are people with a particularly strong connection to their own mythic past, achieved either through training, practice, or dumb luck." She made a mark on her paper. "You seem like the dumb luck type, to me."

"I'm going to take that as a compliment," I said. "Look, I'm okay with not being like Tembo, or any of the others. Sure, I like medieval stuff, I go to ren faires and play at swords, but there are thousands of people like me. You shouldn't have brought us here."

"Thousands of people, sure. How many of them have killed a dragon?" she asked.

"How would I know? Like you said, reality breaks itself to hide these things. There could be hundreds."

"I can assure you, there are not hundreds. I know of twelve mortals who have faced a dragon in battle and survived. Six of them were on that field. Including the two of you." She folded her arms and stared at me. "How do you explain that?"

I opened her folder and pulled out the picture of my mom's wrecked station wagon, then pushed it in front of her. "Two tons of Swedish steel and gasoline. It's not a miracle."

"It is, actually. That's the part you don't understand. Driving your car into the dragon's skull shouldn't have killed him. It should have killed you, and whatever scraps of reality clung to you. There should have been a rupture in the mundane world. This . . ." she gestured to Kracek's dead body, lying next to the car's bumper. ". . . is impossible."

"You have a funny way of using that word," Chesa said.

"Which parts are impossible?" I asked. I took the photo and turned it to face her. "If you could just circle the parts that are impossible. I'll start. The dragon that used to be an accountant, he's impossible." I pushed the photo toward her. "Now you go."

"You're awkwardly clever, Mr. Rast," she said, then snatched the picture off the desk and filed it away. "This is what you're not understanding. Reality breaks both ways. It protects itself from the myths by twisting into something it can explain. And it protects the myths from us in the same way. I don't know how they perceive our world, but modern technology cannot affect these creatures."

"So it's like werewolves?" Chesa asked. "You need a silver bullet?"

"Werewolves aren't real," she said, then held up a hand at my obvious exasperation. "But if they were, guns wouldn't hurt them. Any type of gun. They stay true to their mythological origins, whatever they may be. A werewolf, if it comes from the First Nations lore, would only succumb to the weapons the original storyteller had to hand. A spear, a bow, a club . . . but not a gun. And since most of these creatures come from pre-gunpowder eras, guns are the least useful weapon you can imagine."

"Then why all the soldiers in the hallway? They looked like the gun-toting kind," I said.

"Mundane Actual's task is different than that of Knight Watch. Tembo's magic, Bethany's agility, even Clarence's sword are no good against bullets. They protect us from normal threats, human threats. Some of these myths have spent generations developing a mortal following. They have lackies, guards, human resources departments . . . MA handles that side of things. And we protect them from monsters."

"So, if guns don't work, what does? Wishful thinking?" Chesa asked.

"To kill a dragon, you need a sword, wielded by an elite. Or a magical spear, or the right combination of spells . . . the stuff of folklore. The weapons of mythology. You need a knight," she said, leaning back in her chair, face splitting with a smile. "Or, you know, its culturally appropriate equivalent. Spiritwalker, samurai, night hunter . . . you get the idea."

"You fight dragons. With swords," I said.

"We do."

I took a deep breath, rubbed my face, then sat down.

"That's crazy," I said.

"No," she answered. "It's unreality. It's the Knight Watch."

CHAPTER EIGHT
MANY QUESTIONS, NO ANSWERS

I sat there quietly for a while, letting my mind wrap around all this nonsense. Chesa was abuzz. She peppered the air with questions, most of which she answered for herself, the rest of which Esther just ignored. And for her part, the head of Knight Watch spent the time going through her papers, making notes and muttering to herself. After a while, Esther cleared her throat, squared and closed the dossier, then folded her hands on the table.

"Well, I think we're done here. Do either of you have any questions?" She held up a hand, stopping Chesa's barrage. "Questions about this side of things. Who we are, what we do? Stuff like that."

I had so many questions. If dragons were real, what about wyverns? What about wyrms? Drakes? How about hydras? Were they related, or was there some kind of draconic hierarchy that just used different names depending on culture? Oh, what about the dude in Loch Ness? Dragon! It could be a dragon!

Reader, I hadn't even gotten out of dragon-related questions before she interrupted me. And in case you're wondering, they're all different things, except for kirin, which are a whole other thing, and might be the origin of the entire family.

Oh, and dinosaurs aren't real. It's complicated.

"I think you misunderstood me, Mr. Rast," Esther said sharply. "Unless you're actually a loremaster you don't need to know about every gob-bobbin and draco-lich. What you do need to understand is that you're going to be making a sacrifice. If you accept this job, your life is never going to be the same. And it's not all rainbows and water nymphs on the other side of this door."

"Ma'am, look at us," Chesa said, sitting up straight. "We spend most of our disposable income on chainmail and weapons training. I compare every single real-world relationship I have to the Lay of Leithian . . ."

"This explains some stuff," I muttered.

"And I only really feel at home on the weekends, when I'm in some commandeered forest preserve pretending to be something I will never be." Chesa leaned a little bit forward. "I have lived my entire life in anticipation of this moment. I am ready. Utterly, utterly ready."

"Everyone feels that way to start," Esther says. "We will have this conversation again when you miss your father's funeral because there was an oni in a comic book store. But I appreciate your enthusiasm. And what of you, John? Are you ready to be the hero you were born to become?"

I sat back in my chair. *Of course*, my brain said. *Of course I am.* But was I? Did I even know what was involved? I didn't want to miss funerals, or birthdays, or . . . anything, really. But mostly, I didn't want to miss out on being a knight.

I looked over at Chesa. She was watching me with slight disapproval, kind of the way she looked at me ever since we broke up. I couldn't decide if she wanted me to say yes, or if she was hoping I'd scuttle back to the real world and stop ruining her dream job.

"Yeah, I'm up for it," I said. "How could I not be."

Chesa deflated a little. So that was definitely a hopeful no.

"Excellent. You'll be meeting the team soon enough. You'll be getting assigned an extraction team. They're responsible for getting you into and out of real-world situations, so you can deal with the unreal world problems. For now, we'll return you to your homes and let you recover. I'm sure your families will have some questions."

"What are we supposed to tell them?" I asked. "I don't think 'I'm joining an army of mystical heroes' is going to cut it with my mom."

"Lies. You're going to tell them lies. To be honest, your life isn't going to change that much in the short term. Our operatives have to live in the real world, even as they acclimate to the mythic dimension. I'll leave it to your mentors to explain how that works later on. For now, just go home and enjoy your time off. Quit your jobs, get some life insurance . . . treat it like a little vacation."

"Life insurance?" I asked.

"You're going to be fighting dragons, John. People die." Esther stood up and shook each of our hands in turn. "Miriam, cut the tape. Their consent is on record."

For the briefest of seconds, the control room behind the glass was filled with a maelstrom of ghostly cloth, bones, and glowing fog. A shattered porcelain mask hung at the center, its pieces spinning slowly like a windchime. The speakers squealed to life, and the room was filled with hideous, mind-scraping laughter. I dove under the table, barely beating Chesa into shelter. The lights in the room flickered, and the temperature in the air dropped twenty degrees. The speaker snapped off.

"A simple yes would have sufficed, Miriam," Esther said irritably.

"Let me have my fun, Esther." Miriam's voice sounded like honey slowly pouring over organ pipes, which was a frightfully specific image that imposed itself in my brain. Her laughter came again, this time just inside my skull. I swatted at the air.

"Cut it out, Mir," Esther snapped. "They've had a hell of a day."

"Sssspoil sporrrrrt," Miriam groaned. Then the lights settled down, the chill left my bones. Esther rapped on the table.

"Come on out. She's occasionally a fright to deal with. But she means well. Believe me, she's not the scariest person you'll end up working beside. I mean, you've met the janitors."

We crawled out from under the table and looked around. Chesa tried to look composed, even as she smoothed out the ruin of her plastic chainmail dress.

"Okay," Esther said. "Are you guys ready?"

"Ready for what?" I asked.

"The grand tour. The parade. The guided walk around the heart of mystery and wonder that is Knight Watch." She stood up. "Just don't touch anything. Or anyone."

We were definitely in the weird part of Mundane Actual. MA

tactical squads filed through the hallways, armed for bear, but they were joined by guards in high-tech armor and long swords, and the doorways that led off in all directions were . . . strange. Iron grates led into misty chambers, or archways that flickered with blue flame. One door looked like a thousand faces melted together, their mouths working in wordless torment. Several doors were bricked over and heavily guarded. I half expected to see Tembo, or one of the other elites, but everyone we saw wore the MA badge and dull gray coveralls.

"Where are the guys?" I finally asked. "Tembo and the others?"

"Already down the hole," Esther said. "Except Clarence. He's not quite up to speed, just yet. A lot of his injury was mundane. You clipped him with that cursed station wagon of yours. We're working on it. Hopefully he can make the trip later today."

"What's all this talk about a hole?" Chesa asked.

"Every one of the elites has their own personal domain. It's a fragment of their mythic past that allows them to interact with the unreal world. The longer they're in the mundane, the more contaminated their mythic selves become. Matthew starts missing coffee and blue jeans, Bethany remembers videogames, Clarence . . . well, Clarence has been with us for a while. But he still needs to spend time in his domain to recharge his batteries."

"Is that why Matthew only had so much light left?" I asked. "He talked about getting back to the brilliance, but I didn't know what he meant. Just figured he was a special kind of nuts."

"Yeah, he might be. But his domain contains a spark of the divine. Lets him heal and do other stuff. And it turns his skin into sunlight," Esther answered.

"Wait, what now? There's a glowing guy?" Chesa asked.

"Oh, yeah. Forgot you weren't there for that. It's pretty crazy."

"Point is, the team has to get there as quickly as possible. The fight with Kracek took a lot out of them, so they're on their way to their domains. It takes a little while to adjust to it, kind of like a diver returning to the surface. It's not a literal hole," she said. "Nothing around here is a literal anything."

Esther said some more stuff about domains, how they were all about the mythic self, our true identity in the unreal world . . . something about dying. Not really sure. The last part of her speech went a little over my head, not because I'm dense, or because it wasn't interesting. No, I lost focus because there were ladies. *Hello, ladies.*

Two of them marched down the hall, dressed in form-fitting body armor that looked like a cross between tactical gear and ring mail, heavy on the wing motifs, and boots that looked like they could crush skulls. The lead had light brown skin and freckles sprayed across her cheeks, with eyes the color of amber and long, black hair gathered in dreads. Her companion was pale and muscular, with short silver hair shaved on the sides, except for half-a-dozen thin braids tucked behind her ear. She carried a double-bitted battle axe cradled in her arms like a child, and her eyes were the color of dew-speckled moss. She was beautiful.

I mean, if you notice that sort of thing. Which I did. Gods, did I.

Oh, and they both had wings tucked against their shoulders, feathers speckled with every color of the rainbow, and deeper tints shifted under the surface, like the face of the most precious of jewels. They stared at me as I passed. Actually, I guess I was staring, and they were just returning the insult. They went around a corner and disappeared.

"Hot damn," I whispered. "So angels are real."

"God, John, have some class," Chesa muttered.

"Valkyries," Esther corrected. "Angels can't walk around like that. Cancer risk. Trust me, you wouldn't like angels half that much." She grabbed me by the shoulder and escorted me down the hallway. "And if you're done offending our royal guests, we need to get on with the tour. Mysteries don't reveal themselves."

"I'm going to like this gig more than I thought I would," I said.

"Don't worry. You'll screw it up in the first few weeks," Chesa answered. She glared at Esther and added, "I speak from experience."

"Are we going to need to keep you two in different containment chambers?" Esther asked. "Because that can be done."

"Let's just get on with the tour," I said.

Esther gave us a minute to settle down, then started up where she had been before the divine intervention.

"The farther we get from the mundane, the stranger things get. You're going to have to let your mind get a little loose if you're going to stick around here." We passed a final intersection and came to another corner. "Here we are."

A broad set of shallow stairs led up to a set of double doors, the largest I had seen in this place. The doors looked mundane enough, but the closer we got, the more unreal they felt. Not magical, really. Just out of place. Dented steel plates slid into the walls as we approached, and I could tell that the doors were almost a yard thick, with interlocking teeth that ran in a channel along the floor. The room beyond was a massive bowl, with rows of ancient terminals that flickered in green and amber, leading down to a machine that looked straight out of the movies. Pipes and tubing surrounded an iron tank, speckled with thick glass portals bound in bronze and dozens of gauges. Technicians sat at the dozens of terminals, taking notes or fiddling with controls, talking into brass speaking tubes as they worked. A handful of them surrounded the tumor of machinery in the middle of the room, dressed in old time pressure suits, with rubber breathing tubes that led back to the terminals. The whole room looked like mission control for a steampunk rocket team. The only things missing were top hats and actual steam.

"Welcome to Reality Control," Esther said. "The heart of Knight Watch."

CHAPTER NINE
DOWN THE HOLE

The thrumming machinery at the center of the room got quieter the closer we got to it. Esther led us down the stairs, stopping to chat with several techs along the way, never bothering to introduce us. Chesa looked really out of place in her charred elvish princess costume, but none of the collected technicians seemed to mind at all. Honestly, they were probably used to much stranger dress, if the way Tembo and company comported themselves was any indication.

"I don't like that thing," Chesa said. She had to raise her voice to be heard, but it was like she was muffled, or far away. I leaned in to hear her better. "It doesn't belong here."

"None of this belongs here," I said. "I think that's the point."

Chesa blanched and hesitated. Esther took her by the hand.

"This is important to see," she said, leading us forward. "Just try to remain calm."

At first, I could feel the engine's vibration in my chest. It reminded me of a ship's engine room, the kind of place where everyone wore ear protection and talked in barely heard shouts, but as we descended toward the floor of the arena-like room, the sound faded away. I thought I was going deaf, but I could still hear Esther's questions about pressure levels and anomalies, the techs' responses, even though the numbers meant nothing to me. About halfway down, an eerie silence fell. I stared at the engine.

"What is that thing?" I asked, but even I could barely hear my voice. Esther drew the three of us together. When she answered, I

59

could see that she was yelling, but her words were the barest whisper in my ears.

"Anomaly Actuator," Esther said. "Leftover from the last big war. There's a lot of history in this thing. Gods help us if it ever breaks down. The last engineer from the original team died ten years ago. There are schematics, but not in a math anyone living understands."

We were close enough now that I could see words stenciled on to the side of the engine, big block white letters and arrows and warning symbols. There was a star in a circle near the top, the same one used by U.S. forces in WWII. I had painted enough Sherman tanks to be familiar with it.

"I thought you said this wasn't some kind of military agency," I yelled, pointing to the star. "That sure looks government issue to me."

"Knight Watch is one hundred percent private, from nuts to guts," Esther said. "You won't find Washington anywhere in this business. Half of Mundane Actual's job is keeping the government off our back. We've got more accountants and lawyers than guards. Here, you're going to need this."

She handed both us a brass diving helmet, taken from a rack of similar devices, then settled another one on her head. I watched Chesa maneuver the rigid dome over her delicate crown of leaves, then I followed suit. The helmet's heavy mantle pressed into my shoulders. The air in the helmet smelled like oil, and a steady chugging sound came through a pipe in the top. My view through the glass and iron grate at the front was severely limited. I felt like a toy in an aquarium. Esther tapped my elbow, then pointed toward the engine.

We walked past the three techs in the deep-water diving suits who were monitoring the machine and approached one of the portholes. The glass was thick and bulbous, distorting the view inside, but as I leaned my helmet against it, I could see something moving inside the engine. Green fields and bright sun, windswept grass, and trees blowing in the breeze. Reminded me of summer. If I squinted, I could see a circle of rough stones in the center of the field, each one a knee-high pillar with mushrooms growing at their base. Chesa tapped me on the shoulder. I gave way, letting her get a look. Even through the foggy glass of the diving helmet, I could see her eyes go wide.

"This was a field in Amherst, New Jersey, circa 1925. Appeared in the middle of a busy street, swallowed maybe twenty people before the National Guard was able to establish a perimeter. Every once in a while, the poor bastards show up in the display. There's a horse in there that, to all appearances, is slowly changing into a unicorn king. The rest seem to be having a worse time of it." Esther's voice was coming through my breathing tube and sounded terrible. But there was no other sound, not even my own heartbeat. It was freaky. "An early version of Knight Watch was able to contain and transport it. When the war started, the military commandeered the entire operation, just long enough to screw it up royally. We reclaimed it in the 70s, moved it here, started our own missions and recruiting."

"I don't understand. What does this do?" I asked, hoping she could hear me. There was a long silence, but eventually Esther answered.

"It's systematically weird," she said. "In a predictable manner. So any variation in that pattern indicates unreal activity in the mundane world. We've learned to navigate by those variations."

"You put a grass field into a giant tank and moved it here, wherever the hell here is, so you could track weird shit happening in the world?" Chesa asked.

"You should have seen the German operation," she said. "We kind of assume the Russians got that, after . . . well, anyway. It was a great deal more horrific."

We worked our way back up the stairs, stripping off the helmets and ascending the stairs. Sounds steadily returned, the clatter of keys strangely loud in my ears after such crushing silence. When we got back to the top, one of the techs tapped Esther's shoulder.

"Sword is awake, ma'am. He wants to talk to you."

"Already? I didn't think he'd be ready for another couple weeks."

"Someone told him about our guests," the tech said, her eyes sliding to me and Chesa. "He's very interested."

"I'm sure he is. Well, I guess you get to meet Clarence now."

"We've met," I said. "He's kind of an asshole."

"He's also going to be in charge of your training," Esther answered. "So maybe keep that opinion to yourself."

Mundane Actual's hospital existed in a strange borderland between the clean zone maintained for the elites, and the drab hallways of the real world. There was an airlock going into both areas, leading into a long room that was sectioned off with curtains. Machines beeped in several of the curtained cubicles, and the air smelled like antiseptic. It could have been cut and pasted from any modern hospital in the world, except for the massive cartoonish dragon moping in the center of the room.

"This is nicer than where I was. You couldn't have brought me... oh," I said as I noticed the dragon. "Hi."

"Matthew's pretty lights don't work in this place," Esther said, ignoring my reaction to the dragon. "Or at least, it's easier where we had you. That hallway was modeled after a monastery from eighth-century France. Peak miracle space. This room is all about the medicine." She turned around and noticed I was staring at the dragon. Chesa was frozen in place, just inside the door. "Guys, this is the least strange thing you're going to see today."

"Sufficiently strange, thanks," Chesa said tightly.

"Sure it is. Kyle, this is John Rast and Chesa Lazaro. John, Chesa, this is Kyle." Esther walked past the dragon and into one of the cubicles, leaving us alone with the creature. Chesa started to whimper under her breath.

First off, this guy was nothing like Kracek. His tiny wings could never have gotten him off the ground, and the purple scales that covered its body somehow looked soft, almost plush. His thick neck brushed the ceiling before bending low, leaving his barrel-wide head nearly scraping the floor. Kyle looked at us both with wet, dinner-plate eyes, and a curl of smoke puffed out of his wide nostrils. He was the definition of cute, to the point of being pathetic.

"You're the sonuvabitch who killed Kracek, aren't you?" he asked, zeroing in on me. I nodded, and Kyle grimaced, a look of forlorn dismissal that didn't really fit on his bubble-smooth face. "I never really liked that guy. Still, it would have been better to let Clarence handle it." He laid a massive clawed hand on the curtain wall, bending the iron supports and snagging his talons on the fabric. He sighed, and the room got about twenty degrees warmer. "Clarence would have done it better."

"Clarence was lying on his back, bleeding from a bunch of new holes. I think maybe the only thing he would have done better at that point was bleed to death."

"Yeah," Kyle answered. "And now we'll never know how he would have overcome that challenge and won the day. A pity."

"Sure," I said. "A damned shame."

"John? Is this okay? Is he okay?" Chesa asked.

"Near as I can tell, he's the picture of safe. But don't worry, I won't let him—"

Chesa flew across the room and threw her arms around Kyle's neck. The sound I had mistaken for whimpering was actually barely contained giggles. Chesa squeezed and squeezed, until Kyle looked like he was going to pop.

"My lady!" he squeaked. "This is hardly appropriate for a dragon of my stature!"

Esther stuck her head out of the curtain and shot us all a schoolmarm's look. "You woke him up. I hope you're happy."

Kyle's horns perked up, and a grin crawled across his toothy maw. He shook free of Chesa's embrace and leaned forward. "Awake, you say? He's awake!" The dragon shoved his bulbous nose into the cubicle. "Clarence! Clarence, are you awake?"

"Good morning, Kyle." Clarence's voice was softer than I remembered, though there was steel in it. He sounded very tired. "They brought you here, I see. Marvelous."

"Marvelous!" Kyle agreed. "Do you think we can go home now?"

The small but still quite impressive dragon pushed forward into the cubicle, upsetting the curtain wall and lifting its supports off the ground. The whole line of attached curtains staggered, folding to the ground like playing cards, their steel wheels clattering against the linoleum. Very anxious nurses, all dressed in white versions of the same tactical gear everyone around here seemed to wear, appeared from the shadows and started rearranging the furniture. A few distressed patients huddled under the collapsed curtains.

"Kyle! Kyle, behave! You're making it very difficult..." Esther's exasperated voice trailed off as Kyle arched his back and shook like a wet dog. Hollow steel rods and displaced curtains flew everywhere. I ducked behind an IV stand. When the shaking stopped, Clarence and his bed sat exposed at the epicenter of this draconic catastrophe. Kyle loomed over him, massive head inches away from the knight's face.

My meeting with Clarence had been brief and in the middle of dangerous things, but I would never have recognized him in his current state, even if he had been my father. The tall, handsome man I had seen face Kracek was wasted and thin. Deep lines etched his face, and his eyes burned with fever. The bed seemed to swallow him. He lifted a hand to the dragon, and I was shocked to see it as gnarled as a root branch and spotted. Clarence brushed Kyle's nose affectionately.

"Leave him alone, Esther. This is difficult for him to understand," Clarence said. A puff of smoke from Kyle's mouth swathed the frail knight, "It's alright, friend. We'll be home soon enough." The old knight's eyes trailed across the room, lighting first on Chesa, then on me. He smiled. "Are these the two I've heard about?"

"I'd like to know who's been talking to you," Esther said. "We need you to get your rest."

"What you need is to fill the team," Clarence said weakly. With a wince, he pulled himself into a sitting position and peered at the two of us. "Well. Come closer. This old man's eyes aren't what they used to be."

I nervously shuffled closer. Clarence looked us both up and down. I had trouble settling this old man with the hero I had seen face Kracek. He looked fifty years older, if a day, and his hands shook as he rubbed his chin.

"Yes, they'll have to do. You're sure they're the right type?"

"The boy has a gift for the sword, and the girl . . . well, you can see she was born for it."

"Aren't we all?" Clarence said. "It's just the damned world, with its autowagons, and speaking tubes, and diesel conveyance jets. No one even speaks proper Latin anymore."

"How long has he been in here?" I whispered to Esther.

"The damned modern world!" Clarence said over my question. "That steals the mythical world from us. Get 'em young, I say, before they end up in a factory, sewing chapeaus for some French bastard!" Chesa and I exchanged glances, but Clarence bulled on. "Yes, with Marcus gone, and Ophelia on walkabout, you're going to need new recruits!"

"I'm going to assume Ophelia and Marcus are dead, and he's just forgotten?" I asked Esther.

"They are most assuredly not dead," Clarence said. "I would know. I would *know*."

"It's okay, Clarence. They've already signed the paperwork," Esther said.

"Grand! Then what are we waiting for?" he asked.

"For you to be well enough to go down the hole without dragging corruption along with you. And that isn't going to happen—"

"That isn't going to happen at all. We'll have to take the risk. Kyle?" The dragon arched its back, looming over us. Clarence beamed up at him. "It's time to go home."

It was only a few moments before we were on our way. They loaded Clarence into a wheelchair, one of the tactical nurses pushing him into the hallway. Chesa and I followed, with Esther between us. Kyle bumbled through the hallway behind us, regularly knocking tiles out of the ceiling and bumping into the walls. The sound of his passage was terrifying, and every time I looked behind me, I expected to see a furious death engine charging close on my heels. Instead, Kyle looked like a puppy dressed in scale mail, dipping his head into each room we passed, sometimes drawing screams of terror, sometimes greeting the occupants in his cheerful, childish voice. I was beginning to think he was just a dog from the real world, somehow transformed into a fearsome beast.

"I still don't like this," Esther snapped. "If we put you in too early, you could corrupt your whole domain. Are you sure you're ready?"

"I've done this enough to know. Besides, what's the worst that happens?" Clarence waved a thin hand dismissively. "It's not like that one time with the spiders."

"Worst case? The three of you disappear into a nightmarish hellhole, and I'm down to three elites and no backup," Esther said.

"Wait, what?" Chesa asked. "What's this about spiders?"

"The domains have to be shielded from the real world. Elites can't just go straight in," Esther said. "Remember what I said about how the elites have to work their way into their domains slowly? Well, Clarence has a lot of the mundane world clinging to him right now. We got him stabilized with modern medicine, but he's supposed to spend some time in medieval medical care before he enters his domain. And he's badly enough hurt that we were hoping to let him recuperate here for a while before we turned him over to the barbers."

"There's nothing wrong with me that your leeches can fix, Esther!"

"They're not leeches. They're antibiotics, and if you just let them work—"

"Right, right, little bugs in my bloodstream," Clarence said. He leaned back in his chair and fixed me with an amused look, then rolled his eyes. "Not leeches. As you say."

"The point is that we're taking a risk letting him go straight back in. It could corrupt the domain, and then pretty much anything can happen."

"You worry too much," Clarence said.

"Worried about what? Should I be worried, buddy?" Kyle asked, poking his head between us, his horns nearly knocking us to the ground.

"Not at all," Clarence said. Satisfied, Kyle went back to terrorizing the hallway.

Esther mumbled to herself, but then the nurse pulled up short and turned Clarence's chair to face a broad wooden door. Clarence clapped his hands together.

"This will be fun," he said. "Come on, Kyle!"

Kyle bowled past us, knocking the door open and disappearing through the other side. I couldn't see anything in the room beyond. Like, literally nothing. The floor disappeared.

"What the hell?" I asked.

"Most of the portals are deeper in MA, but we keep a spare near the hospital for cases like this," Esther said. "It's not ideal. But it's the best we can do."

"Come on, you're going to love it," Clarence said cheerfully. "Not like Tembo's miserable place."

"It's not the domain that's dangerous, it's the transition. John, Chesa, are you listening? Just keep your feet moving and try to not think of anything scary."

"Like trolls," Clarence prompted. "Or dragons. Especially not dragons, given your history. Oh, and zombies! Gods, what would happen if you thought about zombies. I shudder to imagine!"

"Do you guys not understand how thinking works?" Chesa snapped. "Just . . . I can't . . . now my brain is all zombies, all the way down now!"

"Then we'll get in some early practice," Clarence said gleefully. "Tally ho, old boy! Let's get to it."

"It's not as bad as he says," Esther insisted. "And neither of you have a domain yet, so it's not like you'll get lost on the way there. Just . . . keep moving." She pulled a face, squinting at Chesa out of one eye. "And . . . maybe try to not think about zombies?"

"Damn it, people!" I swore. Clarence laughed heartily, then started rolling himself toward the door.

"Don't let him get away from you!" Esther said, pushing me toward Clarence's chair. I wrapped my hands around the grips. The inertia pushed us forward. We crossed the threshold into nothingness. I felt Chesa's hand on my shoulder, and then nothing.

All I could hear was Clarence's laughter, echoing distantly in my brain, getting creepier and creepier with each iteration. And all I could think about was zombies. And dragons. And zombie dragons.

But there was nothing but darkness, and the cold steel of the wheelchair under my hands.

CHAPTER TEN
PRACTICE DYING

There's this hobby called freediving. I looked into it one summer, not because I was ever going to do it, but because I couldn't imagine anything that would be more terrifying. Basically, freediving consists of tying yourself to a stone and throwing it into a very deep body of water. The diver sinks through colder and colder depths, the pressure ratcheting up as their lungs collapse, slowly drowning as the light fades above them. There are long moments of complete darkness as you're dragged down by this relentless stone. I'm sure there's more to it than that, but that's as far as I got in my research. I still had nightmares about it, and all I'd done was read a book. I couldn't imagine actually submitting to this activity in the name of entertainment. Or rather, I could imagine it all too well.

This felt like I imagined freediving felt. There was no light, no ground under my feet, no way to move forward or backward, but I was being dragged forward by this relentless Clarence. His wheelchair was no longer in my hand, but I could sense him in front of me, drawing me into the darkness. Chesa was somewhere over my shoulder, a presence sensed but never truly felt. This seemed to last forever.

The first relief from the gloom was a dim, green glow dancing overhead. It reminded me of the northern lights. The light grew, a slow trickle of illumination that spread across the sky, until it stretched from horizon to horizon. The shimmering slowed, until I realized what I was looking at.

"Trees," I whispered. Clarence's answer came from just ahead of me and slightly above. He was standing.

"Dappled sunlight through the primeval canopy," he said, and the strength was fully back in his voice. Leaves rustled above us, and birdsong filled the air. A warm breeze touched my face. Twigs and gravel crunched under my boot. I heard Chesa stir just to my right. We were walking on a forest path. Clarence's tall form appeared ahead of me. He walked confidently through the forest, his hand resting easily on the sword at his belt, chainmail jingling like Christmas bells. He turned and smiled at us. "It's the most beautiful morning in the world. It always is. One of the rules of domains. Every domain has three things: a door for opening, a path to travel, and a hearth to call home. This is my door." His eyes darted to the sky. "The path will find us soon enough."

"Is this Valinor?" Chesa asked, her voice hushed.

"That is not my mythology, child," Clarence said. "I have more of Arthur in my blood than Aragorn. The old tales, before the French got involved. When it comes time to build your own domains, you'll have to find your own path into the mythic realm. Build your own legend." He smiled at her, and I was shocked at how young he looked, how vital. "Though it looks like you're well on your way, my lady."

I glanced over at Chesa and had to restrain my shock. She stood in the middle of the path, her head cocked toward the canopy of trees overhead. She was holding an intricate bow of fresh yew wood, carved with leaves and feathers, the grip shielded by a gilded hawk of bronze and steel. Her costume, which had always been top notch, was suddenly and absolutely real. The plasticard scale mail of her leggings and greaves now glowed like polished starshine, and her cloak rippled with inner life. Her crown of feathers was suddenly a helm of finely worked steel, each feather so delicate and realistic that they looked alive. When she turned to look at me, I noticed that her eyes were purple, and her features had taken on an unworldly beauty, delicate and fey.

"Holy shit, Ches. You're an elf!"

"Not quite," Clarence answered. "The fae are jealous of their blood and wouldn't countenance a daughter of Adam in their ranks. But she is surely something more than she was." He glanced at me. "And you, Sir John. That doesn't look like the dress of a servant."

I glanced down at my feet and found that my clothes were also transformed. Like Clarence, I was in chainmail, with a leather doublet underneath, and a plain tabard of simple cloth. My boots were well-worn leather and looked about as expensive as anything I had ever worn, with buckles and straps and velvet-soft lining. My heart fell.

Don't get me wrong, it was better kit than my paltry income could ever afford. But it wasn't anywhere as cool as Chesa and her purple eyes.

"This is . . . it's amazing!" Chesa said. "Where did it come from?"

"Inside your heart," Clarence said. "That is an expression of your mythic self. The truest form of your intentional being. It's the first step toward tapping into your heroic powers, whatever they might be. And that's what we're here to find out."

"I thought I would be . . . taller," I said. A life spent slightly taller than everyone else, but not tall enough to be noteworthy, was one of my secret frustrations. I would rather have gone all in, one way or the other.

"You're in the intro kit right now. Building your own domain will change you, for better or worse. Some people go into their domains and come out as completely different people. Or they emerge as their true selves, the lie of modern life stripped away."

"If this is the intro kit, I can't wait for the full package," Chesa said. She lifted her empty hand, cupping the air in front of her face, and blew into her palm. Lines of light flared across her fingers. They twisted into the air, knotting together until they formed a flower. She gestured, and the blossom spun away, shedding glowing petals as it flew down the path. It disappeared into a fog of luminous specks that lingered in the air.

"Can I do that?" I asked. I blew into my hand, harder and harder, until my palm was coated in a thin glaze of saliva and desperation. Chesa chuckled.

"You're going to have to build your own legend, John," Clarence said.

"It just seemed like a good trick, that's all. I wish—"

Clarence shushed us, then cocked his head to the sky, shielding his eyes from the shafts of light. A shadow passed over the sun, dropping us into brief darkness. Clarence stopped and followed the shadow's path with his gaze.

"The wyrm has found us. We should get moving."

He picked up the pace, leading us down the forest path. Chesa ran effortlessly at my side, but I was starting to learn exactly how difficult it is to jog in heavy chain and leather. I hadn't taken ten steps before I broke out in a heavy sweat.

We started to descend, heels digging into the soft earth. Ahead of us the light grew. I could see the forest's edge, and beyond it, green fields and a tall gray structure. At first, I thought it was a mountain of stone. When I realized what I was looking at, I stumbled to a halt. Chesa brushed past me, saw what I had seen, and came to a stop as well. She gave a long, low whistle.

It was the largest castle I had ever seen, larger than anything I had even imagined. Tier after tier of stone walls piled up like layers of a wedding cake, each wall hung with thin, flowing yellow and blue banners that cracked in the breeze. The top of the castle bristled with towers, and a pair of heavy gates were at the foundation of this monstrous structure. I wasn't far wrong in thinking it was a mountain. Clouds ringed the highest towers and danced across the face of the walls. Horns sounded from the castle walls as we emerged from the forest.

"Do the two of you have horses?" Clarence asked urgently.

"I don't think so," I said.

"That's something we will have to work on. But for now, we will ride together," he said. He drew something out of his belt, a leather harness tightly folded, with reins and an ornamented bit. With a crack, he unfolded the entire thing, almost like a whip. Fog shot through with twinkling stars formed inside the bit, swirling larger and larger, until it started to take the shape of an animal. For a brief instance, the form could have been any creature; I saw a lion's mane, the claws of a dragon, wings and jaws of unimagined beasts. The fogs continued to swirl, and the creature's form solidified. In the flash of an eye, there was a horse pulling at the reins, fully saddled and caparisoned in the same yellow and blue that flew from the castle walls. Clarence threw his leg over the saddle while the horse was still forming, riding the mount's sudden growth into the air. He held out his hand.

"Come on," he snapped. "We don't have time to screw around."

"How are we both supposed to—" Chesa started.

There was a roar of sound, thunder and crashing trees. A shadow flashed overhead, flying inches over the treetops, tearing at the canopy with the force of its passage. Blood-red wings and black claws ripped through the sky. Flaming eyes turned to look at us as the shadow passed. The dragon swooped down the valley. It let out a terrifying shriek that pierced my ears and shook the forest leaves. Turning, it rose high into the air on a pillar of flame.

"Kyle?" I asked.

"Seriously, John. We need to fucking go!" Clarence grabbed my wrist and jerked me onto the horse, nearly pulling my shoulder from its socket. I landed belly first on the saddle, the high horn knocking the wind out of me. Chesa leapt effortlessly onto the horse's rump. *Of course, she is preternaturally agile*, I thought. *Of course.*

I was barely able to squirm into a seated position, still gasping for breath, when Clarence spurred the horse. We flew down the valley, the hammer of hooves jolting my bones, the wind tearing the breath from my lungs. With each bounding gallop, I felt like I was about to fall from the mount. I clung desperately to the horse's mane. It was only Clarence's iron grip that kept me seated. When I glanced back, I saw that Chesa was perched daintily, her deep amethyst eyes watching the dragon's flight. Kyle's deafening roar came again, as close and as terrifying as a lightning strike. Clarence bent close to the saddle, pushing me down. The dragon's shadow passed over us.

"What the hell is going on?" I shouted.

Clarence didn't answer. We were getting close to the castle gates. I watched as they slowly rose. A jet of flame rolled over the ground next to us, but Clarence didn't balk. We charged through the gatehouse.

"Drop the gate! Drop the gate!" Clarence yelled. Chains rattled as the gate boomed down. He did something with the reins, and I felt the horse turn to smoke between my legs. I crumpled to the ground, but Clarence landed smoothly, whipping his sword out of its sheath as he ran toward the gate. Chesa rolled, drawing an arrow from her quiver and knocking it before she even got to her feet. The whole courtyard shook with the dragon's roar.

Kyle slammed into the gates. The mighty doors boomed, wood groaning as the dragon's bulk pushed against the wood and iron. Kyle roared his fury, and flames erupted over the wall's height, rising in a pillar toward the sky. Clarence stood just inside the gate, shifting lightly on the balls of his feet, sword ready. I scrambled to my feet and grabbed for my belt, but there was no sword there, not even a dagger. I backed nervously away from the gates.

There was a moment of silence, then the roar of wind and leathery flapping of wings. Kyle rose above the walls, his sinuous neck twisting to bring his massive head into the courtyard. Flames flickered between his black teeth. Chesa drew her arrow to her cheek, sighting at the dragon's chest. Clarence noticed, and gestured for her to hold her fire. Kyle, massive and muscular, smiled at us malevolently.

"Hiding behind your stone walls, hero? That is unlike you." The dragon's voice sounded like the breaking of mountains. Just the noise of it put me on my heels. Clarence didn't move.

"I have no time for this, wyrm. Your blood will have to wait to be spilled."

Kyle huffed, and a cloud of sulfurous air filled the courtyard, choking me. The dragon's head shifted, bringing its burning gaze squarely on me. His lips curled back in an insolent grin. His hide was covered in scars, and the broken blades of dozens of swords hung buried in his flesh.

"Some other day, then, champion. Your flesh will keep for another dawn."

He rose on battered wings, spinning into the air, his shadow passing again and again over the castle. With a final shriek, Kyle turned and flew toward the distant, foggy mountains, disappearing as quickly as he had come.

Clarence turned to us with a jaunty smile, sheathing his sword and walking toward the castle interior.

"That was pretty good, wasn't it? The ride and all. Bracing. That's the path in for my mythology. The draconic threat. Kyle takes it very seriously. Well, we've got a lot to do. Put some hop in your step, you two."

I watched him walk into the keep, then turned to stare into the empty sky, looking for any sign of the dragon. Birdsong filled the forest again, and the breeze swept away the stink of the monster's breath. Chesa came to stand next to me. She was still in her elven glory, but there was a look of dull shock on her face. It was unsettling to see such a familiar expression on that otherworldly visage.

"They have an interesting relationship," she said. "I really thought he was trying to kill us."

"Oh, I'm certain of it," I said.

"I can promise you this," Chesa said. "My domain's not going to have any of this almost getting killed bullshit."

She returned her unused arrow to the quiver and slung the bow across her shoulder, then followed Clarence into the castle, leaving me alone in the courtyard. I scanned the distant mountains one last time. There was no sign of the dragon.

"What the hell, Kyle?" I whispered. Then I turned and joined my companions.

The castle appeared empty, although I heard servants in the distance, and the evidence of their passage was everywhere, but I never saw anyone. When we stopped our practice to eat, the banquet hall was filled with food. When we passed through that room later, the tables had been cleared and the fire stoked. And there was a choir somewhere, chanting day and night.

That first day, Clarence led us directly to the practice yard. It was a long field of packed sand, with a jousting list down the center, and on one side a line of quintains, man-shaped practice dummies balanced on poles that would spin when struck. These quintains were different, though, and moved of their own accord. They saluted Clarence when he entered the yard, then settled into various guard positions.

"Live blades today, gentlemen. No need for your service," Clarence boomed, and the quintains went limp. He drew his sword, slicing the air with a dozen practice swings before turning to face us. "Neither of you seem to have swords."

"I guess it's not part of my mythological ideal yet," I said.

"I'm more of a bow and arrow girl," Chesa answered.

"To each their own. But you can't depend on being able to stay away from the enemy forever. You will need a blade eventually, even if it's only out of desperation. And you," he said, pointing to me. "The sword should be the first thing you imagine. I expected that much of you, after your performance at the shinty pitch. A pity. We will have to make do."

He gestured to a rack of blades that folded out of the wall. Dozens of swords of every shape bristled out of the shelves. "I don't think I have much in your particular style, my lady. Perhaps this?" His fingers danced in the direction of the rack, then pointed toward Chesa. A pair of short blades sang through the air, landing crossed in the sand at Chesa's feet. She stared down at them with distaste.

"Two blades? No. I'll leave that to the rogue." She plucked one of the swords up and cut the air with its curved blade. Kind of a scimitar, with an open grip and a spiked pommel. "This will do. For now."

Clarence nodded and turned to look me over. "And for you . . . a little more medieval. Longsword, double edge, hand and a half. Do you usually fight with a shield?"

"Sword and board," I said proudly. He grunted, then made the same gesture. A sword jumped off the rack and flew to my hand. "How does it feel?"

My palm stung from the impact of the hilt. I shook it out, then gave the blade a few swings. It was heavier than my rattan blade, the difference between steel and wicker, but the balance was superb. The edge was razor sharp.

"Very nice. But how are we supposed to practice with these?"

"Like so," Clarence said, then lunged forward.

I barely got the blade up in time, my reflexes naturally moving into a tent guard. Clarence's sword sang off my steel, but the impact nearly twisted the hilt out of my hand. No sooner was his blade clear of mine than he twisted it back, thrusting hard at my chest. I spun laterally, drove my hilt against the forte of his blade, then thrust it to the side. Clarence's shoulder went into my chest. I stumbled back.

"Not bad, but you still stink of the mundane. You battle for points, and the touch. It will take more than a touch to kill." He drew the blade behind his back, then danced forward and struck in a series of downward strokes. I grabbed my hilt in both hands, blocking and blocking again, catching Clarence's blows on hilt and forte. My shoulders sang in pain as he hammered down. Each strike set my skull ringing. By the time I scrambled out of range, my entire body was sore, and we had just started.

"So that's what it looks like to be outclassed," Chesa said with a smirk. She stood at the edge of the practice yard, sword held loosely in her hands.

"It will be your turn soon enough, fae-child," Clarence said with a jaunty smile. "You're doing well, Sir John. But I don't think you understand the point of this exercise. We're supposed to try to hit each other. So far, it's just been me hitting you."

"Come on, man! Be a little careful, will you?" I shook out my arms, trying to get some feeling back in my hands. My own sword was so sharp that I managed to nick my shin with the tip, drawing blood. "Damn it! Why are these swords so sharp? You're going to kill somebody if you don't watch out."

"Yes, I suppose we should get that out of the way, shouldn't we?" Clarence asked. Before I could answer, he lunged forward, thrusting his sword smoothly into my chest. I heard Chesa scream in shock.

The steel tip passed cleanly through my ribs and into my heart. The pain burned so hot and bright that I couldn't feel anything else. Blood bubbled out of the wound, splashing on my face and down my chest. Clarence whipped the sword free of my chest, and the blood flooded out. I went to my knees. The pain was unimaginable. Chesa's shocked face stared at me as I went to my knees, hands pressed against the wound. I looked down at my chest. The last thing I saw was my lifeblood soaking into the sand between my fingers.

I woke up on a meat rack. My chest ached, and my arms and legs were stiff. I blinked dry eyes, squinting against the light, trying to get my bearings. I could smell blood and cured leather, the sweet smell of pipe smoke, and stale sweat. Birdsong filled my head. I tried to move my arms. There was a moment of resistance, then my hand pulled free of some sort of restraint, and I lurched forward, falling to my knees, then my hands. There was sand under my palms. Back in the practice yard.

"Ah, good. That took longer than I expected. Of course, I'm never around to count the hours when it happens to me," Clarence said. My vision was still blurry, but I could see the yard finally, and the line of quintains. Finally, I made out Clarence, sitting in a wooden camp stool in the shadow of the wall. He was smoking a pipe and reading the world's oldest book. He marked his place and stood up. "Shall we start again?"

"What the hell happened?" I asked. My voice was as dry as dust. I looked around the yard. Chesa hung on a rack next to me, a pair of deep wounds on her arms, and a final blow in the middle of her chest. Her clothes were soaked with blood. "Chesa! Chesa! What did you do, you monster!"

"Settle down. You're fine, she's fine." Clarence got to his feet and strode toward me, scabbard in hand. "She had a poor reaction to your loss. Nearly got me, she did. That girl fights like a banshee." As he got closer, I saw that his face was scarred, and his armor sported several deep gouges across the chest. "I don't think we're going to have to train her too much. Killing seems to come natural to that one."

"What do you mean we're fine? I thought I was dead! She sure looks dead as hell!"

"You were. Both of you. Mythically dead. Hurts, doesn't it?"

"Like a son of a bitch!" I snapped. I went to Chesa. The blood on her chest was dry, and if I looked closely, I could see that the three wounds were nothing more than scars. Even as I watched, those scars started to fade. The blood started to fade as well, like disappearing ink. "Are you sure she's okay?"

"Capital O, capital K. Though she's going to be pissed when she comes to. I might need your help with that. In retrospect, it might have been better to warn you." Clarence rubbed his face. "Oh well. Next time."

Slowly, I worked my way up to my feet. My whole body ached. "Was that necessary?"

"Yes, completely. This is not a game played for points, John. The masquerade is over. You are starting on a serious road. There will be pain, and misery, and most certainly death. For your enemies, hopefully many times. And for you, only once. Except here." He drew his sword again, the rasp of steel loud in the silence of the yard. "Do not waste these deaths. Learn from them, so that when the true death comes, you will not fear it. So. Stand up. Retrieve your sword. Join the fight again."

"I'm not so sure about this," I said, rubbing my chest. There was no blood on my tabard, no evidence of the wound that had killed me. But I could remember the steel passing through bone and flesh, the startling heat as it pierced my heart. I shook the memory from my head. "Isn't there a better way?"

"If you want to fail, yes. But I do not train the sword to fail. En garde!"

He lunged forward. I barely managed to get my sword up in time. The sound of steel on steel filled the practice yard, mingling with birdsong and the distant chanting of unseen monks, echoing off the castle walls.

A few minutes later, Chesa flinched, and her eyes fluttered open. She locked on to Clarence and started screaming. Clarence and I stopped circling and ran to her.

"You son of a bitch! You monster!" she screamed. "I'm going to tear the heart from your chest and—"

"Ches, Ches, it's alright. I'm fine," I said. I moved between her and Clarence. A moment of surprise passed over her face, quickly replaced by even more anger.

"So this is some kind of joke?" she shouted. "You did that just to freak me out?" Chesa tore free of the rack, coming swiftly to her feet. She scooped up the bow that lay nearby and drew, magically summoning an arrow from her quiver, drawing a bead on Clarence's chest. The big knight took a step back, holding out his hands.

"Whoa, whoa, let's not—"

The bow hummed, the arrow zipped, and Clarence went down. He lay on his back for a long second, staring up at the sky.

"Oh, bugger," he said. "I suppose . . . that's . . . fair."

Then he died. I turned to Chesa. She shrugged.

"Tell me that isn't fair," she said.

CHAPTER ELEVEN
BLEED, RINSE, REPEAT

Over the course of the next three days, I died thirty-eight times, once because I fumbled sheathing the sword and put the tip into my thigh. Chesa only died twice more, but after the second time she gathered up her bow and spent her hours on the quintains, filling them with arrows. Their tiny wooden voices screamed each time she killed them. It was disconcerting, in a way that my own repeated deaths were not.

Every time I woke up, Clarence instructed me on how I had failed and what I needed to do to improve. We spent the daylight hours on the hot sand of the training yard, and our evenings in the banquet hall, listening to far off music and talking about Knight Watch. Clarence was a better guy than I thought at first. Much older than I expected.

"This is a pretty good place you've got," Chesa said. "Kind of lonely, though."

"I have what I need. And it's better than the life I left behind," he answered. "Tembo, Bethany, and Matthew are better friends than I ever knew before. At least the two of you are already close. It's good to go into this with people you love."

Chesa snorted derisively. I hurried to change the subject.

"So how did you get involved in this?" I asked. "Surely Knight Watch's recruiting method has to extend beyond waiting for someone to be attacked by a dragon."

"Esther MacRae hired me. I don't suppose 'hire' is the right word." Clarence sat thoughtfully at the head of the long table in the banquet room, one leg thrown over the arm of his chair, leaning back and staring at the ceiling. "Enlisted me is more accurate. Duty to king and country, fight the Viking threat, all that sort of business. There was a war on, you know."

"Which war was this?" I asked, thinking about Esther's age.

"The big one. The second one. I understand there have been others," he said, sipping from his goblet of wine. "I've lost track."

"World War II? How old is she?"

"Let's just say she didn't have to lie about her age to enlist, and our branch cared little for gender. Something the mundanes are still figuring out, I understand." Clarence nodded to himself, lost in thought. "By the time we landed in Europe, she was the best warden they had, already leading her own team. And she has changed less than you think."

"I guess . . . I guess I'm learning to believe in unbelievable things," I said. Clarence snorted, then set his wine aside and folded his hands together. "You talk about the service, and branches, but Esther insists this isn't a military operation. I have trouble believing it."

"She has some grudges. The service made some mistakes, refused to believe the war wasn't over. Higher-ups didn't like having faeries on the payroll. Esther hadn't wrangled the actuator out of government hands, yet. There were still elements who thought . . . well, it doesn't matter what they thought. They're dead, and the actuator belongs to Knight Watch. There's no one else doing what we do. At least, not on this side of unreality."

"What's that supposed to mean? This side of unreality?" Chesa asked.

"We've made a few alliances. Among the dead, the elder races, certain mythological factions who don't want to see the mundane world getting fully involved in their affairs. We have friends among the monsters."

"Like Kyle?" I asked.

"Kyle is a special case," Clarence said. His face grew still, almost melancholy, but then he quickly changed the subject. "You're making nice progress, Sir John. Once you put the points system aside and started finishing your swings, that is."

"There are penalties for striking too hard," I said. "Too much finesse, not enough full-on smashing."

"Finesse will always have a place in the swordsman's art. Even in full plate. You will learn to land a proper blow in the exact right spot and with enough power to pierce your enemy's steel without overreaching if you miss. In time, all things in time."

"Which is why I prefer the bow," Chesa said. "An arrow in the eye at a hundred yards is way better than crossed steel so close you can smell the other guy's blood."

"To each their own. And to be honest, I'm the wrong person to train you. We haven't had an archer for . . . well, I lose track of time. A long while," Clarence said. "It feels like you're going to learn more in your domain than you could ever learn from me. Assuming the elves grant you an audience. They're particular."

"That doesn't seem fair," I said. "I have to sweat my way through sword practice, wear armor, risk my blood, take a blade in the belly. Meanwhile, Chesa's conjuring light-flowers with her breath and shooting magic arrows like it was nothing."

"You are working on fundamentals, Sir John. There are things you have learned in the mundane that must be unlearned. Bad habits that are not true to the way of a real knight. Once you have the basic skills correct, then the magic will begin."

"So there is magic in the sword?" I asked.

"Of course. You can't honestly expect to kill a dragon with nothing more than a yard of steel and a stiff upper lip. All the elites have access to a particular form of mystical power. Ours is simply more brutal, less beautiful."

"Some of us get all the luck," Chesa said with a smile.

"Oh, I wouldn't count yourself lucky just yet," Clarence said. "The path of the fae is difficult. They ask a price I would not be willing to pay."

Chesa grew quiet. She stared into the flames for a while, clearly thinking about the kind of costs a knight wouldn't be willing to pay, when so much of his life seemed to involve almost getting eaten by a dragon, and risking death by steel on a regular basis. I cleared my throat.

"Is it the same for the others? Matthew, and Tembo?"

"I don't know the specifics, of course. But the basic rules are the same for all of us. Our powers depend on staying true to our mythic selves. Going into the mundane world risks contamination, and the longer we're there, the more our powers are eroded. Some of it is discipline . . . avoiding modern conveniences, that sort of thing. But it's a balance. Given my druthers, I would stay here all the time. But that risks losing ourselves in the fantasy. And that's just as bad, if not worse."

"How so?" I asked.

"There's a delirium in the unreal. We have to stay grounded, or we just become another myth, adrift inside our own minds. Esther will teach you more about this. The point is that you will have to seek balance. It's difficult."

"Sounds like it," I said. "I can understand wanting to stay here all the time. It's an attractive prospect."

"It is. And speaking of that . . ." Clarence stood, the meal at an end. "I think I have taught the two of you all I can for now. I need to recover, and frankly, you're both barely out of the mundane. You're contaminating the domain and making it difficult for me to recuperate. Report back to Esther, maybe work on your own domains. We'll take up your training at a later date."

"Fine with me. I'm ready to be back in the real world for a while," Chesa said, getting up. She looked around the empty hall. "This place is starting to give me the creeps."

"Can I ask one more question?" I asked.

"Of course."

"Why are we training to fight like this? Sword to sword, armor against armor. Dragons don't carry swords."

"It's not all dragons and trolls, Sir John," Clarence said. "Some among the myths resemble us; the Valkyrie, the seelie and unseelie courts, even the usual panoply of elves and dwarves and other literary creations, though they are much rarer these days than they were in the Professor's day," he said, without explaining who the Professor might have been. He seemed about ready to go on when he thought better of it. "It's a strong foundation, John. You will learn to fight monsters later on."

"There's something you're not telling me," I said. He grimaced but did not deny it. I stood. "Knights shouldn't lie to their squires."

"No. No, they shouldn't." He rested his hands on the back of the chair and thought for a long minute, choosing his words carefully. "There are others. I said no one else was doing what we do, and that's true. But it doesn't mean there aren't people who seek to use the unreal world for their own purposes, if you know what I mean. Some of them were friends once. Some were comrades in arms, gone astray. The lure of the unreal is strong. And that is all I will say. Good night, John." He turned and started toward the door.

"How do we get back to Mundane Actual?" Chesa asked.

"The way you came. There are horses waiting for you in the courtyard. Kyle will pay you no heed. Give Esther my greetings."

Chesa and I walked out to the courtyard. She pulled on my sleeve as soon as we were out of Clarence's earshot.

"What do you think that was about?" she asked. "They were comrades once?"

"Beats me," I said. "But there's a lot of power here. If you can become anything you imagine, don't you think some people have pretty dangerous imaginations?"

Chesa grew quiet. It was hard to read her new face, but I could tell she was bothered.

"Hey, don't worry about it. We're with the good guys. Everything's going to be fine."

"I didn't like seeing you die," she said. "I don't care what he said. I think that was too much."

"Well. I didn't like it either."

We didn't say anything else. The horses waiting for us outside looked solid enough. Chesa hopped up effortlessly, but it took me a few attempts. Four, to be exact, and I almost died again when I landed on my shoulder and spooked the horse, nearly earning an iron-shod hoof to the throat.

It was night, and ten thousand stars glittered in the sky, though none of the familiar constellations. Even the moon seemed bigger. Kyle's silhouette wheeled in the distance, but true to Clarence's word, the dragon came no closer. We followed the path into the forest. After a while it got too dark to see, and Chesa had to lead us with her amethyst eyes. As we entered the trees, I looked back at the castle one last time. Hundreds of lights shone throughout the towers and along the walls, torchlight flickering against the stone, an earthbound constellation of burning stars. But one light shone brighter, in the highest tower. I thought I could just make out Clarence's form in the window, watching us leave.

The trees closed around us, and with them came the sounds of the forest. Insects creaked and whistled, leaves stirred, joined by the strange, distant sounds of the forest at night. I couldn't see where I was going, but Chesa seemed confident in the path. I gave my mount his reins and enjoyed the ride. The light from the moon grew dimmer and dimmer, the trees less distinct, and soon we were riding through pure darkness.

I woke up with my head in a bag, and ropes cutting into my wrists. It was pretty much what I was expecting. Dreams end. Hope fades. And burlap tastes like regret, especially when you're eating it in the trunk of a car, and your hands are tied behind your back, and the shocks on the car have apparently been replaced with concrete. Or maybe I was just regretting the series of decisions that landed me in this situation. That was probably it. Yeah, burlap just tastes like burlap.

In all fairness, this was not the worst place I had woken up. I spent my first couple months at college befriending progressively less gainfully employed artistic types, leading to a period of regrettable parties that always ended in forests or abandoned warehouses. I slept on a lot of trash in those days and I woke up in my share of moving vehicles, religious communes, and at least one hostage situation. But never all three at once.

I was just contemplating the depth of this error, whether this might be the mistake my mother relates in hushed tones to her friends at the funeral while they shake their heads and tut respectfully at the tragedy, when the car rattled to a halt and the engine shut off. *This is it,* I thought. *This is the end of the road.*

Turns out the road had ended a while ago. The trunk opened, and bright light flooded through the burlap bag over my head. Strong hands grabbed my arms and levered me out of the trunk, setting me on my feet and holding me up while I struggled to regain my balance. They ripped the bag off my head, leaving me blinking and blind in the bright sun. Two dark shadows lurked nearby, though I couldn't make out their faces.

"So it was drugs, then?" I asked. "You put drugs in the mead at the faire and I imagined all that?"

"I'm not that kind of saint," a voice said. I recognized Matthew's disappointed voice, coming from the taller of the two shadows. "Things are weird enough around here."

"Where's Clarence?" I asked.

"Still down the hole. You and your friend are being discharged for a while. Try to not be weird about it," Matthew answered.

"Sure. Nothing weird about this," I said, holding up my bound hands. "Perfectly normal way to treat your new friends."

"Are you going to run if we take these ropes off?" the other shadow asked. That was the girl. Bethany, I think.

I shook my head, and suddenly the bonds were gone. I regained just enough vision to see her closing the longest folding knife I had ever seen. The ropes lay in a heap at my feet, their ends cut clean. I blinked down at my wrists to see if she'd nicked me. My arm hair was shaved clean where the bindings had been.

"Thanks," I said, looking around. The three of us were standing next to the most nondescript car I could possibly imagine. We were in the middle of a cornfield. Literally the middle. I couldn't even see a road on the far horizon. A lane of battered stalks led into the distance. "Where are we? What happened to Clarence's domain? And where's Chesa?"

"We're someplace boring, Clarence's domain is the same weird golden age fantasy it's always been, and Chesa is taking a different car," she said.

"I don't...I don't understand," I said. "I was riding a horse, coming back to Mundane Actual, and then..."

"And then you woke up in the trunk of a car," Bethany said. "Is that really so difficult to understand?"

"Esther has a policy. We keep the location of HQ secret, even from new recruits," Matthew cut in. "Especially from new recruits, actually, after the whole—"

"Not something he needs to know about," Bethany said. "Point is, we pulled your body out before your mind caught up. Tied you up to keep you from hurting yourself."

"And the burlap sack?"

"That's just for my amusement," Bethany answered. "Now get in the front seat. Look happy to be alive."

"You're not going to leave me here?"

"Leave you here? I don't even know where here is," Matthew said. "I don't think that's what we're supposed to be doing. Beth?" Bethany shook her head, and Matthew looked relieved. "Good, good. They don't usually send me on the 'abandon innocent people in the middle of nowhere' missions. I issued a complaint the last time that happened, and Esther really doesn't like paperwork."

"We're taking you home, John. Back to the mundane. You're going to need a few days to recover from the unreal before you can do your next bit of training. Both for your safety, and for ours," Beth answered. "We can't have you knowing where the base is, but we also can't drive you up to your front door with your head in a sack. So," she gestured around. "A cornfield for the transition. And the car is magically dull, so don't try giving our description to the cops. You'll literally be unable to describe it. Now let's get going. I want to get back to my domain, and the longer I'm here, the longer that's going to take."

"Sorry to inconvenience you," I mumbled. We got back in the car, Beth in the driver's seat, Matthew stretched out in the back seat. I was so distracted by the crash of cornstalks on the front window that I didn't notice what was wrong at first. Finally I looked over at Beth and nearly jumped out of the car. "You're not driving!"

"Hm?" she asked. She was sitting crosslegged on the bench seat, picking at her nails with a bowie knife that looked like it was made out of stained glass. The wheel and pedals twitched without her interference. "Oh, we can't drive, man. Deeply against protocol. We'd be stuck in this hellhole of a dimension for weeks."

I dove for the wheel, and nearly lost my hand to her blade. She batted me aside with the spine of the knife, then popped me in the middle of the chest with the pommel. I sat back, gasping for air and staring at the windshield. Matthew's face appeared over the seatback, an amused smirk on his mouth.

"That's the BIZ, kiddo. Bethany Interdiction Zone. Don't put anything near her you don't want to lose," he said. "Especially if she's not paying attention."

"Noted," I wheezed. Matthew chuckled and sat back.

We burst out of the cornfield and pulled onto an empty strip of asphalt. The car straightened itself out and started accelerating. Within moments we were merging into traffic on familiar streets. I sat up.

"You're not driving, and this is my neighborhood," I said. "There are no cornfields near my neighborhood."

"Everything in America is about five minutes away from an empty cornfield," Bethany said. "At least metaphorically. And that's what counts." The car snapped to the right, and we pulled into my parents' driveway. "Here we are. Home sweet boring home."

The house of my origin story loomed over us. It was an old Victorian, on a street where all the Victorians had been torn down for loftier, more sterile abodes. To be honest, I took offense at Bethany calling my parent's home boring. It was anything but. The halls and stairways of this home had served as the staging areas for a hundred childish misadventures. I knew every creaking floorboard and dusty cabinet, every weird shadow, the view from every window and landing.

"What am I supposed to tell them about where I've been? God, how am I supposed to explain what happened to Mom's car?"

"You'll think of something. Boring people always find a way to explain away the interesting things in their lives. The Incident was two days ago," Bethany said, in a manner that made the capital I really obvious. "Tell them you've been staying with friends. Too much mead. Keep it simple, and they'll get tired of asking. Unless you want to answer some very awkward questions."

"My mom doesn't ask anything but awkward questions," I said.

"You'll manage," Bethany said. "Now get going. Someone from MA will be in contact soon enough. And welcome to the team."

"That was heartfelt," I muttered. She snorted and went back to digging under her fingers with her peculiar blade.

I climbed out of the car and slammed the door shut, then leaned down to the open window. Matthew (saint or not) smiled at me placidly, then jerked a thumb toward the back of the car.

"Rest of your stuff is in the trunk. Take a couple weeks off, try to relax. Acclimate yourself to the real world. Good luck, man! Be seeing you in the unreal!"

I fished for something clever to say, came up empty, and retreated to the trunk before my tongue lost the war for me. My rattan sword, crumpled sheet metal helmet, and singed shield lay in state on a bed of discarded newspapers and waterlogged paperbacks. There was a burned strip of linen around the hilt of the sword. I picked at it and came away with a scrap of black material. The white runes stood out starkly against the ash. *Eric's silly flag,* I thought. *Apparently, the arcane banner of whateverthehell isn't dragonproof.* Then I realized I hadn't given Eric a second's thought for days. *Man. Hope he's okay. What the hell am I going to tell Eric? He's going to be so jealous.*

I snatched up my equipment and closed the trunk, then trudged up the driveway to my parents' porch.

CHAPTER TWELVE
A COMPLICATED EXPLANATION

Mom was waiting just inside the screen door with her arms folded. I clambered up the stairs and gave her a half-hearted wave. She frowned at me as if her life depended on it.

"Your friends don't want to come inside?" she asked. "I could offer them some lemonade. Maybe they could tell me where my son has been for the last two days."

"Mom—"

"No, no, it's okay. They're not your friends, I know. They're just people who drove you home from your fairy tale adult camping time, because your car . . . I'm sorry, my car . . . wouldn't start. Is that right? I assume they stole your phone, as well?"

"Mom—"

"Because I heard about your dragon thing. It's all over the news. Three dead!" She threw her arms up in the air in exasperation. "And I'm stuck here wondering if maybe one of them is my son, but who knows! Because he can't call, and he can't pick up his phone, and the police won't give out the names—"

"Mom! I'm fine. Whatever you heard . . ." the specific words she'd spoken settled into my brain. "Dragon thing? What . . . what did you hear?"

"The dragon! The stupid float thing, or whatever it was. From the parade!" She pushed open the screen door, and for a brief moment I was worried Mom would bull rush me off the front porch. "The propane explosion! Were you even there?"

"I was . . . yeah. It was terrible." It was the first time that it occurred to me that people had died and, again, I felt guilty for having not thought of Eric until now. I looked down at my mom. There was a thin glaze of tears in her eyes, which was something of a shock. "I'm sorry I didn't call."

"It's . . . it's fine. I was just worried." Her bluster disappeared. Mom swooped forward, gave me a swift, bony-armed hug that threatened to crush my ribs into their component elements, then retreated to the doorway. About the best I could expect from her. "As long as you're alright. And I'm sure we can get the car towed. I assume the police sealed the scene, or something?"

"We . . . have to talk about the car."

"Hm," she said, and the time for motherly affection passed. "You broke another one?"

"No. I mean yes, but not in the way . . ." I looked around. The neighbors on both sides were on their porches, surreptitiously watering plants or reading newspapers, definitely not listening in on our conversation, certainly not gathering fodder for the evening's gossip session. I sighed. "Can we go inside? I'll explain everything."

"I suppose," she said. "Can't have you living on the porch, after all. Come on. Your father is sleeping in front of the baseball. Dinner's in half an hour."

The screen door slammed shut. I looked back at the driveway, just in time to see the Knight Watch car pull into the street. Even though I knew its trick, that it was the most inconspicuous of all possible cars, I was still surprised when it disappeared before my eyes. I was sure the neighbors hadn't noticed. I barely had.

Shouldering my sword and shield, I went inside. How was I going to explain all this? I wondered. Why was I going to explain all this?

Mom insisted on eating before talking. Dinner was soft and warm and served in a casserole dish. I sometimes wondered if my parents ever chewed their food anymore. We ate in relative silence while the television blared in the next room. Father asked a few broad questions about my weekend, seemingly satisfied with the propane explanation, blanching when I said I wasn't sure if I knew any of the dead.

"Is Eric okay?" my mother asked.

"I think so," I said. I was nervous about seeing Eric again. Of all my friends, he was the only one I could imagine telling about Knight Watch. Hell, of all my friends, he was the one who should have been recruited. "I kind of lost track of him when I . . . when the . . . there was an explosion."

"Yes, dear," my mother said patiently. "But you're saying you haven't seen Eric?"

"I'll ask Chesa if she's heard from him. They've apparently started hanging out," I said. "I ended up giving them both a ride to the faire."

"Oh! Chesa!" My mother perked up, saving me from one awkward conversation and dumping me into a different one. "Was she there as well? Such a nice girl. You know, I really think you should—"

"Yes, yes, biggest mistake of my life, a great disappointment to you, etc. I'm pretty sure she and Eric are a thing now. Or something. Or nothing." I too another bite. The casserole in my mouth was turning cold, and a pit was forming in my stomach. I swallowed without chewing. "But Eric. Man, I hope he's alright."

My father shook his head sadly.

"Kids these days . . . I don't know," he muttered, as though rock and roll or soda pop were somehow the culprit in this situation. "When I was a lad, we did healthy stuff. Baseball! Apple pie!"

"People choke on apple pie all the time," I said bitterly.

"Well, next time you choke on pie, please just call," Mom said. "We don't pay for that phone so you can download pornography all day long."

"Mom, my God! I couldn't call. It was . . . there were problems. But I'm here now, and I'm fine." I chewed my food angrily, which was both equally unnecessary and unsatisfying. My jaws made loud slushing sounds as they worked through the world's softest casserole. "I'll drop by Eric's tomorrow. See if he's okay."

"It just would have been better if you had called, that's all," Mom said. "You didn't lose your phone again, did you?"

"No, of course not," I said. I reached into my pocket and produced the phone case. "It's right . . . here . . ."

The case, a nice leather one with a sword embossed on the front, again a gift from my mother, folded open. A musty deck of tarot cards slid out, spilling across the table. My parents simply stared.

"Or not," I said. "I'll have to . . . someone must have . . ."

"Kids!" father exclaimed, then clambered laboriously to his feet.

"Baseball," he said, though I wasn't sure if it was warning, exhortation, or simple statement of fact. He went into the living room and turned up the already loud television, then settled into his couch and fell asleep. I turned to Mom.

"I'll find the phone. And about the car, you don't need to worry. I'll get it back."

"Back? Back?" she squawked. "Is it gone? Has it been turned into a giant pinochle set?"

"No, it's just . . ." I paused, as a familiar sound filled the front room. Mom and I turned toward the front door just as the Volvo's horn sounded a second time. "Hang on a minute."

The Volvo was in the driveway, looking considerably better than it had when last I saw it. There was no sign of damage, either to the front or side, and someone had given the Viking bitch the most thorough detailing job of its long and previously tedious life. A second car waited at the foot of the driveway, nearly as inconspicuous as the one that had dropped me off. A black woman with the sides of her head shaved, wearing gray coveralls and a suspiciously taped badge on her sleeve, got out of the Volvo and smiled in my direction. My heart fell straight through to my heels.

"So I guess this is my contact. Could've waited until I finished with dinner," I muttered. My mom looked at me out of the corner of her eye, then jabbed me in the ribs.

"There is someone else driving my car, John," she said.

"Yes, yes . . . I can explain everything," I said as quietly as possible. The woman by the car was looking through a notepad and jingling the car keys in her hand. Finally, she found what she was looking for and looked up.

"John Rast?" the woman called. When I didn't answer, she strode (no other word for it. She was a strider) across the driveway. "Are you John Rast?"

"Stay here," I whispered to Mom, then hurried across the porch, intercepting the woman before she could reach the sacred ground of my front porch, and the boundary of my mom's willingness to engage with strangers. "That's me," I said. "Rast comma John. Mister."

"Not sir?" she asked with a twinkle in her eye. I groaned inwardly, glancing over my shoulder and hoping Mom wasn't close enough to hear. "I was asked to return your car."

"This couldn't be my car. My car was—"

"Totaled, yes," she said. "A complete ruin. So here it is!" She dangled the keys between us, waiting for me to take them.

"But how?"

"Do you really want me to explain it in front of a mundane?" she asked, her bright smile plastered across her face, eyes darting to where my mom was creeping closer across the porch.

"No, no," I said, snatching the keys from her hand. "Thanks so much, uh..."

"Gabrielle," she said. She plucked a business card from an inner pocket and tucked it into my hand. "Local operator, Mundane Actual. I'll be your contact in case of real-world emergencies. Owen and I..." she stabbed a thumb at the waiting car, "We're the ones who will dig you out of whatever real-world trouble you fall into."

I glanced over at Owen. He had gotten out of the car at the end of the driveway and was leaning massive elbows on the roof of the vehicle. His shoulders towered over the car, and the thick slabs of his arms rippled with muscle. Even his bald forehead looked like it could bench-press a small cow. He grinned at me with all the affection of a white shark.

"He's one of them, isn't he?" I whispered. "Troll or something. A myth, making his way in our world."

"Owen? No, he's from Iowa. High School wrestler, then the military, then us. Lot of those skills transfer pretty well, especially on the creeps who don't answer to bullets." She glanced over her shoulder at Owen and gave him a smart wave. He glowered more aggressively. Gabrielle turned back to me. "Look, there's something we have to get out of the way. Owen and me, we're the last call you make. Got it?"

"Last call?"

"Yeah. You only call us if everything has gone to shit. Complete shit. A lot of the new recruits panic when they get a pixie in their garden, or a water elemental clogs up their toilet, or whatever. Weird things are going to happen to you from now on. That's your problem. Buy them some cupcakes or something. Figure it out."

"So what do I call you for? What constitutes complete shit?"

"Firestorms, icestorms, hellstorms... really, any kind of storm that doesn't come up on your local weather channel. Also, zones of intense negativity—"

"Like . . . people are being down on me and making me feel bad?"

"Like . . . the real world is turning upside down and the sun is sucking the light out of the sky. Negativity," she said.

"And is that likely to happen?" I asked.

"Esther says you're a live one, so I wouldn't rule anything out. Just stay alert. But also only call that number if it seems like the world is ending. Got it?"

"Got it," I said. "And, so, if I see something you can't handle. Something . . ." I hunched my shoulders and glanced behind me. Mom was staring at us through the screen door. I lowered my voice to a harsh whisper. "Something dragony. I can just take care of that myself?"

"If that's how you want to die, sure. Knock yourself out." She flipped through the notepad one more time. "Says here you've just gone through basic training, but you don't have a domain yet, so until one of the other elites has shown you the ropes, you probably just want to run and hide. Let the professionals handle it. And if a dragon shows up, you can bet Clarence won't be far behind."

"Well, I mean, I did kill a dragon. You know." I tried to draw myself up straight, but also stay hunched down so Mom couldn't hear me. I failed on both accounts. "I'm not completely helpless."

"Sure, you're not," she said, patting me on the shoulder. "You're like a hero, only more dangerous to yourself than anyone else." She pointed to the card in my hand. "You have the number. Try to never call it."

She turned and marched down to the waiting Owen, then paused and turned around.

"Be seeing you!" I called after her.

"Not if I'm doing my job right," she answered, then got in the car. Owen asked her something through the open window, glared up at me, then somehow folded his bulk into the vehicle and drove off. I watched them go, straining my eyes as the car's trickery took hold, trying to keep it in sight. When they were gone, I pulled her business card out of my sleeve and tapped it against my palm. *Gabrielle Rodriguez*, it read. *Mundane Actual*. The Knight Watch logo was embossed in the background.

"They're making mechanics a lot prettier than they used to," my mom called from the porch.

"Soldiers, too," I muttered, then spun on my heel and walked up the stairs. Mom was staring at me with funny eyes. "What? Your car's back. Be happy for one minute, will ya?"

"Mm hm," she said as I passed. "Maybe the young lady has your phone, as well."

"Oh! Hadn't thought of that. Maybe she does," I said. "Is there any dessert?"

CHAPTER THIRTEEN
BARD HAS LEFT THE PARTY

I tried calling Eric first thing in the morning. Since my phone was MIA, I used the landline in the kitchen downstairs. Mom was baking an apple pie, which is quite possibly the most Mom thing she could do. My mom, at least, was deeply in touch with her mythic identity.

It took me a minute to remember Eric's actual number, since these days I just pushed a button on my screen to get ahold of him. The phone rang and rang, long enough that I began to wonder if I had somehow broken their answering machine just by calling, or maybe misdialed. Mom walked through the kitchen to check on her pie. She was still busying herself at the stove when someone finally picked up. There was a long moment of silence on the line.

"Hello?" I said. Whoever had answered took a deep breath. "Hello, Mrs. Cavanaugh? Is Eric there, please?"

The line hissed. For a second, I thought I had been cut off, but then a tumbling, hissing, static-laced avalanche of sounds came out of the phone. I heard the line disconnect, then pick up again.

"John?" Eric's voice cut through the clutter. He sounded like he was at the bottom of a well, and maybe not an empty one. "John, where have you been? I've been trying to get a hold of you, but . . . but . . ."

"Eric, what the hell's going on?" I asked. My mom straightened and looked over at me reprovingly. I turned away from her, tucking myself into the hallway for a little privacy. "Eric? Can you hear me?"

"There's just so much darkness, John. I don't know what to—"

The line went abruptly dead. The cacophony of other sounds

lingered in my head like an echo. I hung up and immediately redialed, fingers fumbling through the keys. Not even a ringtone this time. I gave it two more tries before my mom stuck her head around the corner.

"Is everything alright, John?" she asked in a voice that made it clear she knew something was wrong.

"Fine, Mom. It's fine. No one's home." I held the receiver against my chest and smiled at her unconvincingly. We stood like that for a long time before she sighed and went back into the kitchen. I called Chesa.

"I swear to God, John, if I ever wake up in a trunk with a bag on my head again—" she said on picking up.

"Chesa, please, just listen," I said quickly. She didn't hang up, so I rushed forward. "I think something is wrong. With Eric."

She didn't say anything for a long moment. Finally, "I tried calling him first thing when I got home. Didn't even get a ringtone," she said. "I figured he didn't pay his bill."

"Well, someone or something just answered," I said. I tucked the phone against my chest and made sure Mom wasn't listening, then continued in a whisper. "Something Esther might be interested in."

"So call Esther. Or that cute soldier girl, assuming you have the same contact I do. She might be willing to fall for this kind of nonsense, but I have better things to do."

"Ches, I'm serious. I think we need to check it out."

"This isn't some kind of trick, is it? Some ploy to get me to spend time with you? Because that ship's sailed, John. The only reason we're still talking is because it might finally get me into elvish princess heaven. Don't take advantage of that."

"I'm not, I swear. I just think something's wrong. All we have to do is head over there and check it out. If it's serious, we call Knight's Watch. Honest. I'm sure it's probably nothing. But we owe it to Eric to look."

Another long pause. She sighed.

"I'll meet you there," she said, then hung up.

"Mom," I yelled over my shoulder. She was standing right behind me, like some kind of creepy corn child. I dropped the phone. "Mom! Jesus!"

"How is Chesa?" she asked.

"Justifiably pissed," I said. "I need to borrow the car again. We're going over to Eric's for, uh . . . for something."

"Not a chance, young man. I just got that car back. There's no way I'm giving you the keys." She turned her back on me and went into the kitchen. "Maybe Chesa could give you a ride."

"To hell, maybe," I muttered. I followed her into the kitchen. The smell of apple pies was nearly overwhelming. I had to wonder what sort of nostalgia demon my mom was trying to summon. "Well, how am I supposed to get there?"

"Your bike is in the garage," she said. "Last time I checked, you still had two healthy legs."

"Mom, I haven't ridden that thing since high school. Surely—"

"Bike or walk. Or call Chesa back," she said without turning around.

I thought about calling Ches and asking for a ride, then shivered.

"Bike it is," I said.

Shadowfax was mounted on the wall in the garage like a stuffed antelope made of rust and decaying foam pads. I reached up and unhooked the bike. A cloud of dust and the dry husks of dead bugs filled the air. It took a while to get the wheels reinflated, and by the time I started clanking down the driveway, I was both sweating and late.

Shadowfax had seen me through a lot of long rides, especially in high school. Eric and I used to ride our bikes out to the park and ride in circles, talking about the things guys that age talked about. And sometimes we would stop talking about girls long enough to venture into books, or knights, or games.

Honestly, I was scared to see Eric again. I was scared to tell him about Knight Watch, and even more scared to try to hide it from him. I had it on my mental checklist to talk to Esther about him, try to convince her to let him into the club. I still wasn't sure why they had picked me and Chesa off the field and brought us into their little secret, but not Eric. Something to worry about later, I suppose, because now something might be wrong with my wayward, semi-literary, bard-aspirant friend.

Something was definitely wrong with my bike, though. At first, I thought it was just the fact that it was old and in disrepair, but it soon became clear that Shadowfax was ailing. That's the kind of day it was.

I have a history of breaking technology, from toasters to cell phones to videogames and beyond. I spent most of my freshman year of college trying to convince my science professor that I wasn't intentionally ruining everything I touched, that centrifuges just naturally pirouetted across the floor whenever I got close to them, but he never believed me. And my glorious and undoubtedly successful career as a major player in the eSports world was cut short when my Call of Duty account somehow developed a catastrophic error that briefly gained sentience and crashed the system's servers worldwide.

That kind of nonsense usually only affected complicated technology, but ever since my brush with Kracek the Hosier, things had gotten worse. Today, that worseness included my trusty bike, Shadowfax. Misery knows no bounds.

I tried to change gears, and something popped off the rear wheel and went bouncing down the street. My feet spun wildly for a few revolutions, then the chain caught and I lurched forward, nearly tumbling over the handlebars.

"Damn it, Shadowfax!" I shouted. The same trio of soccer moms that had been loitering on the corner when I came by to pick up Eric three days ago were still at their posts. They lowered their macchipoccolitos and narrowed their eyes as I, slowly, passed. I gave them a wave. "Ladies," I called. They turned sharply away.

Something gave deep in the heart of Shadowfax. The gearing, drive chain, pedals, frame, brake lines, spokes, tires, and rims all surrendered their grasp on this mortal realm at the same time. Shadowfax went in a dozen different directions. A handful of gears circled sadly in the street, a tire bounced over the curb and started its new life as trash in someone's yard, and the seat skidded across the asphalt like a base runner. I stood in the middle of the street, holding the tasseled handlebar in my clenched fists as I watched my bike settle into a pile of junk.

"And so his soul goes to the far shore, and leaves us here to feel the ache of his absence," I said solemnly. "Fly on, Shadowfax. Your journey is at an end."

A car rolled up next to me. Another embarrassment, but at least I didn't know many of Eric's neighbors. And what did I care what a stranger thought?

"That was impressive, Rast," Chesa said. She was in full regalia, feathered crown brushing against the ceiling of her hatchback. I wondered if I should have brought my knight's kit, then realized that would have only made this entire situation more intolerably embarrassing. "A real shitshow of a bike trick."

"Yes, of course. Of course, it's you," I said, nodding. "Hi Chesa. Gimme a lift?"

"No way. I've seen what you do to cars," she said. "But you're free to walk alongside."

We went the next couple blocks that way, me carrying Shadowfax's handlebars in one hand, Chesa's hot hatch idling at my side. We got our share of stares, even without an elvish princess in the driver's seat. I wondered how long it would be before someone called the cops on us. It was that kind of neighborhood, where you might draw a SWAT team for wearing white after Labor Day.

"So, how are your parents taking the news?" I asked.

"That I'm going to be an elvish princess? They've known that for a while. What did you tell your parents?"

"Nothing, really. I'm trying to find a way to explain it."

"Dear Mom and Dad, I know you paid for my college, but instead of being a doctor or lawyer, I'm going to live in your basement and pretend to be a knight." She pitched her voice into high geek dialect. "It'th importanth!"

"I don't live in the basement," I grumped.

"Uh huh," Chesa answered. She sped up just enough that it was awkward for me to walk beside her. I broke into a jog, so she slowed down again. She gave a deep and bone-rattling sigh. "Look, I'm just going to meet you there. This is weird."

"But we're almost—"

She sped off, laying rubber for the two houses remaining in our journey, before turning hard into Eric's driveway, tail-end drifting wide in a long, screeching arc. I sighed and jogged the final dozen yards. I tossed the last of Shadowfax's mortal coil at the foot of Eric's yard and followed Chesa's car up the driveway.

Except Eric's house was gone. I stumbled to a halt next to Chesa's car. She got slowly out of the car and stood next to me, gawking up at the spectacle before us.

There was a period of American exceptionalism when a lot of

people suddenly found themselves with a lot of money, or at least access to the kind of debt that looked like a lot of money, but without the taste that good money requires. This led to vast tracts of the American wilderness being converted into houses that were very large, if not very nice. Vast foyers with corkscrew staircases led to beige carpeted hallways that bristled with bedrooms whose only purpose was to serve as the host organ for enormous bathrooms and closets larger than most apartments. Chandeliers were big back then, especially the kind of chandelier that looked like it was in the process of falling painfully apart in midair.

All of these houses shared one distinct feature. They all had a single layer of bricks across the front. The rest of the house was cheap siding, seen only by the underpaid lawn service, and of course the neighbors, who also had cheap siding. It was the clearest expression of fake money. They had just enough money to look like they had money, all built on a shell of tricky banking and down payments and linoleum.

Eric's house was such a house. Or it had been last week. Before it was a tree.

The trunk of this particular tree was as wide as Eric's former house, erupting out of the manicured Elysium of the Cavanaugh front lawn. It rose into the sky like a cloud, branching out into a cloud of twisted, writhing branches, bare of leaves and bark. A storm crowned its boughs. Lightning flashed through the naked canopy of the tree, scoring the hardened flesh of its wood and filling the air with smoke. Thunder rolled down the gnarled bark of the trunk and echoed over the yard.

"What. The. Hell," I whispered.

"Don't think we're going to have to explain things to Eric after all," Chesa answered. The thunder grew second by second, echoing like the laughter of a mighty god. "Do you think—"

A car horn beeped behind us. We turned around to see two luxury minivans/urban combat vehicles, both of whom were driving right on the centerline of the road. They patiently beeped at one another, slowly rolling closer and closer, until their bumpers lightly brushed together. Both drivers rolled down their windows and started yelling about right of way, car horns stridently sounding. We stared at this spectacle for long minutes before realizing something strange.

"The thunder?" Chesa asked.

"It stopped," I said. I turned back to the tree and was immediately buffeted by thunder and the cackling of a mad sky god. I looked back to the street and heard nothing but rich mothers squabbling in the street, hugging their babies and complaining about whiplash. Back to the castle and it was thunder.

"Huh," Chesa said.

"So we call MA for this, right?"

"Seems like it."

I took out my cell phone which was obviously still a deck of tarot cards. I shuffled the cards between my hands, hoping one of them was the Seven of Oh God Help, or the Nine of Esthers, but no luck. Chesa stared at me for a long moment.

"It's complicated," I said. "You better make the call."

Chesa sighed and reached into the open window of her car, fishing her much larger and much nicer phone out of the center console.

It was now a much larger and nicer tarot deck. Embossed leather, gold-foil illuminated face cards, even a suede case. But still equally useless in this situation.

"This is somehow your fault," she said.

"Probably. Guess I'll call from home." I looked at Shadowfax's handlebars, sticking out of the shrubs nearby. "Um. Can I get a lift?"

CHAPTER FOURTEEN
LEVEL ONE

There were a couple of fraught moments when it didn't seem like Chesa's car was going to start. She glared at me out of the corner of her eye while the engine grated and moaned, then finally it roared to life and we rolled down the street. We rode in silence. When she pulled up to my house, there was a long pause.

"What are we going to do?" I asked. "Call MA?"

"My contact didn't seem too interested in hearing from me," Chesa said. "Something about not calling until Fenris' unholy jaws were closing on the moon."

"Sounds familiar. Maybe we just mention it to Esther the next time we go in for training?"

"We could call the police."

"And tell them what? That our friend's house has been replaced by a giant tree? We're better off just checking directly into the mental ward." I shifted in my seat. Mom was in the front window of the house, grinning ravenously at the two of us. "I gotta go. Mom's going to get the wrong ideas."

"Yeah, well. Let me know when you hear from Esther," Chesa said. "And don't you go disappearing on me, too."

I wasn't sure what to say. The last time I had disappeared on Chesa, it was by text message from college as I was leaving another girl's apartment. Finally, I just cleared my throat, muttered something noncommittal, and got out of the car. She drove off without another word. At least her car didn't magically disappear before my eyes.

I spent the rest of the day trying to get myself grounded in the real world again, and nowhere was as real as my mother's kitchen. I ate a chicken sandwich, took a nap, and only woke up screaming about dragons and attorneys and janitors maybe twice that night. That seemed normal enough. Everything seemed normal. Dad slept in front of the television, Mom worried about everything I ate during dinner, and the rest of the day passed.

My phone arrived in the middle of the afternoon, stuffed into our mailbox in a tattered envelope covered in fading ink script and a pair of day-glow orange stickers that warned CONTAINMENT HAZARD and REAL WORLD across the front. I stuffed the envelope into the trash before Mom could find it, then tossed the replacement tarot deck in after and hoped the whole incident would be forgotten.

Chesa didn't call. Chesa didn't text. Chesa didn't do anything but lurk in the back of my mind, along with a lot of guilt and a fair share of karma. I thought again about calling the police about Eric, but I managed to come up with enough excuses that I never did.

I woke up the next morning in my old room. *Thursday*, I thought. I've always liked Thursdays during the summer. As good as the weekend, without the need to make plans or the disappointment those plans always produced. The breeze was blowing in through the open window, the air smelling of cut grass and woodsmoke, the curtains fluttering lazily against my childhood bed. The room was full of the artifacts of my well-spent youth. Plastic knights and Soviet tanks, clumsily assembled and painted with more enthusiasm than skill. The collected armada of WWII fighters, early era rockets, fanciful spaceships, and improbable zeppelin gunships that hung over my bed rattled quietly against one another. I sat up and spun one, the cracked Saturn V booster that I had broken during a failed launch, involving four bottle rockets and an imperfectly cut fuse.

This is what I liked about coming home. Every one of these ridiculous models was dusted, and the bookshelves that lined the walls were straightened and clean. Mom maintained the space of my childhood better than I ever did. I owed my parents a lot. It couldn't have been easy raising a knight aspirant, while the rest of the parents were grooming future doctors or firefighters or . . . whatever it is that people dream about becoming that ends up with going to business school. Rich, I suppose. They had never questioned my imagination, never restrained my creativity, never balked, even when that meant fitting their son for a suit of armor and sending him off to jousting camp. And even though I hadn't been home all that often since I left for college, all of this stuff was still here. Waiting.

Birdsong drifted in through the window. I swung my feet out of bed and went to the sill, kneeling to stick my head outside. The gray asphalt tiles of the porch roof stretched out ahead of me, covered in acorns and twigs. I pulled on a pair of jeans and a sweatshirt, then crawled out the window to crouch on the eaves. The porch creaked under my heels. When I was a kid, I made frequent escapes across this roof, shimmying down the oak tree at the far end of the roof and away to the yard, or just lying out here and staring up at the stars peeking through the branches. The tree had grown, but I could still see glimpses of blue sky and puffy clouds. Mom's voice carried through the house, followed by Dad's rumbling response. I settled against the asphalt tiles and sighed contentedly.

The sky rumbled. Thunder, I thought at first, but then it continued to get closer. A shadow passed over the house, and my heart jumped into my throat. The gentle breeze shifted into a sharp wind, then a gust that whipped the branches of the oak against the house, showering me with acorns. I shielded my eyes from the sudden wind and squinted into the sky.

One of the clouds was descending, its swirling wall forming into a stone tower before my eyes, white marble with a blue slate roof, like a castle out of Disney's pristine imagination. There was a balcony just beneath the tower's eaves, and a woman dressed in lightning, with hair that twisted in the wind. She was holding a travel mug in one hand, and a glowing sword in the other. Even at this distance, I could see the hatred in her eyes.

She was staring right at me. The sky rumbled again, and the sun disappeared behind the descending cloud. A tornado siren sounded down the street, and heavy drops of rain mixed with hail splatted against the roof. The wind blew hard, thrashing the oak and rattling the house. The woman jumped sword first from the balcony.

"So much for Thursday," I muttered, then scrambled inside and slammed the window. The walls groaned as the winds rose. Downstairs, my mother was yelling. I grabbed Gabrielle's card from my dresser and started punching her number into my phone.

The phone came apart in my hands. A tarot deck again, the cards shuffling out of my shaking fingers. I threw them against the wall and screamed.

The wind answered. I threw open my bedroom door and ran.

The walls shuddered as I ran down the hallway, and lightning flashed through the open windows. I slammed them shut one at a time, battered by hail and wind. At the top of the stairs, I paused to look out the bay window that dominated the landing. Debris rolled through the backyard, and the dozen ornamental fruit trees from my mother's garden whipped back and forth like whitecaps. A small woman bounced past, her arms folded, wings wrapped tight against her back. She looked supremely inconvenienced. I stared at her passage, then shook my head and ran down the steps. My mother's urgent voice met me by the front door.

"Your father is already in the basement," she yelled from the kitchen. "Grab the storm bag and get downstairs."

"One moment. I need to . . ." I peered out the front windows, squinting through the sheet of rain cascading off the porch roof. The lightning-clad woman touched down at the base of our driveway. She took a dainty sip from her mug, like a soccer mom waiting for her kids to finish practice, then strolled toward the house. As she walked past the Volvo, she casually lifted her sword and buried it in the hood. Lightning arced through the metal frame, scorching the paint and setting the interior on fire. "Damn it, how am I supposed to explain that?" I muttered to myself. My mom appeared from the kitchen.

"John! This is no time to dawdle!"

"I just need a second," I said, scooping my boots up from beside the door and twisting them onto my feet. "Go downstairs. I'll be fine."

"John!" she shouted again, but then I was out the door, and the wind stole the rest of her protest.

I hit the curtain of falling rain, jumping down the stairs and sliding across the hail-slick walkway that led to the drive. The woman was still involved with the Volvo, wiggling the sword loose and plunging it into the engine time and time again, each blow bringing a cascade of sparks and peeling paint. The shifting stones of the tower dangled over her head, thirty feet off the ground and shimmering slightly, depending from a dark cloud that didn't extend beyond the immediate area. Blue skies stretched from horizon to horizon, interrupted only by my personal tornado.

"Hey!" I shouted, shielding my face from the battering hail and screaming wind. "What the hell do you think you're doing?"

She glanced over her shoulder at me. Eyes the color of blue flame passed over me, barely registering my presence before turning back to the car. Thoughtfully, she set her travel mug on the driveway, then took the sword in both hands and lifted it high over her head. With a look of supreme concentration, the lightning lady took stock of what remained of the car, then buried the blade in the hood. The front of the car peeled open, lightning strokes traveling down the length of the vehicle, turning the whole thing into rubbish. A teeth-rattling clap of thunder rolled across the yard.

"I said, what the hell—" I reached out to grab her shoulder. The instant my fingers brushed the sun bright cloth of her robes, the whole world lit up. I felt a sharp hum go through my bones, and my brain crackled in my skull. Next thing I knew, I was staring up at the swirling clouds of the storm, flat on my back, with every inch of skin on fire. "Uhhhrruh . . . uh, uh . . . ah. Ow . . ."

"Holy hotcakes, can you see me?" The woman's voice rang like a church bell. I lifted my head to see that she was leaning against the wreckage of my mom's car, sword resting at her side, both hands wrapped around her travel mug. Her eyes were narrowed in concern. "You're not just an idiot or something, out in the storm?"

"I think maybe I am," I said through gritted teeth. The pain was really settling into my nerves. My entire body buzzed. I sat up, blinking against the rain running down my face. "What are you, anyway?"

"You can see me, but you don't know what I am." She carefully balanced her mug on the ruin of the hood, then snatched up her blade and strode quickly to loom over me. "So it's probably safe to kill you. No one's going to miss a delusional idiot."

"Whoa, whoa, whoa!" I covered my face with one arm, trying to scramble back with the other. "Lots of folks are going to miss me. I'm going to miss me!"

"So no one important, then." She closed the distance again and pressed the point of her sword into my chest, flattening me. She drew back the blade. "Time to feed the worms, mortal!"

"Esther MacRae will miss me!" I shouted. The woman hesitated for half a breath, long enough for me to roll away and scramble toward the front porch. She screamed in rage.

"It was you, wasn't it? You're the one who killed my husband!" she howled. I glanced over my shoulder. A nimbus of burning light surrounded her, trailing arcs of lightning like a wedding gown as she marched toward me. "Kracek, King of the Outlands, did not deserve to die at the hands of a coward!"

"He was an asshole, lady!" I shouted, taking the three steps to the porch twelve at a time, stumbling as I hit the landing and going shoulder first into the front door. Her travel mug slammed into the wall next to me, splintering the siding and spraying scalding coffee in my face. I turned to face her. She swept toward the house like a squall line.

"You will pay for your crimes, mortal! Death is too good for someone who has dared to touch the divine. They will tell tales of your misery in the halls of hell, devils trembling as they recount your suffering. Mothers will scare their children with the legend of . . . of . . ." she stopped at the bottom of the stairs. "What is your name, child-of-dust?"

"I don't feel like this is the time for introductions." I wrenched the door open, straining against the howling wind that washed off the storm goddess on my porch. I screamed into the gale. "We can discuss this when you're in a better mood!"

I stepped inside, slamming the door on her response. Inside the house, the sounds of the storm were strangely muted. My mother was still standing in the kitchen door, apparently frozen in place. She held a wooden spoon in her hand, as though she meant to paddle me for misbehaving. I backed away from the door. Outside, the wind howled, sending sheets of hail against the windows.

"John?" Mom asked quietly. "Have you lost your mind?"

"Absolutely," I said. "But I think we're safe now. I think there's some kind of rule about invitations, and what they're allowed to do. It's going to be okay."

The entire house groaned, and the old oak tree in the front yard splintered into a thousand pieces. The sound was like a punch in the chest. Seconds later, the grinding roar of the tornado filled our heads. I turned and ran, scooping up my mom and carrying her into the kitchen.

The windows of the front room exploded, showering glass across the furniture and shredding the curtains. A second later, the door disintegrated in a blinding flash of light. The woman, now barely more than the sketch of a figure drawn in lightning and hail, stood in the open doorway. I hit the ground and rolled, sheltering my mom's frail form, wincing as I heard her scream out in pain. I got back on my feet, carrying her to the basement door.

"Get downstairs," I said, balancing her gingerly on the top step. "And don't open this door for anyone. Not even me."

"What ... what ...?"

"I'll explain later," I said, then slammed the door. Part of me hoped that I wouldn't have to, but that would mean one or the other of us was dead. "Later," I muttered to myself, "If there is a later." Then I turned to face the front room.

The woman stepped through the door, bringing the storm with her. Newspapers and photographs swirled through the room, along with couch cushions and the remnants of my mother's best plates, torn from their place in the china cabinet. Her eyes flashed like gold coins, and sparks traveled the length of her sword. When she saw me, her face twisted in rage.

"I warned your petty little circle of upstarts to stay away from him. The rule of dragons is not to be tampered with by the likes of you! You shall pay for your impertinence!"

"And you're going to learn how to knock," I said. I reached up and grabbed the little four-ten shotgun Dad kept over the sill of the kitchen door, thumbed the hammer, and put both barrels of rock salt into her face. It splattered across her skin like raindrops on stone. She laughed.

"At least you are brave. That's good. I find no joy in killing cowards."

"That's hardly comforting," I said, backpedaling away. She stalked after me, leaving destruction in her wake. When she reached the kitchen, the drawers flew open, and a shimmering cloud of cutlery joined the cyclone that was tearing my parents' house apart. A fork buried itself in my knee. The back door was already destroyed, so I rolled through its ruin and limped across the backyard toward the shed. Outside, the skies were maddeningly clear in the distance, though dark clouds swirled directly overhead. As I reached the shed, the woman emerged from the house. Immediately, a heavy downpour slammed down on me, whipped by ferocious wind and the crackle of lightning. I kicked in the side door to the shed and collapsed inside.

The interior smelled like gasoline and yard clippings. Dragging my injured leg, I made my way around the pile of lawn mowers, hedge trimmers, rusted-out grills, and discarded sleds that dominated the center of the shed. I kicked over a can of gasoline, filling the shed with heady fumes and the added risk of immolation. Briefly, I wondered what story my parents would make up to explain my inevitable death. Somehow, I didn't think *"He tried to kill a storm"* was going to make the cut.

The walls of the shed started to shake, and sheets of rain battered the grimy window behind me. I hunkered down behind a lawnmower. The concrete floor was sticky with oil and grass clippings. Through the open door I could see windswept grass and rivulets of rain pockmarked with hail. There was a loud boom, and suddenly the yard was full of tattered asphalt roofing tiles cartwheeling past. A significant portion of my parents' house pulled free of its foundation and scattered into the storm. I gritted my jaw.

The shaking got worse, and the racks of tools overhead clattered back and forth, threatening to fall. I stared up at Dad's collection of hedgewhackers, grass-annihilators, buzzsaws, hammer-guns, pole-splitters, and lawncare artillery with apprehension.

"Probably not the best place to hide," I said. "No good hiding from the storm only to have a maul fall on my . . . head . . ."

A splitting maul. It dangled on the end of a leather thong, the only non-gasoline powered device in the entire shed. Even Dad's hedge trimmer looked like a weapon from a post-apocalyptic gladiatorial arena. But not the maul. It was just an oversized iron head on a wooden shaft, like the lovechild of a sledgehammer and an axe. Nothing fancy about the maul. It was perfectly medieval.

"I don't know what mythos you come from, lady, but I'm pretty sure they had something like this." I stood up and slipped the maul from its hook. It was heavy, I mean, seriously heavy, and about as graceful to wield as a sandbag. I hefted it in my hands a couple of times, trying to figure out how I'd swing it without tearing my shoulder off. Outside, the wind dropped off, and the woman stepped into view.

She hadn't seen me yet, or at least, she wasn't looking at me. Her eyes were narrowed in the direction of my neighbor's house. I could hear sirens in the distance. She held the sword loosely in one hand, spinning the hilt in her palm and squinting against the rain. She looked more human, for some reason. Her dress was soaked through, and her hair hung in damp rings across her face. She might even have been crying. Another gust of wind flattened my mom's gazebo and sent the deck chairs spinning into the air.

No time for sympathy. I leapt over the lawnmower, drawing the maul over my head and screaming. Suffice to say I hadn't figured out how to use this thing yet. The maul's head snagged the shed's low-slung roof, stopping me mid leap and nearly jerking the thing out of my hands. I came down on the lawnmower, slipped on its oil-slick cowling, and stumbled forward, twisting my ankle as I came down heavily in a collection of paint cans and discarded cigar boxes. The whole collection came tumbling down, taking me with it. I took one wobbly step, my leg collapsed, and I slammed into the frame of the door then spun back into the yard. The maul dangled in my hand like a carnival ride out of control.

The storm goddess just stared at me. Confusion and despair mingled in her eyes. When I finally stopped spinning and sat down in my mother's flowerbed, she wiped the hair from her face and shouldered her glimmering sword.

"How . . . the hell . . . did a man like you strike down the great dragon Kracek?" she asked, fury dripping from her lips with every word. "I have seen champions, and witnessed great battles between mortals, but you are no champion. You're a jester, a clown . . . a damned imbecile!"

"I'll take that as flattery from someone married to that oaf," I said. I stood up, squared my shoulders, and held the maul in front of me. Cold mud dripped down the back of my shirt. "Now. Are we going to fight, or are you all out of tears?"

She shouted, a primeval, mad scream, and charged forward. There was a lot of Kracek in her style, but I guess you don't expect nuance from a tornado. I kept my fist tight against the head of the maul, using its iron bulk to deflect her blade. Static coursed through my arm as steel met iron, but since my choices were to either hang on or die, I held my ground. Her sword sang off the maul and buried itself in the ground at my feet. Still holding the maul's head close, I whipped the handle around and cracked it into her jaw. Her head whipped to the side, but as she spun back to face me, I simply jabbed her in the throat with the butt end of the maul, then swung the head down onto her toes.

The bones of storm goddesses make the same satisfying crunch as normal bones when they break. The timbre of her scream changed, and she stumbled back, losing her grip on the sword. As soon as her fingers left the hilt, it sizzled out of existence, burning a sword-shaped hole in the brick pavers of the back porch. She limped away from me. The winds subsided, but the sky grew darker.

"You have made a mistake, mortal. An enemy beyond reckoning. I will hunt you until your last day, and haunt your every—"

"Still talking," I snapped, then muscled the blunt end of the maul into her temple. She fell back flat against the ground. Immediately the storm let up. A ray of sunshine peaked through the clouds. When I looked up, I saw that her tower was rapidly descending.

"Oh, that's nice. Coming down to take mama home, are you? Well, you better hurry, because—"

What I forgot was that the tower was just a metaphor, the false reality of an actual tornado. The wind shrieked around my head, and the shed blew into a thousand pieces. I was thrown into the garden. The sound of the tornado was deafening. I tried to look up, but all I could see was rain and a dark cloud that rippled with lightning. The woman's limp form lifted into the air, carried up with the funnel cloud. I thought I saw feathers pressed damp against her legs, and feet clawed and scaly, one of them bent at an awkward angle. She disappeared into the clouds and was gone.

CHAPTER FIFTEEN
CONSEQUENCES

My parents and I waited at the curb while the fire department went through the house, or at least what was left of the house. The facade still stood, but the inside looked like a giant had come through and scooped it out. Which was literally what had happened, I suppose. The wreckage was strewn across the yard, clothes and furniture and memories littering the neighborhood like confetti.

"This is all my fault," I mumbled. My mother was numbly picking through the detritus scattered across the front yard, looking for anything of value. Her face was scratched up, but other than that, she and Dad had come through unhurt. Dad stood in the street, just staring at the house. I looped my arm over his shoulders and pulled him close. "I shouldn't have come here."

"Act of God, son," was all Dad could say. "Act of God."

"Pretty sure she was some kind of harpy. I'd have to check the monster manual, or maybe . . ." I looked up. Dad's eyes were glazing over. "Yeah," I agreed. "Act of God."

It was no use disagreeing with him, though the theological details were a little different than what he was thinking. Microburst, they were calling it, an extremely rare and completely made up meteorological phenomenon. And exactly the sort of thing reality would do to cover up a storm goddess come to earth to wreak vengeance on her dead husband's murderer.

"I can't believe this. I just . . . can't believe this is happening."

"It is." Gabrielle's voice came from the street behind me. I turned to see her step out of an impossibly nondescript car. "For this you probably could have called."

"I tried," I said. "My phone turned into a tarot deck."

"Maybe we'll need to get you a landline. Something from the 1800s, at least." Gabrielle stood with her arms folded next to me, squinting up at the ruin of my parents' house. "Though in extreme cases like this, sometimes carrier pigeon is the only way to go. How do you feel about pigeons?"

"What the hell's wrong with you?" I snapped. She raised an eyebrow in my direction.

"They're not so bad. You can pretend it's a pet owl, and that you're some kind of special magic person, toiling away in the mundane world, keeping your secret magic owl. Except it's a pigeon, and the only thing it does magically is poop a lot. After all—"

"I've heard enough about your damned bird," I said. "You think you can just roll in here and make a sad face and then offer me a pigeon? Do you not see what's going on around you? Look at my house! Look at it!"

"Kid, I'm perfectly capable of seeing. And yeah, it's a damned shame, and inconveniences like this are part of your life now. But—"

"Inconveniences like this? A damned shame? A damned. Shame. I'll say it is!" My voice was getting louder, and both of my parents were staring at me, along with more than a few of the firemen, but I didn't care. "That thing nearly killed my parents. It nearly killed me, and it did a lot more than inconvenience my house. And the best you can do is offer me a freaking bird? No. No way! This wasn't supposed to happen, and it did, and I'm not going to stand here and listen to you make excuses. We're going to Esther. Now."

I stood vibrating on the curb, my face flushed and red. Gabrielle just stared at me, looking a little disappointed.

"No, we're not," she said, turning away. "You're going to stay here, and keep your head down, and do a better job of calling us the next time this happens."

"The next time? No, there's not going to be a next time. This is Esther's fault for sending me home. And your fault for making me think everything was going to be okay. It's not going to be okay. It's never going to be okay again. So you, and Esther, and that meatwall you call a driver, are going to start fixing this shit. Now!"

Gabrielle stared at me for a long heartbeat. Then she shook her head.

"No, kid. We don't fix the real world for folks. Especially not for people who think we owe them something." She turned on her heel and walked away. "And now you're on your own. So good luck with that."

I waited a heartbeat while she walked back to her car. When it was clear she wasn't going to turn around, I stormed past her.

"Then I'm going to find her myself. Weird shit keeps happening around me. You think I won't be able to just walk right into your silly little secret base? I just knocked out a storm goddess with a splitting maul. Knight freaking Watch doesn't stand a chance."

I got about ten feet past the car before I felt a hand on my shoulder. Well. More than a hand. Two tons of hand, and the kind of pressure you usually find at the bottom of an ocean. I stopped, because the alternative was to have my arm torn from its socket.

Owen loomed over me. I could feel his hot breath on my neck. I tried to turn, but he tightened his grip, pinning me in place. He looked back at Gabrielle.

"Fine," she said. "Better we walk you in than you try to storm the gates. Way things are going with you, that might just be enough to get us all killed." She jerked a thumb over her shoulder. "Give your folks a good story. You're going to be missing for a while."

Owen released me and made a sound like a brontosaurus sighing. I shook the life back into my arm and marched back to where my parents were watching.

"So," my mom said hesitantly. "This seems complicated."

"Yeah. Um . . . I'm going to be helping these folks with some stuff. Just for a little while," I said. "But it's nothing to worry about."

"Is it drugs?" Mom asked.

"It is not drugs," I said quickly. "Or a cult, or the police."

"The government then," Dad said with a wise and knowing nod. "When they take you to the aliens, remember to not look them in the eye. I read on the internet—"

"Be safe," Mom said quickly, cutting off any more of my father's speculation. "And make sure you come home this time."

"I will. And I'll call, I promise."

"Sure you will," she said, patting me on the arm. "Sure you will."

I went back to the car and sat in the back. My mom was already organizing my dad into a recovery effort, collecting the remains of their lifelong home. Father bumbled along, seemingly unperturbed by the destruction all around him. Gabrielle turned around to look at me.

"They'll be fine. Probably better without you around, to be honest."

"Yeah," I said. "Probably," I answered. Owen grunted and started the car. We rumbled off down the street. I wanted to watch my parents as long as I could but made myself look forward. *I'll fix this,* I promised myself. *I'll fix it, and then everything will be okay.*

We picked up Chesa on the way to HQ. Turns out she'd been dialing Gabrielle nonstop since Eric disappeared, and the order had come through to collect her. That's the only reason the MA team was in the neighborhood when the tornado struck. When Chesa heard about my house, she got really quiet. Pretty sure she blamed me for it. I sure did.

This time they left the burlap sack off our heads. It was a mixed blessing. Apparently, this vehicle didn't have access to the mystical powers of teleportation that the car that brought me here contained, so I was subjected to rush hour traffic.

Chesa was quiet the whole way. I didn't know what to say, so I matched her silence. I was worried about Eric, and angry about my house. Angry that I hadn't called MA earlier, angry that Chesa had, and that they hadn't done anything. I was itching to get a hold of Esther and give her a piece of my mind.

Eventually we turned off the main roads and started rumbling down backstreets, gravel pinging off the car's undercarriage as we rolled further and further away from civilization. We finally came to a paved driveway with a faded wooden arch over it. The arch had the word "Camelot" carved into it.

"That's a little obvious, isn't it?" Chesa asked.

"So obvious it's unbelievable," Gabrielle answered. "And it gives the boss a kick every time she sees it." She turned back around to squint at me. "Are you the one who made fun of the name?"

"Yeah, uh, I mean—"

"Don't make fun of the name," she said, then turned back around.

The driveway wound through some dense shrubbery, then climbed a shallow hill before emerging into a parking lot that overlooked some water. A small lake spread out before us, its shores lined with red and white pebble beaches, surrounded on all sides by low berms that kept the water in. An artificial lake, obviously, but why?

"I don't get it," I said. "Where's HQ?"

"Underneath," Owen said, his first words to me. It was so startling to hear him speak that I didn't ask any more questions.

"Explains the mold problem," Chesa said. Owen snorted, then steered us down a narrow cobblestone path, descending out of sight of the lake. The air grew cold, and suddenly we were facing a concrete drainage pipe just wide enough to allow the car to enter. Owen drove into it without turning on the headlights, and soon we were speeding through the dark, the only light coming from the dim glow of the dashboard.

"Are you sure—" I started, just as the car pitched forward, slamming me into the back of Gabrielle's seat. Chesa hissed as she gripped the door. I heard Gabrielle snicker as I yelped. "Guys! Are you sure you know where you're going?"

"You wouldn't believe us anyway," Owen said. He sliced the car back and forth, following unseen roadmarks. My door bumped against a concrete barrier, showering my window with sparks. In the brief light, I saw Chesa's face, her eyes wide with terror. Gabrielle hissed and turned around, staring out the back window.

"Would it kill you to turn on the headlights?" I asked.

"Yeah, it would, actually. That's how it hunts," Gabrielle said. She squinted into the darkness for a long time before continuing. "Don't think it saw that."

"Better pray not," Owen said.

"You don't think what saw what, exactly?" Chesa asked.

"Don't worry about it," Owen answered.

"Since when did you become such a chatterbox?" she shot back, but then the car sloughed to the side, tires screeching.

Owen accelerated, the tiny engine of the car whining in the close confines of the tunnel. He turned once more, then a couple of canvas flaps slapped against the car's hood as we emerged into a parking lot. A handful of cars lined the walls, and three guards stood next to an elevator, talking among themselves. They turned to watch as Owen braked hard, swerving into an empty space. He slapped the car into park, then got out of the car while it was still rocking back and forth, to stand staring at the shifting canvas curtain that we had just driven through. The guards watched silently, just as tense as the big MA agent. Several moments passed.

"I think we're good," Owen said finally. Gabrielle let out a long sigh, then unbuckled and got out of the car. Chesa and I followed.

"That's how what hunts?" I asked again.

"The thing in the tunnel," she said. "It's not ours, but it acts as a pretty good watchdog. If you're careful."

"What do you mean, not ours?" Chesa asked.

"Knight Watch attracts curious visitors. Some of them are very dangerous," Gabrielle said. "Now let's get moving. Esther's really interested in speaking with you both."

Owen grunted, then wrenched open the trunk and started unpacking enough guns to start a small revolution. Gabrielle slung a shotgun over her shoulder and made for the elevator. I turned back to the curtain.

Something slithered against it, black scales and long whiskers that tickled the concrete floor. Owen saw it too, and there was a brief moment when I thought he was going to open up with his arsenal. I wasn't going to wait around to find out. I was already passing Gabrielle, halfway to the elevator before her voice stopped me.

"Hey, we've got notes on you!" she yelled. "No elevator. We take the stairs."

There were a lot of stairs. The walls were gray concrete painted in chipped institutional green, the kind of stairwells you might find in haunted insane asylums, or worse. There were landings every few flights, with doors that looked like they could have survived a direct nuclear blast. The whole place had a government feel to it. I once read a book about missile silos in the Midwest that extended for miles underground, supposedly still lurking under office buildings and soccer fields throughout the middle of the country. None under lakes, though. I asked Gabrielle about it.

"Might have been, but if so, the boss has really expanded it. There's a whole city under here, or so I've heard."

"A whole city? Then why do the elites live out in the mundane world?" I asked. "Seems silly to have someone like St. Matthew slumming it in the second-floor walkup if you've got a secret base under a lake."

"Compartmentalization. Sometimes a domain goes bad, and if the portals are close together, it can spread to the rest of the team. Plus there's a lot of interference between the medievalists, the clockwork types, those guys in the spacesuits..." her voice trailed off. "Actually, that's probably more than you need to know."

"Esther said something about that," Chesa said. "What does that mean, exactly? Clockwork guys?"

"Let's just say there are a lot of different kinds of myths, from a lot of different time periods. Folks like you, you're in it for the fantasy stories. But there are others." Owen tapped her heavily on the shoulder. "Right. Outside my paygrade. If you need to really know that stuff, I'm sure Esther will explain it."

"So..." I paused on a landing, hoping they would stop so I could catch my breath while we talked. They didn't. I gulped air and hurried after. "So this is a big place. I've seen the medical ward, the actuator. What else is there?"

"All MA operations. Servers, barracks, the motor pool. We don't get magic homes like you guys. That's the core. And then wrapped around the core are the various quarantine zones, where the elites go to decompress after missions, but before they can return to their domains. Also where they meet to plan operations, argue about theology... whatever it is you guys do. I've never really seen those zones. Folks like me and Owen, we don't get outside the core, unless it's an emergency."

"What kind of emergency?" I asked, thinking about the black and gray scales brushing up against the curtain in the parking garage.

"Usually the kind of emergency caused by geniuses like you," she answered. "So try to not do anything apocalypse-worthy. Here we are."

She stopped on a landing just like all the others. The door looked welded shut. I leaned against the wall, my breath coming in ragged gasps, as I tried to rub some feeling back into my legs. Owen stared at me with open contempt.

"So do we..." gulp, breathe, gulp. "Do we knock or something?" Neither of my escorts looked even winded, and Chesa was absolutely glowing. I straightened up, tried to contain my breathing, realized I might pass out. "Or is there a doorbell?"

"They'll let us in," Gabrielle said. Just then, there was a series of knocks inside the door, and the portal swung open. Gabrielle gestured at it. "Ta da! Just like magic."

"Not even sure you're joking," I said. Gabrielle motioned us inside. Owen sealed the door behind us. We were in another hallway, this one about as uninteresting as a stretch of carpet could make it. In the distance I could see doors lining the hall, with flashing lights over each one. We started walking. I fell in next to Gabrielle, with Chesa half-a-step behind me. "So, you said something about the core? What's that mean?"

"Home base for Mundane Actual. It stretches straight down the middle of HQ, top to bottom. Your side of things is wrapped around it like the rings on a tree."

"And where I was before, with Tembo and the Saint guy, was that part of the core?"

"Probably not. They don't let the elites into the core. Contamination risk. We had to walk so far down to keep you away from the data servers, the generators . . . all the technical stuff. Don't want you screwing up central processing, do we?" Gabrielle asked. "Not after what happened to noble Shadowfax."

"How do you know about that?"

"Part of the job. Monitoring anomalous ephemera. Trust me, you're lucky to have us watching you," she said.

"Then why'd it take so long for you to get to me? Why'd I have to fight off an angry storm goddess all by my lonesome?"

"That's . . . I mean," Gabrielle narrowed her eyes at me. "We're still looking into that. Nothing came in on the actuator. Almost like you were shielded or something."

"Shielded? And that's supposed to make me feel better?"

"Just be happy your friend made the call," she said, pointing down a crossing hallway. "We'll be handing you off to Esther's team in a minute. Got to process you first."

A door opened to our right, and Jerry Left stepped into the hallway. When he saw me, his watery little eyes lit up.

"You came back," he said. "You make the most excellent sheets!"

"How are these guys not contamination risks?" I snapped. Gabrielle laughed, then handed the janitor her shotgun.

"The janitors go everywhere. Not following the usual rules is kind of their thing. You'll get used to it. How's the kitchen situation going, Jerry?"

"Jerry no longer has a kitchen," he said. "I got to the point when it's simply easier to burn down the rest of the house and start over. So, very well, thank you!"

"Good to hear," she said. "Only way to handle that kind of roach. You've met John and Chesa?"

"Slayer of dragons and his queen of elves!" Jerry turned and offered me the squirming digits of his hand. "I promise to not exude certain secretions, John. Esther spoke to me of your discomfort with the procedure."

Hesitantly, I extended my hand and watched as the janitor's squamous fist enveloped it. The whole process was very much like dipping your hand into a bucket of worms that were trying to mate in the spaces between your fingers. Bile rose as far as the back of my throat before retreating. I tried to smile.

"And how is Mike?" I asked.

"Mike is dead to me," Jerry snapped, quickly withdrawing his writhing grasp. "An unacceptable breach of friendship! There will be warrants!"

Without explanation, Jerry collected the remainder of our luggage, including Owen's considerable burden of weapons and ammunition, and retreated through the door. We stepped through a second later, but Jerry was already gone.

"What was that about?"

"Janitor drama, happens all the time. Hard to avoid when they're basically the same guy in two different bodies. He'll scour the unreal world off that stuff and put it back into the armory. Every time we're exposed to the mythological nonsense, there's a risk of contamination. Can really screw with the equipment."

"Is that what happened to our phones?" Chesa asked. Gabrielle looked at us questioningly, so I related the story of the tarot cards, both when I first arrived at my parents' house and later, at the base of the tree. She shrugged.

"Probably, though I can't imagine Esther sending you out with corrupted artifacts. I'll put it in the report. Anything else?"

"You mean besides the giant storm tree that grew up where my friend's house used to be? No, nothing of interest."

"Don't be bitter. No one likes a sourpuss."

Owen took me by the shoulder and guided me down the hallway. His grip was several foot-pounds tighter than it needed to be, and soon I was wincing at the pressure. The giant leaned down and hissed into my ear.

"It's time to stop whining. You have a great opportunity, a chance most of us would kill for. Gabby in particular. So I won't hear your negativity anymore, will I?"

Before I could answer, we reached another door, with a keypad and combination lock. It was very similar to the one that led to the interview room, oh so long ago. Owen pulled me upright and started punching numbers into the keypad. When he was done, Gabrielle stepped up and fiddled with the combination. The door opened with a hiss.

"This is as far as we go, for the sake of the elites. Contamination goes both ways," Gabrielle said. "Once you establish your own domains, you won't be coming in here via mundane means. Good luck in there."

Owen shoved me through. Chesa followed a second later, looking positively inconvenienced by the whole thing. The door slammed shut. We were in a clean room, similar to the interview room but without the furniture or microphone. Esther entered a second later, hands tucked into her pockets.

"So," she said. "You've got some explaining to do."

"Right," I said. "So I mentioned my friend Eric, who went to the faire with us? I tried to call him, and then—"

"Why the hell do I care about this Eric guy?" Esther snapped. "I need to know what you geniuses did to Clarence."

Chesa and I exchanged glances, then looked back at Esther.

"He's missing, you idiots. Gone. And his domain has sealed itself. So you start talking, or I'm going to throw you into the actuator and see what sort of horrors come out."

CHAPTER SIXTEEN
REGISTERING YOUR DOMAIN

Being questioned by Esther MacRae basically involves being yelled at for ten minutes and then trying to ask a question, which immediately prompted more yelling. But it was informative yelling. Here's what I learned.

Clarence was gone, along with his domain. That much was obvious but also, apparently, impossible. Elites can't die inside their own domains, and a domain exists as long as its owner is still alive. If Clarence were alive, the domain would be accessible, though it would take some doing to get in without his permission. Since the domain was apparently gone, that must mean Clarence is dead, except he can't be dead because he's still inside the domain. Repeat that loop infinitely.

We learned all of this at a very high volume of sound. And Esther didn't honestly believe that we'd killed him. But she sure as hell thought his absence was somehow our fault.

Which finally got us back to Eric. Because once we got it through the wall of yelling that Eric had been with us at the faire, that he was the kind of guy Knight Watch would probably want to recruit, and that his house was now a weird tree-thing, Esther grew quiet. Somehow that was worse. She stood in the middle of the room staring at nothing for long, uncomfortable minutes.

"Do we call someone?" Chesa asked after a while. Esther's lips were moving, but she wasn't making any sound. "I think we might have broken her."

"I don't know. Old people snap sometimes. Maybe she's having a seizure."

"She's not having a seizure," Chesa said. "Probably. But she might have been possessed by a spirit or something."

"I like that you rule out seizure but go straight to demonic possession." I looked around the room. "Can I point out that there aren't any doorknobs in this room? Or light switches, or really anything of any use?"

"That's because sometimes folks get possessed by spirits, and we have to restrain them," Esther said quite suddenly. We jumped. "Not me. But some folks."

"Are you alright?" I asked.

"You idiots really are to blame for all this. I knew there was something weird about your car, but now your friend Eric, and Clarence..." she resumed mumbling.

"If you do get possessed, is there something we can do?" I asked.

"Duck. The agents will come in hot." She smiled wickedly. "Okay, it's happened once. Just once. We had to up security after that. So here's what we're going to do. We're going to find your friend Eric. It's pretty clear that the three of you are somehow involved in all of this."

"Involved in all of what? What'd we do?" I asked.

"You personally? Nothing. Wrong place at the wrong time, and now you've been sucked into a world of dragons and other strange shit. But something's hunting my team. If it can get to Clarence in his domain, it can get to any of us. It might even be able to find a way into the anomaly actuator. We can't let that happen."

"Sounds like your problem, not mine," Chesa said. "I was promised elf heaven, and instead I'm watching this idiot play with his sword while my friends disappear and their houses get turned into trees and wreckage."

"Well, that's precisely the point. Wherever Aaron—"

"Eric," I said.

"Wherever Eric has gone, it had something to do with the attack on John's house. You said it was a big tree with a storm around the top."

"Really big tree," I said.

"Right. And what lives in trees? Mythical trees, especially?"

"Apple people?" I ventured.

"Birds. And harpies. Storm harpies, especially. They look like women, but with some feathers, and clawed feet, and their wings make the wind blow. Sound familiar?"

"Ah," I said. "Ah, yes. So it's connected?"

"Has to be. I'm just not sure how," Esther answered.

"I have an idea," Chesa said. "How about we stop speculating and start doing something? If Eric's in trouble, and it has to do with the old knight and his castle, shouldn't we be, I don't know, calling the cavalry? Riding out to war? Something?"

"Can't yet," Esther said. "The rest of the team is still recuperating in their domains. If the two of you and me and Gabrielle try to take on whatever the hell this is, it'll brush us aside like gnats. No, we need to get you closer to your mythic selves. And that means domains."

"Domains? As in Aelfhome? Valinor? The High Halls of Rivendell?" Chesa asked, perking up.

"That's exactly what it means," Esther said.

"Then what the hell are we waiting for? Why have we waited this long at all?"

"Because there's a very good chance that you could die in the process," Esther answered. She looked from Chesa to me and then back again, then tried to smile. It wasn't convincing. "Or not! You never know! It'll be an adventure!"

Esther led us through a series of increasingly medieval doors, each one locked more and more arcanely, until we reached a gate that looked straight out of Tales from the Crypt. Mist swirled around the base of a rusty portcullis, obscuring the floor. An iron hound's head snarled in the center of the gate, black teeth marred by disturbing stains. Esther stood in front of the gate and held her hands in front of her face. She started chanting.

"This is the part where we find out we should have been going to church the whole time," Chesa whispered. "There's a priest somewhere waking up from a nightmare about D&D. His bed is crawling with flies, and just as he reaches for his Bible . . ."

"Shut up," I hissed. "You're not making this easy."

Esther finished chanting, then drew a knife from her belt and slashed it across the palm of her left hand. Blood streaming from the wound, she thrust her hand into the gaping mouth of the iron hound. The creature's eyes flashed, and the gate creaked open.

"Okay, I have to admit. That was pretty much *a very special episode of Scooby-doo*," I whispered. "We would know if we were on the wrong side of this fight, right?"

"I'll let you know when I find the elves," Chesa answered.

"Stop chatting and go through," Esther said. Sweat glistened across her forehead, and her skin was growing pale. "I can't hold this open forever."

We hurried past the gate. Esther followed, snatching her hand from the hound's jaws. She pressed a bandage over the cut. I took her elbow and was shocked at how cold her skin was.

"Bastard gets hungrier by the year," she muttered. "I'll be fine. Matthew will take care of it."

I didn't ask any questions. The passage we were in was narrow and dark, and there didn't seem to be any torches. I stumbled forward, Esther by my side, each step threatening to be a dead end. Eventually, dim light appeared in the distance. I could barely make out Chesa's slim form ahead of us. She was much further along than us.

"Chesa, wait up!" I called. My voice echoed off stone. She paused and looked back. Her eyes burned purple. I had to suppress a shudder.

"What's taking you guys so long?" she yelled. "There's a room up ahead. I think I hear voices."

"It's the meeting room," Esther said quietly. "But no one should be there yet."

My ears perked up, because now I could hear voices too. I could just make out an archway at the end of the hall, and flickering light beyond. Chesa was nearly there.

"Ches, wait for us!" I shouted. I guess whatever surprise we could have offered the voices in the room was already ruined. Chesa ignored me and disappeared through the archway, then returned a heartbeat later.

"It's empty," she said. By then I was nearly there. We went through the archway again, together this time.

We entered a barrel-roofed room, long and tall with a dozen archways flanking the sides, each one supporting wide wooden doors. Six of the archways were hung with banners, suspended from fancy coats-of-arms. The doors in those archways sported iron figures, like the room numbers at a hotel, only pictures. A long table ran down the center of the room, and at the far end blazed the largest hearth I've ever seen, flanked by two more doors of thick wood and banded with iron. There was no sign of anyone else.

Esther pulled free of my arm and went to the table, supporting herself with the chair backs as she hobbled to the head of the table, by the fire. She sat down heavily and wiped her face.

"Are you going to be alright?" Chesa asked.

"Fine, fine, I'm fine," she said impatiently. "Nothing a little blood magic won't heal. For now, we need to get the two of you started on your domains."

"What are all these doors?" I asked.

"Portals. The rest of the team lives offsite, but each of their domains opens here, as well. Only use them in emergencies, or if we can't risk the trip through the mundane to get home. Only the domain's owner can open these, and then only with great effort." She pointed to the nearest door. It had a sword on the door, and the banners overhead were a familiar yellow and blue. "That's Clarence's door. That's how I knew something was wrong."

The door was warped and broken. Ash lined the wooden planks, and a thin scree of debris fanned out from the base of the portal. The lock was shattered. A blossom of sickly vines was growing out of the keyhole at its center.

"I take it you didn't do that?" I asked.

"No. Found it this way. Or rather Matthew did, when he came down for his nap. Probably happened about the same time you were fighting off that storm harpy." Esther coughed into her hand, wincing as her shoulders shook. "We're going to have to skip the rest of the lesson. Time's catching up. You need to go through one of these doors and establish your domains."

Chesa and I looked around. I went to one of the marked doors and looked it over. Twin daggers, crossed, and a winged boot. I pointed at it.

"Bethany?" I asked.

"And Tembo, Matthew, Tabbie . . . you haven't met her," Esther gestured in frustration at the rest of the doors. "Claimed portals. Use one of the unmarked doors."

"Should we each use a different door, if we're going to different domains?" Chesa asked.

"Despite Mr. Rast's tendency to break reality, and your . . . eye situation, I doubt either of you is strong enough to open a portal by yourselves. Go in together. As you work toward your mythic selves, the path will split. I'm sure it'll be obvious."

"But . . . what does this even mean? Establishing a domain? Finding our mythic selves?" I asked. I was used to very straightforward instructions. Block the sword like this. Strike like this. Move and countermove. "Shouldn't you go with us?"

"Can't. No soul. Long story," Esther said, gasping for breath. "Just go through. You'll figure it out."

"Okay, fine," Chesa said sullenly. "Together. How does this work?"

Esther struggled to her feet and took my arm, then led me to one of the empty doors, opposite Tabbie's bow and arrow, and next to Matthew and his cast-iron sun. The door was made of rough, fresh wood. There were brackets for a hanging, but no icon. She motioned Chesa over.

"What do I do here?" I asked. "Clear my mind? I took some meditation classes in college, but I kept worrying I was going to fart, and that stressed me out, and stress makes me gassy, so—"

"Yeah, I get it. Can we just focus on the task at hand?" Esther asked. "It's no use trying to clear your mind. The domain needs your essential self, not the premeditated image you have. Just . . . walk through the door. Both of you. Together." She turned the wrought-iron handle and pulled the door open. The space beyond was solidly dark, like a wall the color of night. There was no sign of anything beyond. "The domain will take care of the rest."

"Is this dangerous?" Chesa asked.

"Incredibly," she said. "Which is why we usually delay until later in the process. But we don't really have a choice, do we?"

"I mean, I have a choice," I said, pulling away from the slow pressure of her hand. "I could not do it. That's a choice I could make."

"No, you can't," she said, twisting her iron-hard hands into my jerkin and pushing me forward. She shoved me through the open door.

The last thing I saw was Chesa jumping in after me.

My first step felt a lot like falling. I kind of stumbled on the floor just before Esther propelled me into the darkness, so my legs were already curled under me as I entered the void. There was no light, and apparently no air. Even though I remembered a similar sensation when I entered Clarence's domain, my lizard brain only registered that I was suffocating and started filling my bloodstream with panic molecules. My heart started to beat a tattoo in my chest, and a cold sweat broke out across my entire body.

I fell for a long time, without really moving, and with no sensation of air whistling past my face. My body could tell I was falling, though. My stomach kept trying to squeeze its way into my mouth, and my guts tightened, then loosened, then tightened again. I might have been screaming but, again, no air. Just silence and the endless drop.

The first glimmer of light appeared beneath me. I immediately recognized moonlight reflecting off the tops of trees and the soft movement of branches in the wind.

The tops of trees, I mourned silently. *Seen from a great height. This is going to hurt.*

They came rapidly closer. The darkness slowly peeled away from my body, allowing the wind, and the sound of animals howling at the moon, and the shimmering light of an enormous moon hanging low against the horizon. I felt like I could almost reach out and touch the pitted face of the moon as I raced past.

Oh, and I was definitely screaming.

There was a moment of peace as I fell. Terror-addled and filled with the ragged sounds of my own howling voice, but peace nonetheless. I was able to look around and survey the land that would hold my pulverized body for all eternity. It seemed like a nice place, if a bit primeval. Forest stretched in all directions. Rolling hills to my right led to jagged mountains, reminiscent of the sharp peaks of the Tetons, their slopes dressed in snow and wretched-looking clouds. To my left, a delta of thin rivers carved their way through the trees, the silver light of the moon reflecting off their waters like quicksilver among the shadows. Between them, league after league of unbroken wilderness, the trees so closely packed that I could see no sign of the forest floor. There were no buildings, no roads, no castles silhouetted against the moonlight, or ancient towers breaking through the canopy. No sign of human habitation at all.

Do I have to build my bloody castle? I mused. Somehow, I doubted that Clarence had constructed those expansive walls on his own, brick by brick, crenelle by bloody crenelle. Not that it really mattered. I was about to die of a very abrupt stop. Still. It would have been nice to see my unrealized fantasy home before I went splat.

I reached the tallest treetops. Branches tore past my head, leaves the size of tower shields slapping my feet as I went. Any second I would crash into a branch, and that would be that. But I didn't. The moon disappeared behind the canopy, though its silver light continued to follow my descent. I screamed past a bough as thick as a country lane, draped with vines and bristling with elephant ear fungi the color of warm bread. A pair of eyes followed me down, and I realized part of the branch was actually some kind of creature. It looked like a cross between a snake and a centipede, its hundred clawed legs twitching against the bark. Its yellow eyes blinked in shock as I whistled by. I was so surprised that I stopped screaming.

The creature disappeared a second later, hidden behind more branches and the rapidly thickening trees. And now that I wasn't screaming, I realized that the forest was filled with animal sounds. Long growls, high-pitched wailing, the chirruping scream of... something. I used to camp a lot as a kid, and I remember lying awake at night in my tent, wondering which of the hundred noises echoing outside the thin canvas walls were worth worrying about. The foolish fears of a child, unfamiliar with the world.

Except now I knew those fears were justified. Monsters were real, or maybe unreal enough to be dangerous, at least to me. It didn't comfort me much to think that if a troll found me in the woods and tore me limb from limb, the park ranger who found me would assume it was a bear. Horrific death was horrific death, after all.

Doesn't matter, I reminded my worrying brain. *The ground can't be all that far away, and then none of this will matter in the—*

The ground wasn't far away at all. I saw it for the briefest of seconds before I hit. It was just enough time for every muscle in my body to clench in terror, and then I slammed into a mat of moss and broken twigs. The earth bent around me, flexing like a bow as I impacted. My descent slowed rapidly, stopped, reversed. I shot back into the air, my limbs flailing as I tried to get my bearings, my body slowly twisting as I rose into the lowest branches of the forest. I slowed, hung in the air, then fell again. This time I braced my arms and legs, holding myself ramrod straight as I went in. The ground below me didn't look particularly soft, but once again it flexed beneath me, gradually snapping back to flat and sending me into the air. This cycle repeated a couple times, each launch slightly lower, until I finally came to a stop.

I stood there, trying to catch my breath. I gave the ground an experimental stomp. Hard as packed earth. I looked up. The distant branches of the forest canopy waved in the wind, moonlight flickering among the branches. I remembered the gentle arrival in Clarence's domain, the soft light of the forest and the fresh smell of pine branches, the distant birdsong. I shook myself. I jingled.

My clothes were gone, replaced by the fine chainmail and leather I had worn in Clarence's domain. The only difference was a tabard across my chest, quartered in red and black, and emblazoned with a dragon rampant. I chuckled.

"Kracek wouldn't like that," I said.

Chesa appeared a second later. Screaming, as you might expect, though not exactly *what* you'd expect.

"John Rast I'm going to fucking kill you!" she howled as she bashed her way through the tree limbs, trailing a comet of broken branches and fluttering leaves. She hit the ground ten feet to my right, distended the ground, and bounced back into the air. She was windmilling her arms, but as soon as she caught sight of me standing casually to the side, her motions became more . . . violent.

"I'm going to tear your eyes from your head! Your hair from your skull! Your teeth—" Whump, she hit the ground again, and this time she stuck. Ripples flew out from her feet, upsetting pebbles and tickling my toes. When the ground grew still, she jumped at me, hand extended for my neck. "If I have to fall to my death one more time, I swear, it's going to be the death of you!"

"Okay, okay, I get it. This isn't going like you hoped," I said, backpedaling as I batted her hands away. She stopped just short of strangling me, mouth still open, purple eyes blazing. But she wasn't looking at me. Her gaze was fixed over my shoulder.

"John?" she whispered. "Did he come with us?"

I turned slowly around. There was a tree, maybe fifteen feet away, swaying with the movement of our entrance. Except this tree had a mouth, and two long arms, and it was eating a deer. Loudly. Bones cracked under its woody teeth, and blood splattered its bark. As we watched, it pushed the last bit of deer into its maw, swallowed loudly, then turned to us and grinned.

"Welcome to forest, new food," it said in a clumsy rendition of English. "We friends now."

"No, I don't think we are," I said.

"Okay, friends!" the tree answered. It wiped a bloody antler from its chin, then reached for us.

Reached for me, actually. Chesa was already running. I followed.

CHAPTER SEVENTEEN
WILD, WILD
WORLD OF KILLING

It's hard to get a reasonable impression of a forest when you're running through it, especially if you're running away from a slightly friendly carnivorous tree for the express purpose of not getting eaten. Pretty much the only thing I could tell you about this forest was this: it was not made for running through. The trees were densely packed and trackless, the ground was choked with underbrush, and every branch and bough had been custom designed to slap into my face and hands. What good is armor if everything seems to hit the bits of you not protected? It was miserable, but still markedly better than getting eaten.

Also, running in armor is terrible. I was huffing and puffing after the first dozen steps, and my feet sank into the soft loam, nearly tripping me with each stride.

Despite the thick roof of interwoven branches, moonlight managed to trickle through the trees, so while I couldn't see very far, my immediate surroundings were almost as clear as day. I was reminded of night shots in older movies, magically bright enough to let you see the faces of the heroes, but utterly dark a dozen feet away. Constant night sounds filled the darkness, an endless cacophony of whistles, hoots, growls, and screams.

Chesa was right in front of me, but she was slowly pulling away. Some of that elf magic, I suppose. She jumped over fallen trees, skidded down hills, leapt creeks in a single bound, and danced over gullies like she had been born in the forest. I did not. I stumbled, fell, ran into trunks, tripped over uneven ground, and finally fell headlong into a bramble patch that Chesa had somehow skirted over like a ballerina. The chain protected me from most of it but falling down still hurts.

The slow, ponderous thud of the approaching tree-monster shuddered through my bones. Chesa's glowing form disappeared into the forest.

"So much for doing this together," I whispered. I untangled myself from the brambles as quietly as possible. The trees around me started to shake.

"Meat friend? Where am meat friend?" The tree-monster hove into view like an unwelcome party guest. He wrapped his gnarled hands around a tree and uprooted it, peering under the dangling trunk. "How can I eat you if you hide, meat friend? Meat friends are for eating."

Someone doesn't understand friendship, I mused. *I mean, I'm not exactly an extrovert, but at least I've never tried to eat my casual acquaintances.*

It quickly became apparent that I wasn't going to be able to outrun this guy, especially now that I was lying face down in a bramble patch. I vaguely remembered Esther saying that a domain's owner couldn't die inside their domain, but I also wasn't sure I was in my domain yet. And even if I was, I didn't really want to test the theory. I also remembered the feeling of Clarence's sword scraping past my ribs on its way to my still-beating heart. I didn't want to repeat the experience with wooden teeth and the slow digestion of a hungry oak tree.

Tree-monster discarded the uprooted trunk and looked around desolately. Maybe if I waited long enough, it would get bored and just go away. I burrowed deeper into the brambles. Hardly the most comfortable hiding place, but certainly better than the pit of a wooden stomach.

"Meat friends are the worst friends," it grumbled. "But tasty. So tasty. Oh, well." The monster gave out a tremendous sigh, then settled onto the bramble bed. It tore out a handful of thorny vines and started to eat them, reeling the tangle into its mouth like cold spaghetti. "Gotta get my fiber, anyway. Stupid fiber."

This isn't going to work out. A coil of thorn wrapped tight around my ankle. I was just barely able to wiggle free of the vine before it ripped out of the ground and was drawn into the tree's mouth. *Time for plan B. And plan B is . . .* I looked around desperately. *Plan B is not coming to me.*

A trio of arrows hammered into the monster's woody jaw. The creature paused in its ponderous chewing, then raised a finger to brush the fletching. Another arrow thudded into its knuckle, and a look of shock washed over its face. It flinched back, eyes going wide. It stood up, vines still trailing from its mouth.

"Tag!" it shouted. "Tag! I'm it!"

"Hey root head! Over here!" Chesa yelled. She was balanced precariously on the limb of a distant tree, bow drawn and purple eyes blazing. Another arrow whistled through the forest, landing heavily right in the monster's pupil. It stumbled back, nearly crushing me as it pulled the shaft free. "You want a friend? I'm the friendly type!"

The monster started laughing, a deeply disturbing hacking that sounded like stones tearing apart. It crashed into the forest toward Chesa. She paused long enough to make sure she had the creature's attention, then somehow looked directly at me and nodded. I waved back, but she had already disappeared from view.

I stood up. Brambles had stitched their way into my hair, my clothes . . . even my underwear. I started the delicate surgery of freeing myself from their attention without taking off the chainmail. No chance I was going to spend even a minute in this place without my armor. In the distance I could see trees waving and hear the occasional booming laugh or whistling arrow. Chesa seemed fine. I just hoped I would be able to find her later.

"I know we're not supposed to complain," I complained. "But this doesn't seem fair. She has the eyes, and the elfy grace thing, and a bow, and I guess she can climb trees like a squirrel now? I don't know." I winced as a thorn dug into something that was never supposed to see a thorn in the natural order of things. I carefully reversed the situation, then let out a long, weary sigh. "All I seem to have is a tendency for things to fall apart around me. Oh, and I fall down well. Lots of practice. Champion of falling down."

Once free, I gave the surrounding forest a long and distrustful look. I didn't really want to go anywhere. Every inch of this place seemed incredibly dangerous, almost like it was conjured to push every fear response I had available. There were some directions I could eliminate: Where Chesa and the monster had gone, because eventually she was going to slip free and then you'd have an angry and hungry tree-monster to deal with, and the direction I had come from, because maybe that's where the tree-monster lived. Oh, and I couldn't stay here, in case the tree-monster decided to come back.

Picking one of the other directions at random, I started walking. Without Chesa to choose a path with her elfy vision, and with no monster on my heels to motivate me, my going was slow. I eventually found a creek and followed it downhill until I reached a shallow pond. The stream bubbled playfully over a waterfall of smooth, mossy stones, casting the surface of the water in ripples of silver moonlight. Despite my recent terror, it was a very peaceful scene. I pulled off my boots, finding a new collection of thorns to extricate, then dipped my toes in the water. The water was cool and refreshing, but not so cold that it was uncomfortable. I sat down on the shore and found that it was surprisingly soft. I lay back on the spongy moss, comfortable for the first time since Chesa and I had fallen out of the sky. The insect song from the surrounding forest took on a comforting rhythm. I was reminded of summer nights in my youth, sleeping with the windows open as a warm breeze whispered through the curtains. Warm air and the overwhelming smell of fish tickled its way through my . . . through my . . .

Overwhelming smell of fish?

My eyes snapped open. A glowing lantern hung a few feet above my head, bobbing gently in the darkness. I tried to focus on the hand that was holding it, but all I could see was a slimy stalk of dull skin. A gust of wind washed over me, and the ocean stink returned, turning my throat into bile. I looked down at my feet. My toes poked out of the water, floating on the gentle current of the pond. A row of jagged teeth emerged just beyond them, each one as big as my foot, pale and curved and inching ever so slowly closer.

"Holy shit!" I yelped, sitting bolt upright and scuttling my way backwards out of the pond. My head bumped into the lantern, sending it bobbing high into the air. Light flashed across the clearing, illuminating the pond, the shore, the tiny stream and the waterfall of mossy stones.

And also lighting up the fish head, twenty feet across and consisting of nothing more than two bulbous eyes and a gaping mouth, lined with row after row of curved teeth. A long stalk sprouted from its forehead, from which dangled a glowing, luminous orb that looked a lot like a lantern. The whole monstrosity barely fit into the pond.

We stared at one another for half a heartbeat, fishy eyes unblinking, mouth hanging open. I screamed. It pounced.

Crab-walking backwards across a stony shore is apparently my fastest mode of transport. I flew over that beach like lightning. The fish-thing snapped down on the empty air where I had been, then surged forward, teeth cracking shut twice, three times, each report as loud as thunder in my ears. For a fish the size of a bus, it was really fast, and really hungry. Its flaccid body slapped against the pebbled ground, sending a plume of water and torn moss into the air. It chased me all the way to the treeline. Trees bent and shivered as the fish slammed into a pair of trunks, sending a shower of leaves onto the ground. The fish lay on the shore, gills flaring as it stared at me, just out of reach. I got to my feet.

"Not today, little buddy. Not today," I said.

The glowing bulb of its lantern slipped between the trees. It bobbed over my head for a long minute before slowly drawing back toward the creature's mouth. I smiled.

"I'm not falling for that," I said. "It's a very nice light, but it's not worth getting eaten for. Good try."

The fish let out a tremendous sigh, then slowly retreated into the water. It disappeared beneath the surface of the pond, first gills, then bloated eyes, and finally gaping jaws. Finally, the glowing lantern dipped into the water. It turned the pond into a shimmering bowl of golden light, descending, descending, growing dimmer and dimmer until it was completely gone. The insect song resumed.

"So I guess that pond is deeper than I thought," I said.

"You just going to lie on your back all night?" Chesa asked. She dropped as light as a leaf out of the shadows at my side.

"Chesa! You're okay!"

"Of course, I'm okay," she said. "That guy was about as slow and as dumb as a rock. He doesn't even make a good tree. What happened to your shoes?"

"Oh, uh . . ." I glanced toward the pond. They were still sitting next to the pond. "Lost them."

"Isn't that them over there?" she asked. She started toward the pond. I grabbed her shoulder.

"No, no...I mean, yes. But they weren't very good shoes. I, uh... I don't think they're part of my mythic self. You know? I'm more of a barefoot hero."

She stared at me for a long moment. I could feel the disappointment in her gaze.

"Did something scare you, John?"

"Very badly. But I think it was a rational reaction."

"For you, maybe. But you're not you anymore."

"I'm not?" I asked.

"No. You're here to be a hero. And heroes don't go around barefoot because they're scared of the water, or a tree, or whatever it was that put some bump in your night."

"This is not a great pep talk, Ches. There's a monster in that pond."

She looked over at the pond and sniffed.

"Anything that can fit in that pond isn't worth being scared of. Now go get your boots."

"Honestly, I'm perfectly fine—"

"Damn it all, Rast," she snapped. "Boots! Now!"

I stared miserably at the boots and the pond for a few moments. I really wish I had a sword, or at least a knife. Chesa had the full kit, double scimitars, a bow, elven armor, the grace of a goddess. I had soggy chainmail and muddy feet.

"This is some bullshit, I tell you what," I said, then tromped damply toward the pool.

The surface of the pool was absolutely still. If I stared directly into it, I thought I could see a dim light in the depths, but that might just be the reflection of the moon, or a trick of the deeper shadows all around. About ten feet from my boots I slowed to a crawl. Chesa sighed in exasperation.

"I'm doing this at my own pace, Ches," I said. "You want me to go faster, you can—"

She marched past me and grabbed the boots. She held them away from her body, grimacing at the deluge of dirty water that poured out.

"What the hell did you do to get so wet?" she asked.

Just then, the surface of the pond swelled, like a boil about to burst. Warm light shimmered through the rising water. A single bulbous eye pressed against the water.

"Chesa!" I yelled. She knit her brow together, then turned to look at the pond.

There was no time. The creature's teeth sliced out of the pond, yawning wide to swallow Chesa whole. I leapt at her, hoping to at least knock her aside before the monster's jaws closed on her. But of course, she was already moving, elf-fast and silent. I glanced off her hip as she vaulted clear of the pond, sending me reeling to my knees. Those terrible jaws sliced shut inches away from my face, sending a flood of cold water crashing over me. It surged forward, gnashing its teeth, that glassy eye staring at me, both of us quite surprised to be here again.

I got to my feet, standing in about a foot of water, the muddy bank slippery under my bare heels. The fish reared back, swinging its jaws in my direction. I caught a glimpse of Chesa behind it, face slack with shock, still holding the soggy cuff of my boots. I didn't really want to die with her watching. Especially with that look on her face.

With one hand I pushed against the fish's snout. As it swung toward me, I rode the momentum farther up shore. It flapped toward me, dragging itself forward on spiny fins. I punched helplessly at its nose, the frilled veil of its gills, but my mailed fist bounced off its scales like a drum. Its jaws snapped shut once again. Teeth dragged along the mailed cuff of my sleeve, pulling me toward the gaping jaws. I put my naked heel against the squirming mass of its fin. It bucked up like a bronco and threw me to the ground. I barely got a hold of the stalk of its lantern. As it reared back, my feet left the ground. When the stalk whipped back, I landed heavily on the side of the fish, feet first, one heel planted on each side of the beast's eye.

"Shoulda left me alone," I said, then jumped up, tucked my legs, then kicked them directly into the creature's eye.

There aren't a lot of things less pleasant than burying yourself to the knee in recently burst eyeball. Jelly and red gore splattered across my chest. The monster howled, a terrible, gurgling sound that echoed through the trees. I landed with a thump on the shore, corkscrewing out of the monster's ruined socket like a thrown shot. The beast flopped against the shore and then, still screaming, descended into the pool.

I lay there for a long time, gathering my breath. Slick gel covered a good portion of my body. Chesa came to stand over me.

"You okay?" she asked.

"Uh huh," I answered, very quietly.

"Do you want to wash off?"

"Yes."

"Maybe not here, though," she said.

"Yeah. Maybe not." I extended a hand so she could help me up. Chesa stared at it for several heartbeats before I realized my glove was covered in varying shades of red and black. "Fair enough." I scrambled to my feet and stood, arms extended, staring down at my clothes.

"I'm sure that'll wash right off," Chesa said, without a trace of optimism.

"Sure," I said. "You know, I think the modern convenience I'm going to miss the most? Scotchgard."

"Just don't bathe in inhuman ichor," Chesa said.

"Good call. Hey, can we find that other pond? For the washing?"

"Right, sure. Absolutely." She tried to hand me my boots. I waved them away.

"Hang on to them for a minute," I said. "Until my feet are a little less . . . eyebally."

Chesa looked at me skeptically. Finally, she shrugged and turned back into the forest. I followed, picking my way gingerly over the ground.

We found our pond. It was one hundred percent less infested with gnashing teeth. I dipped myself, chain and all, into the water. Miraculously, the eye stuff washed off pretty easily. When I was done, I pulled on my boots and Chesa and I wandered back into the woods. My feet squeaked damply, but at least I was clean.

"Thanks for your help back there," I said after a while. "I was in a pretty tough spot."

"It's what heroes do," she said. "You know, you're going to have to start doing that kind of thing. Hero stuff. You've spent a lot of time screaming and getting chased and so forth. We're supposed to be finding our true mythic selves in here. Not sure what kind of hero is always running away."

"Running away is natural," I said. "These are scary things."

"No, being scared is natural," she answered over her shoulder. "Running away is mundane. Standing up and giving a good account of yourself . . . that's what heroes do."

I opened my mouth to answer, thought about it for a long moment, then shut it again. She was right. I shoved my hands into my pockets.

"Easy for you to say," I grumbled. "Look at you. The eyes, the bow, the clever armor. You're halfway there. Easy to be brave when you're already magical."

"Don't blame me, John," she said. "This is your problem to solve."

We marched in silence for a long time. The forest whistled and chirped around us, growing louder the farther we got from the stream. But nothing else tried to eat us. That was an improvement.

Finally, we saw a dim light through the trees. The forest grew quiet, and the air took on a still quality. It reminded me of libraries and churches, though without the walls and judgment. Chesa slowed down.

"If there's anything I've learned about this place, it's that lights are not worth checking out," I said. "We should probably just go around."

"It's . . . calling to me. I think this is it," Chesa said.

"Yeah, the pond called to me, too. There are probably teeth involved." I plucked at her shoulder. "You can tell by the way the insects have stopped singing. Always teeth after that."

"Quiet, John. This isn't for you." Chesa pulled free from my grip and slipped through the trees, chasing after the light. I hesitated. She was the one with the fancy bow, not me. If this was another trap, there wasn't much I could do other than fall down. But I couldn't let her just disappear.

The forest changed in short order. Up until now, the trees had been tall and thick, with rough bark and gnarled, twisted roots that grabbed at my feet. The trees we passed now were aspens, their pale bark as smooth as butter, golden leaves fluttering in the breeze. Golden light filled the air, replacing the harsh silver of the moon. Birds chirped in the distance. We came to a clearing. There was a single tree in the middle, as tall and straight as a tower, with steps cut into its side, spiraling up into the boughs. A constellation of golden leaves filled its canopy, the source of all the light in the clearing. Soft music came from the tree, a cross between windchimes and angel song.

Chesa and I stood in awe. The terror of the forest retreated behind us. The world was full of glory and light and joy. I cleared my throat.

"So, uh . . . this is your thing, huh?" I asked.

"This is very much my thing," she said.

She started walking toward the tree. The ground underfoot was soft grass and wildflowers. Wherever she stepped, fresh blossoms sprouted, twinkling like fireworks before fading away seconds later.

A figure appeared on the stairway. It was a man, or an elf, or an elf man. He was dressed in silver clothes and a deep green cloak. His hair hung in golden waves across his face, a face that was chiseled to within striking distance of perfection. His shirt hung open to the middle of his chest, a chest that rippled with muscles. He walked with unearthly grace, dancing down the stairs. When he reached the clearing, he took a couple steps toward Chesa and then went to one knee, flourishing exquisitely with cloak and palm.

"My queen," he said. His voice rumbled like thunder, sang like silver bells, echoed like a dream on waking. I almost threw up on the spot.

"So, hey . . . who's this guy?" I asked. "Kinda cheesy, don't you think? Do they not make top buttons where he's from? Right? Chesa?"

Chesa strode toward the kneeling elf-god-man and held out her hand. The vision of beauty took it in both his fists (large, strong, but soft as velvet. I could tell even at a distance) and pressed it to his face. Chesa shivered.

"This is what traps look like, Ches," I said. "I'm just saying."

"Quiet, John. Just . . . be quiet." She pulled the man to her feet, their hips touching briefly as he stood. The elf backed away, gesturing to the tree.

"Your realm awaits," he said. Chesa looked over her shoulder at me.

"Good luck with your domain, John," she said. "I can't save you anymore."

Together, they processed (no other word. It had all the glory and ceremony of a royal wedding) to the tree, climbing the stairs with gentle grace. Higher and higher they went. I watched until the glow from the leaves was too much for my mundane eyes and I had to look away. The music continued for a little while longer, rising into a crescendo as Chesa reached whatever secret door was nestled into those glowing boughs.

When they were gone, the music faded, and the light with it. The clearing grew dark, and the sounds of the forest imposed themselves on the calm that had reigned just moments ago. Just before the golden light winked out completely, the tree withdrew into the sky. Roots burrowed up out of the ground, tearing apart the soft turf, reeling back into the trunk. The tree shriveled up, growing thinner and thinner, finally spooling into the canopy. The golden leaves closed like an umbrella and then disappeared.

The forest was back, and dark, and full of terror.

CHAPTER EIGHTEEN
THE WORLD DOG

I lingered in the remnants of Chesa's clearing as long as I dared. When it became clear that she wasn't going to pop back out of her newly found domain anytime soon, I turned and walked back into the forest.

It was still a terrifying place, made more so by the knowledge I was absolutely, utterly alone among the trees. I began to wonder what it would look like when the entrance to my domain opened up. Would it be a sun-dappled path among the trees, like that of Clarence? Some kind of gate? Maybe just a swirling tornado of stress and disappointment. Who knew? I certainly didn't.

And that was my problem. I didn't really have a clear sense of my mythic self. I knew what I wasn't... particularly brave. Notably handsome. Unrelentingly... relentless? What kind of hero is that? Chesa was right. I wasn't much of a hero. Maybe Knight Watch screwed up in picking me up at the faire. Maybe it was supposed to be Eric, and they got me by mistake.

My pitiful reverie was interrupted by yet another disaster. A horrific growl filled the air, echoing off the trees and shaking my bones. In the midst of the forest's cacophony, it was a piercing, terrible sound. I nearly jumped out of my skin. To my left, I could see the tops of the trees start to shake and heard the dull thump of a heavy body brushing against their trunks. The earth hummed under my feet with each resounding crash. At first, I thought it was tree-friend, but no, even it hadn't made this much noise. Whatever this was, it was bigger than big. It was enormous. And it was coming straight at me.

I'm kind of tired of running through the darkness, I thought. *Maybe*

I should stand. Maybe I should do what Chesa suggested, and find my hero. Maybe I should—

On the next ridgeline, the forest parted like a curtain, and revealed a beast larger than the Caneville Valley Mall. I didn't get a very good look at it, but it was look enough to stop my heart.

"So, to my right, then," I said, turning away from the shuddering forest. I hurried into the darkness, as fast as I could without risking a tree to the face, or a misstep over an unseen cliff. The growl sounded again. It was getting closer.

"What's a little tree to the face?" I mused, picking up the pace. I held my arms in front of my head, wincing as branches whipped against my hands, lashing my cheeks and drawing blood from my scalp. The crashing sound was now distinctly footsteps, giant loping paws. The creature howled, and the whole world shook. "Kyle?" I shouted hopelessly. "Please be Kyle!"

Another howl, and now the beast was running. Its breath filled the forest, thrashing the underbrush and nearly leveling me. Its eyes appeared, huge and red, thirty feet off the ground. It saw me. I ran.

Judging by the sound of its passage, I was being pursued by three school buses welded together and then strapped to the top of a herd of stampeding elephants. The trees behind me crashed aside, trunks as wide as houses shattering like kindling. The beast's growl turned my knees to jelly and the air into a humid funk. I looked back only once, to see those red eyes and the slick glint of slavering jaws, framed by matted black hair. I didn't dare to look back again.

I crested the hill I had been climbing and vaulted down the opposite slope. It was steeper than I anticipated, and my medieval-chic boots were not designed with parkour in mind. I hit the ground heels first, and had to pinwheel my arms to stay upright, my boots clomping into the loose earth. My descent was more of a fall than anything, but it got me down the hill good and quick. When I got to the bottom, I went down like a sack of potatoes. *I am the best at falling,* I thought.

The footsteps of the monster boomed through the ground. But as it got closer, it felt like each step got less distinct, like a single drumbeat diffusing into a concert of smaller instruments. They washed into a steady roar of tramping paws. I lay at the bottom of the hill, staring in horror at the ridgeline above.

A single wolf appeared at the top of the hill. No, not a wolf at all, but a dog. A husky, its bicolored eyes flashing in the moonlight, the majestic floof of its tail wagging noncommittally. It was joined by a schnauzer, then a German shepherd, and finally a whole wave of dogs of every size and variety. The husky licked its enormous jaws and then strolled down the hill in my direction. The rest followed, a rolling, bouncing, yammering tide of dogs. A pug tripped and rolled ahead of the others, ridiculous mouth smiling as it bowled the husky aside. They played as they ran, nipping at flanks and pouncing at tails. A low carpet of puppies swept down from the side, a squirming mass of wild eyes and lolling tongues, their too-large paws flailing in the air as they fell, jumped, ran, tackled, and romped.

As they approached, something strange happened. Stranger than a pack of a million dogs, which is very strange indeed. The dogs began to merge. The husky and the German shepherd ran together for a bit, and then the husky jumped, colliding with the shepherd. But instead of knocking the other dog aside, the husky disappeared into the shepherd's fur, and a new dog emerged; more wolf-like, and larger.

This started to happen all over the hill. The pack of puppies swarmed into a single bulldog, which grew into a wolfhound, and then into something larger and more feral. Soon the woods around me were haunted by a dozen enormous, slavering wolves, with black fur and red eyes. They flowed around me like an inky whirlpool, dodging between tree trunks and appearing a dozen yards away, or simply hiding and letting another of its brethren take up the prowl. I struggled to my feet, turning slowly in place in an attempt to keep them all in my sight. One brushed past my leg, a dog the size of a horse, its fur tangled with twigs and dry leaves. Just that casual contact was nearly enough to knock me down.

"Guys, guys . . . I'm a dog person, okay?" I said, hands up. "I've had dogs. I love dogs."

A rumbling growl filled the forest. The beast was down to four incarnations, each one as big as a soccer mom's SUV. They loped around me in a steady orbit. Red eyes burned at me from all directions.

"Let's not do this. We can both just walk away. Look, I don't even want to be here. I don't even know where here is," I said. Two of the dogs merged right in front of me. The resulting beast was the size of a truck. It padded to the top of the hill and loomed over me. Filtered moonlight turned its black fur into silver down. Lowering its head, the beast raised its hackles and let free a long, rumbling growl that shook my bowels.

"Ah, shit," I muttered. "I knew I should have brought a sword."

My hand brushed my belt where a sword should be, and it was. Believe me, no one was as shocked as me. *Mythic self, kicking in!* I thought. I drew the blade and held it up. Steel sang from the scabbard, drawing sparks.

The blade gave light to that place. A shimmering vein of golden fire ran down the runnel, like lightning frozen in steel. After the dim silver of the moon, the illumination coming from my sword was like a flare at midnight. The wolf squinted at it, then turned his enormous head to stare at me.

"I . . . I claim dominion over this realm," I declared. It seemed like the kind of thing Esther would expect me to say, might even have been what I was supposed to say, if she had given me even a moment's instruction. I held my left hand in front of me, still trying to placate the wolf. "This is my domain now. I don't want to fight you. But I will, if I must, and I've slain dragons before, so—"

There were three dogs. See, that's what I forgot. I was talking to the big one, but the other two were still out there somewhere.

Jaws closed on my sword hand, sharp teeth pricking my skin through the chain of my mitt. I yelped and tried to jerk away, but that only drove the teeth tighter into my wrist. I whirled around. One of the dogs was holding my arm in place. It stared directly into my eyes. I yelled again, panicking as terror filled my head, then reached for my dagger with my other hand. Rather than grabbing the hilt, though, my hand slid smoothly into the third dog's waiting maw. Hot breath hissed up the cuff of my sleeve as the dog's mouth closed gingerly on my hand. I could feel teeth pressing into chainmail, steel links cutting into my skin. I tried hard not to move.

When I looked up, the largest wolf was only feet away. It lowered its head, coming closer and closer. I tried to pull back, but its companions held me pinned in place. Its breath smelled like fresh meat and excitement. I didn't like the look in its blood-red eyes. The wolf huffed at me. Its face was less than a foot in front of me, then inches, then its furry head was pressed against my body. It spoke.

"This is not your world. It never will be. We serve no master. Do not threaten us again." Its voice growled through my bones, felt in my lungs and the hollow places of my belly. It backed away, and the anger in its eyes faded into dismissal. "You are welcome to cower among us. But never to rule."

The wolf turned and loped away, back up the hill. Shortly after its haunches passed me by, the two dogs pinning me in place dropped their holds and scurried after. They ran like puppies chasing a ball in the park, exactly the same except for their size and the pain throbbing in my wrists. I watched until they had disappeared over the hill, then dropped to my knees and had a nice, peaceful breakdown. When it was done, I examined my wrists. There was no blood, only the swollen indents where they had held me fast, and a slick coat of drool that covered me from the elbows down.

I shook off my hands, splattering saliva all over the place, then tried to wipe the rest off on my pants. When I was as clean as I could be, I sheathed my sword and turned back to the forest.

"World of bloody dogs," I muttered. "Clarence gets a castle and a dragon, Chesa walks a stairway into heaven, escorted by Ranger Pectoral, and I get dogs." I let out a long sigh and shook my head. "At least they seem friendly. And maybe he'll make a good pet, someday."

A piercing howl shook the trees around me. I scurried off into the forest, afraid the beast had somehow heard me. It was probably too early to be challenging the authority of a wolf made up of literally every dog in the world. But maybe someday. Sure.

A short time later, I came to a creek. I was scared of water now, which was reasonable, but also not conducive to heroism. And hey, now I had a sword. Surely that was a step in the right direction. So I washed off my hands and thought about what I should do next.

Remembering the view from my descent, I turned upstream and started to follow the winding course of the water. I didn't like the idea of the river delta. I associated that much water with places like swamps, and if the forest was ruled by a wolf the size of three school buses, I really didn't want to meet the mosquito that called that swamp home. Besides, the mountains appealed to me. I always wanted a mountain view. Maybe at least that part of my dream had found a place in the domain.

The creek splashed through mossy valleys and gathered in large pools, sometimes narrowing into whitewater or tumbling over smooth stones in a loud waterfall that filled the air with moonlit mist. Swallowing my fear, I cleaned up in one of those pools, stripping off my armor and washing in the crisp, clear water. It was so cold it took my breath away, and I was forced back to shore, gasping for air. Gooseflesh prickled my skin. I dried off with my tabard, then dressed and continued on. I wondered how much time had passed. It was hard to tell under the canopy, but I didn't feel like the moon was moving all that much. Hours passed. Then hours more. I started to climb rolling hills, and the forest thinned.

Night never ended. And somehow I knew, as I climbed out of the forest, that it never would. The sky spread out above me, a vast tapestry of unfamiliar constellations, dominated by the glowing face of an enormous moon. The mountains rose behind me, their jagged peaks cloaked in snow. I sat down on a grassy knoll and took it all in. It was beautiful, and at this distance, not completely terrifying.

A glimmer of light back down in the valley caught my eye. At first, I thought it was a trick of the distance, or maybe moonlight reflecting off a pool, but after a solid minute of staring and blinking and staring again, I saw that I was wrong. It had the flickering red and orange of firelight, warm and inviting. Something in primal humanity was drawn to fire, especially in a world of eternal night, ruled by a giant wolf and gods knew what else. It wasn't that far away.

I hopped onto my feet and ran down the hill toward the light, hoping that it wasn't another bobbing lantern, dangling from a smooth, pale stalk.

The flame was closer than it looked. Just as I re-entered the forest, I came to a smooth hillock with a short, squat pillar of stone in the middle and a precipitous dropoff on the far side. The light that I had seen was coming from the cliffside of the hill and reflected off the trees that surrounded a small clearing at the base of the cliff. The hill wasn't more than fifteen feet high at the apex.

With visions of dragon's dens and other fire-breathing ghoulies crowding for equal anxiety in my head, I crept around the edge of the hill, sword drawn. The blade still pulsed with a muted light, dim enough that I was confident it wouldn't give away my presence to whatever waited at the base of the cliff. I quickly learned that the cliff face was artificial; wooden beams protruded from the grass along the base of the cliff, like pilings in a dock. I came around the edge of the hill, ready to face whatever waited for me.

The hill was a house. The cliff face was simply the front elevation, overhung by timber eaves that supported a roof of sod and grass. The front of the house itself was made of thick timber, roughly hewn, with a sturdy wooden door and two shuttered windows. The shutters were open, and the light of a bright fire flickered through dense glass panes. The glass was so distorted that I couldn't see inside clearly. I looked around the clearing and saw signs of habitation. There was a woodpile tucked under the eaves at the far side of the hill, a well, and a hitching post that was so old it looked like it might rot away at any moment. The smell of woodsmoke filled the front yard, and I could now see that the stone pillar on top of the hill was a chimney. I sheathed my sword.

"Hello! Is anyone home?" I shouted. There was no immediate answer. Then there was no eventual answer, and then it was clear that there was never going to be an answer. I waited for quite a while, occasionally greeting the vacancy on the other side of the door in various pitches and with various amounts of pleading and threat. Finally, I resolved to enter the house uninvited.

"Surely there's nothing suspicious about an empty house in the middle of a hellish forest, right?" I mused. "Certainly the safest place in the whole world. Sure."

I stood nervously in front of the door for another few minutes, flexing my wrists and wondering if there was a way out of this. It certainly felt like a trap, in the sense that, other than Chesa's glowing tree of pectoral-delivery, it was the first peaceful and inviting thing I'd seen in this domain of terror since I'd arrived.

It started raining on me. A few heavy drops at first, followed closely by an absolute deluge. I was just thinking that I hadn't noticed the sky cloud over when I saw that it hadn't clouded over at all. The moon and stars twinkled happily at me through the thinner forest canopy, oblivious to the fact that it was raining cats and dogs. Just my own personal rainstorm, minus the clouds and the promise of a rainbow at the end. Looking up to confirm this drenched my face and started a river down my breastplate. Chainmail is cold when it wants to be, and my chainmail really wanted to be frigid. I shivered once, stubbornly telling myself that I wasn't going to go in, especially now that the entire domain was conspiring to put me through that door, but then it really started to rain.

"Fine, fine, you've made your point," I muttered.

The door opened easily. The smell of hot food and woodsmoke wafted out the door, filling my head with memories of my mother's kitchen. The room was low-ceilinged, with exposed beams and a clutter of heavy wooden furniture gathered around a roaring hearth. There were a pair of overstuffed chairs that framed the fireplace, and a long, sturdy table to one side, with enough chairs for half a dozen diners. A rocking chair looked out the front window, and two sets of doors led out of the room. A quick tour revealed that the far door led to a long hallway of bedrooms, along with a dry storage cellar at the end of the hall that smelled of fresh dirt and pickled onions. All the bedrooms were small and cozy, with wardrobes, nightstands, and soft, clean beds.

The other doors from the main room led to a kitchen. There was a second fire here, this one contained in the largest and oldest stove I've ever seen. Heat radiated off the black iron of the stove's massive belly, and a pot on top bubbled and murmured contentedly, the source of the delicious smell. Inside was the heartiest stew I've ever tasted, and taste it I did, immediately and to the detriment of the roof of my mouth, as it wasn't cool enough to eat. I fished a crock out of one of the cupboards, filled it to the brim, tore a hunk of crusty bread off a loaf in the corner, and returned to the main room. I laid the latch over the front door, then settled into one of the chairs by the fire. It was very comfortable, and it wasn't long until I was mopping the last vestiges of stew out of the crock with the crust of my bread and sighing contentedly.

I wondered at the origin of the stew, and the occupant of the house. I was reminded of Clarence's unseen choir, and the workings of his invisible staff. Food had arrived, rooms had been cleaned, blood mopped up (I suppressed a shiver at the memory of my seemingly infinite deaths on his ruthless training grounds) and clothes laundered, all without sight of another human being. Maybe that was the nature of domains. Maybe they were attended by spirits unseen, or forces that mimicked human helpers but had no physical form. I set the crock aside and settled deeper into the chair, letting the warmth of the fire wash over me. When I looked up, I noticed there was a shield hanging over the fireplace. I stood up to get a better look.

It was an amazing shield. There's not usually a lot to admire in a shield, not like the sword that rested comfortably next to my chair, or the dagger at my belt. But this was a beautiful shield. It was a heater, quartered black and red, with a golden dragon rampant at the center. I lifted the shield from its moorings and flipped it over. The shields I was accustomed to using usually had three simple straps, allowing it to be held either across the body or with the hand at the point. This shield had . . . more straps. Many more. I spent a few minutes trying to wrestle them into something that would hang comfortably, when suddenly the leather web shivered and wrapped itself around my arm. Smaller thongs wove themselves between my fingers, almost like a glove.

"That's odd," I said. I made a few practice blocks with it and found that the straps expanded and contracted as if by magic. "Oh, right. Actual magic. Right." With a flick of my wrist, the shield switched to a center grip. Another flick and it was firmly against my forearm. I chuckled.

"Don't think this would pass marshal's inspection," I said. "But neither would Kracek the Hosier, so I guess that's fair."

The more I played with it, the more tricks I found. The glove-like wrapping around my fingers acted like levers. I could twitch a finger and trigger panels that folded out of the top of the shield, extending its height. Another flick worked similarly, flashing additional armor along the sides and bottom.

"Well. Ain't that the damnedest thing," I mused. I set the shield back above the hearth and settled into my chair. The rain hammered against the windows, and the smell of stew and woodsmoke filled the cabin. I gave a long and satisfied sigh.

"Perhaps I never wanted a castle," I said to myself. "Perhaps this is all I could hope for. And really, what more could you want?"

I sat there for a long time, listening to the storm hammer against the eaves, the fire hiss and pop in the hearth beside me, and wondered what sort of power my domain would bestow me with. There had been a lot of terror getting here. Maybe that was my new strength. Facing fear, and overcoming it, to return to a place of warmth and comfort. It wasn't quite the same as summoning fire, like Tembo, or mastering the sword, like Clarence, or disappearing, teleporting, stabbing, and smirking, like Bethany, or . . . whatever it was that Matthew did. But I could be content with this. I could be happy.

CHAPTER NINETEEN
FAKE FRIENDS AND REAL ENEMIES

I must have fallen asleep in the chair by the fire, because when the knock at the door came, my head jerked up off my chest and it took several seconds for me to remember where I was. The knock came again. I jumped to my feet and scrambled to draw my sword. In my haste, I knocked a chip out of the low beams of the ceiling. My visitor knocked a third time. I threw aside the bolt and swept open the door, stepping back in case I needed to defend myself.

It was Eric. His ridiculous bard's hat was crumpled against his head, and his costume was torn and muddy. He was completely out of breath.

"Eric! What the hell are you doing here?"

"John . . . John, my man." Deep breath, and a shaky laugh. "There's this dog out here. You would not believe how big it is."

"Yeah, I know about the dog. What I don't know is how you got here. This is . . ." I wasn't even sure how to explain where we were. It was still night outside, and the forest moaned menacingly. "This isn't a place you should be."

"No kidding. I thought I'd just hide in the woods until the cops came, but then it was nighttime, and I hadn't seen anyone since the explosion." He took a deep breath and straightened up. He was seriously a mess. There were twigs in his clothes and scrapes and bruises all over his body. "So then I tried to get back to the parking lot but . . . John, I think the parking lot's gone. I think something terrible has happened."

"Terribly wonderful," I answered. Some trees beyond the clearing started to sway, and I heard the growl of that damned dog. "Look, let's get you inside, get you cleaned up. When did you eat last?"

"Vodka is just a kind of potato, right?" he asked.

"Not exactly." I clapped him on the shoulder and ushered him into the cabin. "Just go inside."

"Thanks for the invitation, friend," he said, then slipped past me. Just in time, too. The dinner plate wide eyes of the world dog appeared in the shadows, flashing red and angry. I slammed the door shut. The house shook with the force of the monster's growl.

"Wow, man. This is pretty swell," Eric said, looking around the cabin. "A real love shack. This where you take all your college sweeties?"

"It's not a love shack. It's ... never mind. Have a seat. I'll get you some food."

He settled into the chair by the fire. I went into the kitchen and got a pot of stew and some water.

"There has to be beer in this place somewhere," Eric called from the other room. I shouldered my way through the door. He was standing in front of the fire, looking at the shield. He glanced over at me. "This is pretty nice."

"Yeah, it's ... It's a custom job. Made especially for me."

"Heck of a lot better than that plywood shingle you've been fighting with. Get it for the championships?"

"I'm not sure I'm going to champs," I said, setting the food down on the table. "Eric ... some stuff's come up. Things have gotten weird."

"You and Chesa get back together behind my back?"

"No, no, gods, no. Nothing like that. What do you remember from the faire?"

"The explosion? You and that lawyer were fighting, and then the dragon—"

"Dragon," I repeated. "You saw a dragon?"

"Yeah, the parade float. Someone must have lost control of it, and it careened through the fence and into the lawyer. And then it blew up." He was eating the stew this entire time without really eating it, just stirring it around and putting the spoon near his mouth, then dumping it back into the pot and stirring some more. It was unlike him. Usually he just talked right through the chewing. "Lots of fire, lots of screaming. I ran into the woods. Man, I thought you were dead."

"I'm not. Or at least I don't think I am. Though that would explain some stuff."

"Yeah, well. Like I said. Hid in the woods, waited for the fire department to show up. Would have kept running, but . . ." He paused, put some food in his mouth. "I forget. Something about guards."

As he talked, the stew dribbled out of his mouth and down his chin. Without missing a beat, he stirred his food, brought another spoon to his mouth, then put it back in the bowl without touching it.

"So that's a really nice shield," he said. "Where'd you get it?"

"Eric, are you alright? You're not eating. And I'm pretty sure you already asked that question."

"Right, right." He looked curiously around the cabin. I couldn't blame him for acting a little weird. This was a weird place, and I hadn't exactly been forthcoming in my explanation. But something was off about my friend.

"John. How did you get here?" he asked. "How did you do it?"

"There's a lot of stuff to explain. Starting with the dragon. That wasn't a float, Eric. It was—"

"Did you make it in your mind? Did you write it out?" Eric asked. "He's written it out a hundred times, but it's never quite like this. It's wrong, somehow. Can you show him?"

"Show him? Show who, Eric?"

"Me. Show me how you did this." He stood up, spoon still clenched in his hand.

"Eric? Are you sure you're feeling alright?"

"I always make the first mistake," he said. "But not this time."

Then he slid forward and stabbed me in the belly.

There were two things that surprised me about this. Maybe three. First, I'd never seen Eric move like that. It was like his body was an afterthought, and the knife was the only thing moving. Second, the knife. I'm pretty sure I gave him a spoon, and a second ago I had seen Eric clutching that spoon like it was a lifeline. But now it was a knife. Surprising.

Also, my friend just stabbed me in the stomach. So I guess that's three.

A word of advice that is both good and something you should maybe ignore. Never sleep in your armor. It's uncomfortable, it's bad for the armor, it's bad for you. There's no situation in which you should be wearing your armor to bed. Except for one. If you plan on getting stabbed first thing in the morning.

Eric's sudden knife went under the lip of my breastplate, catching me in the low belly. My chain turned the blade, but not before the impact of the blow knocked the wind out of me. I doubled over in shock. Eric leaned close to me and put his lips right next to my ear.

"You should have helped him when you had the chance," he whispered. Eric's voice sounded suddenly ragged, but I was in too much pain and shock to really register it. He pushed me toward the fire. I landed heavily in my chair, knocking Eric's crock onto the floor, where it shattered into a hundred pieces.

"Clarence would never give him what he wanted. Too noble. Too knightly," Eric snarled. He stalked through the room, picking up knick-knacks and heaping scorn on them with his eyes before throwing them away. "But surely you'll help. If only to save your friend!"

"What the hell, Eric," I squeaked. He whirled on me. "What are you doing?"

"What am I doing? I am taking what is mine. What should have been mine from the beginning. Why did they take you? You, of all people! This should have been Eric's domain! Not yours. Never yours."

"Well, we're going to have to talk about that later," I said, finally getting my breath back. "Maybe when you're in a better mood."

I stood up, drawing my sword from where it lay next to the chair, and slung the heavy scabbard across the room. Because this wasn't Eric. I should have known right from the beginning. Eric would have used more adjectives.

My empty scabbard slammed into the faux Eric's face, breaking his nose and spraying the room with blood. He screeched and fell back toward the door. I pounced. My sword sliced through the air, dancing off his knife and throwing sparks in the gloom. I shoved him back and elbowed him in the face.

Faux-Eric had a second knife. It appeared from under his robes (the illusion of a bard's costume was fading before my eyes, to be replaced by grayish robes that covered pale, gaunt flesh) and flashed in front of my face. I leaned back, off balance, giving him the chance to wrench his knife away from my blade and attack again. It was all I could do to get the forte of my sword in the way, catching the blade with the crossguard. I fell backwards, hitting the table with the small of my back. Rolling over the table, I landed on the other side with my sword up. It was a lot cooler than I thought it would be. Eric grinned at me. His teeth were small and pointed.

"You're looking less and less like Eric every second," I said. "So why not drop the act and tell me who the hell you really are?"

"I'm never really anyone, not completely. Maybe I'll be you tomorrow. Maybe not," he said, as though we were discussing what to have for dinner, rather than the fact that he was trying to kill me. "It doesn't really matter, does it? You won't be around to see it happen."

We circled the table, guards up, Eric's daggers swaying back and forth like cobras looking for the perfect time to strike. As much as I loved my sword, I had to admit that it wasn't the ideal weapon for this environment. Too long, and too difficult to swing. My butt brushed the fireplace, and I remembered the shield.

I kicked the table between us. Eric dodged it easily, but it gave me just enough time to pull the shield down from its place on the mantle. The enarme strapping whipped across my hand just in time, forming a center grip. Eric pounced, leaping over the upset table. I punched him with the boss of the shield, then followed up with a downward stroke with my sword, sliding the blade along the edge of the shield. He faded back, wary eyes on my blade. Backing toward the door, I kept the sword close to my waist, point resting against the shield. I had to get him outside, in the open, where I could swing my blade around like a maniac, as was my way.

"We've hardly started, and already you're trying to get away? Come play, Sir John of Rast. Come and die!"

"Heroes can't die in their own domain," I said, with a lot more confidence than I felt.

"Clarence said that, too. But there are things worse than dying, hero," Eric snarled. His body popped and strained, as his arms grew longer, and his back became stooped. The daggers in his hands looked more and more like talons by the second. "You should ask him about that. If you ever see him again."

The Eric-thing leapt at me. There wasn't a lot of room inside the cabin to maneuver. Panic seized me, and I brought my shield up, then staggered back when he slammed into it. Claws scrambled around the edges of the shield, scratching at my face and shoulder. I triggered the panels on that side, smacking the creature back and buying myself a little space. I tried to drag my sword into the fight, but every time I swung, Eric was somewhere else. Finally, I forced him toward the fire and settled into a solid guard.

"I'm starting to think we're not friends anymore, Eric," I said. The creature cackled.

"Were we ever? He sees the way you look at him, the way you listen to his stories. He knows what you think of him. But I'll never leave him, not like you did. I'll never leave him! He's the perfect vessel!"

"We'll see about that," I said. I shuffled forward, thrusting my sword in a series of short strikes, filling the space between us with dangerous steel. The creature jumped back, but there was no place to go. His foot went into the fire, and he yelped in pain. Immediately, any illusion that this thing was Eric, could ever have been Eric, disappeared like a morning fog. The flames turned its skin to ash.

Enraged, the creature threw itself at me, heedless of its own safety. I flicked my sword sideways and landed a good blow, points in the old system, but not enough to kill. The tip of the sword glanced off its arm, stuttered across its chest, then slipped free. The blood that came out was black as pitch, hissing against the wooden floor. The acrid smell of burning gore sent me reeling. The creature shoved me aside and ran out the door.

It no longer looked like Eric. Hell, it no longer looked like a human at all. The creature that fled from me wasn't wearing gray robes, it was a bundle of gray robes wearing the scraps of a human. A hollow arm flapped limply from its neck like a scarf, and tattering layers of graying skin trailed along the ground. When I grabbed at it, a tuft of crumbling hair came away in my hand. It looked back at me with a dozen faces, each one stacked inside the other, like masks hanging on a peg. I wouldn't have known it was the same creature, if one of those masks hadn't been Eric's face, and a bunch more I didn't recognize. It laughed with a hollow voice.

"What's the matter, little man? See something you don't like?"

I punched at it with the edge of my shield. The hollow face crumbled, and suddenly Eric was back, just for a second. He looked around the room with wide eyes and clear shock. When he saw me, he nearly screamed.

"John! John where the hell am I? John, you've got to help—"

And then the monster's face returned, pale eyes and needle teeth. It snapped at me, then barreled through the door and was gone, disappearing into the rain like mist. I shook myself out of my horrified stupor. I wasn't sure what I had just seen, but I was glad it was gone. I slammed the door, then looked around the cabin. Every piece of furniture was broken. The floor and ceiling were spattered with stew and the monster's burning blood. Even the crocks were shattered. I sighed and sat down heavily in the ruin of my chair.

My best friend was either a monster or in trouble. And all I had to do was figure out which it was and save him. Or kill him.

Or both.

CHAPTER TWENTY
WAKING UP ON THE WRONG SIDE

I braced the front door with one of the chairs from the kitchen table, then passed a fitful night in the embrace of my lounge chair, sword in one hand and shield across my chest like a blanket. In the morning...it was still night. But at least the rain had stopped.

I stood up and stretched, or at least I tried to. Remember what I said about not sleeping in your armor? This is why. I couldn't feel my hands, my arms, my legs, my feet, and portions of my head. I don't know if you've tried to stand when you're that numb. I certainly hadn't, and promptly fell on my face. I felt my nose pop, and a warm spray of blood started to trickle down my face.

I found a rag in the kitchen that I promptly ruined. The bloodflow eventually stopped, and I became steadily aware of my surroundings. The pot of stew was gone, replaced by a sizzling rasher of bacon and a kettle of the strongest tea I've ever smelled. I fell into it, not even bothering to carry my breakfast into the next room, just shoving bacon and tea into my face while standing over the sink. I splashed cold water from the basin on my face, then wiped the skillet clean with a chunk of warm bread.

"Okay, this is worth it," I said. "Give me food like this every morning, and I'll suffer an assassination attempt any time."

The cabin grew warmer, as though it were blushing, and I felt a smothering happiness waft down from the rafters. But as much as I liked it here, it was time to get back to the mundane. I know I was supposed to stay here and get more in touch with my mythic self, but frankly I needed to get home and tell Esther what I had seen. Maybe murder-Eric was part of the domain, but I suspected not. And he had mentioned Clarence. Surely Esther would want to know about that.

Thing was, Esther had never talked to me about how to leave my domain. Maybe that's something that would have come out in the training, or maybe she expected me to figure it out. Learn by failing. But I didn't have time for that. I needed to get back to MA, tell them what I knew about Eric, and get on with the business of saving my friend.

I packed a leather satchel with the remainder of the bread and a wedge of soft, orange cheese, along with a waterskin filled from the basin and a wool blanket, in case I got stuck in the forest. I gave one last look around the bedrooms, then went outside. There was no lock on the front door. That would take some getting used to, but in theory there wasn't anyone else here.

"A theory that's already been proven wrong, of course, but..." I gave the cozy cabin one last look, then set off into the forest.

I had some theories about how I was going to get out of here. Clarence's domain had an established trail, directly connected to the front gate of that cartoonishly large castle, always patrolled by the resident dragon, Kyle. It was part of the schtick. A knight and his dragon. But that wasn't my gig, and it wasn't the gig with this domain. So what was?

I was the kind of guy who didn't do stuff, mostly because it was different. I wasn't a coward, but I was stubbornly uninterested in the outside world. I spent a lot of time not fitting in, and that had created a barricade of fear around my childhood; fear of rejection, fear of ridicule, fear of even getting noticed. I was afraid a lot of the time. Which is why the world of dragons and knights and castles appealed to me. There was something comforting about a house with stone walls, a suit of armor, and a visor that covered your face. I could be anonymously brave, and just as anonymously afraid under my steel suit.

Which is why I didn't get that fantasy when creating my own domain. That was Clarence, and always would be. I was something else. I was the guy who had to face his fears and overcome them, so other folks could face their fears as well.

Hence the constant night, the forest full of monsters, the sky that flickered with leather wings and distant howls, with just enough light that my eyes were fooled into seeing things that weren't there and blinded to the dangers that were. It was a trial, a place to come to sharpen my bravery, not by being a safe place, but by being a dangerous place. No one gains courage in the embrace of crushing safety, but in the face of overwhelming terror.

That was all good to know. But what did it mean for my escape plan? What was the way out of a realm of constant fear?

Courage, I thought. So I wandered the forest looking for something to be scared of. I found what I was looking for at the top of a waterfall. Now, I'm not a terrible swimmer, but I'm not the kind of swimmer who can survive a dip in icy water while wearing full armor. I'm not sure anyone can survive that, despite the hours I've spent exploring deep sea caverns in various videogames, all while wearing plate mail, carrying a spare set of armor for my healing spec, and lugging around three million gold pieces, twelve platters of spicy shrimp surprise, and a sack full of shattered crystal medallions, which I was hoarding to buy that sweet reputation mount. In short, gaming had not prepared me for the unreal world.

The waterfall was about forty feet high, and I could see a deep, rocky pool at the bottom, barely visible through the cloud of spray. The fall could kill me, a rock could kill me, or I could drown. Hell, I could do all three. Or maybe, just maybe, I could hit the deepest part of the pool, drag myself out from under the pummeling waterfall, and crawl to the shore. It was possible.

"Bloody unlikely, but possible." I stood at the top of the deluge staring down at certain death. "The point is courage, not suicide. I mean, I could just stick this sword down my throat and stand on my head if I wanted to kill myself." I shied away from the edge, bounced on the balls of my feet a couple times, then rushed forward. My heart stopped halfway there, and I pulled up short. "Nope, nope, no . . . no way. This is a terrible idea." My sudden stop dislodged a handful of stones, and they were still falling when I looked over the edge. "That doesn't look like forty feet. That's more than . . . they're still going. Damn it, why are they still falling!" The stones disappeared into the mist, and I was left alone with my incalculable fear and an unpleasant drop. I took a deep breath. There it was. Complete terror. Absolute, knee-buckling fear. There was no way I was doing this.

Three steps and it was over. The edge was closer than I thought, so my foot was still reaching for stone when I found nothing but air. I got to a good speed in those three steps, so I cleared the waterfall and avoided being dashed against the stones. My eyes wanted to squeeze shut, but the point of this whole exercise was courage, so I forced them open, staring with grim determination at the rapidly approaching ground. The pond was the color of carved agate, a jewel set in a ring of broken rocks. It was coming fast. I clasped my hands together and held them over my head, staring down my death. The impact, when it came, was a cold hammer against my skin.

I immediately knew this was a mistake. The driving roar of the waterfall pinned me to the bottom of the pool. The air squeezed out of my lungs, and the force of my landing was still humming through my bones. I blinked, but there was nothing but darkness. I was dying. I could feel the cold oblivion creeping into my limbs.

Maybe death would be a relief. Let's be honest, I'm not really cut out for the hero business. Maybe if I just lay here and let the water crush me into a pulpy, cowardly, worthless . . .

Fuck that. That's what old John would do. Mundane John. And I was no longer that guy. Not because I finally had a cool sword, or because I had killed a dragon or fought off a storm harpy or even briefly walked past a super-hot Valkyrie. Not because I was part of a team of miracle workers, all of whom seemed to believe I was capable of miracles myself, despite all contrary evidence. No, I wasn't going to die here because I didn't want to, and I was going to do something about it.

I pushed myself up off the floor and started crawling forward. I had no idea which way the shore was, or if I was dragging myself deeper into the pond, but I didn't really have a choice. The pressure was incredible. It was all I could do to get a few inches between my chest and the rocky bottom. My legs were completely numb, but I kept sending them signals to kick, to push, to drive. I made progress. My lungs were burning, and my head was a fuzzy cloud of pain and determination, but I kept going. I. Kept. Going.

The darkness started to fade. Either I was getting closer to the surface, or I was finally seeing that tunnel of light people always talked about. The pressure on my back let up, so maybe I was getting out from under the waterfall, or maybe my body was losing the last traces of feeling. I could see my hands. They were bloody rags against the gravel of the pool, but I could definitely see. I was hunched over, rather than crushed flat, and the weight of my armor was the only pressure on my shoulders. Scrambling forward, the sound started to change around my head, and then my face broke through the shining surface of the water.

I was alive. Because that's what I do in the face of fear. I survive.

I stumbled out of the door Esther had pushed me through the day before. I was soaked from head to toe. I fell to the floor and emptied a gallon of water from my lungs, sputtering and vomiting and crying the contents of my body onto the stone floor. Finally, I was empty, and lay there gasping for breath and gathering my dignity. I needn't have bothered. A soft giggle brought my attention to the rest of the room. I wasn't alone.

The whole team was gathered. Esther stood at the end of the table, with Matthew and Tembo on either side. Bethany was several chairs away, and the closest to me. She was just covering her mouth . . . the source of the giggle. I stood stock upright and said, "What's so damned funny, Beth?" Except I didn't, because my lungs were recently full of water, so when I opened my mouth a jet of gray sludge came out, along with a chorus of burps. Bethany went down hard, floored by her own amusement.

"You're not looking so hot there, champ," Tembo said. His brows were knit in concentration, as though he was trying to remember if I usually breathed water, or if this was unusual for me. "Y'alright?"

"I'm fine," I gasped, hands on knees, staring down at the contents of the bottom of the pond, along with several small fish and bits of stew. I glanced back up at the saint.

Then I stared at Matthew for a while.

I wouldn't have recognized him without his hair, and because his costume generally matched the dingy white blazer and blue jeans I had seen him in earlier, though of a more medieval cut. A cream half-cape draped his shoulders, and the rest of his outfit was brown and gray, very similar to a priest's vestments if priests regularly had to run marathons as part of their duties. But that's not why I had trouble recognizing the saint named Matthew.

Matthew's face was hidden behind a featureless steel mask that sat close to his skin, while a high collar covered his neck and tucked into the bottom of the front part of the plate. Thick leather gloves protected his hands. Not an inch of Matthew's skin showed. But it was the blank steel of the mask that bothered me the most. It was like staring at an empty canvas.

"What's the deal with the mask, man?" I asked. Matthew mumbled something, but it was difficult to understand.

"Our saint has been in the presence of his radiance, if only briefly," Tembo said. "Believe me, if he wasn't covered up, you couldn't bear to look at him." Matthew mumbled something else, and Tembo waved him off. "Not like that. And use your divine voice, Matthew. No one can hear you." He turned in my direction. "His skin glows, Sir John. Like fire."

"I swear there's a cancer risk involved," Bethany mumbled. Matthew sat back and turned his head in her direction.

"You let me worry about that," he said, more clearly this time. His voice almost seemed to echo off the stones, though it wasn't terribly loud. "I heal faster than I burn."

At that, my stomach did a quick flip against my intestines, and I leaned forward again.

"Oh, God, I think I'm going to be sick," I said. Bethany laughed again, and I looked up miserably. "What's so funny?"

"There's a fish in your boot," she said. "It's staring at me."

I looked down. The fish blinked at me, nonplussed by its current circumstances. I pulled it free and tossed it on the table.

"My contribution to the meal," I said.

Esther walked past me to look at the door from which I had just emerged. Glancing back, I saw that the rough wood of the door was newly decorated. A cast iron shield hung like a door knocker, and a banner of dark blue and gray draped across the archway. The door was still open, and I could hear the roar of the waterfall. Esther pulled the door shut, then ran a finger over the black face of the shield.

"Hm. Warden. I was a warden once, before..." her voice trailed off with a note of unaccustomed uncertainty. She looked over at me. "Before. Good luck with that. I was hoping you might replace Clarence, but apparently not." She looked at the door next to mine and chuckled. "And Chesa has clearly found her way to the courts. No surprise there."

The other door had an iron tree on it, but instead of leaves, the boughs were hung with arrows.

I nodded, then looked back at my shield.

"What does that mean? Warden?"

"Guardian, bastion, bulwark . . . they're all the same. You protect the team. Clarence was more offence, you're more defense," she said. "Not as glamorous. But important."

"Can we stop talking like Clarence is dead," Bethany said. "And can we do something about this bloody fish!"

She drew her knife and stabbed at the flopping trout, burying her blade a good inch into the table with each strike. The fish slapped its way across the table.

"Let's not be cruel." Tembo stood and took the fish in both hands, then drew his palms together. The fish disappeared. "Did you find your domain? Is it mostly fish?"

"No, it's . . . it's kind of frightening, actually," I said. "I don't like it. Can I use yours?"

"You would like mine even less," Tembo said.

"Point is, you got your domain up and running," Esther said. "But you're back kind of early. Training not go well?"

"I don't know what going well would look like," I said. "But I do know that someone . . . something, actually, tried to kill me. And it looked like Eric Cavanaugh."

This didn't have the effect I was hoping it would. Esther nodded sagely, Bethany was still recovering from her fits of laughter, and Matthew and Tembo just stared at me.

"That's what domains do. Conjure tests to sharpen your mythic identity," Esther said. "Every hero has to go through a series of trials to reach their full potential. Your domain just keeps that cycle of your journey on repeat. I suspect you have some issues with your friend that might need to be addressed in therapy, but I'm sure—"

"No, you're not listening. It really was Eric. I mean, it really wasn't him, it was a monster that looked like Eric. But it knew things only Eric would know. And after its cover was blown, it started referring to Eric in the third person. And it knew about Clarence!"

That got their attention. I had to relate the whole fight, moment by moment, at least three times before they would settle down. By then I was starting to shiver. Finally, Esther noticed my discomfort and sat me down in front of the fire.

"Get out of those clothes. Tem, one of your cloaks or something?" The mage did something with his robes, a flourish and bow, and was suddenly holding a sturdy cloak in his hands.

"I'm more than a wardrobe, you know," he grumbled quietly.

"I know, I know, but it's such a good trick," Esther said, taking the cloak. She held it up so I had a modicum of privacy. I stripped fast, then wrapped myself in the cloak. It smelled like dry grass and beaten dust. When I was situated, Esther leaned against the table and started thinking out loud.

"So, the thing that got to Clarence came for you, too. I hope Chesa—"

"Oh my God, Chesa!" I shouted, standing up a little faster than the cloak would allow. It took Matthew's hand to keep me from falling into the fire. "She's still in her domain! We should go save her!"

"We're doing no such thing," Esther said, gesturing to the door from which I had emerged. "Both of your domains are still hot. She's fine. Or at least, she's better off than Clarence. For now, that will have to do."

"Sounds like a fetch, doesn't it," Tembo said gravely. "That's some serious business."

"Is that a dog joke?" I asked.

"No, he's right," Esther said swiftly. "A Fetch, more commonly called a doppelganger, or the Twin Stranger. That didn't come from your domain. It was sent. By someone who has access to Eric. Or his memories, at least."

"Memories? He could be dead?" I asked. Esther and Tembo exchanged grave looks, but it was Matthew who answered.

"If he's lucky. Getting a bit of your soul spliced into a Fetch is nasty business. Devil stuff." He shook his head. "Not the kind of thing I can heal."

"Then we need to help him. Eric . . . the Fetch, I mean . . . said that he hid in the woods after the dragon attack. And when he tried to find his way back to the parking lot, he couldn't find it." I turned to Esther. "Maybe he was sucked into some part of the unreal?"

"Maybe, but it doesn't make a lot of sense," Esther said thoughtfully. "Someone pushed Kracek over the edge. Made him manifest while the two of you were fighting. And that same someone has now attacked both Clarence and you in your domains. So they're after something. But what?"

"Could be us. They might have been trying to draw us there. We have plenty of enemies in the unreal," Bethany said.

"But there was no resistance. No fight. Just Kracek," Tembo said. "He was an asshole, but he never wanted to destroy Knight Watch."

"Well, whoever it is, they have Eric. And we need to get him back," I said. "I know I'm new to the hero game, but it feels like saving your friends is top of the list."

"He's right. We find this Eric loser and we save him from whatever's gone wrong in his life," Bethany said. "And hopefully the assholes behind it will be there too. And we give them the fight of their lives."

"Great," I said. "So how do we do that? How do we find Eric?"

"Easy," Bethany said with the kind of smile you might find on a hungry tiger. "We tie you to the roof of the car and drive around until your nose turns red." I flinched back.

"Don't worry," Esther said. "She didn't mean that literally."

CHAPTER TWENTY-ONE
S.S. HANGNAIL

She meant that almost literally. What ended up happening is that they asked me a bunch of questions about Eric, then Esther went away for a while. When she came back, they put a blindfold on me and led me through the halls of MA. Eventually I smelled exhaust and engine oil and heard the familiar sound of tires squealing in the distance.

"This is the garage," I said.

"Yeah. Owen and Gabby are almost here. They're going to follow behind with a containment team," Esther said. Seconds later I heard their car hit the tarpaulin flap and screech to a halt. "Good. We're ready. John?"

"Yeah?" I was getting annoyed with being blindfolded but had learned not to complain. Outside my head at least.

"Have you forgotten how to drive yet?"

"Nope. Like riding a bike. I can manage." I pulled at the blindfold, only to have my hand smacked away. "Ow! What are we doing here?"

"You're going to drive something like a car. But the less you think of it as a car, the better this will go. And you can't look where you're going."

"This is not going to go well," I said. "Unless it's a Tesla."

"Nik heads up his own team. Completely different mythology," Esther said. "Just get in, have a seat, and relax. But don't think about where you're going. And don't forget you're driving. And don't think about zombies, or horror movies, or girls. And try—"

"God, lady, I get it. Think about everything and nothing. Pay very close attention to not doing anything and have your mind so blank it's completely full." I felt forward, found what was probably the edge of a car door, and slowly patted my way into the seat. The shocks had a lot of give in them. But at least there was a wheel. The smell of ripe feet wafted up around me. "We're all totally going to die. I'm sure you're aware of that."

"We have made our peace," Matthew said from somewhere behind me. The conveyance swayed and dipped. Esther tapped me on the shoulder.

"We're all in. Get going."

"How do I—"

"By doing it," Esther answered.

"Right. Just doing. Every motivational poster ever." I gripped what must have been the steering wheel and settled back. There were pedals under my feet. I pushed one of them.

"God ALMIGHTY!" Tembo screamed. "Are you trying to kill us?"

"SORRY! SORRY! I JUST—"

The rest of the team burst out into laughter. Esther shushed them.

"You're doing fine," she said. "Just go."

I went. Don't ask me where. I just know where we ended up, and what it looked like when we got there.

But we went to the mall. And we were flying.

The Caneville Valley mall was an anomaly unto itself. To begin with, there isn't a place named Caneville in driving distance of the mall's cherry-pink walls, and the nearest valley is an erosion ditch that cuts through the crumbling parking lot. Once fortified by nationally branded department stores and populated by armies of teenagers anxious to use their freshly minted driver's licenses, the Caneville Valley Mall has fallen on hard times. The anchor stores are gone, the food court has gone to seed, and the teenagers have abandoned cars for cellphones and selfies. Makes for a quiet mall. And quiet malls are creepy as hell.

We came at the mall from above, about twenty minutes after we left Mundane Actual. We were riding a Viking longboat made of toenails. Which explained the smell, I suppose.

"This seems about right," I said when Esther loosened my blindfold. I snatched my hands off the wheel, which was a normal car wheel, attached by a series of pulleys and gears to the tiller, while the makeshift pedals at my feet ran the sails. The ship listed heavily to the left. Esther grabbed the wheel.

"We've been circling this place for the last ten minutes," she said. "What we're looking for must be inside. You want me to land?"

"I want anything that gets me off this thing. Do we have parachutes? Because I'll jump. Like, right now."

"Just chill out for a second. We'll be down soon enough."

"Looks like a fortress of some kind," Tembo said, peering down at the mall. "Do your people still build castles?"

"Only the kind that distribute cheese," I answered. "No, it's a shopping mall. Like a market, only sterile and angsty."

Esther took us down. We landed next to a pair of minivans, and across from the food court. I swung down the ladder (still toenails) and tried to gather my nerves.

"Yeah, this has to be a mistake," I said. There were only about a dozen cars parked in the lot, spread out across seven acres of weed-cracked asphalt. The mall rose before us like a mountain range painted the color of strawberry ice cream that has started to curdle in the sun, its walls stripped of once familiar store names, the only remnant of those missing signs a slightly less-filthy spot on the ramparts. I looked around the parking lot. "We're not going to find monsters here. This place is about as magical as a court subpoena."

"Do not underestimate the power of abandoned places," Tembo said as he climbed down from the boat. His deep blue robes unfolded voluminously around him as he straightened. "This is the storehouse of a million dreams. Just because the dreamers have woken up doesn't mean their visions have left the world."

"Don't know that I want to cross swords with the dreams of a million teenagers," I muttered. I stretched out my shoulders, trying to get the armor to settle back into place. Plate mail was not made for flying. There was a place in the middle of my back that I was sure I would never feel again, and my left leg was coming up with new and exciting ways to cramp. I walked back and forth in the abandoned lot while the others collected their gear and got ready for whatever it was we were planning on doing.

"I'm staying with the ship and coordinating with Gabby and her team," Esther said. She nodded to the entrance of the parking lot. A remarkably inconspicuous car pulled across the road, and Owen got out, directing traffic away from the mall. "I'll ring if we need to pull out fast."

"Or just in case someone notices that a longship of human body parts is parked next to their minivan. You know. As typically happens at the Caneville Valley mall," I said.

"The point is that this could be a place of considerable power. We won't know until we get in there and start peeling back the layers of reality. So keep your eyes open, and your sword ready," Matthew said. He popped the trunk and rummaged through the equipment. "And ... I forgot my censer. I need to go back."

"No. Not having you on hand for Kracek nearly cost Clarence his life," Bethany said. "You're going in without it."

"I wondered why I didn't see you at the faire," I said. "Were you seriously on an errand? Running out to the corner store for some milk or something?"

"The incense heightens my awareness of the brilliant. Without it, I'm going in blind."

"Might want to cut some eye holes in that mask, then," I said with a smirk. Bethany chuckled, but Matthew only shook his head.

The rest of us got our gear out of the car and strapped up. I had my new shield, along with the sword from my domain. The rest of my armor was slapdash, the bits and pieces of armor and heraldry that Esther had been able to scrounge from the storeroom, but the rest of the team looked like professional ... something. Cosplayers? Employees of Medieval Times? Reenactors with CEO budgets and Tolkien aspirations? The point is that I felt a little out of place as we started the march into the mall, not because I was carrying a sword, but because my cuisses didn't quite match my sabatons, my pauldrons were mismatched, and I was missing a vambrace on my left arm. Nerd problems.

We walked up to the food court entrance, past the empty fountain and the cracked trellis of the beer garden. A faded sign welcomed us to Caneville, *Where Fun Comes to Life!*

"Any fun around here died a while ago," Bethany said. "I always hated these places. Glad to see them rotting away."

"Maybe the fun is coming back to life. Zombie fun," I said. Tembo hissed at me.

"Not the kind of joke we make, Rast," he said. "I nearly lost an arm to a possessed merry-go-round once. Damned horses had teeth like saw blades."

"That is disturbing. I am disturbed. I'm beginning to wonder about my career choice, my friends."

"You don't pick Knight Watch," Bethany said. "Knight Watch happens to you, and you try to make the best of a weird situation."

"Good talk," I said. "Let's get this over with. Are we sure Eric's in here?"

"You were driving," Matthew said. I bit my tongue. Everyone knew I was blindfolded. If I wanted to point out the ridiculousness of this situation, I shouldn't be talking to the guy with a steel mask and glowing skin.

Inside, the Caneville Valley Mall was as sterile and as clean as a desiccated body left in the desert, picked over by years of rodents and bleached white by the burning sun. The scattered planters held the dry husks of palm trees, their leaves withered in the half-light of the mall. Of the dozen food vendor stalls, only four remained open, though I couldn't see any employees. Flickering neon signs offered Kebob Paradise, or Fried Fries on French Flapjacks, surrounded by exclamation points of questionable sincerity. I averted my eyes.

"The days of fast food are behind us," I muttered. "Thank the gods."

"You'll miss it eventually," Matthew said. His voice still rang with divine power, though I was learning to hear him through the mask, as well. "We eat pretty well, but at some point, you're going to want something that isn't boiled or burned."

"There are monasteries that live on beer," Tembo said. "You could give that a try if you don't like my cooking."

"Why do you think I'm so chill all the time?" Matthew answered.

"Can we get on task, people?" Bethany asked. "We're not here to recover precious artifacts of nostalgia. Someone in this place is screwing with the unreal, and I for one want to rearrange their insides."

"And save my friend," I said. Bethany shrugged.

"Yes, the mission," Tembo said. "Form up. Rast, you're on point."

"The guy who doesn't know what he's doing? Cool. Tell my mom I loved her."

"You're not really on point, idiot," Bethany said. "You're just the first one in line. If there's trouble, the rest of us will see it long before it eats you."

"Eats me," I repeated. "Cool, cool, yeah. Eats me. No problem."

With my nerves thoroughly ruffled, I started through the food court and into the depths of the mall. The others fell in line behind me, with Bethany darting back and forth to the sides, stalking through the shadows of empty storefronts. More than once I thought I saw her ahead of me, her form flickering among dead palm trees or reflected in the overhead mirrors, but every time I looked back, she was still behind me. I shook it off.

We emerged from the food court and into the labyrinthine corridors of the greater mall. Most of the stores were closed, and the few functioning lights took on an oppressive quality, like the unsettling green of a storm cloud. We passed a brightly lit toy store whose interior chirped and sproinged, but I saw neither customers nor employees. Winds moaned along the upper concourse, and the dappled sunshine coming through the peaked skylights turned sour. My heart was in my throat.

"There were cars in the parking lot, right?" I asked, confirming I hadn't imagined it. "So where are those people?"

"We're getting into the strange," Tembo answered. "I'm not sure why this didn't show up on the actuator, but this is clearly an anomaly. No place is this empty."

"You haven't been in a mall recently," I mumbled, but he was fundamentally right. The mall felt beyond empty. It felt evacuated, as though a pestilence had swept through and consumed all life. No longer concerned with running into a security guard, I drew my sword and huddled behind my shield. Creeping forward, I kept my eyes active and my balance forward. The air smelled like a fight waiting to happen.

We found our first body around the corner. Like everything else in this place, it was stripped of any humanity. Bones and clothes, the skull grinning up at the ceiling, bony hands gripping three shopping bags and a set of car keys.

"There's one," I said. "But none of those cars have been here long enough for a body to erode this much. I think." Truthfully, I didn't know anything about rates of decay of human flesh. It just didn't seem natural for a skeleton to be here. Nothing about this felt natural. Which was kind of the point, I suppose. "Do you think they're all like this?"

"The dead usually are," Tembo said.

"I mean, do you think they're all dead. All those people whose cars are waiting outside."

"That's a question that's going to answer itself," Bethany said. "But not if we keep standing around."

Swallowing hard, I stepped over the body and continued down the corridor. We were getting toward the middle of the mall. Some part of me expected to find the source of this strangeness at the heart, like a spider in its web. But the confluence of hallways was empty, other than the flying stairs that led to the upper concourse, along with elevators, a dry fountain, and a vendor's cart selling jigsaw puzzles. There was a body on the stairs, spread out and disjointed, as if the victim had fallen apart while fleeing upwards. I stared at it for a long time.

"We need to pick a corridor and clear it," Bethany said. There were three ways to go, each twisting out of view within a few stores. "That means splitting up."

"That never works out," Matthew said. "We should stick together. Let's try this one."

"You can if you want. But Rast is too slow for me. I do better on my own, anyway." She turned and marched toward one of the other paths. "I'm going to scout this way. I'll scream if I need you."

"Bethany, wait—" Tembo said, but the girl flickered and disappeared. I saw a sketchy image of her leaping up to the walkway, her body stretched thin as it arced through the air. She was gone in a heartbeat.

"Impatient child," Tembo spat. "We'll have to follow her, now."

"No, she's right," Matthew said calmly. "We'll only slow her down. Come on." He started toward the chosen corridor, and I followed, but Tembo hung back. The big mage stared in the direction Bethany had gone. "She's a big girl, Tem," Matthew said. "She can manage. And if she can't, well, I'm full of light."

Tembo grimaced, then shook his head and strode across the empty fountain. Matthew and I hurried to catch up.

I immediately assumed we had made the right choice, or perhaps the very, very wrong one. The sterile linoleum floors and fluorescent lights quickly devolved. The ground was covered in a loose scree of dry leaves that swirled in lazy eddies under our feet. The air took on a fetid quality. Even the light turned sickly. I stopped in front of an open storefront.

"Aeric's Alchemystery," I read. "That feels like we're going in the right direction."

The sign was painted wood, with a shingle that depicted a boiling green beaker. Inside, all manner of stills, cauldrons, flasks, and potions bubbled and hissed, emitting a noxious stink that hung in a low cloud over the floor. Strange music pinged and tinkled from the back of the shop. I saw movement. "There's someone inside!"

"For their sake, I hope they wake up in one piece, hopefully in a Sephora," Matthew said. "We have to press on."

"Should we go back for Bethany?" I asked.

"She will catch up to us. Or she won't. Come on." Tembo seemed anxious. He clutched his staff in both hands, holding it in front of him like a prow. I caught a look of fear in his eyes.

"Have you seen this kind of thing before?" I asked. "Do you know what's ahead?"

"I have seen everything before," he answered. "Mostly in dreams. And sometimes nightmares. But no, I am not sure of what lies ahead. Sir John, you must take the lead. If we are attacked, neither Matthew nor I can fight hand to hand. You will have to keep them off of us."

"Keep who off of you?" I asked, but he had no answer. Thoroughly unsettled, I started forward.

It wasn't long before we left the mall behind completely. The walls were now stone, covered in twisting vines, lit only by guttering torches and the dim light of the sun, peeking through a fractured roof. The ground underfoot was spongy, and thick fog lurked close to the earth on all sides. We squeezed through a wall of narrow pillars, turning sideways to get past. Beyond them, the air was thick and sour. Blood was hammering through my head, and each breath I took tasted more and more like bile. I was pretty sure I was going to throw up before we found anything interesting.

"There is something ahead of us," Matthew said quite suddenly. I jumped, but Tembo's heavy hand came down on my shoulder to steady me. Swallowing a little bit of my lunch, I looked around, my eyes darting around the corrupted mall. Even with my hair-trigger imagination, I couldn't see anything.

"Are you sure?" I asked, happy that my voice only cracked a single octave.

"Yes. The light is being expelled from this place," Matthew said. He raised one hand and removed his glove. His hand looked like it was carved from glowing marble, except the light was streaming off his fingers like a candle in a stiff breeze. Motes of bright light trailed down the corridor in the direction we had come. "There is great darkness waiting for us. It knows we are coming."

"Now's when we get Bethany, right?" I asked.

"Yes," Tembo said. He turned to look back. His voice boomed louder than any human voice possibly could. "Assassin! Your blade is required!"

No sooner had Tembo spoken than the passage behind us groaned and shook. An avalanche of loose stone tore free from the surrounding walls and started to fill the hallway. I took a step in that direction. Tembo grabbed my arm.

"It is too late," he said gravely.

"But she'll be cut off!"

"Concern yourself with the teeth, rather than the throat," he snapped.

"What? What the hell is that—"

The hallway shook, and I had to grab the mage to stay on my feet. When I looked back, I understood.

The hallway wasn't collapsing. It was closing. What I mistook for pillars were actually teeth. They splintered apart, revealing their true nature, each one as long and thick as a human body, glistening with saliva and sharp as knives. For a brief second, they yawned open, and I thought about dashing past them.

The next heartbeat, they slammed shut with a thunderous crash, with enough force to break stone. The mouth closed around us, and with it, the light was gone. Only the dim illumination from Matthew's exposed hand remained. And then that, too, disappeared.

Everything was darkness.

CHAPTER TWENTY-TWO
MALL ADJUSTED

The darkness broke on the fury of Tembo's flame. The mage drew a swirling cloud of fire out of nothingness, wrapped it around his fist, and shot a spear of light into the air. The cavern was painted in harsh shadows and burning red flame. The heat of the eruption washed over me, forcing me to turn aside.

"Rast, to the front!" Tembo shouted. "You have to keep them off of us!"

"Keep who . . ." my voice trailed off as I whirled around. The sudden light of the flame had blinded me to the darkness. All I could see were shadows upon shadows, and the bright coruscating fire spearing out of the mage's hand. St. Matthew was nowhere to be seen. "Who am I supposed to be fighting?"

My answer came in the form of a whipping tendril. It lashed against my shield, wrapping around the edge and nearly ripping it from my grip. I stumbled forward, left arm nearly to the ground as I fought the shield free from my unseen attacker. Before I could regain my balance, another tendril lashed at my right foot. I screamed in frustration.

A blossom of flame washed over my shoulder. I had a brief glimpse at the creature I was fighting. I was briefly reminded of tree-friend from my domain, but whereas he was a solid trunk of wood, this creature looked like a wall of roots, barely humanoid in shape, with stumpy legs and a broad chest and no head. Its two eyes were vacant holes near its shoulders, and its arms consisted of writhing tendrils of root and vine that branched into dozens of individual

187

whips, prehensile as snakes and twice as fast. Both the lashers attacking me came from the same wrist. Its other arm was drawn back to strike.

Tembo's bolt of fire struck the creature in its drawn-back arm. Flames crawled through the gnarly mass, erupting in clouds of cinder that started new fires elsewhere on its body. It howled, the sound coming from a gaping mouth in its belly, a void that seemed to have no bottom. The shriek chilled my blood. As flames rushed up its arm, the monster released me, and started thrashing its burning limb against the stone floor, raising geysers of blackened roots and ash, limned in burning embers that flew through the air.

"Rast!" Tembo screamed. I tore my eyes away from the burning monster and saw that the creature wasn't alone. Another of its brethren loomed out of the darkness, knocking Tembo to the ground with a branch-like arm. I ran toward him but tripped over the uneven floor and went down.

"Can we get some light in here?" I shouted. My sword had bounced into the darkness, and as I was feeling around for it, I could hear more creatures advancing on us. Their movements sounded like the creaking wood of a forest caught in a windstorm. My fingers closed on the hilt of my sword. I rolled to my feet and lifted the magical shield. I felt safer behind it, much safer than I actually was.

"Let there be!" Matthew said, and there was light. He was standing on top of a pile of rocks, which looked like it had once been one of the mall's planters, now broken granite and moss. The saint had removed his mask. His face was brilliant, shining with the kind of light you might see reflected from the heart of a diamond. It was difficult to look directly into his eyes. Fortunately, I had lots of other things to look at.

The room we were in was narrow and long. There was no sign of the mouth that had closed the way behind us, only a wall of broken rubble and tumbling scree. The only remnants of the mall were neoclassical pillars of crumbling marble in the walls, and the faintest sketch of storefronts between them. Trees grew out of the walls. I once saw the aftermath of an avalanche out west, where a plain of ice had ravaged a forest. Trees poked haphazardly through the broken snow, as though they were trying to reach through a cloud. That's what this looked like. Some of the trees were moving. As I watched, one of them stepped out of the wall, its trunk splitting open into eyes and a mouth, its branches curling down into massive arms, roots boiling underneath until it rose up on two thick legs hardly a foot high. The creature looked at me and roared.

It was not alone. Other than the one attacking Tembo and the flame-wreathed husk of my assailant, at least three of the creatures lurked in the hallway. They advanced on us with the slow patience of the forest.

"Drue-kin," Matthew said. "Guardians of ancient forests in Ireland, and sometimes Wales, though there they are known as..." Matthew pronounced a word devoid of vowels, then paused while one of the creatures tore a stone from the ground and hurled it in his direction, forcing Matthew to duck. "They aren't usually this angry."

"They aren't usually this real," I snapped. "So let's start with that." I hacked at the swarm of tendrils holding Tembo in place. They were as hard as iron, and it took several strong blows to sever them. Tembo fell backwards, and I stepped quickly forward to protect him. "How do we beat them?"

"Fire and steel," Tembo said. "And I'm low on both."

The closest drue lunged forward. They were surprisingly quick over short distances, though the rest of them were lumbering closer as fast as changing seasons. If I could keep them separated, I might stand a chance. I still wasn't clear how I was supposed to kill them, though. Do trees have vital organs?

A swinging branch glanced off my shield, then a tangle of roots slammed into my shoulder, tearing at my armor and scratching my helm. I pulled on the straps in the shield and flipped the shield wide on that side, batting the tendrils away. I slapped my visor shut, which had been open to improve visibility, but immediately regretted it. The drue-kin disappeared, replaced by heavy shadow and a narrow band of vision. I swung wildly, blade landing on tough vines, then dancing off stone. The jolt of the impact ran up my arm. I felt vines close around my chest and start to squeeze. The steel shell of my breastplate groaned. I hammered at the restricting vines with my shield.

"Where's that flame, Tem?" I yelled. His answer was muffled by the thick steel of my helm, but a blast of heat and light was response enough. The pressure on my chest didn't let up, though, and now I could feel it in my ribs. I slashed down, hacking like a maniac until I could draw a comfortable breath.

I stumbled away from the drue-kin, twisting my helm off as I fell. Charred streamers of vine and twisted wood hung from my pauldrons, and the steel was hot to the touch. The seared stump of the creature's arm waved at me ineffectually, but even as I watched, fresh green shoots sprung up from the ashes. It was regrowing its limb.

"Flame's not enough," I said. Tembo didn't answer. I looked back and saw that he was on one knee, his bald head beaded with sweat. The mage's hands were shaking. "Tembo, man, you doing okay?"

"No," he said, and that was it.

"None of us had enough time in our domains," Matthew said. "But we can't let up. I'm sorry, my friend."

The saint spread his hands. An orb of pure light blinked into existence, rolling across the broken floor to surround Tembo. He screamed, quickly biting it off, though his clenched fists and wide eyes spoke of his pain. The orb of light poured into him, shrinking in size as it filled Tembo's flesh with its brilliance. His eyes and teeth glowed, along with his skeleton, bones flashing through flesh like an x-ray. When the light was gone, Tembo stood up. He was sweating blood.

"Finish this, Rast," he said. "Before Matthew kills us all."

I turned back to the drue-kin. A shrub of fresh flowers and bright green leaves sprouted from the creature's gnarled limb. I set about hacking it to pieces. A cloud of chopped greenery flew into the air, the soft branches of the new growth offering little resistance to my hell-forged blade. My blade bounced when I reached the old limb. The drue swung at me with its other arm, but it seemed sluggish, either from the energy needed to grow or because the flames had taken some essential power from it. I danced aside, wincing as the limb tore gouges in the floor, spraying me with shards of stone. I hacked at it while it was on the ground, chopping several ropey strands off its arm. They fell off, writhing like snakes against my boots. The drue pulled the arm back, but I kept at it, hacking and cutting, the bound edge of the limb fraying like cheap rope with each blow. Tendrils tried to weave themselves back together, forming a dozen smaller limbs. I cut these off in a series of quick blows, leaving only the hard core of the limb behind.

"Sword's not made for this!" I shouted. "Does anyone have an axe? Even a hatchet would be better than—"

The drue's other fist punched into my chest. I flew back, sliding past Tembo and into the collapsed ruin at the end of the corridor. The creature lumbered after me. Tembo stepped between us. He pressed his palms into the forest spirit's chest, just below the gaping darkness of its eyes.

"I am sorry, brother. But this is not where you belong," Tembo said. "Return to ash and be reborn."

Flames outlined his hands, and then a tremendous roar filled the air. Fire jetted into the drue-kin, cutting through wood and vine and soul in colors of red and redder. Soon the core of the drue was immolated. The flames looked like a sunset seen through the trunks of a forest, angry fire glimpsed through black trunks. Its eyes and mouth flickered with deep coals, and ember clouds spilled out of its bark as the creature started to collapse. Like a paper doll thrown into the fire, the tendrils of its limbs curled inward, and the trunk turned black as coal. The screaming stopped. The drue-kin settled to the ground, its heart still glowing with bright embers, as hollow as a shadow, and just as dead.

Tembo stepped back. His hands were blistered, and the frenetic energy of his eyes looked now like madness and disease. His chest was heaving.

"I am done. You must handle the rest, Sir John."

"I . . . I can't possibly . . ." There were four, though one was already charred by Tembo's earlier attack. They stood in a circle around their hollow brother, then turned to us and shuffled forward with renewed rage. I twisted the sword in my hand. "Matthew, you need to do something! This is too much!"

"I have my limits," Matthew said. "But such as I have is yours."

I felt the saint's light more than I saw it. The brilliance was harsh, like the coldest winter air. It cut into my skin and filled my head with a stark hum. Up until that moment I had assumed the source of Matthew's power was fundamentally good, but now that it was upon me, I began to wonder. There were limits to good, after all, and this light felt too pure for a human body to bear. But it was too late for me. The brilliance was in my bones.

Everything stopped. I blinked in wonder. The drue-kin lunging at me stood frozen in place, the wild crown of its vines as still as a leaf frozen in clear water. Tembo stood with his back to me, but his clenched fists and the bunched muscles of his jaw might have been carved from wood. Briefly, I wondered if I was also frozen in place, but then I turned around and saw Matthew. It felt strange to move, as though something resisted me, though I could see nothing. Matthew's hand was stretched out toward me, and his face was calm. No, more than calm. The look on his face was that of a man slowly dying, who has made peace with his end, a man who has already seen the worst of life and now looks toward death, and whatever lay beyond. The brilliance of his skin flickered with faceted light, sparkling like distant stars.

"Well, this is a special kind of crazy," I said. My voice echoed in my head, but I couldn't hear myself speaking. My mouth felt strange, like I was chewing something as I spoke. *Air*, I realized. *Not even the air is moving.*

But as soon as I thought it, I could see that I was wrong. Because Tembo was moving ever so slowly, and when I looked back to the drue, I saw that their whip-thin fingers were inching closer. A burning leaf floated slowly toward the ground, the trails of embers crawling through its veins as slow and bright as the lights of a city seen from far above.

Quickly. Matthew's voice filled my head. *Five heartbeats. No more.*

The first beat of my heart shuddered through my chest. One down. I leapt forward.

The air felt like a thick jello that I had to shove my way through. My first few steps were sluggish, but then I got the hang of it, turning slightly sideways to ease my passage through the thickened air. I slithered past the burning husk and sprang into the air, landing hard against the closest of the drue-kin. Its vines gave slightly under my boots. I started to cut, chipping a wedge into its forehead. The outer layers were dry bark and springy wood, its flesh as green as new grass, but as I got deeper in the rings got closer together and the wood turned soft with rot. A final blow tore a huge slab away. It was hollow inside. I stared down at nothing.

"How the hell do you kill this?" I asked, but my voice caught in my throat. There was something in the core, black and glittering, hanging in open space like the filament in a lightbulb. Even with the world slowed down around me, this strap of darkness shimmered and danced. I stabbed down at it. The closer I got, the thicker the air, and my sword slowed to a terrible pace. My heartbeat slammed through my chest again. I could actually feel the blood moving in my veins. I pressed harder, and the tip of my blade touched the darkness. It snapped out, like a candle snuffed.

The drue-kin died. Or worse, the drue-kin had been dead the whole time, but now its body was released from some foul grip. I don't know how I knew. It was moving too slow to fall. All I can say is that something essential left it. I jumped to the ground. The thick air held me aloft, and an idea occurred to me. When I touched down again, I jumped differently, floating through the soup of atmosphere like a dart.

This must look so damned cool, I thought. I drew back my sword, imagining the movie trailer as I flew. Damn, I look amazing!

The second drue-kin drew close. I swung hard, chopping at a point just beneath its eyes, figuring the rotten core must be closest there, based on what I'd seen of its brother. My sword cut into the bark and stopped.

I kept going. My fingers twisted off the hilt, and I started a slow spin through the air, pirouetting past the drue like a child's top flung from its string. I beat against the thick wind, but it was nothing like swimming, and whatever laws governed the stillness didn't award points for cool. I finally touched down, but the force of my landing twisted my ankle. I felt things pop, but for some reason the pain didn't reach me. Steadying myself, I slithered my way back to the tree, dragging my foot. Another beat of my heart. Three. The ratio of killed drue to pulse rate was unacceptable. I had to pick things up. Fast. But how much faster could I possibly move?

I reached my sword and twisted it out of the drue. Bark peeled away. No time to get to the core the same way. I stabbed the sword into the flesh, then leaned into it. The drue-kin's own momentum worked for me, and the unnatural force of Matthew's blessing. The sword sank slowly, so slowly, into the bark. It felt like stabbing loose dirt, each inch taking twice as long as the inch before. I braced the pommel against my chest and shoved.

A jolt went through my body. There was a moment when I could taste darkness, not cold, but empty. I stumbled back and would have fallen if not for the soft cloud of air that surrounded me. A look of pain flashed in the drue-kin's eye, and then its spirit was gone. Heartbeat. I was down to one, and the last drue-kin was still up.

I scrambled for my sword. The hilt was flush with the ruptured bark of the creature's skin, and when I pulled it was as if the whole blade had fused with the wood. I put one foot on the drue-kin's forehead and pulled so hard I thought my head was going to explode. Nothing. The sword was stuck.

I let go and looked around. A weird pressure built in my temples, the precursor to my next heartbeat. Odd what you notice when time stops. The drue-kin was close, but my only weapon was gone, and I was pretty sure I wasn't going to be able to punch a tree until it died.

Just then a shimmer caught my eye. It was like the reflection of light through a prism, just to the side of my head, and more all around. I squinted and looked closer. Light bent madly through the air in a trail that followed my own movements. Compressed air, the oxygen I had shoved out of my way as I flew and ran and stumbled. It formed a tunnel that I had burrowed through. Now that I knew it was there, it was obvious. I could trace it all the way back to where I had been standing when Matthew cast his spell. The closer the tunnel was to that point of origin, the narrower it was.

What's going to happen when that closes? I wondered. *Thunder? Isn't that all thunder is, the collapse of air into the vacuum of lightning? Man, that's going to be loud.* I looked back at the final drue-kin. *Destructively loud.*

Through all of this, I had been keeping my shield edgewise, like a ship turned into the waves. Now I put it in front of me and started running. The resistance was hard, and the faster I ran, the harder it became. But I was shoving great lumps of air out of the way. I ran in circles around the drue-kin, staying as close to its skin as I could, burrowing a tunnel in the air around it. With each step, the shield in my hand got hotter and hotter, until I could feel my knuckles blistering against its surface. I had to duck around the vacuums I had already created, navigating by the shimmer of bent light and the drag on my shield. My veins were swelling, and my legs throbbing, but I kept pushing through.

Thud-whump. My heart beat one last time, and the world came loose from its prison.

I stumbled forward half a step, landing on my crippled ankle and crumpling to the ground. The two dead drue-kin disintegrated, shuffling apart into piles of broken bark and twisted wood. And Matthew took a deep breath as the last of his light faded from his skin, plunging the room into darkness.

I only remember all of this in retrospect. In the moment, the only thing I felt was thunder, and the only noise was my own screaming.

The tunnels of empty air collapsed with a horrific crash. It must have followed my path, because there was a sound like paper ripping, only ten thousand times louder and with the force of a god's hammer. It zipped around the two dead drue-kin, a single line of vacuum collapsing, a final memorial to the fight. But when it reached the last forest spirit, the world crashed in all at once. Even before Matthew's light died, the shattering song reached its crescendo. The force of the blast turned the drue-kin into dust, like a lightning stroke of noise.

And then it reached me. There was no more sound, only the hollow roar of my skull, and pain, such pain. My skin turned to fire, and tears streamed down my face. I gasped for air, but my lungs filled only with bile that burned my ribs and bore a hole in my chest. I dropped my shield and fell to the ground, trying to tear my burning skin off, trying to extinguish the agony of my flesh. But there was no fire, no flame, only the delayed friction of every movement. I went to my knees and started screaming.

CHAPTER TWENTY-THREE
DEEPER IN

Tembo bent and touched my shoulder. I was choking on my tears. Even the soft brush of his hand was like a brand against my skin. He grimaced at me.

"There wasn't time to warn you," he said. "But you want to move as little as possible when Matthew does that."

"No shit!" I said. I stood up, holding my arms away from my body, wincing at the rustle of fabric against my skin. It was like having the world's worst sunburn over every inch of my body, and maybe a few inches inside, too. My lungs certainly felt pretty raw. "How am I supposed to fight if I don't move?"

"That's why I didn't warn him," Matthew said. He left the mask on top of his head. The saint looked pale, even for a man who lives inside a mask, and the beads of sweat streaming down his face shimmered in the torchlight. There was a bare amount of brilliance still in his eyes, but for the most part he looked like anyone else. He shrugged apologetically. "You couldn't get the job done if you knew the rules."

"Thanks a ton," I said. I bent to pick up my sword, which had tumbled from the dying drue-kin, but that sent bolts of pain down my legs and through my back. I froze and let out a long, wheezing breath. "You got any of that healing left?"

"None of your injuries are fatal," he said. "I need to save what little brilliance I have left for more critical patients."

"But we've won, right? The drue-kin are dead."

"Whoever sent them is not," Tembo said. "And this anomaly is still intact. Your friend is somewhere inside. We must press on."

197

"How the hell are we supposed to fight anything else? You're tapped out, Matthew has only a glimmer of hope, and I . . ." I shivered as some new pain flickered through my skin. There was a breeze. It was excruciating. "I'm not exactly at the top of my game."

"And this is what makes us heroes," Tembo said. He slapped me on the shoulder, nearly blacking me out. When I was able to open my eyes again, he was staring right at me. "We do difficult things. Now stop crying and start fighting it. The pain is not going to go away."

This sounded way too much like the jock-tough bullshit my father used to peddle before he developed a gut and an increasingly atrophying social consciousness. I didn't respond well to this kind of thing. I was just about to tell Tembo off when he turned and walked away. Matthew nodded to me sadly.

"He's right. Suffer and die or suffer and live. But bitching about it isn't going to solve anything."

"What the hell happened to holy mercy?" I snapped.

"Mercy would let you die here. You don't want to see my mercy."

He followed Tembo. The pair of them rapidly disappeared, the light of the mage's torch barely enough to illuminate the ground around them. I realized that I was either going to be left in the dark, or I was going to pick up my sword and follow them. If I could find it.

Pain coursed through my body as I felt around in the dark. By the time I had retrieved it, the torch was a mere pinprick in the shadows. I limped hurriedly after them, tripping over the shattered remains of the drue-kin in my haste. My ankle hurt badly enough that the pain in the rest of my body started to recede in my mind. Not because it hurt less, but because it wasn't going to hurt any more than it already did.

"So what now?" I asked through gritted teeth.

"Your friend is still here, still in need of our help. We find him and get him out. If the anomaly is still intact after we extract him, we will have to come back," Tembo said.

"I hope Bethany is alright."

"You don't worry about her. You worry about you. Bethany can handle herself," Matthew said. "Besides. She's not the one trapped in a hell-mall with no light and little hope. Not yet, at least."

"Better and better," I muttered. They ignored me. We walked in sullen silence.

I swear we must have already walked the length of the mall at least twice. The corridor had been slowly widening, and now the walls on either side were outside the circle of light cast by Tembo's torch. By the echo of our footsteps and the breeze swirling around our heads, I could tell we were in a pretty big cavern. Tembo drew us to a sudden halt.

"This is it," he said, lifting the torch. "This is the source."

"I don't see anything." The gloom in front of us was impenetrable. Even the torchlight seemed to bounce off it.

"Because there is nothing to see. Literally nothing." Tembo motioned to Matthew. "My flame cannot penetrate this. Dispel the shadows, Saint."

"You're sure? If one of us gets hurt, I won't have any light left to heal with."

"This is the way forward," Tembo said. Matthew shrugged and stepped forward.

A beam of light emerged from his chest and pierced the veil of darkness. The shadows swirled around it, slowly dissipating as the glowing shaft bore through them. The murk parted, revealing what was behind.

It was a bookstore. The display windows were broken, and dark vines spread along the walls, spidering out into the corridor. Mildewed stacks of books tumbled out the doors, and a haphazard barricade of shelves choked the entrance. There was no light inside. I chuckled.

"Man. We're deep in the unreal. A bookstore in a mall. That's just delusional."

"This is where your people keep their tomes of magic?" Tembo asked. "Then we face a great sorcerer. Perhaps we should turn back."

"More likely whoever kidnapped Eric is feeding off his imagination. He always had a thing for these places." I chopped through the vines hanging over the door and stepped inside. "Though if you see something that could only be described with, like, thirty disjointed adjectives, let me handle it."

The interior was a mess. Rearranged bookshelves formed a maze of dead ends and looping corridors, their shelves sometimes neatly filled with row after row of books, sometimes stacked in chaotic piles of mildewing pages and fading covers, sometimes barren of anything but dust. The floors were littered with torn paperbacks and the jagged bindings of coffee-table books. And throughout the chaos, the store was filled with invading plant life. A rotary display of comic books had been stuffed with crumbling leaves, while an abandoned shelf was sprouting branches that reached up to the ceiling, pushing through the tiles and spreading into the space beyond. Insect song clicked and chirruped in the distance, though the bookstore wasn't large enough to have a *distance* to it. I pushed my way forward, wading through piles of discarded literature. It made my heart break to see so many books in such bad condition. Through it all, my skin throbbed and twitched. I wasn't looking forward to encountering my first mirror. The sunburn must be epic.

"Have a care, Sir John. There's no telling what awaits."

"It's a maze, Tembo. Do you think there will be a minotaur?" I joked. Then I remembered that yes, there could be a minotaur. That was the shape of my life now. I crept forward, sword and shield at the ready.

The interior of the maze was much larger than the store that contained it. Always under that tiled ceiling, and with the broken display windows always in sight, we wandered hither and yon, coming to dead ends, turning back, always going right, then always going left, and finally choosing our path based on whichever way seemed to lead away from the doors and into the store's interior. Yet whenever we tried to return to the entrance, we were there immediately. The maze was anxious to eject us, and unwilling to let us inside. We were getting nowhere.

"It keeps changing," Tembo said. "We haven't passed the same stack of books, and yet we are no deeper into this labyrinth. I would say we were going in circles, but even a circle has a far end and a near end."

"Perhaps we split up to—" Matthew started.

"No! I'm not going to wander alone through these stacks for the rest of my life. We've already lost Beth, I'm not about to let the two of you out of my sight." I kicked at a pile of remaindered paperbacks, immediately regretting my frustration as a jolt of pain reminded me of my bad ankle. I soothed myself by kicking a different, much softer looking, pile of books. The resulting mess was very satisfying. "In fact, I'm starting to think—"

"Quiet!" Tembo snapped. I immediately shut up. If I had learned anything in my time in Knight Watch, it was that Tembo knew when everyone should shut up. I peered down the aisle we had been traveling for the last ten minutes, waiting for the inevitable attack.

"What was it?" I whispered.

"Didn't you hear that?" he asked. "There, again."

This time I heard it. A low groan, like a restless sleeper. My eyes lit up.

"Eric? Eric!" I almost laughed. "That's him! I'd know that incoherent mumbling anywhere!"

"Sounds more like someone talking through a gag," Matthew said, tilting his head to listen more carefully. "If I had any light left, I could find it."

"This way," I said, facing a half-empty bookcase. "I swear it's just on the other side of this thing."

"For what good that does us," Tembo said. We had already tried to climb over a case; the shelves had sunk into the floor while the case kept growing taller, like walking up the down escalator. "It's not like this maze leads anywhere."

"No," I said. "It doesn't. But this does."

I kicked the case hard, toppling it backwards and spraying musty pages and clouds of dust into the air. The whole thing crashed to the ground. Immediately, the adjoining cases started to grind together, closing the breach.

"Quick!" I shouted and jumped through. Tembo followed, with Matthew close behind. There was a flicker of movement out of the corner of my eye, but then the pain of my ankle filled my head, and I was rolling around on the floor. The cases slammed shut behind us. I hit the ground and rolled onto my knees. The saint was staring just above my head.

"Nobody. Move. A muscle."

Matthew's words cut through my pain. I looked around. There was Eric, kneeling in the center of a circle of open books. Arcane symbols were crudely painted in black paint on the crumbling pages. Gnarled roots ran from the circumference of the circle toward the center like spokes in a wheel. They encased Eric's kneeling form, binding him in place, pressing into his eyes and covering his mouth. A terrifying scene, especially for Eric, but I wasn't sure what was so dangerous about it. I stood up.

"What the hell, Matthew? You need to calm down before—" I turned to look at the saint and nearly swallowed my tongue I shut up so fast.

The room was lined with spiders. Thousands of them. Tens of thousands. They clung to the interior of the surrounding bookcases on delicate webs. None of them moved.

"This is a trap, right?" I asked. "It feels like a trap."

"Yeah," Matthew whispered. "This is a trap."

"Luckily, I know how to spring it." Bethany's voice came from behind us. I turned just in time to see her appear amid the far shadows of the room, stepping through the tangled roots of the circle to stand behind Eric. She took his chin in her hand and twisted his head up, exposing his neck. The roots around his face tore free. Eric blinked slowly, his eyes sticky with sleep. Bethany put her blade to his throat. "What's a trap without the cheese?"

"Wait!" I shouted, and the thousands of spiders suddenly tensed. "You're not going to kill him! That's the guy we're here to rescue!"

"John?" Eric asked, his tongue thick. "Why are you still in costume? And what's with this knife at my throat?"

"Have a little faith, Rast," Bethany said. "Let the hero do her job."

"Beth, you psychopath! You can't just stab your way out of—"

Ten million tiny legs shimmered down the walls at the sound of my voice. They flowed in an inky blanket over our feet and up our legs. The flicker of their passage was agony on my skin, but I hardly noticed in the midst of my rising horror. They reached my waist, my chest, crawling under my armor and between my fingers. Matthew was screaming with his mouth closed, and Tembo was waving his torch around like a madman. The surrounding books caught fire, and the smell of smoke and burning paper filled the room. Bethany stared at me with calculating eyes.

"You boys are going to need a hand," Bethany said. "Good luck with that."

She ran her blade down Eric's chest, popping open the circles of vines that held him in place like a Christmas present. He started to tumble forward, but she pulled him to his feet and cut a hole in reality with the shimmering blade of her knife. Eric screamed as she shoved him through, then followed after. The blackened strap zippered closed.

"Well don't fucking leave us he—" but then I felt the dancing legs of thousands of spiders on my chin, and snapped my eyes and mouth shut. They swept over me in a wave of sheer terror. I screamed through clenched teeth.

Then it stopped. The pain of spiders on my super epic sunburn, the smell of fire, the horror of crawling bodies working their way through my clothes. I held completely still. When nothing further happened, I took a deep breath through my nose and spoke, opening as little of my mouth as I could manage.

"Tem?"

"Hm."

"I think it's over."

"Hm."

"They're gone."

"Hm."

I peeled open one eye and looked around. We were in the mall again. A lady was watching us from her place on a bench. Sun filtered through dirty skylights, and the dusty branches of palm trees waved in the air conditioning. I let out an explosive breath.

"They're gone. We're fine," I said. Tembo and Matthew stood nearby, arms and legs held close to their bodies. "Guys, you can open your eyes. The spiders are gone."

Slowly they relaxed. Tembo shook it off faster than the saint, seemingly embarrassed at having overreacted. The lady stood up and marched off, pushing a baby stroller while she muttered to herself. Matthew waved at her, then turned to me.

"What happened? I clammed up as soon as you shouted."

"I thought Bethany was going to kill him. But instead she cut him free and kind of . . ." I made a cutting motion with my hand. "Disappeared."

"Breaking his hold on the dream. Good. Quick thinking," Tembo said. "Though it would have been quicker to kill him. I wonder why she didn't."

"Because it was Eric, you idiot. Eric, my friend from the faire. Are you both psychopaths? I mean, I suspected the kid with the knives, but you seem so normal, Tem."

"We have to go. That lady's going to call security," Matthew said. "I know that look. Come on."

"Well, where did Bethany go?" I asked.

"Over here," Bethany hissed. She was tucked behind a planter, with Eric at her feet. I ran over to them. "I set an anchor here in case things went shit-ways. Which they did. So this is the guy we came to save?"

"It is. And you almost did the other thing."

"No, no. Just because I put a knife to a guy's throat, it doesn't mean I'm going to kill him. Kidney's cleaner. Damned carotid sprays everywhere." She pushed Eric onto his side and stared into his eyes. "I think he's going to be fine. Just a little out of it for a while."

Eric looked bad. Deep lines creased his face, and his mouth hung open. A thin trickle of blood leaked down his neck from where Bethany must have nicked him. He was still dressed in his bard's costume from the renaissance faire. Tembo came to stand next to me.

"How do we know it's not another Fetch?" I asked.

"We don't. Not until we get him back to MA. Matthew, can you get anything on this guy?" Tembo asked. Matthew came over and knelt next to him. We were really drawing a crowd now.

"Has a soul at least. Most Fetch's feel like a pile of sticks bound together. Someone might have cut a little piece of his soul off to create the Fetch, but he's probably mortal."

"Oh, he's mortal enough." I pulled Eric to his feet. His breath stank of vodka. "Yeah, this is our guy."

"Mommie, that man is red!" I looked up to see a child pointing at me. "Why is he so red? Is he a socialist?"

"Time to stop freaking out the mundanes. Looks like we're carrying him out," I said. I hauled Eric up by his left arm, while Matthew took the right. I winced as his weight settled against my super-sunburn. We started for the doors.

CHAPTER TWENTY-FOUR
BREAKFAST OF CHAMPIONS

Unfortunately, our nightmarish toenail boat was right where we had left it. The parking lot was much busier now, as if the abandoned version of the mall was part of the anomaly all along. Esther was waiting by the keel of the longboat, glaring at the minivan parked one spot over. The door of the minivan was dangerously close to scraping the side of the boat. We got some odd looks; four cosplayers who looked like they had just been in a fight with . . . well, giant trees, carrying a drunk and portly bard between them. But no one seemed to care about the shaggy gray boat exuding a fume of sweaty feet and toe cheese.

"Explain this to me, Tem," I said as we passed a gaggle of teenage girls. They were taking pictures of us with their phones, and at least one was trying to get a selfie without looking like she was getting a selfie. "How do they see us, but not the Good Ship Hangnail?"

"We are within their definitions of weird. They will find it strange that a group of friends came to the mall dressed like their D&D characters. They might even call the police. But they will still see us," he said. "The Naglfar is outside of their ability to believe. No one expects to see a Viking longboat made of the nail clippings of dead warriors, especially in a parking lot."

"A reasonable expectation," I said. "But annoying as hell."

"You get used to it," Bethany answered. "Especially the phones. But it takes forever to wash the Instagram bullshit off. We're going to be decompressing for a long time. Gods, I can't wait to get back to my domain."

"We don't have a long time, and none of you are going down the hole," Esther said as we strolled up. "Gabby and Owen had to head back to MA. Word came through the anomaly actuator that we've got another situation. They've found the Fetch. It dropped into the real world somewhere south of here and is scrambling to return to the unreal. They're moving now to cordon it off."

"Probably got expelled from the unreal when we collapsed this anomaly," Tembo mused. "Which means they're both definitely connected."

"And that makes it all the more important that we corner it, capture it, and find out who or what created it," Esther answered. "Sooner we do that, the sooner we get Clarence back, and put an end to this whole bloody mess."

"Esther, we're tapped out," Bethany said. "We can't handle a stiff zephyr right now, much less a doppelganger."

"Which is why I'm pulling in the other recruit," Esther said. "She's made good progress on her domain. The rest of you are going to have to make do with a quick recharge."

A collective groan escaped the lips of the rest of the team. I looked at Tem.

"What's that involve?" I asked.

"Nothing good," he said.

"Hey, um ... I think I'm going to throw up?" Eric, hanging between me and the saint, started tapping my shoulder. "Yeah, yeah, definitely throwing up soon."

I set him on his feet and stepped quickly away. Matthew directed him away from the ship and the minivan, staying at arm's length as Eric started making retching sounds. Eventually a wet ball of squirming roots dropped from his mouth and plopped onto the asphalt.

"That's ... disturbing," Eric said. He spat, and slowly stood up. "I don't remember eating a houseplant, though it could have ... John?"

"Hi, Eric. Remember? We rescued you from the bookstore, and the spiders. Do you remember any of that?"

He looked slowly around the team, his eyes finally settling on the Naglfar. He followed the blood-trimmed gray beams all the way to the prow, then looked back at me.

"John? I think I need to stop drinking."

"Always a good plan, buddy. But this is real. Or as real as anything else. Come on, I'll try to explain on the way home."

"He's not going home," Esther said. "He's coming with us. If he knows something about who kidnapped him, and sent that Fetch after you, we need to know it."

"Probably for the best," I said. "His house is a big tree now, anyway."

"A tree? What about a tree? John?"

"Just get in the boat, man."

Eric wobbled up the side of the boat, trying desperately to avoid touching any of the toenails on his way up. I was about to follow him up when I noticed the rest of the team had grown very quiet.

"What's the matter?" I asked "What's going on?"

"Itchy eyes," Esther said. "Happens to me every time an anomaly is manifesting. It's coming back."

"But I thought you said—"

"Nevermind what I said," Tembo whispered. "Something's coming. You know your job, Rast. You're the warden. Get to warding."

"Right, right." I swung the shield off my back and looked around. The rest of the team was standing in a loose mob, and I couldn't see anything that looked even remotely like a threat. "Um. Where are they coming from?"

A mound of cracked pavement shivered on the other side of the lot, kicking up dust as it grew larger and larger. The asphalt spiderwebbed, then split open like an egg. A vine flopped out and started to writhe against the ground. It reached toward the sky, climbing straight up, higher and higher until it was ten feet tall, then twenty, then it was towering over the parking lot.

"So, we got a Jolly Green Giant situation going on here?" I asked. "I feel vastly underwhelmed to learn that's a real thing. Dragons, harpies, djinn, Valkyries..." I waved my hand at Matthew. "Whatever the hell you are. But Jolly Green Giant? Feels weak."

"This is not of the Jotun," Esther said. "Though it may be one of those late-sixties jam bands. They are notorious for their bean magic."

The vine grew darker, taking on the appearance of bark, and a thousand limbs corkscrewed out of its trunk. Clusters of golden leaves blossomed from the branches, each one holding the light of a dying star. Stairs unfolded from the trunk, spiraling down to the ground.

"Oh, hey. It's okay, guys. This is fine." I rested my sword on my shoulder and hooked a thumb on the hilt of my dagger. "I know this show. That's where Chesa went. You said you were pulling her in, right, Esther?"

"She should not be able to manifest her domain so readily," Esther said. "I was expecting her back at Mundane Actual. Not in a suburban parking lot."

"Yeah, well. Ches is pretty much good at whatever Ches decides to do. And there's nothing Chesa wants to do more than be an elven princess," I said.

Sure enough, Chesa's delicate form descended from the golden bough. She looked pretty much the same as when she had left, though perhaps a fraction more otherworldly, a touch more fae. She came down about halfway before stopping. I waved like a maniac.

"Hey, Chesa! We found Eric! Check it out," I shouted. When she didn't respond, I jerked a thumb at the good ship hangnail. "We were just heading back to MA. How has your domain been?" I cleared my throat and strained my neck, trying to peek up into the canopy. "Captain No-Shirt somewhere around? Or is he, uh, oiling his pectorals somewhere?"

"Get away from him," Chesa commanded. She unslung her bow, drawing and nocking an arrow in one smooth motion. She leveled the flight at my heart. Even at forty yards, I had no doubt she could put it on target. Instinctively, I raised my shield and fell into a guard position. "John, you have some questions to answer."

"I think we both have some serious concerns right now, Ches. For example, why are you pointing that thing at me?" I edged closer to the cover of the boat. Chesa responded by drawing the bow fully to her cheek and shaking her head. "On second thought, that's pretty much my only question."

"Mine too," Esther said. "Stand down, Lazaro."

"He tried to kill me," Chesa said. "Or something very much like him. I thought it strange that John would follow me into my domain, but when my rangers found him wandering the border marches, he told a very convincing story. But when they brought him to the Everthrone, he answered my trust with a knife. Iondel gave his life protecting me. You will answer for that death, Rast!"

"Ches, it wasn't me. In fact, the same thing happened in my domain, only it was Eric. It was a Fetch, Chesa. A doppelganger. Someone kidnapped Eric, stole his face, and sent it to kill me."

"And it sounds like the same Fetch came for you," Tembo said. "I assure you, this is the real John Rast. Not the monster who betrayed you and killed your lover."

"Lover?" I asked. "Who said anything about lover?"

"And how am I to know the truth of that?" Chesa asked, ignoring my very reasonable concern.

"You'll have to trust us," Esther said. "That's part of being a team."

"The worst part," Bethany murmured from the lee of the boat. She was crouched against the ground, peering at Chesa with narrow eyes. "I could probably reach her before—"

"We don't have time for this," Esther snapped. "Whoever sent that Fetch is still out there. And unless the world is made up of a series of unbelievable and unlikely coincidences, this new anomaly that Gabrielle and Owen are tracking has something to do with it. We need to recharge, regroup, and get moving."

Chesa held stock still for the longest thirty seconds of my life. Then she lowered her bow with a sniff.

"Oh, thank God," I said. "This is all getting to be a bit much."

"What of Eric," Chesa asked. "If he's been kidnapped, shouldn't we be looking for him?"

"Right here, Chesa," Eric said. He was hiding behind the longboat's shield wall. He waved at her meekly. "You're looking . . . sharp."

Chesa didn't respond. Instead, she danced down the remaining stairs and stepped lightly to the ground. When her foot left the final step, the tree folded up like a magician's trick and disappeared back into the earth. Only a scattering of sun-bright leaves remained.

"Glad we got that figured out," Esther said with a sniff. She turned to the rest of the team and waved her hand in the air. "Saddle up, folks. Daylight is burning."

We got reluctantly into the boat. Chesa sniffed at the hand I offered, bounding up the ladder in a single jump. I scrambled after, settling on a plankboard seat next to Eric, with Chesa immediately in front of us, the rest of the team spread out. Esther took the wheel.

Flying in a boat made out of toenails is much more terrifying without the blindfold. At least blind I could pretend that I was inside something safe, or maybe on the ground. But as the tattered sails billowed upwards, and the prow lifted off the earth, there was no hiding what was going on. We were hundreds of feet up in a matter of seconds. Eric clung to the side of the boat, staring down at the ground with wide eyes. Only Chesa seemed nonplussed. After a bit, Eric tore himself from the scenery and turned his attention on me.

"John, man, you look like hell. Actual hell. It's like you've been using a blowtorch as a tanning lamp." He smiled, but it was interrupted by a look of confusion on his face. He fished a leaf out of his mouth. "Man. What the hell happened to me?"

"That's what my friends are going to try to find out. What do you remember?"

"Well, for starters, you killed that asshole accountant. Oh!" He looked nervously around the car. "You killed a guy! John! Did you . . . are you a criminal now?"

"Certain of our actions are covered under the 1098 draft of the Danelaw, as well as the armistice of Krakow, the Atlantis Accords, and the peace agreement of 1939," Tembo turned a piercing eye on Eric. "The lunar peace, that is. We still uphold our end of the deal, even if the Germans couldn't be bothered."

"Sure, okay," Eric said placidly. "But like, normal criminals. Here and now?"

"Some laws do not apply," Tembo said stiffly.

"So much for not being crazy," I muttered to myself.

"I don't know, man, this is pretty cool. I'm not sure how the boat is flying. Helium, maybe, and a well-hidden engine. Dude, your immersion standards are epic!" Eric said. "I mean, I assume this is part of some game, right? You're all gamers?"

"God," Bethany moaned. "Spare us, sweet Laverna, from the wisdom of dice."

"Back to the subject at hand," I said. "We were at the ren faire, I was fighting Kracek . . ."

"Who?"

"The accountant . . . lawyer guy. Hosier," I said.

"Oh, right. The guy you killed."

"No! I mean yes, but not . . ." I turned to Matthew who was watching out of the corner of his eye. "How am I supposed to explain this?"

"I have never tried," Matthew said. "Not worth the grief. To me, or them."

That seemed to close the matter for the rest of the team. Eric kept asking questions, but they deflected everything and allowed nothing. Finally, he settled in next to me.

"Your new friends are kind of dicks," he whispered.

"Yeah, well. They lead strange lives," I said. "So, Esther, where are we going?"

"Fulham Recreational Park and Marina. We'll do the recharge on the way. Tem, can you pass out the supplies?"

"It is against my better judgment," he said. The big mage pulled a cooler out from under his seat and produced a series of vials. Cold fog wisped out of the open container, and the vials bubbled maniacally in his hands. He passed them around, one for each member of the team.

"That address sounds familiar. Fulham Rec Park. Why do I know that address?" I mused. Chesa turned and looked back at me, her eyebrow arched smartly. "Guys, what day is it?"

"In the conventional calendar, it is the day of binding Saturn and sacrificing him to the sun," Tembo answered as he handed a vial to Chesa. He turned to face me. "By old Martian, we are facing the downgrade of lament, and—"

"The calendar day. In mundane terms."

"In the U.S., it's Memorial Day weekend. And I'm pretty sure we're still somewhere in America," Esther said, leaning over the side of the boat. "I can see cornfields, at least."

"Oh, yeah. I know where we're going," I said. Chesa shook her head and sighed.

"Where?" Matthew asked.

"Let's just say it'll look familiar," I answered. Tembo handed me a vial. It was cold in my hand, but the liquid inside looked like it was boiling. The vapor coming out smelled sweet and a little bit sickly. I grimaced.

"Oooo, libations!" Eric said. He tried to pluck one from Tembo's hand, but Tem snatched it away.

"These are not for mundane hands," he said. "It is the purest dream-stuff, gathered from the dew of the first tree."

"So, like, Mountain Dew?" Eric asked.

"It is nothing like dew from a mountain," Tembo said. "There are no dreams in that dew. That is only for burning at a wight's funeral, and also polishing the mirror of atonement. If anything—"

"No, he's right," I said, licking my lips. "It's pretty much exactly like Mountain Dew."

"You weren't supposed to drink that yet!" Tembo snapped. "We have done none of the rituals. You haven't even filled out your will, or the employer indemnity form!"

"Hey, you pass out drinks, I drink!" I said. "Besides, what's the worst that could . . . MY HANDS! WHAT IS HAPPENING TO MY HANDS!"

And then the worst happened.

CHAPTER TWENTY-FIVE
THE FRIENDASSAINCE

Dreams are great. I like dreaming so much that I'll sometimes do it while I'm awake, rather than interacting with other people, or paying attention to my job, or . . . anything else productive. If there was a way to make a living by dreaming, that's what I'd be doing.

Well. Wait. Maybe that's what I *am* doing. Hm. Hadn't thought of it like that. Knight Watch as professional dream fulfillment. Interesting.

This was not dreaming. First off, I was awake. And screaming. And nothing that I was seeing was *dreamy*, by any definition of the word.

Recharging felt like having a barbed sunbeam shoved through your forebrain, down your spine, and out your ass at a million miles an hour. I was happy and scared and nauseous and more than a little sweaty. My heart burst a dozen times. My brain . . . my brain . . . my brain did a verb. I don't even know what it was, other than uncomfortable.

And then it was over. I slumped against the side of the boat and stared down at the swirling clouds. My skull was several sizes too small for my beautiful brain.

"That was . . . that was horrible," I said peacefully. "I'm never going to move again."

"It is worse every time," Tembo said. The mage sat in a meditative pose in the center of his plank, hands folded in his lap, eyes closed. "But it does not kill."

"You'll wish it did," Bethany said from the floor. She was lying

213

face up on the deck, her body wracked with hiccups. "And you haven't even gotten to the hangover yet."

"Enough bitching," Esther said. "We're coming in for a landing. Time to do the hero thing."

Grumbling, the team moved slowly around the deck, collecting their gear and preparing to land. Eric sat despondently next to the cooler. Esther kept her eyes forward, working the pedals of the Naglfar. We clipped through a cloud that briefly covered the deck in a drenching mist, cloaking us in an eerie silence. When we burst through the other side, a steady rain was falling.

A medieval encampment spread out beneath us. Bracing myself on the rigging, I went to stand at the side of the boat. Tembo came to stand next to me.

"This could be trouble," he said.

"Because there are a lot of people down there with swords?"

"No. Because if anyone is going to see a Viking nightmare ship swoop down from the clouds to deliver judgment and war," he nodded to the crowds swirling below. "It's this lot."

The banner that hung over the entrance welcomed us to The Friendassaince, The Fortie-Therd Gathering of the Houses. The misspelling was done in an attempt to be historically accurate, by people who didn't know much about the Renaissance, or the Middle Ages, or really even spelling. But that didn't matter. The houses were gathered. I was back among my people.

Friendassaince, or the Fren Faire, as we called it, was the largest assembly of medieval reenactors on the continent. Everyone was welcome, from filthy casuals walking around in jeans and a jaunty hat, to hardcore medievalists pronouncing knight like Chaucer did and wearing uncomfortable underwear under their uncomfortable clothes. It was worth going just to watch these groups interact. You could almost see the temporal distortion waves rippling through the air.

I've been coming to the Fren for ten years, ever since I was one of those vaguely uncomfortable casuals in a cape my mom made out of a blanket, with stern instructions to keep it out of the mud, or I'd be "sleeping in the dark ages," whatever that meant. If all this other nonsense hadn't happened, and I had defeated a perfectly mundane

Douglas Hosier in a perfectly mundane competition, I would be participating in the sword and board tournament this weekend, defending the honor of the Elderwood and fighting to win my place on the platform. I would also be drinking, because what's a weekend in the mud without a little ale, other than a very dirty weekend.

But that's not what was happening. Unlike everyone else here, I had been to a real castle, trained with a real knight, died on a real sword, fought a real dragon, and had my well-being threatened by a real Bethany. My life had changed in impossible ways. Glorious ways. And I couldn't tell a damned soul.

"Just once. Just a hint. Come on," I begged. My words came out in a muffled wheeze. I was wearing full plate, with the visor stuffed with cotton to disguise my voice. It wasn't a bad plan. I knew everyone here, and as far as they knew I was dead, either in that initial explosion at the soccer field or later, when a tornado hit my parents' house. My demise must be legendary by now.

"No. You can't say anything to anyone about anything," Tembo whispered. He had one hand wrapped firmly around my arm. "Now stop looking around like a moron and march!"

"And stand up straight," Chesa ordered. "You have a particular way of slouching. Someone is going to recognize you."

I threw my shoulders back and tried to walk straight. Chesa was on the other side of me, striding in all her elfish glory. I was a little jealous. She wasn't wearing a disguise at all. Chesa Lazaro finally looked like the elf she had always aspired to be. Her glowing eyes, flowing hair, starlight-silver armor, and faewood bow got a lot of attention.

Seriously. People were bowing as she passed. The small faction of faux-elves that populated every ren faire was following us around, marching in solemn procession and singing songs of the ancient places. It was deeply disturbing.

"Did you bring these guys from your domain?" I asked her, glaring over my shoulder. "Because that doesn't feel fair. I have followers in my domain too, you know. A dog, for example."

"You could have brought your dog, if it made you feel better," Chesa said.

"No, I don't think I could have, actually. He's pretty big."

"I'm sure he is." Chesa waved to a chorus of elven maids who fell in line as we passed. "No, these are my people by another meeple. Dreamers, aspirants, the hopeful fae. And I am their queen."

"It's actually a pretty dangerous distraction," Bethany muttered. "We're not supposed to draw attention to ourselves. If people start treating us like royalty, we're not going to be able to do our job."

"What am I supposed to do? Disperse them?" Chesa asked.

"Look, there's Thomas Tomasson. I don't know him that well." Truth was I had been stalking Tom's career since I first got involved in the Faire. Known as Sir Tom, Dubbel Tom, or Tom Tom among his fans, Tomasson had developed a clever forte guard technique that won him four national sword and board championships, and which had gotten me killed by Clarence on his training ground no fewer than twelve times. "Just a quick passage of swords. What can it hurt?"

"Do you really have no idea the danger we're in here?" Tembo asked. He dragged me stiffly away from Tom Tom and his gaggle of admiring squires. "These people are only a hair's breadth away from triggering an anomaly or falling into their very own hell realm."

"Hey now, be nice. They're just having fun." A group of wandering bards pushed their way through our little group, serenading Bethany and Esther as they passed, eyes lingering on Chesa, making a joke about my sword, and finding three rhymes for holy as they circled Matthew, all of it improvised and in perfect iambic pentameter. Eric applauded as they left, dancing and nearly joining their parade. Esther dragged him back into our group.

"They mean well," Esther said sharply. "But the game is over for you. We're here on business. Focus up."

The rest of the ready team was as tense as a drawn longbow, and twice as dangerous. Matthew's mask barely hid the glow of his face, and the deep illumination of his skin gave his white clothes an aura of silvery light. If I hadn't known it was true magic, I would have been really impressed by his use of LEDs and semi-translucent cloth. Bethany was buttoned up and stiff, her usual swagger replaced with guarded caution. The guards at the gate had tied peace knots over each of the twelve daggers on her twin holsters, but I knew there were another dozen blades hidden in her boots, cloak, belt, gloves... literally anywhere a knife could fit. I was surprised she didn't clatter when she walked.

Even Esther had gotten into the act, though I didn't fully understand her costume. Faded green fatigues with frayed cargo pockets and a scattering of burn marks contrasted sharply with a few pieces of traditional armor. A doughboy's helmet, like the troops wore in the First World War, hung from a strap around her neck, and a complicated leather harness held a simple sheath, along with a metal shield and the widest sword I've ever seen across her back. The shield was painted olive drab, and had a military badge in the corner, framed by an obscure rank insignia that I didn't understand. At one point she caught me staring.

"There have been wars you didn't learn about in school," was all she would say. When I pressed further, Tembo tapped a bony finger against my helm. I left it at that.

Tembo was the only one who seemed relaxed. The mage had descended from the Naglfar with a look of deep calm on his face and a looseness to his gait that was typical of the tall mage. I wondered what it took to rattle the man. But now that we were on the faire grounds, his grip on my arm had gotten progressively tighter. I glanced over at him once, but his face was hidden in the deep shadows of his hood.

Eric was having none of this doom and gloom. My friend still wore his bard's costume, though he had added a cloak he had rummaged from the Naglfar. He danced his way through the muddy streets of the faire. It was good to have him there. We had met at the Fren, always went to the Fren together, used to plan our summers around the annual trip. It would have felt weird to be here without him, even in these extreme circumstances. He caught my eye and winked, then buried his face in a leather beer stein.

"So what are we looking for?" I asked. The crowds were thick and the faire in full swing. A parade of bards and bawdy dancers wound its way through the press, filling the air with music and muddy flesh. I don't usually get to see this part of the faire, especially once the tournament begins. I could hear the clash of metal and the roar of the crowd in the direction of the tourney grounds. "We don't know whose face the Fetch is wearing, or why it's here. How are we supposed to find it?"

"It takes a great deal of magic for a Fetch to change its form, so it probably still has the shape it had when it attacked Chesa," Tembo answered. "Which means we're looking for you. Or something that looks somewhat like you. It is probably here, drawn to the Friendassaince—"

"Fren Faire, man," Eric said. "Don't act weird."

"It is drawn here because the veil is so thin," Tembo continued. "Just as the barrier between the mundane and magical worlds was pierced when you fought Kracek, so may it be pierced here. If our villain exists in the magic world, the Fetch may need to come here to cross over. And if they live in the mundane realm, and are trying to manipulate events in the unreal, this is the ideal place to do so."

"Man, I don't understand the first damned thing that's happening, but you guys are a lot of fun to hang with," Eric said. "You're taking all of this very seriously."

"We flew here in a magical boat, buddy," Bethany said. "Maybe you're not taking it seriously enough."

"Enough screwing around," Esther said sharply. She was facing away from us, slightly separated from the group. There were a lot of people admiring her getup, though she didn't seem to notice. She looked over just long enough to make sure that she had our attention, then nodded toward the beer hovels. "Chesa, is that him?"

We all followed her gaze. There was a guy who could have been my brother, lurking behind a flickering neon sign that proclaimed Ye Olde Style. He was dressed for the faire, with one glaring exception. The twin daggers at his belt weren't peace knotted.

Chesa didn't answer directly. Instead, she dropped to one knee and drew her bow. Tembo hissed and pulled her arm away from her quiver.

"Not in this crowd," he said.

"I wouldn't miss," she said. "I never miss."

"Because of magic," Tembo said. "And this whole place is trembling on the verge of anomaly. If you do the elven thing, we will have a full-scale anachronism on our hands."

"That doesn't sound so bad," Eric said with a smile. "Take the shot, Ches."

"I've got this," I said. "Bethany?"

"Already on it," she answered. She slipped into the crowd, dodging between legs and over barrels. Chesa cocked her eyebrow at Bethany's fleeting form.

"That's not magic?" she asked.

"No. That's talent," Esther answered. "Don't lose sight of her, Rast."

I started after the Fetch. It was shrouded in shadows, almost as if the sun couldn't quite reach it, even though it was the middle of the day. The crowds were pretty thick around here, and I was forced to shove my way through without causing too much of a commotion. The others were half a step behind. I heard Eric say something about "staying behind to ensure I drink everything here first," though I suspected I was finally seeing my friend's true colors. He just wasn't the heroic type.

But I was. Damn it, I was a hero. No matter how badly I'd screwed things up with Chesa, or how thoroughly I'd messed up the whole domain thing, this was something I could do. All I had to do was catch that doppelganger. I could do it. I could be heroic.

I was halfway across the yard before it looked up and saw me. There was a flicker across its face, like a dozen different visages looking out from those cold, dead eyes. It grinned that small toothed grin and grabbed its daggers.

For the briefest moment, it seemed like it would stand and fight. I had one hand on the hilt of my sword, working the peace knot free as I ran, swearing at myself for not tearing it off the second I was inside. But that would have attracted attention, and we were trying to avoid that. Unfortunately, running through the crowd in a flying wedge formation, with half our company drawing swords and daggers, while Tembo's staff was bathed in an aura of living flame, wasn't the best way to avoid attention.

The Fetch looked past me at the rest of the party and did some quick math. It ran, disappearing among the hovels like a whisper in a concert. I caught sight of Bethany just as the Fetch disappeared. A second more and she would have had it.

"Halt in the name of the King!" I shouted. A passing bard hissed at me.

"Did you just assume the royal gender?" he shouted at my back.

"The law, then! Halt in the name of the law!"

That caught the attention of the crowd. The Fren Faire was the kind of place where yelling about the law while in costume would be part of an act, rather than some kind of legal declaration to halt. A half dozen middle-aged men in black leathers and well deep in their cups stumbled away from the shade of a nearby tree. They sloshed half-empty steins in our direction and struck a pose in our path.

"The law has no place in this ... place!" Their leader declared, planting his fists on his hips and thrusting his groin in our direction. "We, the Black Band of Bawdy Bards, will put an end to your oppressively tyrannous tirade! Gentlemen, to arms!"

They produced an arsenal of pool noodles and established a defensive perimeter.

"Not today, sweetheart," Esther snapped. She slid past me, bowling through the drunken band, shield up and head low. They went down like soggy bowling pins, flopping to the ground with noisy consternation. We followed her through the breach. I apologized profusely, for all the good it did.

"The marshals shall hear of this!" the Bawdiest of the Black Bards shouted at our retreating backs. "They shall know of your impertitudinousness!"

"That's not a word!" Matthew shouted.

"I am a bard!" the man responded, which seemed to be all the answer that was necessary.

Having witnessed Esther's negotiation skills and the impact her shield could have on the soft flesh of the other faire goers, the crowd scattered before us. We had a clear path to the beer hovels where we had first sighted the Fetch. Unfortunately, by the time we got there, the doppelganger was nowhere to be seen.

"Does anybody see anything?" Esther asked. We stood in a circle, weapons out, looking like a bunch of crazed cosplayers who had taken the act a little too far.

"No. But I think we have other problems," Tembo said. He pointed.

The marshals had found us on their own. And when I say marshals, I mean bouncers ... guys who missed their calling as battering rams and human sledgehammers and were forced to settle with roughing up rowdy tourists at ren faires. They were carrying batons, but at least one of them had pepper spray, and I knew those robes concealed all manner of taser-related paraphernalia.

"We gotta go," I said. "Those guys won't screw around. And I don't want the kind of incident we'd cause by knocking out civilians with fireballs."

"Now you're thinking. But we can't go yet," Esther said. "We need to find that Fetch."

"Then we need a new plan," Matthew said.

"Everyone scatter!" Esther shouted, then jumped into a beer hovel, crashing through the cardboard back and bringing the false front down.

"Got it," Bethany said, and then literally just disappeared into a cloud of smoke. Tembo wasn't far behind, whipping his hands around in a growing pattern of light that surrounded him, then shot off into the air, apparently taking him with it. Matthew lowered his hood and strolled away. No one ever suspects the healer.

Chesa looked over at me.

"Good luck, dude," she said, then shoved me toward the marshals and started running in the opposite direction.

"What the hell!" I shouted, but then the nearest marshal put his hand on my shoulder and spun me around.

"Alright, asshole!" he yelled in a voice that probably didn't have any other settings besides Loud and Louder and Oh my God Loudest of All. "Fun time's over!"

"Sorry, man," I said, then finally freed my sword from its knot. I punched the pommel into his belly without fully drawing the blade, then dodged to the side when he tried to grab me again. I heard the jagged discharge of a taser and saw the device in the marshal's meaty fist. Getting tased in chainmail long johns was something I'd never experienced, but I imagine it sucks pretty hard.

A knife appeared in the marshal's chest. At first, I thought it was one of Bethany's, but when I whirled around, I caught a glimpse of the Fetch just as it disappeared into the crowds once again. I turned back to the marshal. The man went to his knees with a look of shock on his face. He stared down at the blade buried in his heart.

"The hell?" he whispered, then fell forward. The crowd of marshals stumbled to a halt, staring down at their fallen friend. Their shocked faces quickly turned red with fury.

"Get that sonuvabitch!" the largest brute yelled.

I turned tail and ran.

CHAPTER TWENTY-SIX
A FAIRE FIGHT

I stumbled through the narrow alley of the beer hovels, upsetting brew carts and barreling into drunken celebrants like tomorrow's hangover. A few of the marshals stopped to attend to their fallen comrade, but those who followed were gaining fast.

"Stop that guy! He's got a knife!"

I had a great deal more than a knife, but I wasn't going to stop to argue the point, not when there was a marshal possibly bleeding to death in my wake. The shouts were enough to draw the attention of the crowd. My sword was enough to keep them away. In the rapidly clearing lane, I caught sight of the Fetch, just as it ducked through the last hovel and onto the tourney grounds. By some chance I had caught up to it. As I reached the picket fence that marked off the grounds, a trumpet sounded, followed by the raucous shout of hundreds of voices.

The grand melee was starting. Perfect.

The capstone of any decent Fren Faire, the grand melee was an enormous clash between two forces, mass combat at its finest and most well-padded. Hundreds of thoroughly insulated maniacs on each side rush forward, battering one another with rattan blades and flimsy spears, shouting in agony when one of the roaming judges declared them wounded or dead, or simply keeling over when the moment felt appropriately dramatic. I had done my share of melees, and always found them terrifying. The crush of bodies, the screams of my enemies, the rush of charging across the field waving a heavy stick . . . it was an intense experience. There was a time when I would have called it the most exciting thing I had ever done, but that was before the whole dragon incident.

The point is, this was the worst possible place for two people with very sharp weapons to be. But then, I imagine the Fetch knew that.

The field was lined with judges, each one dressed in bright white and carrying red and black flags, to signal injuries and disqualifications. The Fetch ran right past one of them, carrying a wickedly barbed knife in each hand, the strange gray robes of its body fluttering behind it. The judge raised one of his flags.

"Sir John Rast?" the man said, apparently recognizing me in the doppelganger's features. "Those are not approved weapons, Sir John! You must clear the field immediately. If you do not clear the field—"

"He's not going to stop," I yelled as I passed. "And neither am I."

"Sir . . . John?" There was more yelling, but I was completely focused on the chase. I felt the weighted bag of a disqualification flag thud into my back. I kept running.

The melee was just starting, so the two sides had yet to join. Padded bodkins fell around me as I ran, their soft heads bouncing off the ground, a couple thumping me in the head and chest. A few red flags arced in from the perimeter, indicating my faux injuries. When I didn't slow down, they were joined by black flags. I bent my head and rushed forward, more determined than ever to end this before it got messy.

First, my parents' house. Then my friend Eric. But now the unreal world was screwing with my Fren, and that was a step too far. I was going to tear this guy's face off when I caught him, no matter how long it took, or how many faces.

The Fetch was in front of me, running right down the middle of the field, where the opposing armies would eventually meet. The distance between the forces was rapidly closing. Unlike the light steel and cotton padding of the ren faire crowd, I was humping my way across the field in authentic plate, designed and forged in true medieval fashion. It was built to withstand actual warhammers and dragon claws and had the weight to prove it. I was struggling. My breath came in whooping gasps, and the sweat running down my face and back was not making this any easier. Black spots crowded my vision. I began to worry that I was going to pass out.

The first lines of the western army reached the Fetch. An enthusiastic rank of skirmishers, wearing only light leather and armed with javelins, surrounded it and started stabbing it mercilessly.

At first, the creature ignored them, but when one of the reenactors grabbed its arm and pointed angrily at the red flags lying at its feet, the Fetch answered by slashing the man viciously across the chest. He went down, blood streaming from his cuirass, the armor parting easily under a blade that it was never built to turn. His friends stared in shock at their fallen friend.

"No!" I shouted, redoubling my effort, pushing back at the rings of darkness that clouded my vision. And then the armies joined, and I lost sight of the Fetch.

A shieldwall crashed into my blind side, pushing me to one knee and nearly knocking my sword out of my hand. I had to tuck the blade against my leg to keep from accidentally lopping someone's foot off, and then I was suffering the hammering of blunt instruments against my helm. I raised my shield and stood up.

"You're dead, man. Don't be an ass," one of the shieldmen said. I pushed him back with my pommel, and he and his friends took offense. "Come on, man. Take the flag and go home!"

"I don't think you understand how serious this is," I said. "There's someone killing people out here."

"Holy shit, that's a sharp!" one of the others said, pointing to my sword. He raised his voice and waved his spear in the air. "Sharp! Sharp!"

"Damn it," I muttered. There were already marshals wading through the fray in my direction. Fortunately, an enthusiastic charge of knights bulled their way into our little circle, and the melee flowed over us.

Given the narrow vision slots of most of their visors, and the frenetic pace of the melee, it was no surprise that the danger my sword presented was quickly overlooked. The alarm was raised, and those marshals would catch up to me eventually, but my immediate problem involved moving forward without sustaining a concussion from the rest of the fighters. I assumed a defensive posture, fighting mostly with my shield, resorting to the sword only when I couldn't avoid it. The blade did its part, cutting through the rattan and padded steel of my attackers, severing a number of swords and leaving confused re-enactors behind. At least I wasn't hurting anyone. Yet.

Suddenly I was standing over the injured skirmisher. His eyes were wide, and he was gasping for breath. I thrust my sword into the grass and took a knee at his side, snapping my visor open to get a better look at the wound. He looked at me weakly as I tore the straps off his cuirass and threw the breastplate aside. A single wound in his shoulder was seeping blood into his Green Day t-shirt. He grabbed my hand.

"Am I dying?" he asked. The sound of his voice, so damned young and scared, was a punch in the gut.

"Not yet," I said. "We're going to get you some medical help. Where are your friends?"

"They went after that guy . . . the one who stabbed . . ." his eyes lost focus and his head lolled back on the grass. I grabbed his shoulder and shook him out of his shock.

"If Matthew were here, he'd bless you or something, but I'm a little short on holy light. So this will have to do." I tore strips out of his ruined underpad, binding them tight and stuffing them in the wound. They started soaking up the blood immediately, swelling to fill the gap. I used his harness as a compress. "Come on, man. Stay with me! Fight it! Fight it!"

"Hey! You get the hell away from him!"

I looked up to see that his friends had returned with a medic. The man clearly didn't understand the seriousness of the injuries, because if he had, the melee would have been halted. As it was, fighters still swirled around us. I stood up.

"You need to call a halt to the fight!" I shouted at the medic. He was dressed in cartoonish priestly garb but carried a modern medical pack. He ignored me and knelt next to the injured boy. "Are you listening! There's someone out here killing people!"

"Someone?" one of the boy's friends asked. "Don't you think I recognize your face? It was you! You're the one who did this!"

"Now, wait a second . . ." I backed slowly away, pulling my sword out of the grass, shield arm raised defensively. "It's not me. It's just someone who looks like me. Honest."

"No way, I'm not an idiot. It was you. Same face, same armor, same shitty grin." He and his friends produced cudgels. Definitely not approved weapons, but I suspect they were beyond caring.

"I don't want to fight you. See to your friend, and just leave me out—"

"Will you people stop screwing around! This guy's really hurt!"

the medic snapped. I could hear panic in his voice. "I can't get the bleeding to stop. It's like . . . it's like . . ."

"It's like the wound isn't real," Matthew said as he appeared out of the crowd. I went to my knees.

"Thank the gods. The Fetch stabbed him. Can you fix it?"

"Sure," he said. Matthew nudged the medic aside and put both hands over the wounds. The boy's eyes were fluttering, and his skin was as pale as spoiled milk. There was a warm cloud of light, and the smell of fresh fields and golden honey filled my nose. Then the cuts were gone. The bloody strips of my makeshift bandages lay over clean skin. I laughed so hard I was crying.

"Snap out of it," Matthew said to me. "You've got a job to do."

"Where are the others?" I asked, climbing back to my feet. I blew my nose on my sleeve, then settled my visor back into place.

"Lost in the crowd. We've tried to get the judges to stop this nonsense, but something's going on. This whole field is slipping into the unreal. They're going to start killing each other for real pretty soon."

"Are you . . . are you serious?" I looked around. The melee was pretty hectic, despite the presence of truly injured and the medics trying to attend to them. I didn't see any flags flying either. When my eyes settled on the band of skirmishers, their cudgels had become short swords. "Huh. Okay then."

"Find the Fetch. Stop this, before we have a real incident on our hands," Matthew said. He stood up and pulled his mask up. The alabaster glow of his skin was barely noticeable. "I'll do what I can here. But get going. Time is running out."

"But, if we could find Tembo, or at least Esther—"

One of the skirmishers lunged at me. His blade skated off my shield, pricking into my shoulder before I knocked it away. Another of them swung, harder this time, yelling as I blocked the blow. And then they were all rushing me, doing their best to put their magically summoned blades into my completely mundane guts.

"Now!" Matthew yelled. There was a wave of light, and the skirmishers fell over like gathered wheat. They lay at my feet, sleeping fitfully in the middle of a battle. I looked up at Matthew. His face was drawn, and the only light was the ember burn of his eyes. "Stop screwing around, Rast!"

I left him there to care for his charges. It wasn't long before I realized how right he was. There was something wrong with the melee. This battle was no longer pretend and was slipping into something more diabolical. I didn't see any more bodies, but the fighting was pitched, and the blades sharp. There were a lot of injuries, a lot of knights and squires limping away from the front lines with blood on their faces and panic in their eyes. No one seemed to know how to land a killing blow, though. Or maybe some part of their minds still hung on to the real world and was staying their hand. Gods knew how long that would last.

Amid the chaos and the crash of battle, I heard more desperate screams. I plowed my way in that direction, using my shield to batter my way through rank after rank of confused reenactors. The screams got closer, and then I was among them. And there was the Fetch.

It stood in the middle of a clearing spotted with blood. A couple of injured fighters were being dragged away by their companions. A shieldwall formed around the Fetch, bristling with spears that poked and jabbed whenever it got too close. Before I could get any closer, Sir Thomas Tomasson, the champion of every tournament from here to there and back again, strode into the clearing.

Whatever magical change had come over the melee, it had done Tom Tom some good. His armor was already a work of art, custom forged and perfectly fitted, with flowing heraldic tabards and pennants, and a wolfhound crest on his helm that looked so real it could bite. Under the influence of the unreal, Tom Tom had become a knight in the truest sense, carrying himself with a nobility that modern man could only aspire toward. His face shone with dignity, and the black curls of his hair spilled out in oiled ringlets. The crowd quieted as he addressed the Fetch.

"I know not what you are, monster. You wear a face I recognize, that of a knave and a scoundrel, whose blade is not worthy of this field. But by the grace of God, I sense that you are not him. You are something else. Something fouler and more base than any man. So," he settled his helm onto his head and lowered the visor, then drew his sword. His blade was as bright as sunshine, the hilt shining with ivory and silver. "Defend yourself, scum. And may God judge the just, and lay vengeance on the unclean!"

For the briefest moment, I was embarrassed. He recognized my face but didn't think much of me. I felt myself blush, both with anger and self-pity. But then I remembered who Tom Tom was, and what he had taught me, and a generation of aspirant knights across the country. He had developed a style that won him countless tournaments.

The same style that had gotten me killed dozens of times under Clarence's tutelage.

"Sir Thomas! Wait!" I shouted. I tried to muscle my way into the clearing, but the shieldwall held me back. "Wait!"

The Fetch didn't wait. It pounced forward, knocking aside Thomas' sword and stabbing quickly at the knight's chest. Thomas didn't skimp, though, and the true steel of his breastplate turned the Fetch's blade. Startled by this attack, Thomas stumbled back, batting the Fetch down and swinging with his beautiful sword. It was a classic Tom Tom move, delivered with the kind of strength needed on the tournament ground, his shield moving to protect scoring opportunities, his feet braced for the counterattack. Only the Fetch wasn't going to counterattack, not in the way Tom Tom expected. No, the Fetch was in this to win.

The creature rolled away from Tom Tom's attack, then grabbed the knight's overextended arm and held on. Thomas tried to pull free, but that brought his feet too close. The Fetch kicked once, twice, and Thomas' knee buckled, sending the knight sprawling. With a scrabble of claws, the Fetch landed on his chest. Tom Tom swatted at him, but it was too late.

The Fetch bent its head and laid tiny teeth into Thomas' throat. Thomas screamed, but the sound became garbled as the Fetch bit through his chain coif, crushing his throat. It leaned back, cheeks slick with blood, and roared. This was an inglorious end for such a decorated knight. But it was the end.

"Get out of my way," I snarled. The circle of shieldbearers, shocked by Sir Thomas Tomasson's sudden death, stood in horrified silence. I pushed my way into the clearing. "You're here because of me, aren't you! So here I am. No one else has to die."

"Am I?" the Fetch whispered. It cocked its head in my direction, and I was momentarily stunned to see my own face, blood dripping off feral, pointed teeth. "I suppose I am, in a way. But if you think your death will sate my master's needs, you have no idea what the true cost is. But as you say, here you are." It vaulted off Thomas' chest, landing with a thud on the ground. It looked disjointed, as though all its limbs were too long, its body hunched over. Daggers dragged on the ground, clutched by gnarled hands, and its spine squirmed under its loose shirt. "And your death will make a fine start."

CHAPTER TWENTY-SEVEN
ARGUING WITH MYSELF

The Fetch loped back and forth in the small clearing, its movements quick and agile, its manner strange. My face hung lopsided on its skull. Its arms hung limp at its side, dragging twin daggers through the grass. It watched me with my own eyes.

"Is this how you thought it would go, Sir John Rast?" it asked. "Did you think this is what it meant to be a hero?"

"This has taken a turn for the dark," I said to no one in particular. "I got into this for the swords and the glory. Not to watch some monster terrorize my friends and murder my acquaintances."

"Ah, but what is a sword for? What is glory without horror?" It peeled its lips back into the caricature of a grin, then motioned to Tom Tom's body. "You don't get to be a hero without a few nobodies dying tragic deaths, drenched in empathy and their own sweet, sweet tears."

"You don't have to do this," I said. "No one else has to die."

"You do. Eventually," it said. "That's the plan, anyway. Once the path is opened."

"What plan? Whose plan? Tell me!"

"I'd rather show you," it said. The Fetch lurched forward. Without thinking, I fell into the guard Clarence had taught me, sword and shield crossed and at the ready.

The Fetch attacked immediately, leaping over the still form of Sir Tom Tom with a scream. I swung clumsily down, forcing it to block my attack with one dagger while thrusting the other into my chest. The blade skidded off my breastplate, lodging briefly in the armor over my shoulder before slicing free. A few of my buckles came loose, and the pauldron with them, exposing my shoulder. I tucked the shield close, covering the gap in my armor.

"Not yet accustomed to true combat, I see. You only beat me before because we were in your domain. But now we are not, and I will cut you down, one piece at a time."

"I'd like to see you OUCH—"

The Fetch was dancing back, having put both blades into the wrist of my sword hand, slicing through the chain link and drawing blood. It ran hot and wet over my fingers and into my glove. The creature cackled at me, circling and weaving its blades through the air. They were already stained red.

"A little cut, a little blood, and I'll have my due. You just aren't good enough, John Rast. Clarence was a challenge. You're nothing."

"I'm not Clarence," I said through gritted teeth. It laughed. *I'm not Clarence*, I repeated to myself, remembering what Esther had said. *I'm something else. Something better. Defense, not offense.*

The Fetch noticed my momentary distraction and pounced. I met its charge with my shield, easily blocking its daggers and using its momentum to brush it aside. It slid off the face of the bulwark to land in a heap on the grass. It was immediately up again, arms and legs scrambling like an upended spider, slashing and kicking at me. My shield intercepted every blow. I could feel the rhythm of its attack in my bones, in the dozen deaths Clarence had drilled through me, in the training and, apparently, in the magic of my domain.

My sword and shield were a blur of motion, moving by instinct and preternatural talent. I caught a cascade of downstrokes on the shield, swiveled to meet the counterstroke that it was trying to distract me from, preemptively blocked a kick by driving the pommel of my sword into the Fetch's thigh, then stepped aside as the creature threw itself at me in a desperate attempt to knock me off balance. It fell against the shieldwall, driving the line of defenders back for a second. They reformed quickly, poking at the Fetch with their spears.

The Fetch stayed down for several long heartbeats. Its breath came in long, ragged gasps that shook its whole body. When it finally stood, there was blood leaking from its eyes, and the mask of my face hung slack on its bones. It ran a forearm across its brow, resettling my visage and wiping sweat from its eyes. It was no longer smiling.

"A warden, eh? That will not be a happy path for you, boy.

Wardens get no glory. Wardens win no damsels and gather no great names for themselves. All that wardens get is killed, and then forgotten."

There was a commotion in the ranks, and then Esther pushed her way into the clearing. The olive drab of her shield was scarred in a dozen places, revealing the bright steel beneath. She rested the wide blade of her sword on one shoulder. It was a strange weapon, the blade as thick as a hand, the cutting bevel only a narrow wedge, serrated on one side, with a flat point, almost like a butcher's cleaver. I wasn't sure how such a slight woman was supposed to wield a weapon like that, especially at her age. But the steel gray in her hair seemed a reflection of the mettle in her blood. She stared at the Fetch with eyes that could have melted stone.

"Not all wardens die," she spat. "Not yet, at least."

"Oh! Esther MacRae, at long last. I was beginning to think you would never show up. And your friends?"

The Fetch looked around the circle hopefully. Bethany blinked into existence between two shields, her daggers loose in her hands, shifting her weight from one foot to the other. Tembo rose above the ranks on a pillar of flame. Three fiery orbs circled his waist, following the subtle gestures of his hands. And finally, Matthew appeared in the crowd. He sheltered between two shields, but the light of his skin was turned all the way up. Without his mask, Matthew looked like a statue carved out of shimmering diamonds.

Even Eric skulked out of the crowd. He was carrying his lute case like a hammer and stared at the Fetch with undisguised terror. He gave me a nod, took a swig from something in his hand, then continued shaking in his boots.

"Very good," the monster purred. "Very good indeed. Everyone is here. Now, which one of you is it going to be?"

"Everyone stay back," Esther said. "It obviously wants to die. We need to capture it. Question it."

"And how are we supposed to do that?" Bethany asked.

"Carefully," Esther answered.

"May I remind you that we are on dangerous ground," Tembo said. "This whole field is plunging into the unreal. If we don't stabilize it soon, these people will never see their televisions or internet pornography again."

"Not a very compelling argument," I said. "Can't we just finish the thing and be done? I don't want to lose more civilians for no damn reason."

"Our warden is right. This ridiculous carnival needs to be stabilized," Tembo said. "We can deal with the doppelganger's origins later. There are innocent lives at stake."

"No. We take it alive. Together." Esther hunched forward. "Rast, circle to the other side. Tembo, give us some light, and make sure it doesn't get away. Bethany—"

"I know," she said. "Do something clever."

"What do I do?" Eric asked.

"Try not dying," Esther said. "That should keep you pretty busy."

The Fetch dropped to all fours. I made my way to the far side of the clearing. Tembo stitched a line of fire into the sky, casting everything into bright light and sharp shadows. Bethany took a half step and then disappeared, leaving a blur of light.

"You are wasting your time," the Fetch said. "Even if you were to take me, I have already served my purpose. You risk destroying all these people, and for what? You can't prevent the inevitable! You can't stop the revolution that is coming!"

"Maybe not, but we sure as hell can shut you up," Esther snapped. "Now!"

She and I closed on the Fetch together. It feinted toward her before rushing me, dancing off my shield and then fading back before I could swing. It dodged directly into the flat of Esther's wide sword. Its arm bent at an awkward angle, and it let out a terrible sound before dropping one of its daggers. We didn't let up. I charged in with my shield up, but I was overconfident, not anticipating that it would keep fighting even with a broken arm. The Fetch slipped beneath my shield, tangling my legs and sending me to the ground. As it leapt over me, it took the time to drag a knife over my chest, just catching the tip of my chin. I started bleeding profusely. At first, I thought it had caught my neck, and crab-walked back, dropping the sword as I grabbed at my throat. When I threw my shield aside, one of the prehensile straps looped across my shoulder, securing the heater on my back.

"Rast! Don't let it—" Esther barked as the Fetch dodged past me and dove for the crowd. "Tembo!"

"Got it," the mage answered. He raised his palm to the creature, as if to grab at it. His fingers curled together, and lightning sparked between them.

A wave of flame lashed down from the sky, kicking clods of earth and grass up into the air and throwing the Fetch onto its back. Realizing I wasn't dying in the near future, I sheepishly collected my weapon and cut off the creature's escape. It was rolling around on the ground, a collage of faces flickering across its features. Its limbs lost their form, changing into amorphous tendrils of squirming flesh, tipped with claws of steel and horn. It crawled to its feet and lurched toward me.

"You cannot kill us you are us we are you and killing you is killing everything—" it slammed into my shield, arms wrapping around the edges to stab at me. I slashed at them, lopping off tentacles and carving ruts into its flesh. It fell off my shield like a leech, leaving bits of itself still wriggling on my blade. The drastic shadows of Tembo's burning sky gave the whole scene a horrific cast. If we were trying to avoid turning this place into a pocket of the unreal world, we weren't doing a great job of it.

"We're done here." Bethany's voice came from nowhere, but then she formed behind the Fetch like a shadow. She struck, hammering the monster in the neck, shoulder, lower back, temple . . . a dizzying series of blows with the brass-tipped pommel of her daggers. A resounding hum filled the air, each strike adding to the cacophony, until the sky was splitting with the music of her attack. Bethany danced back. The Fetch stood frozen in place. Our thief slid her daggers together, letting steel clatter against steel, then drove both blades dramatically into the ground.

Like a puppet cut from its strings, the Fetch collapsed to the ground. The humming sound cut off, leaving a buzz in my ears. The fire in the sky faded as Tembo eased his way back to the ground, and a low murmur ran through the crowd. I could feel the change in the air. Whatever risk there had been of this place dropping into the unreal faded away. The glory of Sir Tom Tom's majestic armor evaporated, reverting to reenactor's padding and the dull steel of a false sword. But he was still dead.

"That was a hell of a thing," Bethany muttered. "Thought it was going to get away there for a second." She bent down and dragged the doppelganger's limp form off the ground. It looked like a collection of gray robes hanging from a mannequin's head. Unconscious, its features reverted to a blank anonymity. "How are we supposed to tie this thing up? Does it have arms?"

"Your little trick should hold it long enough to get it in the trunk. Tembo can put some seals on the lock. Should hold it," Esther said.

Eric and Matthew both emerged from the crowd to look down at the bound Fetch. Matthew leaned over it.

"Ugly son of a bitch," he said. "No offense, Rast. You don't wear a monster well."

"None taken. Is everyone alright?" I asked. They nodded. Eric just continued staring, as though he was working up his nerve to say something.

"So can you do that, Tem? Bind this thing?" Esther asked.

"It'll be the last of my power," Tembo said. "Had to pour most of myself into that blast. So much easier to just burn without control. You doing okay, Sir John?"

"Yeah, I'm fine." I touched the wound on my chin, grimacing at the blood on my fingertip. "Nothing a Band-Aid and a cold beer won't fix. How the hell are we going to explain all this to the mundanes?"

"Madman with a knife, consumed by some murderous fantasy," Esther said. "Most of these folks won't be able to form a memory of this. Not without some extensive therapy."

"If nightmares are the worst thing they have to deal with, I'll be happy with that," I said. "Except for Tom, of course. Damn it." I knelt by the man's shoulder. His eyes were wide with shock and horror, and his throat was a ruin of blood. I closed his eyelids and heaved a sigh. "He was a decent guy. Would have made a good knight."

"Don't focus on the dead. Think about the ones you saved," Esther said.

"Yeah. I'm still kinda new to this," I said. "This warden thing is weird. But it feels good to defend folks who can't save themselves."

"Yeah, until you can't," Esther said glumly. "And then it's just bad memories and regret."

"You're really selling this job," I said. "Can we—"

"Quiet!" Bethany snapped. "What was—"

A soft thunderclap sounded behind us. I spun around to see a seam split open in reality, right behind Eric. We locked eyes for the briefest moment. He smiled.

"There had to be a sacrifice, John," he said. Then he stepped into the tear in the world. It zippered shut, disappearing into thin air.

"Eric!" I shouted. The rest of the team was still turning to face the commotion. I bulled through them, searching the ground where he had been standing. As I shoved my way past Matthew, he crumpled to the ground.

The grass where Eric had been standing was charred. But of my friend there was no sign. Chesa came running up.

"I saw the fight! And Eric, he disappeared," she said. "How did he do that?"

"I don't know. I don't know anything right now. Where did he go? Where would he—"

"Medic!" one of the reenactors shouted. My ears perked up. During the grand melee, no one yelled that word unless it was serious business. I stood and looked over.

Matthew lay on the ground. A dagger was buried in his back. One of Bethany's daggers, but it couldn't have been from her hand. The light was gone from his face, replaced by pale skin and pain.

CHAPTER TWENTY-EIGHT
HEALER DOWN

Matthew was dying. I'm not a doctor, I'm not even the kind of guy who googles lung cancer every time I cough, but I can tell when someone is dying. He lay in the middle of the field, surrounded by concerned-looking reenactors and the rest of the party. Blood was blotting into his robes, and his pale skin was getting paler by the second. He was dying, and there was nothing any of us could do to stop it. The Fetch lay forgotten to one side.

"Shouldn't we be applying pressure to the wound?" I asked. "Isn't that what we do in this situation?"

"Mundane solution to a magical wound," Tembo said, his voice maddeningly calm. His hands were clasped around Matthew's shoulders, and a soft purple haze surrounded them both. Some kind of temporal effect, meant to stabilize the saint, but it could only do so much good. "The only solution is to get him back to Mundane Actual."

"There some kind of miracle waiting for us at MA?" Chesa asked. "A 'break this glass in case of near-death experience' kind of thing?"

"Close enough. Our best bet is to get him into his domain and let the ladies take care of him. They chose him, gave him the light, made him the saint that he is." Esther's face was drawn tight with concern. I got the feeling she was talking just to convince herself. "I can't believe they're done with him just yet."

"What about this guy?" Chesa asked. She toed at the Fetch, grimacing. "We can't leave him here."

"And we don't need to ask him a lot of questions anymore," Esther said sharply. She stood up, drew her sword, and plunged it into the Fetch's chest. The creature exhaled a long, fetid breath, then slowly deflated. When he was done, all that remained was a pile of gray rags and rubbery flesh, like a discarded costume. She moved back to Matthew's side.

"Just like that?" I asked. "I thought we needed something from that guy?"

"We needed to know who had spliced your friend's soul into the doppelganger," Tembo said. "That is no longer a question. It was Eric all along."

"But that . . . that's not possible. Eric wouldn't do this."

"He just did. Or do you not see the knife in Matthew's back?"

"How do we know it wasn't another Fetch? Or some kind of ghost? Or . . ." I trailed off. I knew it wasn't any of those things. But I didn't know why Eric would try to kill the saint.

"We're wasting heartbeats," Esther said. "And Matthew only has so many of those left. We need to move."

"Can we land the hangnail here without causing a major disturbance?" I asked.

"Fuck disturbing the mundanes, my saint is dying," Esther snapped. I flinched away. Even for Esther, she sounded stern. "There's no time for the Naglfar. Tembo? Open a portal."

"I don't like it," Tembo answered. "It's dangerous."

"You have a better idea?"

Tembo was quiet for a long time. Finally, he shook his head. Esther turned to me.

"Get these people back," she said. "I don't care how you do it."

I stood up and cleared my throat. It was a little tough to pull people's eyes away from the dying man in their midst, but I raised my voice and gave it a shot.

"Folks! Your attention, if you don't mind. We need to give the patient some room, so we can . . . we can . . ."

"Damn it, Rast," Chesa muttered. She stood next to me and raised her arms to the sky. "Eldoreath!"

The small patch of grass surrounding us started to squirm and grow. Green leaves twisted up out of the earth, slowly wriggling into the air. A low murmur went through the crowd. They slowly pressed back, just as vines shot out of the earth. The vines grew and grew until they formed a gazebo around us, weaving rapidly together into a canopy that shut out the sun. Dim light leaked between the roots, casting our little party in shades of green and gold. Chesa gestured, and glowing bulbs curled out of the canopy, filling the damp space with soft, pulsing light.

I stared at her. Chesa shrugged.

"She said she didn't care how we did it," she said.

"Get to work, Tem," Esther said. The mage rummaged through his robes.

"This is going to take ritual. I don't have enough mana left to do it off the cuff."

"So, we're forming a portal? Do we need to join hands? Chant? Is that how this works?" I asked. "Are we going to teleport straight to MA?"

"Unfortunately, no. We'll need to take a detour through Tembo's domain," she said. "Portals are complicated."

"And terribly dangerous to go through without proper preparation," Tembo said. He was leaning heavily on his staff. "And there is no chance of preparation here."

"Well, I think we're in pretty desperate territory," Chesa said. "So what do we do?"

"Every domain is anchored in that room in Mundane Actual. Some heroes are able to open gates in other places, depending on their mythic identity. Tembo is one of those elites. If he can get us to his domain—" she glanced in his direction.

"I can," he said grudgingly. "There's enough unreal craziness dripping off of us to muster that much power. But it will be a rough landing."

"Right. So we go through Tembo's domain," Esther said. "There will still be some travel involved to get to the normal entrance from his domain to MA, but we should be able to do it."

"And from there, we stick Matthew directly into his domain," Tembo said. "And hope the angels are willing to do their job."

"Lotta maybes," I said.

"That's the way it is sometimes. You try your best. Sometimes it's enough. Sometimes it isn't." Esther finished arranging Matthew on the ground. "Come on, Tem. He's losing a lot of blood."

"This cannot be rushed," Tembo said. He was walking in a circle around us, scraping his staff along the ground. Outside our weird bower, I could hear loud voices. Someone started chopping on the root walls.

"We're going to have guests pretty soon," I said.

"They're not taking their exposure to the unreal as well as I was hoping," Esther said. "Get moving, Tembo."

"If this goes badly, we lose more than a saint. Domains start collapsing."

Esther hesitated, then nodded. "You're right, of course. You know I wouldn't ask this if Matthew's life didn't depend on it."

"I know what's at stake," Tembo said. He finished drawing in the grass with the butt of his staff. He gestured, and a rapid flame seared the ground into ash. Sharp shadows jumped across the gnarled walls of our shelter. He fixed Esther in his gaze. "I'm just not sure you do."

A thick cloud of smoke erupted from the ground. It surrounded us, filling the narrow confines of our little bower, turning the air bitter. I knelt close to Matthew, to be sure I didn't lose track of him during whatever was coming next. The smoke grew darker and darker, until I couldn't see anything at all.

And then there was no smoke. It was night above and below. In the far distance I could see the horizon. It was a bright spear of light, every color of dawn concentrated down into a single line, fading from black to purple to red and startling orange. A cloud of stars hovered over our heads, so close I felt like I could touch them, so far that looking up made me dizzy. I could hear Matthew's halting breath. Esther moved at my side, adjusting her harness as she stood up. Chesa and Bethany crouched nearby, the shifting purple tones of Chesa's eyes limning their faces in shades of amethyst. Tembo loomed over us.

I mean, seriously, he loomed. He stood twenty feet tall, and though his features were at first hidden in shadow, I could tell that the mage had gained a good deal of bulk. His shape was different, too, as though he had grown rounder and more muscular. His massive head swung from horizon to horizon, looking for something in the distance. I heard a flapping sound, like a leathery banner slapping against a wall, and a warm wind buffeted me. I stood up and stared at him.

"We have to go," Tembo rumbled. "Something has changed. Night has fallen in the land of eternal sun. The herd is restless in this new darkness. If they find us, I will not be able to hold them back."

"Tem? What happened to you?" I asked.

"I am what I am, little man. I am what I have become." He took a step forward, and a long, sinuous appendage brushed the top of my head. The ground shook under his gait. And I could just make out two curling tusks sprouting from his mouth.

"You're an . . . you're . . ."

"Furaha na Nguvu ya Tembo," Esther said quietly. "Very roughly, The Joy and Strength of Elephants. And he's right. I have only been here once, and it was nothing like this. We need to keep moving."

"It's the same sky," Chesa said quietly. I looked over to where she was only now getting to her feet. Her head was craned up at the stars. "The clouds of stars, unnumbered. But I would recognize it anywhere."

"Myths share things. Skies, monsters, catastrophes . . ." Bethany's voice trailed off. She, too, was captivated by the constellations. "We are not so different."

"We don't have time to compare mythologies," Tembo said impatiently. "Quickly now. We go, or we die."

Tembo's heavy bulk leaned down close to us. Now that he was so close, I could see better what he was. An elephant, yes, but still a man. Thick, muscular arms, banded with copper and leather, ending in hands with three blunt fingers. He wore his robes, though now they took on the weight of ceremony. His head and tusks were intricately tattooed, and his wrinkled eyes were all too human, looking at me out of that massive head. Tembo gathered Matthew gingerly up in his arms, tucking him against his chest like a baby. Then he picked up his staff, now the size of a tree, and stood up.

"If the herd comes, stay close to me, and do not run unless I tell you to run. If it comes to that, know that it has been a privilege serving at your side, Esther MacRae."

"The pleasure has been mine, Tem," Esther said. There was a softness in her voice that I had never heard. I was so surprised by it that I was still standing there when the others started to run; Tembo in a rolling lope, the others jogging to keep up. My armor jangled as I ran, each step coming down hard on the dusty earth. I was already beaten down from the fight, and the heavy crunch of steel plate against my shoulders was almost too much to bear. I ran my hand across my forehead to wipe away sweat and ended up scraping steel gauntlets across the narrow opening in my helm, accidently dropping the visor. I thrust it back up with a curse.

"Are we going to be running long? Because this armor—"

"Stuff it, Rast," Esther snapped. "This is hero shit we're doing. Complain when you're dead." I shut up.

As we ran, I heard Esther rummaging in her bag, and then there was a sharp crack, followed by a sudden, brilliant light. She held a flare aloft.

Tembo's reaction was startlingly fast. He whirled around and slapped the flare out of Esther's hand with his trunk, drawing a cry of pain from her, then stomped on the flare until it was extinguished. I was momentarily blinded by the change in light, but I didn't need to see Tembo's face to hear the anger in his voice.

"Fire brings the hunters, child. Fire draws the shadows! We have enough problems without your foolish light!"

Esther didn't answer, and a short while later I heard Tembo walk away, his gait rumbling through the ground. We followed in silence. We must have entered Tembo's domain in a clearing of some sort, because shortly after we started walking, I felt the dry scratch of tall grass on my legs. It grew and grew with each step, until we were pushing through a trackless sea of grass that reached up to our chests.

"Where are we going?" I asked.

"Toward the hearth," Tembo said. "If the way is open."

"Three things," I said, remembering Clarence's description from what seemed like an age ago. "Door, road, hearth. So that's where we'll find the door out?"

"Death is the door out," Tembo answered. "Pray we can find another."

"What's that supposed to mean?" I asked, looking at Esther.

"Don't worry, there's a door," she answered. "I think."

"You've been here before, right?" I asked. She shook her head.

"Gravehome is a dangerous place. We will not be welcome there, the four of us. Matthew they might accept, if only to bury. We'll have to be careful. Tembo knows this, but he doesn't. Once he starts rolling toward Gravehome, he's difficult to shift. Like a very heavy stone rolling down a steep hill. And if the herd—"

Though I think she meant to speak only to me, Tembo answered her.

"If the herd finds us, I will have little choice where I go. And if the hunters find us, none of us will be going anywhere."

"What are these hunters? I thought the domains are supposed to be safe, at least for their residents." I turned to Esther. "You told me I was perfectly safe in my domain, that I shouldn't worry. So what's the big deal?"

"Gravehome is unique. Tembo's power comes from death," she said. "Death lives here, stalking the veldt, manifest in the very air. Anything can die here. Even us."

"And you brought us here on purpose?" I yelped. "Are you out of—"

"Quiet!" Tembo said impatiently. "This is a silent place. Your words are fire for the shadows."

I clapped my mouth shut and glanced over at Esther. My eyesight was finally adjusting to the darkness once again, and I could just make out the gray-haired woman's face, drawn tight with effort and concern. Bethany and Chesa ran side by side. Esther caught my eye, shaking her head.

For the first time, I recognized the truth of Tembo's words. This was a quiet place. At night, in so much grass, I expected to hear a concert of insects, chirping, clacking, whistling, humming . . . but there was nothing. A sky like this should host flights of singing birds, but the cold stars burned down at us in silence, alone. Other than our labored breathing, the rustle of dry grass against our legs, and the muffled thump of Tembo's ponderous gait, we moved through utter quiet.

Except for that shuffling sound. Off to our right, or maybe our left, a soft slither of noise, and then an anxious whimper. It almost sounded like—

I ran face-first into Tembo's leg. He stood stock still in the grass, his whole body quivering with concentration. I caught myself from crying out in shock, sensing somehow that he was trying to hear something. Esther sucked in her breath, realizing what was going on long before it penetrated my dull brain.

"What is it? What's happening?" Bethany asked. Beside her, Chesa was staring into the darkness, her eyes narrowed in concentration.

"There's something there. Something dark," Chesa said.

"They have found us," Tembo answered. "Quickly."

He rumbled off, and I realized how much Tembo had been slowing his gait to let us keep up. He covered the grassy earth in bounding strides, each one swallowing yards and yards at a time. We followed not a second later, but quickly lost ground to the hulking mage's hungry stride.

"Faster, faster," Tembo urged. "They are working around us. If we don't hurry, they will cut us off!"

"I'll hold them," Esther said. She started to slow, swinging her shield down into her arms. "One last stand for the old lady. You go on."

"No! They will lap around and take us all. There is no use in sacrifice. Run!"

Reluctantly, Esther reseated her shield and continued to run. My armor wasn't made for this. Hell, *I* wasn't made for this. But I ran, and despite my ragged breath and the lumbering awkwardness of my boots, we stayed together. Chesa kept glancing back at us. She and Bethany both must be restraining themselves to keep us in sight.

I was just beginning to run out of breath when I saw them. Dogs, I thought at first, or hyenas. But the rippling quivers of their backs, the sawtooth ridges of their spines, with mouths that ran from snout to shoulder, tier after tier of slavering teeth, and a lolling four-tipped tongue that scented the air like a snake and writhed like a squid in water . . . these were not dogs. These were nightmares come to life.

"I need to start having better dreams," I said. "This started so well. It started so well!" I turned to Esther. She was looking straight forward, her focus on Tembo's back, and the way out. "I killed a dragon, you know!"

"Join the club, kid! Now shut up and run!"

Chesa and Bethany split apart, each one taking a flank. It was obvious that they were holding back, merely jogging when they could be flying. Chesa let fly a trio of arrows, but if they found their mark, there was no sound, no cry, no shriek of pain.

They were on either side of us, sliding through the grass like sharks, drifting closer and then away, harassing us like a pack of wolves harasses the stragglers. I would catch sight of one to my left, its leering eyes appearing over Esther's shoulder only to disappear into the thatch. While I was straining my eyes to see where it had gone, I would hear a rattling croak to my right, and whirl to see another of the monsters veering close to my side, almost laughing as I lashed out with my blade, only to fall short as they skipped away into the darkness. I tried to run faster, but there was no faster. My strength was fading, the weight of my armor was too much. My reserves were nearly tapped. Esther was slowly pulling away. Bethany kept pace with her, but Chesa lingered. She looked at me with pleading eyes.

"John, you need to run! You need to keep moving!"

I nodded, too gassed for words. Tembo was a rumbling shadow in front of me, nearly lost among the grasses.

The elevation of the ground suddenly changed, and I stumbled, nearly falling. We were going up a hill, gentle at first, but quickly steep. I went down on all fours, scrambling forward, desperate. Hot breath blasted across my back, and I whirled around, trying to bring my sword up, only to see one of the beasts bounding back into the grass. I turned back to my flight, reaching a plateau. Tembo was already there, standing solidly in the middle, with Matthew huddled at his feet. Esther knelt panting beside him. Bethany and Chesa walked slow circuits around the plateau, looking for attackers. Tembo held his staff across his chest, watching the edge of the low hill we had climbed.

Just as I crested the hill, he swung at me. I held out my hands, tried to yell something along the lines of "It's me, you buffoon!" but only got "Eeets!" before I was forced to dive to the ground. Tembo's staff whistled inches over my head. There was a meaty thump, a yelp, and one of the beasts rolled whimpering down the hill. I got to my feet.

"What the hell are these things?" I gasped.

"The hunters. The cull. That which lurks at the edge of the campfire, luring out the weak, consuming the sick, the foolish, the old." Tembo took a step forward and swept his staff through the grasses again. He didn't connect with anything, but a swishing of grass and that choking, laughing cry told me he hadn't missed by much. Tembo turned slowly in the center of the narrow plateau, watching all sides. "They are the shadow."

"Yes, I . . . I get that part. The shadow, and . . ." *gasp, swallow bile, deep breath* "... the killing. I probably didn't need that part explained, though it does say a lot about your views on, say, social services. But do they have a name?" I struggled to my feet and held my sword and shield at the guard, then decided it was too much effort, and simply rested my hands on my knees, gasping for breath. Plenty of time to draw later. "I need to call them something. I don't want to keep saying 'The Shadow that Lurks at the Edge of the Campfire' every time I refer to them. Makes for an awkward warning."

"Might be a chimisit," Esther said calmly. She was also preparing herself, drawing sword and shield, unbuckling the awkward harness of her satchel and throwing it to the ground. We wouldn't be running from this place, clearly. "Or some variety of the dingonek, though those are supposed to have poisonous tails, and that thing looked too much like a hyena. Or it might be unique to this place. A product of Tembo's domain, and nothing else."

"Call it what you will," Tembo said, his voice rumbling like thunder. "They will kill you just as easily."

"Cheery thought," I mumbled. But it was true enough that I unbuckled my helm and lay it on the ground. If I was going to die here, I didn't want my last breath to be drawn through the stinking smell of sweat and dried bile that seemed to haunt my visor. I spared a glance for Matthew. He seemed no worse for wear, despite the difficulties of our journey. "Do you think he'll make it?"

"Right now, I'd lay even odds on all of us joining Tembo's sun-bleached hearth," Esther said. "Nice enough place. And you've got to be buried somewhere."

"If I fall, the hunters will tear all of this down. Even Gravehome," Tembo said. "Our bones will lie in splinters in their shit."

"And that tops the number one spot on today's list of cheeriest thoughts," I said. "Come back next week for a new countdown to the apocalypse!"

"You're funny when you're scared," Chesa said.

"I'm funny all the time," I answered. "Then again, I'm scared all the time, too. Maybe that's my superpower. Sheer terror and mindless babbling. Now if I could just find some way to harness—"

They came out of the shadows, all fury and teeth.

CHAPTER TWENTY-NINE
A SOUND HERD
ROUND THE WORLD

The first chimisit came right at me. It erupted from the tall grass and arced through the air, gaping maw yawning open. I brought my shield up and braced, but the force of the impact sent me sprawling. I lost my sword and by the time I looked up, Esther was already on the beast, hacking into its spine like it was kindling.

Two more appeared out of nowhere, latching onto Tembo's leg with their long, grotesque jaws. The big mage roared, smashing down with his staff, but before he could free himself, three more of the howling beasts leapt from the grass and started to circle at his feet. Chesa circled close by, shooting arrows into the beasts as they flailed against Tembo's legs, each of her arrows piercing a throat or puncturing a monstrous heart, but for every beast she slayed, two more leapt from the sea of grass. Tembo swung wildly with his staff, managing to tear one from his leg. The wound left behind was gruesome.

"Don't just lie there, Rast!" Esther shouted. She was still tussling with the hound that had knocked me flat, trading blows and hammering away with her shield. "If Tembo dies, we all die!"

"Also, you know, he's our friend," I muttered as I searched the hill for my sword. "It's never good when your friends are eaten by bear-wolf-demons."

Bethany leapt out of the shadows, screaming as she buried a pair of daggers in the back of one of the demons. It howled and bucked, trying to shake her off. The daggers were stuck, but her grip was less sure. Each time she lost her grip on one of the knives, she would draw another blade and stab again, until the creature's back was a pincushion of bloody hilts. It finally charged into the grasses, taking Bethany with it. Her cries of fury filled the air.

The grasses on the top of our little hill had already been trampled flat, which was fortunate, because it gave me some room to look around. The grasses all around us rustled with constant movement, the humpy backs of the monsters appearing and disappearing, like shark fins. I tried to ignore that. Finally, I found what I was looking for. My sword was lying point down in the mud, about ten feet away. I scooped it up and rushed to Tembo's aid.

"Tem! Incoming!" I shouted, hoping he wouldn't accidentally clip me with his whirling staff. The massive weapon whistled through the air, thumping into rib cages and cracking skulls. I slammed my shield into one of the circling demons, then sliced at the creature's head when it turned to face me. It yipped, snapped at my face, then bounded off into the grasslands. The two remaining turned to face me. They spread out, growling and prancing. I backed away, trying to keep both of them in front of me. It wasn't until I felt the grass on my back that I realized how far I had gone.

They launched at me at the same time, two howling missiles of fur and teeth, bristling with quills. I hunched behind my shield, but they were too heavy, too fast. Massive teeth wrinkled the edge of the bulwark and would have torn the shield away if it hadn't been lashed to my arm. As it was, I was tossed back and forth like a rag, my shoulder screaming as the chimisit shook me. The other beast, the one that wasn't playing with my shield, barreled past me and then whirled back. It snapped at my sword arm a few times, but between the shake game and my own attempts to stay in one piece, it wasn't able to grab hold.

Chesa came to my rescue. With a thunderous roar, she hurtled past, slicing with that wicked scimitar Clarence had first given her. Like the rest of her kit, the sword had changed with exposure to her domain, and now looked more like a moon-bright sickle. The blade sliced through flesh and bone like the creature was nothing but fog. The demon dropped in several pieces to the ground, knocking me flat. While I rolled around in the trampled grasses, simultaneously dizzy and frantic, she kicked at the second chimisit, driving it into the shadows. Chesa stood over me while I got my bearings.

"You're going to have to do better than that, Rast," Esther said. She was standing over Matthew's limp form, eyeing a pair of circling chemisits at the edge of the plateau. Our boss was pretty torn up. Long ruts crisscrossed her shield, and the pauldron of her sword arm was gone, revealing abraded skin and tattered fatigues.

I crawled to my feet, still unsteady, but determined to not be the guy lying down on the job. Together, Chesa and I made our way back to the center of the plateau. Tembo loomed over all of us. His massive staff was gouged and bloody.

Bethany reappeared in a rolling tumble. She was covered in the blood of demons and smiling from ear to ear. She held a severed dog's head in one hand. When she landed, she rolled it back in the direction she had come, drawing a yelp from the trees.

"Quite an entrance," I said. "But can you do that blindfolded?"

"Shut up, Rast," Chesa said. "Bee, are you alright?"

"Great, I'm great," she answered, chest heaving. "This is a pretty good way to die. You know, if you have to die."

"Can I ask a question. Because people keep saying that heroes can't die in their own domain, but that," I pointed to Tembo's gruesome wound. "That looks an awful lot like dying."

"Everyone is different. Being able to die here is essential to my myth." He straightened. "It is the only place I can pass from the mortal coil."

"You're . . . you're immortal?" Chesa asked.

"That's a pretty good gig," Bethany said. "Though it makes this a bit perilous."

"It has its advantages, and its dangers." Tembo raised his staff and slammed it into the ground, sending a dull thud through the ground. It rattled my teeth, and apparently unsettled the circling demons. They flinched away, disappearing into the grass, even if only for a second.

"I'm assuming that we didn't drive them off," I said.

"If we kill enough of them, they will slink off into the shadows, where they belong," Tembo said. "But no. We have not killed enough."

"Is there a progress bar we can track? Some kind of milestone I should shoot for? Ten beardogs? Twenty?"

"Is this answer enough?" Tembo asked. He pointed to the

grasslands. Hundreds of spiny backs loped through the prairie toward us, their chattering laughter floating through the air. They were coming straight at us.

"So, like, fifty? Is fifty a good number? Because right now I'm at . . ." I started counting on my fingers, doing some mental math. "Zero. But I have at least two assists."

"What is that?" Chesa snapped, pointing in the direction of the approaching tide of murdering demon dogs.

"Our imminent deaths?" I ventured.

"No, beyond, there's a light."

"Yes, I see it," Tembo said. "We have been followed."

I strained my eyes in the direction she was indicating. Eventually I saw it. Two pinpoints of light, low to the ground and filtered through the grass, but clearly coming closer, and fast.

"Headlights?" I asked.

"That should not be," Tembo said, in a way that expressed horror more than disbelief. "This place is sacred. It is holy!"

"We can't stay here," Esther said. "How far do we have to go, Tem?"

"Too far. And Gravehome would provide no shelter to your kind. It is simply death by another name."

"Not Gravehome," Esther said. "The herd."

Tembo didn't answer at first. The chimisit pack was circling, waiting for their reinforcements, but pretty soon we were going to be in the thick of it again. He shook his head.

"That is not wise," he said. "You could not survive."

"We have three bad choices, and only one of them doesn't destroy this realm or let whatever that is—" she pointed furiously at the approaching car. "Doesn't let it get to us, or the domains beyond. I would rather die than let that happen."

"Yes, but die horribly?" I asked. "Do we have to die horribly?"

Esther ignored me. Tembo ignored me. The girls ignored me. I took my cue and shut up.

"Very well. If that is your wish," Tembo finally said. "It will be a death worthy of your story, my lady."

"Just do it," she said, then glanced at us. "Strap up, you three. This is going to be rough."

Rather than ask how anything could be rougher than the last few minutes, I set about tightening my gear and preparing to fight. My helm was gone, kicked away during the fight, but I was glad for the fresh air in my lungs. Tembo's domain really was a beautiful place, once you got past the murdering bits.

He set his staff in front of him, closing his eyes and breathing deeply. After a nerve-wracking moment, he raised his head into the air and trumpeted. It was a deep, mournful sound, a dirge, the kind of noise you expected to hear at the end of the world. It echoed through the sky. It hummed through the earth. It turned the air into warm honey and filled my head with light.

It was answered by an earthquake and a storm cloud on the far horizon. The thin spear of light was occluded, filtering through a sudden cloud of dust. Trumpets, distant and thin, filled the air. Then I could see them. Elephants. Hundreds, if not thousands, stampeding toward us.

At the first sound of the herd, the pack broke. It wheeled away from the thundering path of the herd, dispersing until it disappeared completely. I laughed.

"It's working! Ye gods, but I thought we were done for." I turned back to Esther and Tembo. "You guys don't look relieved. Why don't you look relieved?"

Tembo took a knee, resting the staff on his shoulder. "Get on. I will pass the others to you. I will need my hands free for the staff."

"We're supposed to ride you?" I asked.

"You will be crushed otherwise," Tembo said. "Now hurry. They are nearly here."

Chesa leapt lightly to Tembo's shoulders, helping Bethany to her side. I looked over at the stampeding herd. It was at least a mile wide, maybe more, and showed no signs of slowing down. The car, which had been driving parallel to the herd's path, had disappeared in the plumes of dust kicked up by hundreds of thundering feet.

"Got it. Trampled alive," I said, sheathing my sword and buckling my shield across my back. Esther scrambled up just ahead of me. I used Tembo's staff as a handrail as I scrambled up the elephantine leg and shoulder. Once I was settled, Tembo handed us Matthew's limp form. Using rope from Esther's satchel of many wonders, we secured him as best we could, then tried to lash ourselves down. Tembo stood. That alone was nearly enough to throw me to the ground.

"Careful, man! It's not like we have saddles up here."

"I am going to have my hands full," he said. "You must adapt."

Slowly, ponderously, Tembo started to run away from the stampede. He gave us time to adjust, time to find the rhythm of his gait, swaying with his stride as he picked up speed. The stampede was rapidly catching up to us. I leaned close to Esther's ear.

"What's going to happen here?" I shouted, my words nearly lost in the wind and the thunder of Tembo's stride. "What's our endgame?"

"All domains have a road. A pathway through, both for getting there and for leaving. It's usually something specific to the owner, something that resonates with their identity, and is really only safe for them." She leaned slightly, hanging precariously from the makeshift harness we had created. She pointed to the rapidly approaching herd. "That is Tembo's road."

"Where does it lead?"

"Gravehome, the heart of this place. From there we should be able to find the door to the mundane."

"And if we can't?" I asked nervously.

"Then we find another way," she answered without looking in my direction.

I had more questions, but then the herd was on us.

The lead elephants overtook us with a sound like worlds collapsing. The ground shook, and clouds of dust washed over us, carried on hurricane force winds. I covered my head and huddled close to Tembo's sloping shoulder, trying to keep the biting dust out of my eyes and mouth. It was hopeless. Fine grit filled my nose and mouth, forcing me to cough, each breath making the problem worse and worse. The winds died down after the initial wave had passed, but by then I was trapped in a haze of dirt and bellowing elephants.

Though really, not quite elephants. The tusks of these creatures were more like elk horns, multi-tipped and curling, sometimes climbing up the elephant's head to sprout around their head like wicked crowns. Their ears and trunks were decorated with tattoos, and their massive flanks were caparisoned with fine silk or hardy leather, jangling with brass and gold. They spared us not a glance as they thundered past. And thunder they did. The sound of their passing was a deafening roar, like nothing I had ever heard.

Suddenly my footing shifted. Tembo lurched forward, like a man running downhill and trying to keep his balance. I grabbed our rickety harness, holding on for dear life. The herd was going past at an incredible rate of speed. Tembo wasn't able to keep up, and the herd wasn't willing to part around him. Elephants, small and large, brushed past, the force of the impact staggering even Tembo's massive frame. And stumbling slowed him down, which led to more unfortunate encounters, which led to more stumbling.

I looked down at the earth passing under our feet. Trampled grass, cracked earth, flying by in a blur. *What happens if I fall?* I thought. *What happens if Tembo falls?*

Chesa started beating on my shoulder. I twisted around to see what fresh horror awaited, but she was pointing ahead. There was something rising out of the grasses, outlined in the purple spear of the horizon. A henge of bones and tusks, their curved archways reaching nearly to the sky. The herd spread out as we approached, winnowing down until we ran alone toward the entrance. The wide stampede of ur-elephants lapped around the structure. The noise of their passage slowly lifted from our ears. Tembo stumbled forward. I turned around, whooping with joy that we had escaped.

This was the end. This was Gravehome. And there, skirting the edge of the stampede, I could see a pair of headlights.

CHAPTER THIRTY
GRAVEHOME

The thunder of the herd faded into the distance, leaving only a cloud of dust and the ringing in my ears. I stood taller on Tembo's shoulders, peering at the rings of bleached bone ahead. Tembo's loping gait slowed, until we were nearly at a standstill.

"This is as far as I can go," Tembo rumbled. "I will lose myself among the herd and return to Mundane Actual once I have recovered."

"You can't go the extra mile, buddy?" I asked.

"Not without dying. That is the gift of this domain, and the curse." Swaying dangerously, Tembo went to one knee and extended his arm. We scrambled to the ground. Matthew rolled gracelessly into the grass. Esther immediately bent to Matthew's side. The rest of us formed a loose perimeter.

"General location of the portal?" Esther asked without looking up, her voice clipped.

"Just beyond the archway," Tembo said. "I have never seen it. I enter and leave out in the steppe, with the herd and the horizon."

"Fair enough. Good luck, Tem," she said.

"And you." The giant bent carefully and put a massive hand on Matthew's head. His thumb, as thick and rough as a loaf of crusty bread, gently brushed Matthew's hair from his face. "Take care of him. See that he lives."

"We will," Bethany answered sternly. "We always do."

Tembo nodded. Then he stood and slowly loped into the swirling dust. His footsteps faded a moment later, and then we were alone. I looked around. Everything was bones and dust. The walls that surrounded the enclosure looked like stacked ribcages, with the occasional tusk or leg bone. The archway in front of us contained rack after rack of sun-bleached tusks and was crowned by an elephant skull. Beyond the entrance, I could see pillars of bone, and lesser henges of pale white, all arranged with mathematical precision. Much creepier than my little cabin and its pot of eternal stew.

"So what is this place?" I asked.

"The heart of his domain," Esther answered. She knelt beside Matthew's still form, working frantically. "John, you're going to do the heavy lifting here. We don't have a lot of time."

"What we do have is company," Bethany said. She was staring into the clouds of dust that swirled across the steppe. The dim pinpricks of headlights burned through the gloom.

"I take it this isn't a matter of those dog things learning to drive, is it?" I asked.

"Most certainly not," Esther said. She looked up from her work long enough to squint nervously at the approaching car. "It must be your friend. If he ever catches up to us, I'm going to have some very sharp questions for him."

"I'm up for the fight," Bethany said. "This guy's screwed up enough of my life. Time to return the favor."

"I can't believe Eric would do this. There must be something else . . . something we don't understand," I muttered.

"Only thing I don't understand is why we rescued your friend in the first place," Bethany said. "I had my knife to his throat. I should have finished the job."

"Nice sentiment, but Matthew can't wait. We need to get him into his domain as quickly as possible. And we still have to find the door to Mundane Actual." Esther finished what she was doing and looked up at me. "John?"

A series of belts and canvas straps crisscrossed Matthew's body, tied in place by Esther's expert hand. She held two loops in her hands and was offering them to me.

"You turned him into a backpack," I said.

"Duffel bag, really. It's the best I can do."

I threw the straps over my shoulder and stood. Matthew slumped against my back. He was lighter than I expected, like a bag full of dry sticks. Esther caught the surprise in my eyes and nodded.

"All his weight is in his soul. And there's not a lot of that left at the moment," she said. "Bethany, you're on point. Chesa, follow close, but keep your eyes behind us. Those monsters shouldn't be able to follow us, but you never know. And your friend in the car will have to wait."

"Do you really think that's Eric?" Chesa asked, staring at the headlights. It looked like he was circling Gravehome, rather than coming straight at us. She glanced at me. "Do you think he's behind all this?"

"I can't imagine it," I said. "Not Eric."

"Well. He's up to something," Esther said. "Let's go."

The ground just inside the archway was littered with loose bones. These were smaller and looked like they belonged to the dogs that had chased us here. I peered at them nervously.

"So apparently those monsters tried to get inside at some point. What do you think killed them?" I asked.

"Gravehome itself," Esther answered. "Look at how they're laid out. Legs and pelvis by the arch, spine stretched out, shoulders, then skull ten feet later. They come apart as they run through."

"And that didn't happen to us because . . . ?" I asked.

"I wasn't sure it wouldn't," Esther said. "So this is starting off well."

I swallowed my protest. Esther was probably used to throwing herself into situations that might get her killed. It was still a novelty for me. But I was determined to not show my concern.

Beyond the dead bones, the enclosure opened up. The pillars and henges I had seen earlier spread throughout, arranged in complicated patterns. It felt like being inside a maze, except there weren't really any walls or doors, just increasingly complex structures that led nowhere. Thankfully, Esther led the way.

"I thought the portal was just inside the archway. Shouldn't we already be there?" I asked.

"Big elephant men tend to forget how long it takes little human feet to walk somewhere," Esther said. "Bethany! Don't get too far ahead!"

"You're slow," Bethany called. The rogue was just at the edge of my vision, sometimes disappearing in the swirling dust that blew through the bone maze. "I have to admit, I've got new respect for Tem. This place is epic."

"Epically creepy," Chesa muttered behind me. I glanced back at her. She was walking backward, bow held nocked in her hands. The archway had already been swallowed by the dust. "This isn't where I want to die."

"Really? Seems kind of perfect," I said. "Maybe a little dustier than I imagined, but you really can't beat the bone pillars and archways of death."

"Cut the chatter," Esther said. "There's something coming."

We froze. A low droning sound cut through the air. It was uncomfortably familiar.

"That's the Viking bitchwagon," I said.

"Your mom's car?" Chesa asked. "But how—"

"I found the portal!" Bethany's voice called out from the gloom ahead.

"Get Matthew through," Esther said, pushing me forward. "Chesa, you and Bethany follow. I'll hold the gate."

"What do we do on the other side?" I asked.

"You'll have to summon the angels," she said. "But don't go through his door yourself. And don't talk to them. And don't—"

"Guys!" Bethany shouted. "He's in front of us!"

Sure enough, the sound of the car was coming from somewhere ahead. Headlights cut through the dust.

"How did that happen?" I asked.

"No time! Move!" Esther shouted. When I didn't immediately run blindly into the darkness, she slapped me on the shoulder. "Move move move!"

I moved, running toward the sound of Bethany's voice. I caught a glimpse of her form just as her twin blades flared to brilliant life. She was crouched in the lee of an archway. The space between the bone pillars was utterly black. Matthew's limp form slapped against my back as I ran.

Mom's car loomed out of the dust, windshield wipers flapping back and forth, headlights stabbing through the gloom. The bitchwagon drifted sideways, kicking up clouds of dust as it spun toward us. I caught a glimpse of Eric behind the wheel. We locked eyes for a brief moment. Eric's face was lined in deep shadows. As he passed, he leaned out the window, as if to wave. Instinctively, I raised my hand to wave back.

He had a gun. A short, stubby, black as hell and twice as real semi-automatic of some variety. Fire blossomed from the barrel. The rest of the team scattered, dropping to the ground and covering up, but I was too stunned to move. Bullets pinged off the ground at my feet, kicking up dust and flakes of bone. I stared in horror.

And then he was gone, barreling past us, the clouds of dust kicking up from the wagon's fishtailing back-end swallowing him like a bad dream. I heard squealing tires. Headlights flashed back toward us as he flipped the car around and punched the accelerator.

"Get through!" Bethany shouted.

"What about the others?"

"They'll follow," she said. "They better."

I hesitated, looking up at the archway. The opening was nothing but darkness. I still hadn't quite gotten over my fear of stepping into gaping voids of emptiness. Call it instinct.

Chesa appeared, sprinting past me at top speed. She vaulted into the archway and disappeared. Esther was a step behind.

"Didn't I give you an order, Rast?" she yelled.

"But . . . but . . ." I looked around in confusion. "He has a gun!"

"Reason enough for me," Bethany said. She turned and ran into nothingness.

Holding tight to Matthew's still form, I squared my shoulders and stepped into the void. There was a moment of weightlessness, falling but not falling, and the weight of Matthew's unconscious form was briefly removed from my shoulders, even though I could still feel his arm in my grip. The next breath my foot was on the stone floor of the barrel-ceilinged room, and my momentum carried me into the table. I swung Matthew's limp body onto the table, wincing as he gave out a low groan. Blood bubbled from his lips, and the wound in his chest reopened. His eyes shot open, and his hands crawled across the ruin of his robes to grab at the dagger still protruding from his ribs.

"Jesus Loving Christ, Rast, what did you do to me?" he gasped.

"I think maybe you should stay still," I said. I looked around. The others weren't here. Where had they gone? "Esther said there would be help once we—"

"Present!" Gabrielle shot through the far door, escorting a pair of nurses. Owen followed close behind. He was carrying a full stretcher like it was a skateboard. Gabrielle looked around the room. "Where's everyone else?"

"I was just wondering that myself. They went through the portal in Gravehome right before me. Tembo stayed. I'm not sure what happened."

"Tembo will be fine," Gabrielle said. She went to Matthew's side, undoing the complicated webbing Esther had created. "Not sure about the others. Let's get him stable and try to summon the girls. We'll start with the knife."

"We can't fix this here," one of the nurses said. "That blade isn't real."

"Sure it's real. It's sticking in him," I said. "Seems real enough to me."

"She means that it's not part of the mundane world. It's magic."

"Where did Eric get a magic dagger?" I asked.

"Eric? Your friend Eric? He's the one who stabbed the saint?"

"I guess. It's complicated. Look, what are we supposed to do?" I asked.

Matthew gave out a low, rattling moan that drew Gabrielle's complete attention. The medics started their work, which led to an entire symphony of misery and pain.

"Definitely a cursed blade," the medic said finally. "It needs to come out."

"Can we do it here? Without killing him?" Gabrielle asked.

"Yes and no, in that order. But it has to be done. Just having the thing in this place risks compromising MA's cordon."

"I can't make that decision," Gabrielle said. "I don't have the authority to risk the life of an elite."

Esther emerged from the door to my domain, followed closely by Chesa, then Bethany. She slammed the door once everyone was through. I looked at her in confusion.

"Why did you ... how ..."

"He screwed up the portals. Not sure how, but I'm pretty sure he was hoping to trap us in Tembo's domain. We need to seal these doors."

Gabrielle nodded and pulled something out of her tactical vest. She started sprinkling the doors with water and muttering incantations. Owen helped her. The doors hissed with steam as they worked.

"We need a decision!" the medic snapped. Esther took in the situation, got a brief update from Gabrielle, then nodded sharply.

"Do it," she said.

"It'll kill him," I protested. "I didn't carry him through all that just to see him die on a table."

"Neither did I," Esther said. She walked to Matthew's door and hammered on the iron sun. The echo carried through the walls like a giant bell. "But it's out of our hands now. Start praying."

CHAPTER THIRTY-ONE
BRUSH WITH THE DIVINE

The medic nodded and bent to her task. The business of removing a cursed dagger from the ribcage of a living (and screaming) human being is complicated and brutal. There was a lot of blood. Mercifully, Matthew passed out about halfway through, but I carried on screaming in his place, just in case that was a critical part of the operation. When the blade was free, the medics packed the wound with gauze and drew some kind of runes around the bandage. Then they stood back and looked at Esther expectantly.

"Now?" Gabrielle asked.

"Now we wait."

"Wait for what? Wait for him to die?" I asked.

"Wait for them to notice," Esther said, and looked to the quiet iron sun on Matthew's door. "Probably takes a while for them to put the suit on."

It didn't take long, though every second felt like a lifetime. I had to call an ambulance for a friend once, and the fifteen minutes it took for them to arrive dragged on for hours. This wasn't fifteen minutes, but it wasn't fifteen seconds, either. I paced nervously at Matthew's side, wishing there was something more I could do, anything at all. Bethany and Chesa stood nervously at the hearth. Minutes passed. Finally, Esther's head perked up. There was a grating sound from the door to Matthew's domain, and then a chorus of horns, low and downbeat, almost a dirge. A line of brilliant light outlined the doorway, traveling from the hinges to the lock, growing brighter and brighter until it was difficult to even look at. The music rose into a crescendo that shook the room.

"What the hell is happening?" I shouted at Esther. Then I noticed that Esther, Bethany, the medics, Gabrielle, even Owen, had all taken a knee. Chesa shrugged and followed suit.

"A little deference, kid," Esther said without looking up. "They can be picky."

I went to one knee, suddenly terrified by what I was about to see, the presence I was about to be in. I remembered the beauty of the Valkyries, and Tembo's casual scorn when I mistook them for angels. *Trust me, you wouldn't like angels half that much*, he had said. I bent my head toward the floor. The door opened.

A vaguely humanoid figure waddled into the room. It was black as night, and at first I thought its skin was shiny and smooth, almost like rubber. Its whole body squeaked as it moved, like a barrel of balloons rolling down a hill. Out of the corner of my eye, I could see a face as featureless as a plate stare down at Matthew's limp form. I dared to look up.

Whatever the angel looked like, this one was wearing some kind of outfit, a cross between a radiation suit and a diving rig. Dials and tubes bristled over the front, and an umbilical of about a dozen hoses trailed from the shoulders to disappear into Matthew's portal. The light, so blinding a second ago, faded into the darkness. The helmet was bound in dark iron, with half a dozen small portholes sprinkled around the dome, none of them lining up with the traditional placement of eyes or faces. I could see the faintest glow through the tinted glass, but whatever was beyond the mask was constantly shifting, like a jar full of fireflies. The angel shuffled forward.

"Saint has a boo boo." Its voice came out of a small grill in the palm of its left hand. "What boo booed Saint? You?"

"No, brilliance," Esther said. "A villain foul and tricky."

"Tricky," the angel said. "Okay." It turned and started shuffling back to the door.

"Wait!" Esther said, rising to her feet. "Can you help him?"

"Help? Help." The angel stood stock still for the longest time, while Matthew slowly died on the table. Finally, it shrugged in a way that was utterly wrong in some unidentifiable way, as though it had too many shoulders, or not enough. "Okay."

It picked Matthew up and went back into the domain. We waited breathlessly until the door closed, and the droning horns faded into silence. Esther rubbed her hands nervously, then stepped forward and locked the door to Matthew's domain. We all let out a breath that I at least hadn't realized we were holding.

"So that was an angel," I said.

"At least one, maybe more. Those suits are bigger than you think. Thank the gods it didn't get bored," Esther said. "Okay, that was good. That worked. Let's all . . ." she looked around the room, eyes lingering on the table, spotted with blood, and the dagger lying beside. "Let's never do that again."

"What do we do now?" Bethany asked. "If Eric was able to follow us into Tembo's domain, then there's no telling where he is, or what he's doing." It felt like she was saying this to me, even though she was facing Esther. I squirmed in my armor.

"First things first," Esther said. "You guys have compromised this place more than a little. We need to start resecuring the unreal half of MA, get Gabrielle and the rest of the mundanes behind the barrier, and seal the heroes inside." Gabrielle started to protest, but Esther held out her hand. "No, it's okay, it was necessary. If you hadn't broken protocol, Matthew would be dead, and who knows what would happen to the rest of us. You did the right thing. But we need to have this place clean before we start looking for Tembo." She made a shooing motion toward the doors by the hearth. "Go on, get going. I want to see what the actuator has to say about all this before I decide what to do about Rast's bastard friend."

The medics hurriedly gathered up their stuff, wiping down the table and stuffing bloody bandages into their bags before rushing out of the room. Gabrielle and Owen left more reluctantly, but Esther was insistent. Chesa and I were about to follow them out when Esther turned on me.

"John, you and Chesa stay here. In case Tembo appears, or the angel, or . . . or anything else happens."

"What else might happen?" I asked.

"Just . . . keep an eye out. Okay?" She glanced at Bethany. "Bethany, with me. I'll need your help with sealing this section."

Bethany snorted something about that being a job for a mage, then she and Esther were through the door. There was the distinct sound of a bolt being thrown. We were locked in here.

Chesa pulled a chair away from the bloody table and sat down. She folded her arms and set about ignoring me.

"Are we going to talk?" I asked.

"About what?"

"About what? About Eric," I said. "And the fact that he just tried to kill Matthew. Hell, he tried to kill me. You have nothing to say about that?"

She sniffed and somehow managed to ignore me even more. I tossed my weapons on the least bloody part of the table and pulled up a chair, turning it sideways in front of Chesa and sitting down. I threw my arms over the back and leaned toward her.

"Because if you don't have anything to say, I sure as hell do. See, I thought it was a little weird that the two of you were suddenly hanging out. But hey, people change. Who am I to judge? Then we get in here, and you're already half a step into fairy land, while I'm still babbling about janitors and dragons. Didn't really strike me at the time, but you didn't seem too surprised by what was going on. Were you?" Chesa clenched her jaw and tried to scrape her chair away from me, but I put a hand on her knee and turned her back. "Were you?" I asked again.

She looked at me angrily, but there was something more. Something scared.

"Chesa, you have to tell me what's going on. Because if you were somehow involved in this—"

"No," she said firmly. "Or, at least, not this. Not..." she gestured helplessly at the bloody table. "Not that. No one was supposed to get hurt."

I leaned back, a little shocked.

"Hurt by what, Ches? What's going on?"

"Eric said he found something. Something from his writing, something that let him make his stories real. I thought he was crazy." Chesa glanced down nervously, wringing her hands. "Then he showed me. Little stuff, like, literally. He had a family of gnomes living in his backyard. He said he could make me a princess. Helped me design the new costume, wrote some backstory... even taught me some enchantments for my bow. Then you came home, and a week later Eric says he has a plan for getting into this world. That you were going to help, whether you knew it or not."

"Holy shit. The favor. And then the dragon. Eric did that?"

"No, you did. Eric just helped it along. He said it would tear a hole in the real world, and we could just slip through. Like Narnia, only we'd be in control." She folded her hands in her lap and sighed. "He promised. I should have known better."

"Ches, this is bad. This is really bad." I stood up and started pacing. "We need to tell Esther."

"John, no. Please don't. She'll kick me off the team, and then I'll never get back to the tree. You can't do that to me."

"I don't know if you noticed, but Eric seems to be breaking that promise he made to you. Those were real bullets he was shooting at us. You're not going anywhere if you're dead. Tree or no tree."

"But . . . but maybe we can fix this ourselves. Maybe we can talk to him, get him to undo whatever it is he's trying to do. Right?" She was pleading, nearly to tears. I felt something twist in my heart. I pushed it down.

"Sorry, Ches. Esther needs to know." I marched to the door. "If anyone can fix it, it's her. Maybe she'll be lenient."

I grabbed the handle of the door and immediately regretted it. Smoke hissed up from my hand, and pain shot through my arms, spreading like lightning through the rest of my body. I jumped back, too surprised to even yelp. I stared at the door.

"What?" Chesa asked. "What's the matter?"

"Door's hot. Very hot," I said. She wrinkled her brow, then walked to the door. Chesa held a hand in front of the door, then hovered her palm just over the handle.

"No, there's no heat radiating off it. Must be—" she touched the handle and screamed. "What the hell!"

"They must have quarantined us, somehow. They think this is our fault!" I said. I went to the door to my domain. Same result, same pain, same burning flesh. Between us, Chesa and I seared our skin on each of the doors, one at a time.

"Damn it all! What are they going to do when Matthew comes out? Or Tembo?"

"Other doors, I imagine. Especially if they think we're compromised." Chesa stood in front of the portal to her domain, tears streaming down her face. "They've cut us off."

We were interrupted by the sound of ripping wood. I whirled to look at Matthew's door, but the iron sun wasn't moving.

"What was that?" I asked. Chesa was stock still. She snatched her bow from beside the hearth, and I grabbed my sword and shield, strapping in fast.

"Not sure. But it doesn't sound good."

The noise came again. I spun around to face the direction it had come from. At the end of the hall there were a handful of unused doors, without symbol or banner. The farthest one was riddled through with dark veins. I got closer, and realized they were blackened roots, spreading through the wood like cancer. As I watched, the roots twitched, forcing a splinter of wood from the door. A small pile of shattered planks lay at the foot of the portal.

"Esther!" I shouted. "There's ... we have ... something's happening!"

As though prompted by my voice, the roots thrashed about like a beached octopus. The door disintegrated, and a figure stepped through, stooped over like a crooked staff.

Eric Cavanaugh straightened his shoulders. He was taller, his beard fuller and more wild. Squirming roots trailed down his cheeks from bloodshot eyes, and his hair was woven through with thatch. He wore very traditional wizard robes and carried a staff of tangling vines. He looked around the room with glee.

"There you are, my darling," he said, raising a hand. The dagger, recently embedded in Matthew's chest and still sticky with his blood, flew across the room and landed in Eric's palm with a meaty smack. "Like a hound to the hare, it has brought me here."

His eyes finally focused on me and Chesa. He smiled. Dirt and blood lined his teeth.

"Hello, Johnny. Hello, Chesa. I'm afraid there's been a change of plans."

CHAPTER THIRTY-TWO
I PREFER THE TERM
TIME LORD

"What the hell, man?" I asked. "I thought we were friends!"

"I've found something better than friends, John. So much better." Eric raised the gnarled head of his staff and pointed it in my direction. "I've found true power."

A bolt of dark, sizzling energy shot out of the staff, narrowly missing my head and cracking into the table. Where the bolt struck, twisting roots grew out of nowhere, digging through the wood of the table like lightning. They expanded in the blink of an eye, tearing the table in half. The tendrils that survived the eruption quickly withered into dust.

"What do you think, John? How would you describe that?" Eric asked. "Whispering willows of fetid destruction, tearing the table into haphazard splinters?"

"I don't—"

"Adjectives, John! Use some adjectives!" he snapped. "Or are you too good to be circumlocutory?"

"Now you're just being an asshole," Chesa said.

She had backed as close to the spellbound door as she could and was fumbling through her quiver for an arrow. I'd never seen her this unsettled, not since we had come to the unreal world. She pulled an arrow, but when she looked up to shoot, her eyes went wide.

"John, look out!" she yelled.

I turned back just in time to see Eric swing his staff at my head. I raised my shield, catching the head of the staff, which had transformed into a squirming ball of roots and sprouting branches. This new growth dragged across the steel face of the shield, catching and pulling, twisting my arm down. Off balance, I could do nothing when Eric stepped forward and punched me in the throat. I dropped onto my butt, gagging. Behind me, I heard the distinct clatter of arrows on stone, as Chesa dropped her quiver.

"Chesa, dear. We had a deal," Eric said. "I'm disappointed in you. Running off with that elf, when I'm the one who brought you here."

"You're not . . . you're not going to stop me," Chesa said, but her voice was quiet. She was on her knees, scrabbling through the pick-up-sticks of her dropped arrows. Finally, she got one nocked and raised her bow. "You're not going to take this from me."

"That's enough, girl," Eric said dismissively. He swept his staff in her direction, and a net of roots flew across the room. They wrapped Chesa tightly around the waist, pinning her arms to her hips. She went down hard. He turned to me. "Women. Am I right?"

"You're a lot of things, Eric," I croaked. "Right isn't one of them."

He laughed, then kicked me in the face. All his fat had burned away into muscle. My head snapped back, and shadows spun through my vision. His voice reached me through the steady hum of my skull.

"This isn't personal, John. For me at least. And I really like your new friends. They seem nice, especially the mage fellow. Pity he had to resist." Eric stepped over me, kicking my sword away in the process. I made a half-hearted grab for the hilt just as it slipped out of reach. Eric shook his head. "You won't need that again. We aren't playing at knights and castles anymore. Typical of you, to get distracted by the pointless shiny trinkets, when there are so much better things right under your nose. There's real power waiting to be tapped in the Imaginarium!"

"Imaginarium?" I whispered through my ruined lips. "What the hell is that?"

"This!" he said, spreading his arms. "A world of magic, and spells, and dragons! A whole world of incredible potential, all of it waiting to be bent to my will. The will of the world's first Anachromancer!"

"You're just making up words, aren't you?" I gasped. "Gods, does this have something to do with your damned books?"

"You would know if you'd finished any of them, John," Eric answered. "Oh, you said you did, but it was clear enough. No matter!" He swept his arms wide. "I will make real the tale of the Anachromancer! I will carve my name onto reality itself! The world will know OOF—"

I had kept him talking long enough to recover, and now launched myself off the ground and into his belly, shoulder-first. Eric folded like a sack of potatoes. I stood up, rubbing my neck and wincing.

"Look, I know I'm not one to judge, but you really do talk a lot," I said. I limped over to my sword and snatched it up. Eric was rolling around on the ground, staring at me as he gasped for breath. I took the time to kick his weird rooty staff under the broken table. Then I bent and started sawing through Chesa's bonds. She was staring at Eric with some combination of burning hatred and honest fear. "Now let's stop screwing around. You and I have been friends for a long, long time. Friends tell each other the truth, and the truth is, you've really screwed up on this. People have died. Hell, *I* almost died. So whatever it is you think you're doing here, you need to stop. I'm sure we can straighten things out with Esther. Okay?"

The last of Chesa's bonds fell free. She stood up and retrieved her bow, then stood to the side. She wouldn't look me in the eye.

"It's going to be alright, Ches. You didn't know what he was planning," I said.

"That's the problem," she answered. "I should have. But I wanted this too much." Finally, she lifted her face, giving me the barest glance before returning her stare to Eric's crumpled form. "I was blind to what he was doing."

"Well. We all make mistakes," I said. "Gods know I have."

"Shut up, John. This isn't about you."

After several moments of wheezing and huffing, Eric regained his breath. He closed his eyes and seemed to collapse a little on himself. I knew a beaten man when I saw it. I extended my hand.

"Come on. Let's go talk to Esther. I'll put a good word in for you."

"You always did care too much about chivalry, Sir John," he said.

Then he pulled a gun out of his robes and shot me in the chest. I barely registered Chesa's scream through the deafening echo of the report.

Let me tell you, no one was more surprised by this than I was. I had a fraction of a second to stare down the barrel of the stubby little gun (an H&K MP5, some gamer-lizard part of my brain screamed) before there was a sound like fabric ripping and a series of heavy impacts in my chest. I spun away, flopping like a ragdoll to the ground. Chesa screamed and dove behind the ruined table. Sparks danced through the air as bullets ricocheted off the stone walls.

"Damn it feels good to be a magesta," Eric sang to himself. I heard him snap the safety back on the MP5, then stroll over to his staff and pick it up, humming the whole time. I lay on the ground in shock. "Sorry about that, man. But sacrifices have to be made." He walked over to where Chesa was curled up in front of the hearth, crying hysterically. "There, there, Ches. I'd never shoot you. Too sweet an end. But once I get to the actuator, you're going to wish you were bleeding out with your ex. Night, night."

There was the dull thump of wood against skull, and Chesa's crying stopped.

The door opened, the door closed, and I was still lying on the ground. *I've been shot*, I thought. *He shot me. With a gun! I can't believe he shot me! That asshole!*

But then . . . *Why doesn't this hurt more? Why doesn't this hurt at all?*

I craned my neck forward and looked down at my chest. There were a half-dozen nickel sized slugs laying peacefully on my breastplate. I sat up, and they slid down into my lap. They were hot to the touch, and deformed, as though they had struck something solid, but there was no mark on my armor. In retrospect, I realized the impact on my chest hadn't been that hard, not even as bad as a paintball. It was just the shock and the fear of getting shot that had put me on my butt.

"That doesn't seem normal," I said. I put my finger in the dent in my breastplate. Esther had said that bullets couldn't hurt the denizens of the unreal, but they could hurt the heroes of Knights Watch. That was the whole point of Mundane Actual, to protect the team from mundane threats. "Huh. Well. Maybe I'm just a monster or something. I dunno."

Just then Chesa let out a dull groan, and I remembered she had been hurt. I slid over to her. She was lying on her back, with a knot the size of Kansas growing in the middle of her forehead. I brushed her hair out of her face and pulled her upright, leaning her against the hearth. She let out a little moan.

"How do you feel?" I asked.

"Like I have twelve headaches in one head," she whispered. "What happened to Eric?"

"Near as I can tell, he's written himself into the story as the villain. Are you going to be okay?" I squeezed her shoulders, and she didn't immediately throw me to the ground, so that headache must have been pretty bad. "I need to go after him."

"I'm fine. Just..." she winced in pain, and her voice grew quiet. "Just get him. Make sure he gets what's coming to him."

That terrible ripping sound came again, followed by screams of panic and pain. Eric's little gun, and a lot of people who probably weren't unexpectedly bulletproof. I grabbed my sword and my shield, then ran out the door.

This part of Mundane Actual was all stone walls and flickering torches, designed to keep the elites safely contained from modern technology while they were out of their domains. But in the distance, I could hear klaxons blaring and the sharp report of gunfire. I got turned around pretty quickly among the twisting corridors. Whenever I thought I was getting closer to the exit, I would find myself at a dead end, or suddenly hearing the gunfire come from the direction I had just come. I began to wonder if there was some kind of glamor on these corridors, meant to keep the elites from accidentally stumbling into the mundane section of the complex.

That's when one of the janitors skittered out of the shadows. He was looking around nervously, the squirming mass of his hand pale with fear, as he crept to a door and started to work the handle. When he locked eyes with me, he yelped and started pulling desperately on the door.

"Jerry!" I snapped. He refused to answer, so I ran at him. "Jerry, what are you doing!" I grabbed him by the shoulder and spun him around. His squamous fingers came off the handle reluctantly, suckers popping like bubble wrap. He wouldn't meet my eye.

"Sorry for the inconvenience, sir, but these chambers are temporarily unavailable due to... the profuse... infestation... of gunfire?" One of his eyes rolled awkwardly in my direction, to see if I was buying it. Scanning the impatient look on my face, he tried a different tact. "I'm looking for a mop?"

"How do I get out of here, Jerry? I'm starting to think there's some serious head-screwing going on around here." A staccato exchange of gunfire cut me short. It was really close, maybe behind one of these doors. "Those people need me!"

"The red zone is for gunpowder only," Jerry said stiffly. He sounded like he was reciting a training video which, considering the nature of this place, was completely possible. "Magical creatures are to stay clear of the red zone during exchanges of gunfire, rocket fire, or in the presence of armed hostiles bearing torches and pitchforks. This is for their own good."

"Well, this is not a red zone situation, Jer. In fact . . . hey, drop that!" While he had been talking, Jerry had extended a sinuous tentacle from the collar of his shirt and was feeling around at the door behind him, trying to keep it out of my sight. I slapped the tentacle away, then pushed him into the middle of the corridor and put myself between him and the door. "This is not some simple assault by torch-bearing hostiles! This is serious business!"

"You clearly do not remember the Cajun Inquisition," Jerry said. "That was some serious business. This is one guy with a dirty stick. And a gun." A muffled thump traveled through the corridor, shaking dust from the ceiling and causing us both to flinch. "And a variety of explosives," he added.

"That one guy is my buddy Eric, and he has a lot more than a dirty stick! Jerry, listen carefully. Eric has gone crazy. He's convinced himself that he's a mage or something, but he also apparently can shoot people, and it's a really bad situation. Really bad! And I need to get out there and help, or a bunch of people are going to die."

"Yes, that sounds important," he said. "So Jerry will let you get on with that. Okay, I need to get going bye."

"Jerry! You have to help me get to the gunfire!"

"Jerry is more of a skulk-in-the-shadows kind of guy. You should try it sometime. It is much safer and does not require getting shot or anything." He motioned to the door. "If you would like to join Jerry in the shadows, you are more than welcome. I have crickets."

"I don't . . . want . . . crickets. I want to help my friends. But I can't, because I can't get out of this godsforsaken place! And if you don't help me, I swear, I'm going to become the most dangerous thing you deal with today!"

"That feels unlikely. I mean, all you have is a sword, and your friend Eric has a gun. It just doesn't seem like an even exchange."

"How many swords does it take to cut you in two, Jerry?" I asked, pressing my blade against his belly.

Jerry's gaze traveled down the length of my sword. He swallowed, a complicated motion that seemed to involve everything from his ribs to the top of his skull.

"My math comes out to one sword," he said.

"And do I have the requisite number of swords?"

"Yes."

"So are you going to help me?" I asked.

He seemed to think for a long minute. Then his face changed, the sulky fear replaced by cheer. He smiled, spreading his lips like an oil slick to reveal damp, yellow teeth. His skin pulled tight against a skull that had too many bumps and not enough muscles. It was by far the most horrible thing I had seen in my time in the Knight Watch.

My God, he's trying to smile!

"Stop doing that," I said.

"Jerry will help!" he said cheerfully, but the stiff rictus of his smile distorted the words so badly it sounded like a threat. "Jerry knows the way!"

"Just . . . just show me the door. And then you can scamper back to whatever hell you call home."

The janitor raised his arm and pointed to the opposite wall. His hand extended with a grotesque schlup, tentacles squirming through the air until they touched the stone wall. They touched a series of stones, rapidly tapping out some kind of code. The corridor rumbled, and a gap slid open in the wall.

"See, was that so difficul—" I heard a splat and turned around to see that Jerry had retreated through his door. The last bits of his extended hand slipped through the opening, sucked in like spaghetti. The door slammed shut. I sighed. "The janitorial staff around here really needs to work on its customer service."

I turned back to the slowly widening gap in the opposite wall. It was very dramatic, almost like a bit of stage scenery, all flashing lights and rolling smoke. A carpet of mist washed out of the gap to flood the corridor. With a rumble, the walls came to a stop.

That's when I realized that the smoke was actual smoke, and the flashing lights were a combination of strobe alarms and muzzle flashes, and not special effects at all. The stink of cordite explosives burned my eyes. I hesitated. Now that I was faced with the actual fight, it didn't seem like the kind of place a guy with a sword should be charging into, even with plate mail and an apparently magical immunity to bullets. Maybe that only worked in the containment zone. Maybe I would step through that gap and get filled with lead before I knew it. Maybe . . .

Esther stalked into view, crouching forward with her shield tilted up, and an assault rifle gripped in both hands. Her sword was slung across her back, the flat brim of her helmet tilted close to her eyes. She fired a roaring enfilade down the hallway, her whole body quivering with the recoil. It was deafening. She shouted something behind her, then locked eyes with me.

"Rast, get over here! Your friend is trying to get to the actuator! We have to cut him off before he reaches the core!"

"But I . . . but I . . ."

A hail of bullets hissed down the hallway, dancing against the stones and sending shrapnel into the air. Esther ducked down, sighted her rifle, and sent three short bursts downrange. Then she stalked forward. There was a muffled thump ahead of her. As I stood numbly watching, a whole fireteam came up in Esther's wake. They were MA troops, olive-drab tac gear caked with dust, rifles up, moving liquid smooth down the hallway, as if they shared one mind, one will. At their head was Gabrielle.

"Owen, we need to secure this door. Whatever that thing is, it came out of the containment zone! We can't afford to get flanked," she yelled. Owen appeared out of the murk. He knelt beside the door and started messing with it. There was a shower of sparks, and the walls started sliding shut.

Gabrielle glanced up and locked eyes with me. In just that brief instant she weighed me, assessed my threat level, and discarded me from her mind. I wasn't dangerous. But I wasn't helpful, either. If anything, she looked disappointed.

"Take a knee, Rast," she barked. "We'll handle this."

The walls were rumbling closed. She and Owen disappeared down the hall, into a rippling exchange of gunfire. In a second, I wouldn't be able to follow. It would be out of my hands. In fact, I might not fit through that rapidly narrowing gap even now. It was probably best to stay here, stay down, stay safe.

I jumped through the gap, landing in a cloud of smoke and whistling bullets. The portal slammed shut right behind me. The klaxons were deafening. I could barely see in the roiling smoke. Muzzle flashes sparkled to my right, answered by a brief blast of machine pistol fire, and Eric's cackling laughter.

To my complete surprise, I ran toward the fight.

CHAPTER THIRTY-THREE
MUNDANE APOCALYPSE

The hallways of Mundane Actual were in chaos. Gabrielle and her team disappeared into a roiling cloud of smoke, taking the running gun battle with them. I tried to follow, but they were moving fast, and clearly didn't want to wait up for a slightly out of shape knight in full plate. There were bullet holes in the drywall, and most of the harsh fluorescent lights were shot out. I passed a few doors, but the keypads next to them were flashing LOCKOUT, and the ones I tried were sealed tight.

Guess that leaves me only one way to go. Where was it Esther said Eric was going? The actuator? What could he possibly want there? I thought. *Wait, didn't he say something about the actuator to Chesa?*

I was coming up on a T-intersection when Gabrielle's team came out of nowhere. They were falling back down the crossing passageway, appearing briefly before retreating to my right. Gunfire stitched the air in front of me, the disciplined fire of an orderly withdrawal, but moments later they opened up with everything. An absolute hail of lead crossed the hallway in front of me, chewing through drywall and zipping into the ceiling. Tracer rounds turned the air bright yellow. The clatter of rounds impacting against something hard and impenetrable rose to my left, and moments later Eric stepped into view.

The self-titled Anachromancer held his staff in front of him with his left hand, and the stubby machine pistol in his right. A dome of spent bullets hovered in the air around his staff, with more piling up by the second. Eric fired back indiscriminately. There was a dry clatter from the gun, then a flash of light around the magazine and the shots continued unabated. Eric was laughing in a very mechanical bark. His feet were swathed in squirming roots that tore out of the ground each time he took a step forward, only to burrow into the concrete whenever he set his squamous foot back down.

The gunfire from down the hall came to a stop. Eric kept shooting for a few seconds, then lowered his weapon and shrugged. He shook his staff, dislodging the field of hovering bullets, sending them clattering to the floor like a thousand piggy banks spilling their coiny guts onto the concrete. That's when he noticed me.

"John! I thought you were done for. Man, I'm glad you're here."

"So you can shoot me again?"

"I mean, eventually, sure. But it looks like your friends have given up." He gestured broadly down the hallway. His eyes shone with madness. "I'm sorry, it looks like they've executed a strategic retreat to gather their thoughts. Maybe come up with a new plan. That's the part of the story we're at, right? The hero forms a plan? Moment of darkness?" He laughed maniacally. "Are you waiting for the big reversal, John? Because it isn't coming."

"What the hell are you doing here, Eric?" I asked. I crept closer, shield close to my body and sword in a low guard.

"John, man, I need you to focus up, here. We're changing history. We're making a new world. A new world! My own world. It's going to be marvelous." Eric stood casually, staff cradled in the crook of his left arm, the machine pistol swinging comfortably in his right, beaming like a drunk at the ren faire. If it weren't for the lingering smell of cordite and trees growing out of his tear ducts, he might have been my old friend.

But he wasn't. All the shit that had happened in the last few weeks, it was all on him. My parents' house, Matthew almost dying, the very fact that I was in this world in the first place. All of it. And here he was strolling casually toward me, grinning like an idiot.

"You're not making anything, Eric. You're destroying things. Does this look like a new creation to you?" I asked, backing up as he came closer. I motioned to the torn-up walls, the smoke rising from burning flakes of drywall, the flashing alarms. "You're ruining everything!"

"Well, not everything," he said. "Not the parts I like. And I don't like this part."

"That's not for you to decide!"

"Sure it is," he said. He stopped by a door flashing LOCKOUT and paused. "I'm literally the guy deciding. This door? Not very compelling." He pressed the MP5 to the keypad and squeezed off a stream of blistering lead. The keypad disintegrated, and the door popped open. Eric pushed it open with his staff, leaned inside and looked around. "Looks like a break room. Break rooms are boring. Gonna write it out of the script." He produced a grenade out of thin air, popped the pin out with his thumb, and tossed it into the room, then kicked the door shut with his heel and walked toward me. There was a muffled thud, and the door blew open, showering us both in debris. I stumbled backward, shield up, wincing as cinders danced off the ground at my feet. Eric was nonplussed. "We'll do something better with that space. Trust me."

"What the hell is wrong with you?" I shouted, backing up. The hallway opened up around me, becoming a larger room. "You could have killed someone!"

"Kill your darlings, they say. My darlings. And I don't even like these people. Too serious. And I have to be honest, John, I'm not really feeling our relationship is going that well. I think it's time for us to see other morality paradigms."

My heel banged into something solid, nearly toppling me. I waved my arms to regain my balance, then took a look around. My heart sank. The smoke was clearing out, and the shattered walls and scorched ceiling made the place difficult to recognize. But one glance behind me confirmed my worst fears. I was standing at the bottom of the wide stairs that led up to the vault that held the actuator. The vault door was closed, and a flashing light signaled emergency conditions overhead. Somewhere, a klaxon sounded. Nothing stood between Eric and his goal except me.

"What's the matter, John? Hoping someone's going to come save you?" Eric asked. I took a step onto the stairs, shield and sword at my side. "Done with being a hero?"

I was about to answer when he lifted the MP and started shooting. There's something primal about being shot at. I reacted the way any sane, nonmagical person would have, by jumping away and cowering. Bullets stitched their way across the floor toward me, and I kept dancing side to side. After several heart-stopping seconds, the little machine pistol rattled empty.

"Oh no, John! John, I'm out of bullets! Oh no!" Eric stared at his gun with open-mouthed horror. "What will I do? My plans are ruined! Oh wait, I'm not out of bullets at all!" The flash of light returned, traveling up the length of the magazine. I could hear the brass shells clicking together, like dominoes being lined up. "I never run out of bullets! Ever!"

"You never run out of being an asshole, either," I said.

"Snappy comeback. Too bad there's no audience." He dropped the barrel, sighting straight at my chest. The muzzle flash nearly blinded me.

A whole magazine's worth of bullets slammed into my chest. There was a long tearing roar as he emptied the gun. I stood there, waiting for the smoke to clear. When the pin clicked down on an empty chamber, Eric lowered the gun and stared at me.

The silver disks of deformed bullets slid off my chest, singing as they bounced off the concrete stairs. I kicked them aside and descended.

"Reversal," I said, rolling my shoulders. My neck popped in a very satisfying yet slightly gratuitous manner. "And now the big reveal."

I raised the shield, blocking Eric from view but also blinding him to the movement of my blade. I drew my sword overhead and charged forward. A few scattered shots ricocheted off the face of the shield, then I heard Eric drop the machine pistol. Impact, and I swept the shield aside, chopping down with the sword. Eric caught the forte of my sword in the crook of his staff and twisted it to the side. I flicked my wrist, magically changing the enarme straps of my heater to single-hand in the middle, then punched Eric in the throat with the rim of the shield. He stumbled back, and I followed up with a sweeping slash. He barely got his staff up to block. My blade bit deeply into the ropey wood of the staff. I punched again with the shield, driving him back, yelling as I struck again and again, each blow hacking at the staff. Sweat broke out across Eric's face.

"It's not all drinking and flirting with pretty girls, Eric," I said. "You might have spent some time fighting, if you meant to be a proper villain."

"Not really my thing," he answered. "Too much sweat." He knocked my shield aside then thrust with the staff, forcing me to retreat. "Besides, magic is easier."

"Yeah, I have that, too." I flexed my fingers in the tight embrace of the shield's leather grip. Panels irised open around the edge, transforming the heater into a round Viking shield.

"Not very flashy," Eric said. "Try this."

He waved his staff overhead in a wide arc, then slammed it down in front of him. A twisting creeper tore free from the staff and rolled toward me, growing as it approached, until it was about the size of a bike wheel. I slashed at it, but the whirling vines twisted up around the blade, tangling the sword. I danced to the side, pulling my sword free, trailing vines, and slashed again. Tangling roots crawled across my hilt and onto my hands. Before I could counterswing, my wrists were trapped, with leafy vines spreading up my arm. I jerked back, but the squirming vines were implacable.

"This isn't your story we're writing," Eric said. He was out of breath, but his cheeks were flush, and his eyes glassy. "No more than it's Chesa's, or your precious Watch. It's my story. My destiny. Mine!"

He approached. Half my body was trapped in vines, but I still had my shield. I swung it at him, the rim glancing off his shoulder. He batted it aside, then circled my wrist in his hand. I tried to change my grip again, but vines burst out of the veins on the back of Eric's hand. They crawled across my hand, burrowing between my skin and the leather straps of the shield. The shield fell to the ground, transforming back to a heater as it hit the floor. Eric grabbed me by the shoulders, then pulled backward. To my great surprise, the fantasy version of Eric Cavanaugh was as strong as an ox. I vaulted over his shoulder, to land headfirst on the ground behind him. I rolled, somehow springing to my feet, though I was woozy from the impact. My sword landed in a tangle of vines, well out of reach. My shield was still at Eric's feet. He kicked it at me contemptuously.

"If all they gave you was a magic shield, you kinda got screwed, John," he said.

Eric shook the staff, smiling as it reformed. Twisting vines grew up in the gaps I had hacked out, the whole shaft growing wide before knitting itself back together. Eric's fingers were intertwined with the staff, as though he was becoming part of it. Roots burrowed into the back of his hand, tapping into his veins, spreading out under his skin.

That doesn't look good, I mused, before remembering that Eric was trying to kill me, and that his well-being was the least of my concerns. I scooped up my shield, then looked around for a weapon. There was a pistol lying discarded in the rubble of a collapsed hallway. I tried not to think about what had become of its owner and snatched it up. Safety was already off, so I leveled it at Eric's face. He raised his brows.

"You think that's going to work, John?" he asked, more curious than accusatory. "I mean, those guys must have shot me a hundred times. What makes you so special?"

"Beats me. I mean, I was able to kill a dragon with a car. Esther said that was impossible. Maybe if I can do that, I can kill an asshole with a gun."

"Oh, but you didn't really kill that dragon. I did. Kind of. See, I figured out this mythological world thing existed, but every time I pressed into it, I got pushed back. Like it was rejecting me. I needed someone else to break the veil and take the brunt of that pushback, and then I could kind of slip in through the gap while everyone's eyes were on you. You remember the favor I gave you? That's what dragged Kracek into our world, and let you kill him with your mom's car." He brushed his fingers off on his robes, strolling casually forward while he talked. "Man, she must have been pissed about that. Did she ground you, John? God, I've been thinking about that for weeks."

"You did this. All of this. My parents' house, Tom Tom . . . people are dying, Eric. Is that worth it?"

"You're being a little ungrateful, John. Without me, you never would have found this place. Don't lie, you've enjoyed the last few weeks. You like being a hero. But that's over now. All of this is."

"Not yet it isn't," I said.

I squeezed the trigger, wincing as the pistol barked in my hand.

Or . . . more like chirruped. Maybe croaked . . . I had inadvertently shut my eyes, and when I peeled them open, I saw my pistol had turned into a centipede the size of a proper Chicago hot dog. It writhed in my hand, tiny legs scratching at my palm. I dropped it with a yelp, dancing away as it scurried back into the debris.

"You always did have a way of breaking things in the most interesting ways," Eric said. "That's what made me think you'd make a good decoy, actually. Like the world was already rejecting you. Like a disease, John. Too strange for the mundane, and too boring for the mythological. But you're starting to get too interesting. Time to put that to an end."

Then Eric shoved his staff into my belly. Even through the armor, it was a hard blow, and knocked the wind out of me. I backed up, tripping over something and came down hard on my butt.

"It's not too late, you know," Eric said as he strode over the wreckage of the hallway. There had been a lot of fighting here, and at least one heavy explosion. "Chesa and I had an agreement. I promised to not bother her, and she promised to not get in my way. But sometimes people break promises. You know all about that, don't you, John? Chesa really thought you two were going to go the distance. But there's no reason you can't have a second chance. Go, build your own place, just the two of you. That cabin of yours would make a good start. All you have to do is walk away."

"I can't," I said, struggling to my feet. "I can't let you get away with this."

"You don't really have a choice," he said, then slammed his staff into the ground. Roots burrowed through the concrete, running toward me in a jagged path, cracking the floor open like an egg. I tried to back away, but they climbed the stairs faster than I could move. I turned to run.

And slammed smack into the closed bank vault of the actuator room. I bounced off the steel drum of the door and fell down the stairs. Eric's twisting roots erupted from the ground, seizing me by wrist and ankle and chest, squeezing until I couldn't move, not even to turn my head. His footsteps slowly climbed the stairs, until he was standing next to me. I stared up at his twisted body, wincing at the thorns poking through his cheekbones and piercing the flesh of his forehead.

"I think we're done here, John. I have more important things to be doing right now." He gestured, and a stalk of roots jumped up to slam into the number pad on the door. Eric's eyes lost focus and the roots squirmed. "It's always something obvious. Just have to feel . . . it . . . out. There."

There was a pleasant chime, and then the vault unsealed with a hiss. The handwheel spun, and then the door creaked open. Inside, klaxons sounded, and frenzied voices started shouting. A string of bullets zipped through the opening.

"This has been pleasant, John. If you'd like to get together later to discuss my writing, I'd be happy to do that. As long as you promise to actually READ THE DAMN BOOK FIRST!" Eric adjusted and calmed himself, smoothing his robes as he approached the door. "Goodbye, John." As he stepped across the threshold, the yelling from inside got louder, and was answered by a peal of thunder and Eric's mad laughter. The door started to close.

I looked back down the hallway, where Esther and Gabrielle and the rest were hiding. There was no time. I couldn't wait for them to catch up.

I jumped through the vault door. It boomed shut just as I cleared the threshold.

I was trapped.

CHAPTER THIRTY-FOUR
FATE ACCOMPLI

Stumbling as my feet hit the ground, I pitched forward into soft earth, taking the impact with my shield and rolling, sword out to one side. I was getting good at not stabbing myself every time I fell down. Leaves slithered under my feet as I skidded down an embankment. *Didn't this used to be stairs?*

At the bottom of the hill I slid to a stop and stood up. Reality Control was . . . different.

There were a lot of trees. In fact, it was pretty much all trees, in all directions, above and below. I was standing on a mat of thick roots. The remnants of the control room were barely evident beneath the underbrush. Office chairs and cracked computer monitors poked out from the grasping roots of the tree-world, like gravestones in an overgrown field. The actuator lay in the center of the room. It yawned open like a broken egg.

A dozen or so tunnels led away, formed out of closely-knit boughs. The whole world shifted and creaked, like a forest in the wind. I swallowed. Hard.

"So . . . he's done a little remodeling," I said. My words disappeared into the shadows. I peered into the darkness, trying to decide which direction to go. Eric's laughter boomed in the distance. At least that gave me a direction to follow.

A voice crackled in the silence. I jumped clean out of my skin.

"John, are you inside? What the hell are you trying to do?"

I looked around, finally seeing a tiny speaker near the door. I went over and pushed a button.

"Esther, is that you?"

"Rast! I knew it was a mistake trusting you and your friends. Whatever the hell you're up to, know that I'm going to stop you! Once I get in there, I'm going to tear your skull from your head and—"

"Whoa, whoa, pump the brakes, boss. Whatever Eric's doing, I've got nothing to do with it." I thought about spilling the beans on Chesa but decided against it. Deal with it later. "I just chased him in here. I don't know what's going on any more than you do."

There was a long silence. I pushed the button again.

"What kind of choice do you have, ma'am?" I asked. "Trust me, or don't. There's no one else here to save the day."

I could feel the sigh through the speaker.

"Fine. What do you see?"

I described the surrounding area, the actuator, the control room, and the dozens of tunnels. When she answered, Esther's voice was scared.

"He's opened the actuator? That's not good. The actuator was designed as a weapon. It's supposed to manipulate anomalies, guided by a team of elites, to impose their version of reality on the mundane world. Think of it as weaponized daydreaming. But that was... problematic. We never had the coordination or control we needed. The results were catastrophic. Mostly for the team."

"You were on that team," I said, realizing how she must have lost her domain, and apparently her soul. She ignored me.

"The program got dropped, the whole operation mothballed. We went back to fighting the old-fashioned way, with swords and clever dialogue, but the larger fight ended before we could resolve anything."

"Which war was this? Because I'm pretty sure I would have learned something about all this in school."

"The German one. By your count, the Second World War. Fifth on the unreal side of the border. Sometime later we acquired the actuator through mostly legal means and started the Knight Watch. But we couldn't use it the old way. So we rigged it for passive running, and set it up to detect anomalies, rather than create them. But I assume it still has that capability. And that seems to be what your friend is into."

"Yeah, that would be consistent with his diabolical monologue," I said.

"Nature of villains. Can't help blathering on about their villainy. Is he some kind of artist or something? Lotta artists go this path."

"Writer. He has ten thousand pages of unfinished fantasy novels on his LiveJournal."

"Gods save us," Esther said. "Listen, none of that matters right now. You've got to find him and stop whatever he's trying to do."

"And how do I do that?"

"Improvise. I can give you a little guidance. Grab one of the isolation helmets near the actuator. If they're still working, we should at least be able to talk."

I looked around. Sure enough, the row of brass helmets lay haphazardly at the base of the broken anomaly actuator. I pulled one off and fitted it to my head. Kind of like a helm, except it smelled like motor oil and rubber.

"Did that work?" I said as loudly as I could.

"No need to yell," Esther answered. Her voice sounded like it was coming from the bottom of a mile-long pipe, but at least I could hear her. "Okay. First order of business is to find your friend. Be careful. If this is his domain, he'll have some control of the environment."

"Like he has his finger on the thermostat? Or more like he can conjure nightmares?"

"More like the conjuring nightmares part."

"Well, that's only going to be a problem when he figures out I'm here, and orders the trees to crush me," I said. "Until then, we're golden."

A quick tattoo of gunfire and muzzle flashes sounded from one of the passages, high up and to my right, followed by Eric's laughter. I started climbing toward it before the sound stopped.

"He's really got the maniacal laughter down," I mused. "Must have been practicing that for a while. Darkness really changes a guy, lemme tell you."

"You have to stop thinking of him as your friend. When the time comes, he's just another monster," Esther said. I heard a chorus of voices in the background. "Bethany has some suggestions about how to kill him, if you need it. They're . . . specific."

"No, it's fine. I know how a sword works," I said. "Eric and I have dueled a hundred times. No match."

That brought me up short. Eric was different, but it was still Eric.

He was still my childhood friend, just crazy, and growing a tree from his hand. And I was probably going to have to kill him. I was musing on that when Esther's voice cut into my head.

"Just be careful, Rast. He's not the same guy, no matter what you think. There will be changes."

"Oh, there's plenty that's changed about old Eric," I said. This place was getting to me quick. Probably not smart to talk out loud, but I couldn't stand the silence. "Used to be he was happy to push words around on a page and drink too much beer on the weekends. I tell you, I don't think even his own mother would recognize him. It's like he's not the same person at all."

When we were fighting, it was easy enough. He had been shooting at me, after all. But now that I was approaching the deed very intentionally, the weight of killing a man I had known for most of my life was starting to crush me.

At the top of the makeshift ladder, I found a broad tunnel, much like the others. Light came from bell-capped mushrooms growing out of the floor. The passage twisted away, disappearing around a curve twenty feet away from the mouth.

Checking the fit on my shield, I started creeping down the tunnel. It twisted and turned for a hundred feet or so. Passages broke off every dozen yards, but they were narrow crevices, barely more than gaps in the pressing foliage. I stayed on the main path. The sound of gunshots urged me forward.

"Who's he shooting at?" I whispered to myself.

"Domains are not formed whole from the occupant's mind," Esther said. "Though they are always a reflection of their creator. Eric may be trying to contain the native inhabitants of this place." A long rattle of gunfire interrupted Esther's lecture. I could see the muzzle flashes reflecting off the walls. I was getting close.

"Or maybe he's just out of his damned mind," I said.

"Also possible," Esther answered quietly.

I crept forward, checking each corner before I rounded them, being as stealthy as I could in full plate. Which was pretty stealthy, considering the deafening gunfire and maniacal laughter up ahead. It's easy to sneak up on someone who's punctuating each breath with twenty rounds from an MP5.

"Rast?" Esther's voice cut into the thunder. She sounded even more distant than before. I had to strain to hear her. "We have a situation. I don't understand what's going on but you need to hurry it up. He's almost done."

"Done with what?" I asked.

"Hard to tell from this end," she said. "A ritual of some..." static "interference. You'll have to..." howling whispers and the chanting of a mad choir "Something big."

"Bigger than a world made of trees?" I asked. There was no answer. The line was dead. "Perfect. I was hoping to face this completely on my own." I tore the bell helmet off my head and tossed it aside as I started to run. I came around the corner at a dead sprint.

What I saw was hard to believe at first, even after everything I had seen. But as we approached, I heard something that started the gears moving in my head.

"Why are you doing this?" Eric pleaded. Then Eric answered. "Because you were weak. I am done with weakness."

"What the hell," I whispered as I rushed forward.

Around the corner was a large, domed room. Tree roots as thick as houses surrounded the perimeter, arching up to the ceiling high above. The floor was the stump of an enormous tree, millions of tiny rings telling of an age older than the universe itself. Vine-twisted braziers dotted the room, burning with cold fire, dead and blue. At the center of the room was an altar. Eric stood over the altar with a dagger in his hand.

Eric also lay on the altar, arms and legs bound. He squirmed against his bonds.

"Hey!" I shouted without thinking. Both Erics looked up. "Don't touch yourself!"

"Johnny! What the hell's going on? You've got to help me! This guy's—"

"Crazy," the other Eric finished. Then he shifted the dagger to his left hand and held out his empty right hand. A staff curled out of the ground, joining with his flesh. "I'm getting a little tired of beating the shit out of you, John."

CHAPTER THIRTY-FIVE
DOUBLE TROUBLE

I swung sword and shield into hand, dropping into a guard position and tightening the enarme straps against my forearm. I flexed my fingers. The steel face of the bulwark blossomed open like a flower in a time-lapse. Eric raised his brows.

"I still think that's a cheap trick, Sir John," he said. "Does the sword get bigger, too? Or is that a little too on point?"

"You're the guy with wood growing out of his pants, weirdo," I said.

"Fair point. I guess we'll just have to fight to see whose compensation mechanism is more authentic."

I was formulating a pretty snappy comeback for this, something really clever, hopefully. But I never got around to it, because I was suddenly beset by a pair of giant fists that rose out of the ground and tried to smash me into pulp. I rolled the lower panels of my shield out and anchored it, bracing it with my shoulder. It took all my force to hold my ground as blow after blow rained down on my shield. The metal grew hot with friction.

"I can't keep this up forever!" I shouted. But of course, Esther was gone, and the rest of the team was on the other side of the vault door. Vines crept along the border of the room, slowly encircling me.

"Hey, John?" That sounded like Normal Eric. Or at least, it didn't sound like crazy magic-slinging Eric. "John, this is all really weird and stuff, but I think you're having a bad time of it."

"Observant," I said through gritted teeth.

"Okay, yeah. Just checking. Do you think you're going to be able to save me or something?"

"Forecast unclear. Ask again later," I answered.

"Cool. Because I think this guy is trying to kill you."

"Sounds right," I said. One of the massive fists came down on the edge of my shield, twisting it in my grip and wrenching it out of the ground. I stumbled back, steadying myself with my sword. Waves of vines flowed in from the flanks, grabbing at my ankles. I ripped my feet free, stomping as vines tangled in my greaves, trying to pull me down. I retreated from the twin fists. They followed me, pulling free from the ground and dragging themselves forward.

"Faster! Faster!" Dark Eric yelled. "Crush him!"

One of the crawling hands paused long enough to flip him off, then resumed its laborious journey across the room.

"Looks like this place isn't as magical as you thought, buddy," I said. "You might want to do some editing here."

"Shut up!"

"I don't think he's your buddy, John," Other Eric said. "Unless I'm completely misreading this situation."

"You're not," I said. "I'm kind of being an asshole. He tried to kill a friend of mine."

"Oh, yeah. That makes sense," Other Eric said.

"Everyone shut up!" Dark Eric yelled. "I need to concentrate! Art is hard!"

"Oh, Gods, you're so damned precious." The vines at my feet had gone limp while Eric focused on his impertinent fists. I gathered several strands up, twisting them around the hilt until they were tight, then yanked them free. The trailing vines tangled around the approaching fist. The motion of dragging itself forward quickly tangled the hand, binding finger to finger and thumb to palm. It tumbled to the ground.

Dark Eric threw his head back and laughed.

"Very good! It's always dull when visitors don't bring games to play." He drove the dagger into the altar next to Other Eric's shoulder, then fished around in his robes. "I have my own, as well!"

He drew the stubby machine pistol and pointed it at me. I had to laugh.

"We've already done this dance, Eric. That shit doesn't work on me."

"Maybe not in the real world. But we're not in the real world, are we, John?"

Bullets tore through the air, the muzzle flash turning the dim interior of the tree into brilliant light. Hot fire cut across my shoulder as a bullet punctured my armor and grazed my skin. I was so shocked I nearly dropped my sword.

"Magic bullets, John! Like that movie!" He waved the gun in my direction and pulled the trigger. I ducked behind my shield, angling the face of the bulwark and bracing myself. Lead hit steel, ricocheting inches from my head. Long scars dug their way across my shield, exposing bright steel under the paint. I had my own magic, but somehow a shield didn't feel as cool as a bullet. But I had to work with what I had.

"I think I've had enough of this bullshit," I said. "You need an editor, Eric. Someone needs to cut you down to size."

I ran forward, dancing past the entangled hand. The other fist rose up and slapped at me, but I was able to roll past the impact and keep going. Eric's eyes got big as I barreled toward him. He lifted the machine pistol and let loose. A hail of bullets spattered across the face of my shield, but I had opened the supplemental panels. I was deep into my mythic self. The shots whizzed clear. I didn't slow at all.

I hammered into Eric shield first. The force of the impact bowled him over. He yelped as his roots tore free of the ground, dripping blood. I slashed at him as he rolled away. The steel of my blade bit into his staff, severing the gnarled tendrils of the haft. It stuck, and I had to throw my shield over my shoulder and grab the hilt with both hands to keep the sword from twisting out of my grip as he rolled away. The shield tightened against my back, prehensile straps hugging my shoulder and chest as it settled into place. Eric and I struggled for a second, then I kicked him in the chest. He fell back. I struck.

Quick slice, blocked by the barrel of his magical gun, then counterstrike and I put the forte of my blade into his shoulder. I drew it out, slicing as I pulled. Flesh parted, and the sword's edge rattled against his collarbone.

The Eric on the altar gave out a squeal of pain, thrashing against his bonds. Blood sprang up on the cheap fabric of his bard's outfit, turning the faux-silk bright crimson. While I was distracted, Dark Eric scrambled to his feet.

He was uninjured. The dirty sleeve of his robe was sliced open, but the flesh beneath was unharmed. There was blood on my sword, but not on his skin. I stared at him in horror. The way my sword had battered his skin was familiar. It was the same as the quintains in Clarence's yard.

"You're nothing but wood," I said, and Eric started laughing. He pistol whipped me, knocking me back on my heels. I brought my shield back, shrugging my shoulder to let it slip down the length of my arm into a single-hand grip. I barely got the shield up in time before he dropped a hail of lead on me. The magic of the warden held up, though. The shield stood up to the punishment, even if the impact was enough to rattle my teeth.

"That's not how this is supposed to work," I said. "Guns against swords! How am I supposed to win that kind of fight?"

"Hey, John?" Other Eric whimpered. "Can you not do that again? The stabbing? Because that hurts like hell."

"Sorry, man. Not sure what's going on here."

"Isn't it clear?" Dark Eric hissed. "Kill your friend, if you want. But you can't hurt me."

"Yeah, I figured that part out," I said. "But I have a question for you. What happens if I cut Eric free? Where does your blood go then?"

Dark Eric paused.

"Did you seriously not think of that?" I asked.

"Of course, I did. I just . . . I'm . . ."

"You're stalling," I said, then ran straight at Eric, good Eric, the Eric that was tied to the altar. When I reached him, I put my sword against his bonds and smiled. "Don't worry, man. It's going to be okay."

"I can't allow that!" Dark Eric said. He raised the charred tip of his staff and pointed it in our direction.

The ground around us erupted with thorny growth, surrounding us and then closing in. There were brief seconds before I was having to batter my way free. Eric gave a horrific cry, and then I lost sight of him. I was fully consumed with keeping the twisting, choking vines out of my throat. Lashing creepers caught my wrists, wrapping around my chest and squeezing until it was a struggle to breathe. I slashed with sword and shield, battering back the grasping vines, until there was a tiny space around me. The bramble wall was going to overwhelm me in a few heartbeats. Desperate, I pulled on all the levers on my shield, all at once.

The shield whirred to life. Panels clattered out, circling me in a ring of steel, slicing through the thorny tendrils that scratched at my back. A dome of steel irised over my head, and pillars shot into the ground at my feet. Darkness enveloped me.

I was in a coffin-sized sanctuary. Panels of magical steel surrounded me, sealing me in place. Dim light glowed from runes across the interior of the shield. Dead vines lay at my feet, their edges cut clean by the shield as it enclosed me. I could hear brambles scratching on the surface outside, but I was completely protected. The webwork of leather straps hung from the interior of my shelter, leading to my hand.

"What . . . the . . . hell?" I whispered. "That's a whole lot of shield."

Sallygate in ten seconds, a voice intoned. The runes began to flash. *Five seconds. Four. Three . . .*

"Is there a pause button? No?" I braced and lifted my sword. "Okay then. Pull!"

The shield exploded. Panels flew straight out, blowing the growing bramble wall into bits. I was left with a tangle of straps dangling from my fingers that stretched into the darkness. I wrapped the straps around my fist and pulled. From the shadows flew the dozen panels of my shield, reeling back to my hand. The heater reformed against my knuckles.

"Okay, that's a pretty cool trick," I said. "Now . . . what happened to Eric?"

There was no sign of either Eric. A bundle of vines lay next to the altar, about the size of a dead human body. I ran to it, pushing it frantically aside, looking for my friend. There was a narrow cleft in the ground, slithering with snake-like roots, and a brief glimpse of Eric's limp hand as he disappeared into the depths.

"Eric! Eric are you in there?" There was no answer from the ground. I looked around desperately and saw a shadow of dark robes disappear down one of the tunnels. He was getting away. I had to choose. Chase Dark Eric or try to save my friend.

I drove my sword into the ground, cutting roots and shoving them aside, always careful to not cut Eric, just in case he was nearby.

Suddenly the root-floor gave way, and I was faced by a yawning gap. Without a second's thought, I pulled my shield tight to my body and jumped.

I had a little time to regret that jump. The walls of the cleft closed on me, and the roots tried to work their way into my armor. It was a little like being swallowed by a . . . throat full of snakes? The metaphor collapses. The point is, it was unpleasant.

I fell for a long time. I kept my sword and shield pressed close to my chest. Last thing I wanted to do at the end of this fall was lose my weapons.

The tunnel ended abruptly, dumping me out into a much smaller room. The walls were close and constantly moving, roots swarming over thicker branches, appearing and disappearing in the blink of an eye. I shook off the squirming streamers of roots that had pulled free during my passage and looked up. The cleft sealed shut.

The only light here was coming from the tunnel in front of me. It was the steady glow of electric lighting, not the flicker of torches or even the purplish fuzz of the mushrooms earlier. No, these were light bulbs. I walked down the tunnel. The ground under my feet slowly turned from wood to stone, and then to carpet. I stepped into Eric's room.

It was a simple space, austere not out of some spartan design sense, but because Eric never bothered to decorate. I had been here dozens of times, to play D&D, or video games, for sleepovers and late-night bitch sessions. This place was a combination of his childhood room and the place I had last seen two weeks ago. The toys he had long ago packed away so we would stop making fun of him were arranged along the wall. The only difference was that the window looked out onto a wall of roots, and there was no door.

There were two of him again. The one I had seen slip away into the cleft was limping, a trickle of blood running down his leg. He was muttering to himself. The other Eric, the real Eric, lay on his bed. There was no need to bind him. He was long dead. The roots running from his open chest reached to the walls and were stained rust-red from drinking his life. His eyes were open, staring dully at the ceiling.

"Goddamn it," I muttered. Other Eric, as false as his magic, whirled around. When he saw me, he smiled. "How many of you are there?"

"I was really hoping you'd go chasing after my golem. But I thought you might figure out that it was just a trick. For the best, honestly. He is nearly tapped. And as you can see, I've gotten everything out of my progenitor that I can." He turned to face me, and that wicked staff materialized out of thin air. "But you're about ripe."

"When did this happen?" I asked.

"At the faire. My Fetch did his job. I swear, when you broke him out of my little circle in the mall, I thought the gig was up. Which reminds me." He gave a short bow. "I have to thank you for bringing him back. He might still be alive, but for you."

"Goddamn it!" I howled, and threw myself at Dark Eric, or whatever he was. I had been so close, so close. I had almost saved him. Part of me expected to journey down that cleft to find the real Eric waiting to be saved. But not this. Never this.

Dark Eric's staff was a whirling spiral of roots, a cloud of blocking, grasping, entangling tendrils. I slashed through them, lopping off woody limbs, striking with all my fury and my grief. Eric fell back, the staff growing shorter and shorter, but he didn't seem to mind. He didn't even seem to care.

"You can't bring him back, no matter how hard you fight, John. Why destroy what little there is that remains?"

"Because you killed him! And you're not him!" Hack. Crash. The sound of breaking furniture as I pushed the monster against Eric's desk. "You're just some cheap copy!"

"Oh, but I am." He diligently blocked my next attack, and then drew more rooty staff out of thin air. I got the feeling he was just trying to buy time, but I didn't care. I was too consumed by anger and the sorrow over poor, dead Eric. "How else would I know about Chesa? And what you wore under your graduation robes? And why you really missed PE in September of your junior year?"

"I don't know how this shit works, freak, and I don't really care," I said. Tears were streaming down my face. "You're not him. You can't be."

"I'm better than him. I'm what he dreamed of being. And he was close enough to the unreal that those dreams took on a life of their own. My life." He raised the staff in both hands to meet a heavy downward chop from my blade, a strike strong enough to cut through the wood and nick the tip of his nose. He stumbled back, angry. "Okay, enough of this nonsense. What's dead is dead. I need blood to live. Yours, his, it doesn't matter."

Throwing down the staff, he raised both hands and gave me the most horrific smile.

"Besides, wasn't it about time you started putting down some roots?"

His fingers burst open, and branches came out of his flesh. They shot across the room so fast I could barely see them move. I still got my shield up, but even with its magic I couldn't hope to block them all. They crawled over the rim of the shield and lapped around, spiraling up my arms until they reached my chest. Every hack of my sword severed a dozen vines, but for every one I cut, three more grew back. I screamed, but several creepers wrapped around my head, cutting off my voice. They started to peel my armor away. Several of them reached my skin, and started burrowing in.

Footsteps scratched against the floor behind me. Eric's eyes glanced up, and his face fell.

"You've got to stop running away like this," Matthew said. He stepped into the room and raised one hand, then snatched off his glove. "Lights, people!"

The room lit up like heaven itself. Dark Eric hissed and cowered away. The roots choking the life out of me went limp, and I started tearing them away in big handfuls. Bethany wasn't far behind. She jumped into the tiny room like a rocket, phasing in and out of reality as she danced over Eric's dead body, barely touching the bed before she landed behind Dark Eric. He whirled to face her, but she was already drawing blood. When he tried to punch her, she was gone. When he turned again, there were already blades in his back. Even in the tight confines of this nightmare version of Eric's bedroom, Bethany moved like smoke and struck like lightning.

Tembo appeared next. He burned bright, throwing darts of flame that crawled down the length of Dark Eric's rooty limbs, sizzling when they reached flesh. The monster howled, stumbling until his back was against the far wall.

"Enough of this!" Dark Eric screamed. "Time to prune the old growth!"

The room creaked and groaned. The walls splintered, cracks forming down their length, until roots started to peek through. The phantom of Eric's old room crumbled around us, revealing a squirming wall of living wood. The tree clenched tight, closing the tunnel behind us. Eric watched with glee in his eyes.

"You will feed us, one way or another!" he shouted. "There's no escape!"

"For either of us," I said. Then I stepped forward. Roots dragged on my shield and ankles, trying to hold me in place, but I cut my way forward. Eric's body slumped off the bed, to catch in the grinding roots of the tree. I didn't let that distract me. "This is how I know you aren't Eric. He was a nice guy. And you're just a son of a bitch!"

I swept my sword across the bed, slicing through the roots that led to Eric's chest. Blood spurting from the severed tips.

"No!" Dark Eric howled, throwing himself forward. He gathered up the bundle of severed roots and pressed them back against the wound, whimpering as blood leaked slowly onto Eric's teddy bear comforter. "You don't know what you've done! You've killed him!"

"I've killed you both," I said. I battered Dark Eric aside with the face of my shield, then drove my sword into Eric's heart. Real Eric, my friend Eric, the root of all this trouble. And the only person in this room I could still save. Dark Eric, staring in horror, stumbled away from the bed, backing away until he reached the slithering wall of vines.

The roots crawling out of Eric's chest turned black, then turned to ash. The withering hurried across vines that stretched across the bed, hitting the walls like a blight. Soon the whole room was turning to dust. The walls groaned as they collapsed. Eric's bed tipped back, disappearing into a rising cloud of disintegrating ash. I looked up at Dark Eric.

"I don't know which one you are, or if you were ever really my friend," I said. "But this is over."

"Nothing's ever over," Dark Eric said. "Not in the Imaginarium! Not for an Anachromancer! I'll find you, John Rast. I'll find y—"

The wall behind Dark Eric blistered and grew, suddenly enveloping Dark Eric's twisted face. His scream of horror was cut off by the sound of creaking wood and breaking bones. The fissure closed, leaking dark sap.

Bethany appeared at my side, one dagger pointed toward the

bleeding tear in the wall, her other hand free. She looked at the body on the bed, grimaced, then turned to me.

"We have to get out of here," she said. She grabbed my arm and pulled me away. I snatched my arm back, but then she got frantic. "Seriously, there's nothing here. He's gone."

"I can't leave him here like this," I said. "Not if there's a chance."

"There's always a chance, or a prayer. Sometimes both," Matthew said. He shoved through the collapsing room and put both hands on Eric's chest, then took a deep breath. "This is going to be hairy. Hang on."

Apparently, he meant that literally, because the next thing I knew, Bethany and Tembo had linked arms around me and pressed all three of us against Matthew's back. Light burst all around us. As the tree collapsed around us, splinters of wood and root crashed down on our heads, roots pierced our skin. But through it all, wave after wave of light washed over us. Every time a shaft of wood punched into my arm, or knocked me in the head, there was a flash of brilliance, and the pain was gone.

Matthew huddled at the center of our tiny world, screaming and burning bright, healing through it all. Soon he stopped bothering with the little injuries. A limb collapsed on my skull, and I was sure I felt bones crack and brain compress, but just as suddenly I was fine. A barb of wood punched through my lungs and pierced my heart. The pain shot through me like a lightning bolt, but the bright thunder that followed wiped the wound away, though I could still feel it. Thorns tore at my arms, but each time they reached the bone, Matthew sent out a wave of healing that started the process over from the beginning. I died over and over again, the memory of pain lingering, though my flesh was repaired. It was torture. It was madness.

Tembo lent his strength, sending out glowing purple domes that turned aside the worst of the rubble. I threw my shield over our heads and focused what little magic I had absorbed into keeping us safe. It's the least a warden could do. Literally the least. I'm pretty sure I did nothing. But I tried.

At the end of it, the dust settled. We were on a field of grass. The sun was shining, the birds were singing, and a castle shone in the distance. Warily, I raised my head and looked around. Broken trees lay all around us, the remnants of a forest that had gone mad. But there was something familiar about the castle.

"This is Clarence's domain," I said.

"It is," Tembo answered. "Which means the old swordmaster must still be safe. That monster must have snuck in somehow, while you and Chesa were here to train."

"Should we try to find him?" I asked.

"Not now. We'll come back, when we're recharged. No telling how Kyle will react to visitors. But the domain looks intact," Tembo said. "Which means our way out is over there."

"Then let's get to it," Bethany said. She helped Matthew up. The saint was barely able to stand. We hung him between us.

"What about Eric?" I asked.

"What about me?" Eric asked. His eyes fluttered open, and he sat up. He looked around curiously. "Man, the ren faire went all out on this set. Or is that just a big painting? It's so hard to tell." He blinked and looked at me. "Oh, hey, John. How you doing?"

"Good man," I said, trying not to cry. "How are you?"

"Hung over. Tired. Pretty sure I missed all the good stuff. So, the usual." He smacked his lips and smiled. "Hey, what was that about a dragon?"

"Long story. And you wouldn't believe it anyway," I said. "Come on. We need to get back to the faire."

EPILOGUE
MAKE-BELIEVE HOMECOMING

We met in the ruins of my childhood home. My parents moved; too many changes, too much trouble to rebuild. And now that I was taking that big job in the city (I had to tell them something, right?) there was no reason for them to stay here. So they moved south. Somewhere with a beach and the occasional hurricane, you know, for variety. What remained of the property fell into my hands. And from there, it fell into ruin, and the unreal.

Esther taught me how to fold bits of the real world into my domain. To folks walking past, the old property was still there, an empty lot looking creepier and more abandoned by the day. But for me it was a portal into my domain. And today, it was the perfect site for a backyard grill-out.

"I'm still not clear what happened," Eric said. He sat on a cooler by the grill, chatting with Chesa and trying to figure out the rest of the team. "You say you killed me, but I don't feel dead."

"Thank the saint," I said, nodding to Matthew. He and the rest of the team were gathered under the old oak tree, the only thing still standing in my front yard. Clarence was with them, looking feeble. He had come out of his domain a week or two after the Eric incident, completely mortal once again. He was still wearing his medieval finery, but there was no sword at his belt. "Apparently something about the doppelganger's magic kept you from really dying. Just the magic part of you."

"Hm," Eric said, as if I had just told a really fascinating story about a flat tire. "Well, I don't know. I guess I never will."

"What do you remember?" Chesa asked.

"The faire. Some fire. Figured I'd wake up in a hospital." He looked around the vaguely magical grounds of my property. There was something about the Unreal in everything you could see. The sun shone brighter, the grass glimmered, even the smoke from the grill was somehow infused with mystical power. He shrugged. "I guess this could be one of those waking dreams. The beer is certainly dream-level quality."

That's how it was with Eric now. He didn't ask about the scars on his chest, or the dreams of a tree and a dragon. Bethany, Clarence, Matthew, Tembo, and Esther kept their distance from him. It's hard to go back to treating someone like an innocent when their power-mad alter-ego breaks into your home and guns down a bunch of your friends. I couldn't blame them.

It was different for me. Eric would always be Eric. Even after I killed him. It was hard to believe he had survived that.

The biggest change in the guy for me was the stories. I didn't hear anything more about his books. I kind of missed all those adjectives.

"So what now?" Eric asked. "You and Chesa are heroes or something?"

"Something," I said. "We're still getting a feel for it ourselves."

"Speaking of which, I need to get back to my domain. I think we all do," Chesa said.

"One more burger," I said. "It'll be quick."

"You need to stop treating this like a game, Rast," Esther answered. She had strolled over from the main team. "The Unreal doesn't exist for sunny summer afternoons."

"Then why does it exist at all?"

"Myths exist because people need them," Esther said. "And Knight Watch exists to keep the myths in their place. It's not so you can have the perfect backyard barbecue."

I flipped a burger. It spun in the air and landed perfectly on the grill, hissing as it hit the grate. I smiled.